The BOOK *of*

The BOOK *of the* DUCHESS

Alyce Chaucer 2

CHRISTINA HARDYMENT

HAUGETUN

First published in Great Britain in 2023
by Haugetun Press, Oxford

ISBN 978-1-7391980-3-9 hb
ISBN 978-1-7391980-4-6 pb
ISBN 978-1-7391980-5-3 eb

COVER IMAGES daffodil and saffron © Bodleian Library,
University of Oxford, L 1.5 Med., pp. 111, 123; woodcut copied from
the Ellesmere manuscript of Chaucer's *Canterbury Tales* in *A Six-Text Print
of Chaucer's Canterbury Tales*, ed. F.J. Furnival with woodcuts
by W.H. Hooper, Chaucer Society, 1872.
ENDPAPER MAP © Map of London by John Norden (1548–*c.* 1625) from
his *Speculum Britanniæ: an historical and chorographical description
of Middlesex and Hartfordshire*, Daniel Brown, London, 1762.

Designed and typeset in 11 on 14 Dante by illuminati, Grosmont
Printed in Great Britain by Henry Ling Ltd, Dorchester

Contents

*To Claire Bodanis, who gave me the confidence
to finish my first book about Alyce*

Foreword

The underlying theme of this series of novels is the power of women in a world torn by war and faction. 'To thrive, you must wive' ran a contemporary proverb. 'The man is the head of the family, but the woman is the neck; she turns the head' was another.

The central figure is Alyce Chaucer (1404–1475), only known grandchild of the poet Geoffrey Chaucer (*c.* 1343–1400). She was one of the wealthiest individuals in Britain: herself an heiress and married three times, she had estates in every county of England south of the Trent. After the death of her third husband in 1450 she chose to remain a widow. As such, her power did not have to be veiled in apparent obedience to a spouse. She was notoriously proud and strong-minded. There is evidence that she loved books and had a well-chosen library, which included at least two books by Christine de Pisan.

Alyce lived in great state in the Palace of Ewelme, fourteen miles from the city of Oxford. Little of this now remains, but the church, the almshouse known as the God's House and the school that she and her last husband built there are uncannily unchanged. They and the magnificent tomb which describes her as 'Most Serene Princess' (a title allowed to the wives of dukes, who were usually of royal blood) are the inspiration for the books. So too is the never solved mystery of who was responsible for the death of Alyce's third husband William de la Pole, Duke of Suffolk, intercepted on his way into exile in 1450 and brutally executed.

The first book, *The Serpent of Division*, was set in September 1466 and saw Alyce fighting not to lose her Ewelme heartland and learning that she needed to survive the machinations of her arch-enemies, Sir Robert Harcourt and Queen Elizabeth, wife of King Edward IV, a woman intent on dividing York and Lancaster. In *The Book of the Duchess*, Alyce is summoned to London by King Edward's mother, Cecily Neville, Duchess of York, to investigate the murder of a scrivener, only to find herself caught up in a plot intended to ruin her.

In both, much is imagined – these are after all novels – and many of the characters are invented. Those who were real are capitalised in the cast of characters. I have taken liberties with their doings, but I have used known facts about them to furnish their fictional personae.

Who's Who

No need to read now, but useful to remind yourself if muddled.
Historical characters are in CAPITALS.

SIR RICHARD ROOS, a poet knight imprisoned in Windsor Castle.

ALYCE CHAUCER, a lover of literature and gardens. She is the granddaughter of the poet Geoffrey Chaucer and the widow of William de la Pole, Duke of Suffolk. She lives in Ewelme Palace, near Wallingford.

Tamsin Ormesby, Alyce's maid, resolute and rash.

SIMON BRAILLES, Alyce's secretary, timorous and twitchy.

BEN BILTON, Steward of Ewelme, brave and bullish.

William Marton, Master of the God's House.

Farhang Amiri, Alyce's Persian physician, skilled in curing bodies and souls.

Mistress Joan Moulton, eminent London bookseller, four times widowed, as irrepressible as Chaucer's Wife of Bath.

Lady Katherine Arderne, widow of Sir Richard Arderne, forlorn but feisty.

Peter Arderne, her seven-year-old son.

Amice, maid to Kate Arderne, overfond of finery.

Monique de Chinon, Joan's companion, taciturn and tactful.

Sukey, Peter's nursemaid, gawky and brave.

Henry Sewardby, Beadle of Bread Street Ward, plump and pompous.

Agnes Quincy, herbalist with secrets.

Joseph Pek, bedesman, a sturdy one-armed veteran of the wars in France.

Peggotty Lambourn, Chamberlain of Montagu Inn.

Ellen, kitchen maid at Montagu Inn, friendly and flirtatious.

KING EDWARD IV, son of the Duke of York, crowned aged nineteen in 1461; shrewd but lazy.

QUEEN ELIZABETH, his wife, widow of the Lancastrian Sir John Grey; cunning and conniving, devoted to advancing her Wydeville relations.

CECILY NEVILLE, Dowager Duchess of York, mother to Bess and King Edward; cunning and conniving, devoted to advancing her Neville relations.

JOHN (Jack) DE LA POLE, Duke of Suffolk, Alyce's heir.

BESS PLANTAGENET, his wife and King Edward's sister; cleverer than both.

Nancy, taverner at the Mermaid Inn.

Micky, kitchen boy at the Mermaid Inn.

Abel, servant at the Mermaid Inn.

Sir Gervais Arderne, grandfather to Peter.

SIR ROBERT HARCOURT of Stanton Harcourt; a ruthless braggart who covets Ewelme Palace.

Rufus Savernake, his henchman.

Denis Pailton, scrivener and engraver, talented but untrustworthy.

Bronwen, his widow.

Owen, their son.

John Grafton, bookseller in St Paul's Yard; gormless and gullible.

Margaret Grafton, his wife, 'the horse that draws the cart'.

JOHN TIPTOFT, Earl of Worcester and Lord Constable. Unpredictable and secretive. A notable humanist but merciless in his pursuit of traitors.

JOHN WENLOCK, Lord Someries of Luton, diplomat to Edward
    IV; a man of mystery.
Francis Thynne, his secretary, 'close as an oyster'.
SIR THOMAS MALORY, biographer of King Arthur.
James Danvers, a dashing young lawyer.
WILL STONOR of Stonor Park, his apprentice.
JOHN HARDYNG, chronicler, a trimmer to the political wind.
Guy of Yarnton, journeyman at the Sign of the Mole.
Matthew Cobham, chief binder at the Sign of the Mole.
Ned, lad of all work at Moulton Inn.
Brother Pietro of Padua, a Dominican friar.
SIR JOHN DE VERE, Earl of Oxford.
MARGARET (Meg) NEVILLE, his bride-to-be, Alyce's god-
    daughter, Cecily Neville's niece, Richard, Earl of Warwick's
    sister.
Giles Scott, clerk to John Laweley, the Coroner.
GEORGE, Duke of Clarence, brother of Edward IV.
GEORGE NEVILLE, Archbishop of York, an old friend of Alyce's.
Malachi Fryse, an apothecary.
John Doll, Oxford bookseller.
Job, a Wallingford smith.

'By means of books we communicate to friends as well as foes what we cannot safely entrust to messengers, since the book is generally allowed access to the chambers of princes, from which the voice of its author would be excluded.'

RICHARD DE BURY,
Philobiblon, c. 1344

'The lady willingly will read books inculcating good habits as well as studying on occasion devotional books. She will disdain volumes describing vice, never allowing them in her household.'

CHRISTINE DE PISAN,
Treasure of the City of Ladies, 1405

Prologue

Windsor Castle

Sir Richard Roos, once a favoured court poet, now a prisoner, sat at his tower window and looked down through its bars to the stable yard below. The king and his company were setting off into Windsor Great Wood to hunt. He saw the royal huntsman James Forrest, whipcord thin, hounds yapping eagerly at his heels. Three muzzled mastiffs were being led out of the kennels, their collars gleaming with pointed studs. So the king was to hunt boar, fiercest and most feared of forest beasts. How he longed to be with them. At least he was no longer in the damp dungeon in which he'd spent the last few months. He had been moved to more comfortable quarters as a birthday boon a week ago, a day after Edward of York arrived. The young king was eager to win Lancastrians to his own cause. 'I value loyalty, Sir Richard,' he had said with that radiant smile of his. 'And I hope that one day you will do me the honour of giving me an allegiance as certain as you now feel for Lancaster.'

No chance of that, Roos reflected half-regretfully as he watched the gay procession troop through the castle gatehouse and into the woods, the king's broad back pikestaff-straight, his thighs at one with his splendid horse. King Henry of Lancaster had knighted him, and however regal Edward of York might look he was a usurper. And now a plan to gain a powerful new ally in the cause of dethroning Edward was under way and, old though Roos was, he had been given a crucial part in it.

I

Inspired by what he had seen from the window, he turned back to the verses he had composed. Make the message hidden to the casual reader, the Dowager Duchess of Suffolk's emissary had told him. He dipped his quill into the ink and copied them on the book's first page:

Who then is so potent or can do more
    Than honest Truth, whom I liken to a boar?
To this boar he is like not only in strength
    But in nature, for his nature is tenacity.
The lion his lord is at bay and in distress,
    His single cub hides with the lioness.
This boar may well be called the boar of grace,
    Prophecies of antiquity call him to his place.
As do allies ready in each stronghold.
    One word and Fortune will bless the bold.

That should do it. Only the great lord for whom this book was intended, whose heraldic beast was the boar, would recognise the poem as a call to arms. To free Harry the Sixth, England's rightful ruler and restore his wife and son to his side.

Ewelme, Oxfordshire

Alyce Chaucer, Dowager Duchess of Suffolk and one of the wealthiest and most independent-minded women in England, knelt down on the damp turf, poked a thin trowel down beside the long taproot of a dandelion and levered it out with a satisfied grunt. The honey-coloured hound drowsing beside her cocked an ear, then leapt up with a bark. Quick footsteps on the gravel path made her look round. Tamsin Ormesby was hurrying towards her mistress with a frown on her face and a padded leather kneeler in her hand. Alyce looked up, a little guiltily.

'Too late, sweeting. Mud stains on my apron, but it's out. And all in one piece. A fine fat root we can stew with sorrel. Farhang says it cleanses the liver marvellously. Which I need after all our Easter feasting. And the leaves will pepper up the salad he recommended.'

Rising, she handed trowel and root to Tamsin and arched her back to relieve the pain that always seared her spine when she stooped for too long over her flower beds.

Caressing Leo's silky fur, she looked around with satisfaction. Four arcades of carefully trained apple and pear trees led to the fountain at the heart of the garden. Some were already in blossom and at the far end of each tunnel was a plum tree clipped into a frothy ball of white. A low hedge of box encircled each tree, and tulips and fleurs-de-lis filled the narrow beds below the tunnels.

Heavier footsteps sounded on the gravel and Leo slumped down with a bored whine. Her secretary Simon Brailles was advancing towards her, brow furrowed as usual.

'A messenger with a letter, my lady. He says he was to wait for an answer.' He handed her a packet. Alyce frowned as she recognised its seal: the royal arms impaled with the Neville saltire: the arms of King Edward's mother Cis Neville, Duchess of York. Once a good friend, now a thorn in her side. She broke it open.

To my trusty and entirely well-beloved cousin Alyce.

I, Cecily, send greetings and wish you well. You are doubtless planning to remove to London in time to witness your son taking part in the June tournament with Anthony of Burgundy and his train. This letter is to urge you to begin your journey immediately. I have need of you to deal for me concerning a most horrible death. I know that by the love you bear me, you will not shrink from investigating this on my behalf – only you can act with the utter secrecy this delicate case requires. Moreover, I am longing to see my beloved daughter Bess and my new grandson. I desire you to bring them to London with you, so that my own skilful herbalist can tend her and the baby.

The blessed Trinity have you in His keeping,
    writ at Baynard's Castle in the year of Our Lord
    10 April 1467.

Cis had boldly scrawled her name after the scribe's neat court hand, then dashed off a postscript:

Remember my silence about the most secret matter of Newton Montagu. Burn this letter.

Alyce's heart sank. How rash Bess had been to confess the truth about Jack's true parentage to her mother. For the sake of her daughter, Cecily was keeping the secret close of course, but Alyce had quickly discovered that she was now expected to be at the overbearing duchess's beck and call. She'd been looking forward to overseeing the building of the extension to her library that was due to start this week and Bess and her four-month-old baby were far safer here in the country under Farhang Amiri's care than in plague-ridden London with some quacksalver of Cis's choosing.

Tamsin saw her face fall. 'What is it, my lady? Bad news?'

'Only time will tell, child. But it will please you, as I recall that you joined my service hoping to see more of the world. I have to journey to London rather sooner than I had intended and this time I'd like you to attend me. We will need to leave on Monday.'

She saw glee light up her maid's freckled face. Until Tamsin won herself a place as Alyce's maid, she had been condemned to a humdrum village life. Now she was to go to London, a place few Ewelme villagers would ever see.

'Is Ben Bilton coming with us, my lady?' she asked hopefully. Alyce's steward had been her brother's oldest friend and since his death had been all but a brother to her.

Alyce shook her head. 'Bilton is needed to manage matters in the palace and Father Marton those of the God's House.' She turned to her secretary. 'Simon, you will organise the journey and accompany us.'

'Of course, my lady,' said Brailles, paling a little at the prospect of responsibility, but quickly pulling himself together. 'It would be an honour.'

Alyce saw her tiring maid's face fall. Fussy and precise,

Simon could not be more of a contrast to Ben Bilton. Tamsin would be foreseeing Simon constantly carping at her short-comings in the weeks ahead. But, in the long run, keeping Tamsin and Ben apart would be no bad thing. He was utterly uninterested in the girl at present. Seeing her after she'd learnt something of London fashions and London ways might change his mind. And a match between them would delight her.

'Is the Duchess of York's man in the buttery?' she asked Simon. When he nodded, she put down her gardening tools and signed to them both to follow her. Two hours later, Cis's courier had been despatched with Alyce's answer and Simon was laying out the books Alyce wanted copied and bound at the Sign of the Mole for Tamsin to wrap in protective linen cloths.

Watching them approvingly, Alyce had a sudden thought. 'Oh, I nearly forgot,' she said, fumbling in the leather satchel in which she kept personal things. 'I bought you both something to read when I was in Oxford browsing in John Doll's bookshop. Tamsin, I know how you love Arthurian tales. It's a tale of Arthur and the Emperor Lucius. Doll says it's by Sir Thomas Malory, like the stories you were so absorbed in reading last September.'

Tamsin opened and shut her mouth, so grateful that she was lost for words.

Alyce chuckled. 'I'll take that as a thank you. In truth, it is sadly damaged. The binding has been ripped off and so has the ending. But bring it to London and I'll get Joan Moulton to rebind it.'

She handed the shabby bundle of pages to her. 'And ask Lady Bess to be sure that she and her servants are ready to leave straight after prime on Monday morning.'

After Tamsin had hurried away, Alyce turned to Simon. 'I thought you would enjoy Aquinas's lucid commentary on the book of Job. I know you are fascinated by his tribulations.' Simon took the dull little volume and bowed solemnly, hiding his disappointment. He too loved Arthurian tales and dreamt of chivalry, but his mistress saw him only as a dry-as-dust scholar, who aspired to nothing more than taking orders. She was still mourning her former man-of-business Denzil Caerleon, who had left her service in disgrace last September. He'd last been heard of taking despatches to Milan for Sir John Wenlock, before undertaking a pilgrimage to Jerusalem in atonement for his sins. Trust Denzil to make such a flamboyant gesture. He rose in Simon's mind's eye, energetic, charming and reckless.

Oblivious to her secretary's disappointment, Alyce was writing a personal list of necessaries when she remembered that, distracted by its contents, she hadn't destroyed Cis's letter and its dangerous mention of Newton Montagu. Where had she put it when she'd returned from the garden to change? She hurried upstairs to her chamber. It had been tidied, the bedding straightened and the cushions plumped up. The letter was nowhere to be seen. She hurled the cushions onto the floor and searched the bedding. Then she crouched down and looked under the bed. Nothing. Had she taken it into her reading closet? She was walking towards its door when she saw a rectangle of paper folded neatly and tucked under the candlestick on the mantelpiece. Put there by one of the maids, no doubt. Of whom only Tamsin could read, and Tamsin had been helping Bess with the baby. She crunched it into a tight ball, walked over to the brazier of burning charcoal by the window and watched it burn to ashes.

On Monday morning Alyce watched critically as Brailles packed her books into an iron-bound travelling chest.

'Are those the books we're taking to Moulton Inn to be copied when we collect my *Tales of Canterbury* from Joan?'

'Yes. But I kept out your commonplace book and your psalter.' He handed her the two books, one much-worn, the other resplendent in a gilded cover studded with jewels. 'They'll go in this little case, which can be strapped in front of your saddlebow.'

'Thank you, Simon. That was thoughtful. You know just what I like. Would my new Pisan poem about the shepherdess fit in it as well? I'd like to read it on the journey.'

'Easily,' he said, relieved that he'd chosen well. 'I'll get it out of the chest.'

She turned to Ben. 'Send a courier to Reading Abbey to arrange lodgings for us and go to Caversham Manor and tell Farhang that I will need him to join us in Reading and travel with us to London. His patient must surely be well by now. And Lady Bess and baby Edward might need his ministrations on the journey.'

Ben turned to go, then stopped.

'One more thing, your grace. We've received a complaint against Sir Richard Harcourt from one of our tenants in Marsh Gibbon. He's been thrown out and his house and land given to one of Sir Richard's retainers.'

Alyce frowned. 'Sir Richard has no holdings in Marsh Gibbon. This will be the work of his new wife, my cousin Catherine. She thinks she should have inherited the manor. But it has been part of the God's House foundation for over two decades. Write a letter to the Oxford Assize Court with

8

a plea of unlawful dispossession. William Marton can get the tenant to sign it and deliver it to the court. I'll have to sort it out when we get back. Oh and Ben, make sure Leo has some good expeditions. Keep him with you when you can, or I know he'll pine.'

She hated leaving her favourite hound behind, but there was no question of taking him to London. Still, a visit to the city would have its compensations. She was looking forward to calling at the Sign of the Mole in Paternoster Row. Joan Moulton would be full of the latest city gossip. Thinking of London's foremost book-making street stirred her sense of duty. Turning to the small portable altar on the wall behind her, she measured out two paternosters and an Ave Maria on her rosary, then picked up her book of hours and turned to the psalm of the day. But her mind kept wandering uneasily to Cis Neville's letter. What could it be about? Whose most horrible death? And why was utter secrecy required?

Broome Place, London

Joan Moulton heaved her substantial person up into the dark cave of the four-poster bed and stroked the tousled hair of the weeping girl with a beringed hand.

'Don't despair, Kate. A widow is a sight more comfortably settled than a wife. You've got a fine son – he must be seven now – and you can live your own life. A dower of a £1,000 a year, the finest house in Bread Street Ward and a clutch of the prettiest manors in Oxfordshire. Just be careful who you fall for next.'

Kate ducked deeper under her coverlet to block out her godmother's voice. Dust to dust, ashes to ashes. We came into this world with nothing and so out of it we shall go. The priest's words echoed and re-echoed in her head, a lunatic refrain of misery and hopelessness. With nothing, with nothing, with nothing. She recalled Richard's eager face alight with love, his strong arms reaching for her, the nervous fumblings that had become passionately confident: gone for ever. In her last sight of him, he had been ravaged and skeletal, eaten away by the evil crab inside him.

'I'll never look at another man.'

'I doubt that. And they'll be after you like bees round a honeypot, I'll be bound. Full of comfortable words and cow-eyed looks. Strumming on lutes and slipping love letters into your workbasket.'

Kate couldn't repress a wry smile at the thought of her

disorganised and rarely opened workbasket. Sewing had been her mother's passion; she avoided it like the plague, grateful to have a skilled maid like Amice to keep her clothes in repair.

She sniffed loudly and hauled herself up into a sitting position. 'I'd never find them there, that's for sure.'

She blew her nose on a scrap of fine lawn and sat up. 'It's good to see you, Aunt Joan. Thank you for coming. I don't know where to begin. The funeral was a nightmare. And Richard's family were just as horrible as he'd told me they were. They looked at me as if I was a bad smell.'

'I'm not surprised. You're entitled to a third of Richard's lands and a half of his chattels, besides return of your own dower, if I remember your settlement rightly. And the Ardernes have been scraping the bottom of their coffers to keep up appearances for years. Lady Arderne is as proud as Lucifer and she wanted Richard to marry above him, not below. The saving grace was your dowry – and now that's forfeit and the last of their unmortgaged estates are to be made over to you. Marriage is a risky thing when it ends early. It's a risky thing anyway, especially for a woman.'

'But you married often enough.'

'Once for duty, once for love, once for protection and once for fun – only it wasn't. They're all gone now and I'm better off than I've ever been. But I'll always miss Martin.'

'Martin?'

'My second husband. My parents married me to a lordly young ruffian called Nigel Morgan who was only interested in my dowry. He treated me like dirt, as my parents were in trade. Martin was one of his retainers. We fell in love, and when Nigel was killed in a hunting accident we eloped. But it cost me my children, swept away by Nigel's parents. Which is something you must be wary of.'

'Did you ever see them again?' said Kate.

Joan shook her head sadly. 'No. They haunt me still. After Martin was killed in the French wars, I married old Thomas Moulton and learnt to love the book trade. When he died, I built up the business with his son's help.'

'Until you got married again,' prompted Kate, with a little giggle.

Joan was relieved at her recovery. 'Yes, to that charming and unfaithful rascal Walter Caerleon. He tucked me away in the country so he could be free to flirt at court, then died of smallpox two years later. Still, that final folly of a marriage turned out to be unexpectedly rewarding. It brought me Charlbury Manor, my friendship with your parents and you, and Monique de Chinon, a pearl among companions.'

Kate had been ten when Joan arrived in Oxfordshire. Gregory and Anne Browne were wealthy London mercers and owned several manors near Witney, just west of the Caerleon estates. They had done all they could to comfort the disconsolate urban exile. After Walter's death and her return to Moulton Inn and her book business, they had stayed supportive and Gregory had been quick to let her know if neighbours hunted across her closes or encroached on her holdings.

Kate had grown from a quicksilver child with an impish grin to a beauty, but was plunged into misery by the death of her mother when she was fifteen. Asked by Gregory to be a godmother to her, Joan did her best to cheer her up with a combination of motherly sympathy and worldly-wise humour. Three years later, alight with love and her bright self again, Kate married Richard Arderne and disappeared into Warwickshire. The political troubles tearing the country apart meant that cautious bodies travelled as little as they could, but Kate and Richard were often in residence in Broome Place, the imposing Southwark house which Kate had inherited from her father. They renewed their friendship, and when Richard died Joan was the first person that Kate sent for. She had dropped everything and summoned a litter to carry her and Monique to Broome Place.

Now that Kate's mind had been distracted from the lost Richard, Joan decided to remind her about her son.

'But Kate, we must have an eye to the future. Where's Peter? The first thing we must do is to assert your right to guardianship. Families like the Ardernes can turn nasty when money's involved.'

Kate gasped, pushed back her hair and swung her legs out of bed. 'Of course we must. I wonder where he is. Sukey usually brings him up at about this time. He loves helping Amice to dress me. Perhaps they are still at breakfast.' She pulled a robe over her shoulders and ran out of the bedchamber, calling for him as she went.

There was no answering cry. Kate began to panic as she ran down the stairs to the great hall. No sign of Peter. On one side of the fire, her tiring maid Amice was bent over an embroidery frame. Joan, following more slowly, pursed her lips with disapproval at the sight of Amice's tight-fitting, low-cut, apple-green dress, the height of fashion that spring. Much too fine for a servant. No doubt it was one of Kate's, tempestuously cast aside after Richard's death. Sitting on a stool on the other side of the hearth was Monique, never a morning person, looking tetchy and ill at ease.

13

Kate ran up to her maid and grabbed her arm. 'Amice, have you seen Peter?'

'No, my lady. But Sukey isn't around either. Perhaps they've gone for a walk. Are you ready for me to dress you?'

As she spoke, a gawky thirteen-year-old stumbled into the hall, yawning and rubbing her eyes. Kate turned to her. 'Sukey, where's Peter?'

'I don't know, mistress. I've only just woken up and it's past ten of the clock. Must've been the milk and honey Nan Webster made for my cough.'

Kate paled. She looked wildly around and rushed out of the hall, shouting to the servants as she went. 'Look in the attics – and the cellars. Look everywhere. He loves hiding. The stables, the brewhouse – sweet mother Mary, the well – is its cover on?'

Pandemonium reigned. Doors banged, feet thundered on the stairs, excited voices disappeared into the highest and lowest recesses of the vast house.

Sukey stood uncertainly, her eyes oddly glazed. Joan walked up to the girl. 'Where might he be, Sukey? Did he have a favourite hidey-hole?'

Before the girl could answer, there were four peremptory knocks on the door to the street. Luke, the house steward, came up from his hunt in the cellars for Peter and looked through its peephole. He turned to Kate.

'Shall I open it, my lady? There's five men out there, with big staves in their hands.'

'Yes, and quickly. They may have found Peter.' Kate came eagerly forward as the door was swung open and the squad of men moved inside. Joan hung back, less sure that these were welcome visitors. The mulberry gowns smacked of the king's

14

courts and the beadle's office. The stoutest stepped forward, pasty-faced and codfish-eyed, a scroll in his hand.

'Are you Lady Katherine Arderne?' he asked. When Kate nodded, he unrolled the scroll and read aloud.

> Be it known that, in view of the most horrible and outrageous behaviour of the Lady Katherine Arderne in adulterously embracing men without number, the great house known as Broome Place in Bread Street ward and the Oxfordshire manors of Combe, Stonesfield and Hanborough and all her goods and chattels are forfeit, not excepting her jointure and dower, cattle, sheep and horses. And that her son Peter Gervais Arderne, heir to the estates and chattels hereby confiscated, is to be made a ward of the queen.

He rolled it up and looked around smugly. 'I am Beadle of Bread Street Ward. These men are my officers. Two of them will take charge of the house and instruct your servants as to their duties. Two will escort you yourself, mistress, to the Clink until the church court at Lambeth is in session to hear the case against you.'

Kate felt the room wheel around her and her knees buckled. But a brawny, clove-scented arm stopped her fall. Rock-like, Joan held her up and glared at the beadle.

'Henry Sewardby, on my life. I remember you when you were a snot-faced apprentice to Bartholomew Goldsmith. Fouled your britches whenever he raised a hand to you. By whose authority do you imprison an innocent woman without giving her the option of bail so that she can summon witnesses in her defence?'

Sewardby flushed. He knew exactly who Joan was – every citizen of London did. He cursed inwardly but returned to the attack. 'That of the Hustings Court. And since all her possessions are forfeit, she has not the wherewithal for bail.'

'But she has friends willing to stand bail for her,' snapped Joan. 'Namely me. How much is it set at?'

The beadle hesitated. Joan's wealth was legend. But he could name a sum that few could find at a moment's notice. 'Two thousand marks. In coin of the realm and on the instant. We cannot risk the whore absconding.' It was a small fortune and Kate's heart sank. Joan was unperturbed.

'Outrageous,' she said, fixing Sewardby with a stare worthy of Medusa. 'Monique, go to Moulton Inn. Take the litter; I told the porters to wait for us. My stepson is there today. Tell him to count two thousand marks out in those rubbishy new angels our sovereign lord has just had minted and to come back with you. And bring Friar Joseph too. They'll stand as witnesses.'

Then she turned to Sewardby again. 'Show me your warrant for the removal of Lady Arderne's son. And where is he now?'

The beadle glared at her. He knew he was on dubious legal ground. The hurried session at the Hustings had been short of aldermen and the judge an elderly magistrate so deaf and short-sighted that he'd only been aware of the purse tucked into his hand as he dropped his gavel. Neither he nor the Ardernes had reckoned on Kate having a champion as formidable as Mistress Moulton. Worse, the menservants had now returned from the search for Peter and were gathering in a scowling mass behind the two women. But he hadn't got to where he was by giving up easily.

'The paperwork will be shown in court and the boy's whereabouts are not your concern. All that matters is that he is away from his adulterous mother.'

'Abduction of a minor without authority is an offence,' said Joan crisply. 'As is premature confiscation of rightful dower. You remove goods from this house or from any other of Lady Katherine's properties at your peril. The Ardernes will be hearing from Lady Arderne's lawyers. I'm going to give you one more chance. Where is the boy?'

Sewardby smirked. 'At the Mermaid Inn with his grandfather Sir Gervais Arderne – if they haven't set off for Warwickshire already. He'll be with his grandmother at Langley by tomorrow. They are the best guardians for him until the courts decide the rights and wrongs of the affair. There's nothing you can object to in that. He is, after all, the Arderne heir.'

Kate's eyes filled with tears. She fell to her knees. 'Have a heart, your worship. He's only seven years old. He's never met his grandparents. He'll be terrified.'

'Children adapt easily enough,' said Sewardby coldly. 'I had to. So will he. Such is life.'

'Don't waste your breath on this toad, Kate,' said Joan. 'What we need is legal help. At least we know where Peter is and he won't come to any harm with the Ardernes. He hasn't been made a royal ward yet. Come upstairs. While we're waiting for Monique's return with William, you must dress. Then we'll go to Moulton Inn and get some food into you.'

Kate shook her head. 'I'm not hungry.'

'Nonsense. You need to eat. A full stomach brings courage. After that, we'll call on Lord Wenlock, the queen's chamberlain. He owes me a favour or two and no one knows more about the legal ins and outs of wardship. He might even win temporary custody of Peter; he's got a houseful of Lancastrian wards in his charge already. He'll be at the Royal, his old tower house in Chequer Lane. Amice, stop ogling those men and look to your mistress.'

Unstoppable as a warhorse, Joan swept up the staircase, shepherding Kate protectively ahead of her, followed by a sullen Amice. Sewardby, who had blanched at the mention of Lord Wenlock's name, looked helplessly after her. Matters were going badly wrong.

As Joan, Kate and Amice disappeared along the landing, little Sukey broke away from the cluster of maids at the far end of the hall and raced after them. By the time she reached Kate's chamber, Amice was already in the wardrobe looking out clothes for her mistress.

Sukey grabbed Kate's arm wildly. 'I'm sorry, my lady, I'm sorry. It was all my fault. If I hadn't slept in, Peter would be safe.'

Kate put her arms around Sukey's thin shoulders and gave her a comforting hug.

Joan looked at the girl appraisingly. 'From the look of your eyes, I suspect you didn't have a choice, Sukey. There must have been more than milk and honey in the posset you drank yesterday. There's a traitor in this house. Someone who laced your cup and opened the door to whoever spirited Peter away in the night. Which gives me an idea, Kate. We could do with a friend in the Arderne camp, and from what you've told me of your pinchpenny mother-in-law, she won't object to a free maid. Sukey, would you be willing to ride pillion behind one of the grooms to the Mermaid Inn and see if you can persuade Sir Gervais to let you look after Peter? I'm sure he'll be much happier if you're with him.'

Sukey wiped her nose on her sleeve and nodded vigorously. 'I'll pack my bundle and go and find Tom.'

Kate felt her usual energetic self revive a little. 'Sukey, tell him I love him and I'll see him very soon. And take some things for him. That old blanket he loves and the little sword his father gave him. And some clothes. Now I need to dress.' She went into the wardrobe, where she found that Amice had got out a long-sleeved, deep-blue gown of flowered damask with a deep white-edged V-neck filled with a frontlet of black silk. She let her nightgown fall from her slim shoulders and began the slow process of dressing: a fine lawn chemise under her gown and over it, fastened high under her breasts, a wide belt studded with silver roundels holding seed pearls circling sapphires.

By the time that Amice had pleated a starch-stiffened white veil into a pair of butterfly wings arranged over one of the truncated cone headdresses made fashionable by the new queen, Kate felt more in control of her destiny. She put on her favourite necklace, three linked silver chains, which Richard had given her on their wedding day, then inspected herself in the looking glass hanging on the wall. Tip-tilted eyes in a small, oval face looked warily out at her. She sighed. There was a time when her reflection had given her pleasure; now it seemed a meaningless vanity.

She turned to her maid. 'And now a cloak, Amice. The black velvet one with the sable trim.'

Every inch a gentlewoman of standing, Kate came out of her chamber onto the landing. Joan nodded approvingly.

'That's more like it, Kate. And I've given Sukey some money and one of my rings. She'll need to be able to send us a message when she gets to the Mermaid.'

Kate blenched. 'Won't it be dangerous, godmother? She's hardly more than a child.'

'But a brave one,' said Joan. 'And we need to know what's going on.'

As she and Kate descended the stairs, with Amice holding up Kate's trailing skirt, there was a hammering at the front door. One of Kate's menservants opened it and a tall man in an ink-stained green gown surged in, followed by Monique and portly Friar Joseph, perspiring and red-faced in his thick grey habit.

Joan bowed her head in front of the friar to receive his blessing, then turned to her stepson. Looking at his broad, honest face, its blue eyes blazing indignantly and its chin jutting furiously forward, she wished, not for the first time, that she'd had the luck to marry his father when he was in the prime of life.

'William, you made good speed. Thank you. Have you got the bail money?'

'I have, belle-mère.' He glanced at Sewardby and curled his lip. 'But is it wise to give coin to these rascals? Surely a bond, properly witnessed, would be safer.'

'A child's life could be at stake. We need to act swiftly and the witnessing of a bond will take all morning. But with the beadle's signature and you and Joseph as witnesses, our money should be safe enough.'

Kate heard the clip-clop of hoofs leaving the stable and said a silent prayer for Sukey's safety.

Montagu Inn

The ornate tunnel-roofed carriage lumbered down Holborn, turned south along Old Bailey and then east into the city at Ludgate. Occasionally jerking sharply as its massive wheels hit potholes, it still made a brave show, drawn by six well-matched horses, gilded sides gleaming in the sunshine, canvas hangings bright with heraldic devices and two long pennants fluttering from the flag staves slotted into its sides. One showed the young Duchess of Suffolk's complex combination of Plantagenet, Neville and Pole; the other Alyce's preferred device – her mother Maud Burgersh's twin-tailed lion.

Two yeomen rode ahead to clear the way and outriders flanked its sides as it clattered along Bower Row and around the vast bulk of St Paul's, where a mill of people were gazing at a broadsheet attached to the great west door. The huge black capitals of its first and last lines were visible even from the carriage. A stocky man, proud of knowing his letters, was reading it aloud for the benefit of the crowd.

THE PROPHECY OF MERLIN
The usurper York and his traitrous polity
oppress the people.
But remember the words of Merlin:
When the Lion of Justice is dead
It will be the age of strange men
And whatever a man seizes he will hold.
Behold the greed and the effusion of blood.
But the miracle-worker will return
With a great host and honour
And truth and right will be restored.
Look to your true anointed king.
LANCASTER ARISE

The driver slowed inquisitively, but predatory hucksters began to thrust their wares through any gap that they could find in the curtains of the carriage. He stung the flank of the lead horse with his whip and pulled away.

Riding beside the carriage on Larkspur, the dappled jennet that would be Alyce's mount while she was in London, Simon Brailles wondered at such flagrant treason being tolerated on the doors of London's cathedral. But even as he watched, two constables came hurtling out of the gatehouse to the precinct, tore down the broadsheet and hustled the reader away. Simon didn't envy him his punishment. The pillory, if he was lucky. Tyburn gibbet if he wasn't. King Edward of York was sensitive to criticism.

As the horses slowed to negotiate the narrow entrance to Paul's Wharf Hill, a gypsy of a woman in a shabby green cloak was striding up the steep, narrow lane, a basket strapped on her back. The driver bellowed a warning, flicking his long whip at her and she fell into a doorway. She turned and raised an arm to protect herself. Her eyes caught Simon's and her lips hissed something inaudible. Simon crossed himself as he recognised Agnes Quincey, the Duchess of York's herbalist. Was it a curse? What had that notorious witch been up to so near Montagu Inn? Nothing good, he was sure.

He was aching in every muscle. It was four long days since they'd left Ewelme Palace. He loathed such snail-pace journeys. It could have been done in half the time without the carriage, but Duchess Bess was in no state to ride. To make things worse, they'd had to wait half a day at Reading. Farhang, always a law to himself, had refused to leave the patient he'd been treating until he'd seen her out of danger. Thanks to pouring rain and a horse with a twisted fetlock, they'd only got as far that day as the Ostrich Inn at Colnbrook. Princess Alyce had closeted herself in an upstairs chamber with her books and the young duchess had spent the afternoon teaching Tamsin how to address folk of rank and to make a courtly curtsey. Their giggles had made it impossible for him to concentrate on the Tale of Lucius he'd borrowed from Tamsin. They'd been held up again in the morning because the young duchess had insisted on watching the May dances, laughing in a most unseemly way when the maze-witted Moorish men had hoisted Tamsin on their shoulders as their May Queen. He quashed the memory of the girl leaping and skipping among them with shocking abandon but remarkable grace.

At least they had been made marvellously comfortable by the nuns of Syon the next night and he'd enjoyed looking at the books in their library. Elizabeth Muston, the abbess, had presented Alyce with a copy of John Capgrave's *Life of St Catherine*, which she'd long coveted. Farhang had disappeared into their physic garden of course, followed by Tamsin. Fair enough, Simon supposed; back in Ewelme, Tamsin's grandmother Nan Ormesby often did duty as a nurse in Farhang's infirmary and Tamsin used to help out there too. But he'd felt slighted by her woodenness in his presence and her relaxed manner with Farhang. He was, he had to admit to himself, jealous of the old Persian's ease with women, great ladies and common wenches alike. Though he was an ancient of seventy-seven, women seemed to blossom when he spoke to them as if he was an Adonis. He looked across at Farhang, now nodding in the saddle. Just as well he had a steady steed like old Jankin. And a high saddle cantle to support his back.

Soon after the crossing with Thames Street, the horses slowed and the great doors of Montagu Inn, Alyce's London home, swung open. The cavalcade crowded into the courtyard.

Simon dismounted, then held Jankin's head while Farhang slid stiffly to the ground. Then he handed both sets of reins to Joseph Pek, a grizzled veteran of the Normandy campaigns, sometime bedesman of the God's House, but now Marshal of the Stables of Montagu Inn. He had been in Lady Alyce's service ever since he was wounded at Orléans over forty years ago.

'Good day, Master Brailles, good to see Larkspur in fine fettle. And Master Amiri, I see you're riding Jankin. Nice change for him after his fighting days.' The old warhorse bent his head and nuzzled hopefully into Joseph's pocket. He pulled out two wrinkled apples and gave one to each horse, crooning endearments as he scratched their forelocks. The grooms led them away. Farhang made straight for the hall and Simon and Joseph turned to the carriage. Their mistress had drawn back its painted canvas curtain and was putting a slim foot clad in soft green leather onto the short ladder that the driver had propped against it. Brailles held out an arm, but she waved it away.

'Let me be, Simon. I'll tell you when I'm too feeble to get myself down from a carriage. Good to see you, Joseph. How are you finding London after Ewelme? I hope Hugh and Brian are pulling their weight.'

'Shaping up well enough, my lady, though they are a mite too fond of gaming,' said Pek. 'Good to see you back so soon. Peggotty has made your favourite pudding, a Sussex Pond. Cargo came in from Bilbao yesterday and she sent Ellen down for lemons at dawn's crack. Oh and that old beldam her grace of York is in the solar. Came down from Baynard's Castle on the tide.'

Alyce grimaced. 'I guessed she'd get wind of my coming.

24

Cis is never one to waste time. The only trouble with Montagu Inn is that it's so close to her gloomy stronghold. Give Lady Bess a hand, Simon, and join us upstairs when she's settled. Where's Farhang gone to? Planning to get a quart jug to his lips, I suppose. I want him to pot up those seedlings we were given by the sisters of Syon. Come, Tamsin, I'll be needing you to take my things to our chamber.' She hooked her full skirts over her arm with a practised hand, stepped down onto the fresh straw that the yard boys had laid down between the carriage and the house, and swept towards the porch.

Tamsin, for whom the four days of travelling had been an astonishing succession of new experiences, scrambled out after her and looked around the busy courtyard. A girl of about her own age was stretching wet sheets between the tenterhooks beside the south wall. She gave her a hard stare, then grinned. Tamsin smiled shyly back. Once the driver had handed down Lady Alyce's bags, she swung them over her shoulders and hurried after her mistress.

Pek looked after Alyce admiringly. 'Sixty-three years old but still willowy as a linden tree, God save her,' he said to Simon. 'How did your journey go?' Before Simon could reply, a groan came from the carriage.

'Help me, Simon. What a dreadful journey. All that hanging around. And the jolting. If only we could have gone by river.' Bess of York looked exhausted, her blonde prettiness blowsy. She turned to Pek. 'You better give me an arm as well, Joseph. I ache all over. Is my lord here as well as my mother?'

'Not yet, your grace. You made better time than we expected. We've sent a messenger to the Manor of the Rose.'

'In that case, I'll return with mother. Waiting for Jack is a thankless pastime.'

Bess clambered wearily out of the carriage. She was followed by her old nurse Molly, who beckoned Joseph over and handed him a lidded basket from which came a frantic mewing.

'Take these to the kitchen, Joseph. Two new kittens for the Manor of the Rose. It was crawling with vermin last time I was there. These are the Ewelme Palace cat Greymalkin's babies and she's a capital ratter. They'll need milk. Then come back for little Ned. Fast asleep still, the cherub. But he'll need a feed soon.'

It was left to Simon to escort Bess into the porch, along the panelled screens passage and into the great hall. As she hung on his arm, he revelled in her sweet, sweaty scent, and when she turned her lazy-lidded eyes to him and thanked him his pulse raced. Mad dreams of himself as Lancelot and her as Guinevere arose in his mind. Could he be losing his sense of vocation? First those unsettling feelings he'd been having about Tamsin on May Morning and now the young duchess. He urgently needed to cleanse his thoughts. He would make his confession as soon as he could. Lady Alyce had often hinted that if he were to be ordained she would make him her personal chaplain, an infinitely more prestigious position than mere secretary.

Inside the hall, sunbeams danced in the column of smoke rising from the old-fashioned central hearth. A small cauldron hung over it on an iron pole that ran between the tall firedogs on which the logs rested and the air was scented with ginger and cinnamon. Farhang was already settled in one of the high-backed chairs around the fire, enjoying a tankard of the spiced ale. Bess subsided thankfully onto another one and stretched her feet out towards the merrily burning logs. Although it was the third day of May and the cherry trees trained against the walls of the courtyard were white with blossom, there had been frost on the wide verges of the highway from Syon that morning.

'Sweet Mother of God, my feet are as swollen as if I had the dropsy. Get me cushions and a footstool, Molly, and put the kittens in my lap. Is Ned still asleep? Good. That ale smells wonderful. And is there anything to eat?'

Just then Tamsin appeared from the staircase to the solar and bobbed a slightly wobbly curtsey to Bess, who nodded approvingly.

'Getting better. But you'll need more practice to impress the court ladies. Now pour me and Nanny Molly some ale.'

Tamsin giggled, then went over to the sideboard, took two tankards off its middle shelf, ladled ale into them and handed one to Lady Bess and one to Molly. Then she filled a third and handed it to Simon.

'Simon, Princess Alyce said that you were to show Peggotty which bags were which and bring in her chest of books and then take some wine up to the solar for her and the Duchess of York. But that you were to have a tankard of ale first.'

Simon took the mug, impressed but also annoyed at how quickly Tamsin was adapting to London, a place that he himself had found utterly daunting when he came to the city for the first time. As he sipped the hot ale, he watched her inventing games for the kittens, dangling beads in and out of their tiny paws. She didn't even glance up when he replaced his tankard on the sideboard and went out into the courtyard where Montagu Inn's cheerful chamberlain Peggotty Lambourn was overseeing the unloading of the wagons. Women ruled the roost in Alyce's London inn, just as they did at Ewelme. After

27

he'd told Peggotty where to put which bags, Simon asked her if Agnes Quincey had been in the house earlier on.

'That she was,' said Peggotty. 'She came with the Duchess of York on her barge from Baynard's Castle, then went into the kitchen to make a new poultice for Pek's stiff joints. Nice little chit, that Tamsin, ain't she? Quick as a cock-sparrow.'

Simon nodded a little coldly, picked up the chest of books and carried it into the hall. Then he filled a tall silver jug with wine and went upstairs to the solar. Outside its door a disconsolate maid sat on a stool. Evidently the duchesses wanted no witnesses to their conversation. He gave the girl a sympathetic nod as he opened the door.

The room always took his breath away. A series of windows in its south wall looked out onto the Thames. Floor-to-ceiling tapestries in rich reds, blues and greens, gleaming with silver and gold thread, lined the other walls. Looking at the rearing hoofs and rolling eyeballs of the larger-than-life horses and the heroic gestures and plumed helmets of their riders, Simon marvelled, as he always did, at the exquisite weaving. They showed scenes from John Lydgate's *Siege of Thebes*, a tale the old poet had hoped would be worthy of being added to those of Geoffrey Chaucer's pilgrims.

Alyce had admired Lydgate, who had once been her tutor, and she had commissioned the tapestries in Rouen twenty years earlier, when her husband Duke William had taken her with him to France to bring back the French king's niece, Margaret of Anjou, to marry King Henry VI. She was barely sixteen and Alyce had become both mother and mentor to her. But half England had seen the girl as a tool of their enemy France, and when the poor mazed king fell into a trance they'd turned to the Duke of York as Protector rather than

Queen Margaret. Now, after a decade of civil war, she was in exile in Lorraine, queen only in the eyes of her raggle-taggle court at Koeur, and the Duke of York's son was on the throne as Edward IV. How the wheel of Fortune whirled, Simon reflected.

In the longest of the solar's walls was a wide fireplace, its hearth ablaze with sweet-scented applewood logs. But the chairs in front of it were empty; so too were the stools on each side of the chess table beside the window. Puzzled, he turned to go, but then there was a rattle of curtain rings and a high cackle came from the canopied four-poster bed that stood at the far end of the room.

'We're here, Brailles. Too draughty by the fire. Good, you've brought more wine. We can drink another toast to the damnation of my daughter-in-law.' Cecily, Duchess of York, was lounging back against a heap of embroidered cushions, a bright-eyed monkey perched on her shoulder. At fifty, the beaky Neville nose dominated her once-beautiful face more than it used to, but the black eyes that had flashed to such effect through the years had lost none of their fire. The only occasion on which her will had been flouted was two and a half years ago when her son King Edward had told her of his secret marriage to Elizabeth Wydeville, widow of the staunchly Lancastrian Sir John Grey. The argument that followed was legend. Cis's furious shrieks, counterpointed by Edward's defiant bellows, had been overheard by the entire royal household.

'She's five years older than you, with two sons of her own.'

'So much the better. I've fathered two babes myself. It shows that neither of us is barren and my realm needs heirs as speedily as I can get them.'

'She's a Lancastrian born and bred.'

'So's half England. What better way of uniting the kingdom?'

'But Warwick is negotiating in France for Bona of Savoy.'

'A moustachioed trout who squints. No man should be wived against his appetite.'

Presented with a fait accompli, Cis was forced to welcome Elizabeth, but it was through gritted teeth. Nor had Elizabeth even tried to ingratiate herself with Edward's mother. She was much more interested in furthering Wydeville interests. Two years after Elizabeth's coronation, Cis was still burning with resentment.

Simon refilled her goblet, then went around the bed to fill Alyce's. She was sitting up stiffly, a troubled frown on her face, but she gave Simon a weary smile and took a hesitant sip of wine. It was one thing for the king's mother to damn his queen, quite another for a subject to do so.

Cis's second glass of wine brought her to a crescendo of indignation. 'Edward and that trollop are planning to celebrate their third year of marriage at Windsor, in a fortnight's time. She wants a grand ceremony this time, to make up for marrying secretly in Grafton Wydeville church with scarce a witness. Dressed all in green like pagans. Jacquetta's descended from Melusine and the Magi, they say. I'm sure she used sorcery to ensnare my son.'

Simon doubted it. Elizabeth's mother Jacquetta might or might not be descended from Melusine and the Magi, but she had abundant royal blood in her veins. She was a Luxemburg princess who had been married at seventeen to Henry V's brother John, Duke of Bedford, commander of the English forces in France. When he died three years later she'd made a love match, eloping with the dark and dashing Sir Richard Wydeville. Then Bedford's chamberlain and Lieutenant of

Calais, he was now Earl Rivers. All fourteen of their children were startlingly good-looking, but Elizabeth was truly beautiful. Charms and potions hadn't been needed to seduce Edward, just cunning management by the Wydevilles' obliging Northamptonshire neighbour William Hastings. He had invited the king to a hunt and made sure that they pursued a stag through Whittlewood Forest and called in at Grafton for refreshment – served by Elizabeth and her two little boys.

Alyce's eyes had glazed over, but Cecily ranted on. 'And now Jacquetta is using Elizabeth's power over Edward to mate the rest of her brood with the oldest and noblest blood in the land. My fool of a sister Katherine celebrated her sixty-sixth birthday by marrying Elizabeth's brother John Wydeville. He was barely nineteen. She thinks he loves her because he spent a few weeks strumming a lute under her window and penning rhymes to the glories of her eyes and thighs. As if he wanted anything from her but her estates.'

Simon heard his mistress murmur neutrally. He knew that the apparent accord between the two women was illusory. Cecily would not have come anywhere near Montagu Inn unless she wanted something from Alyce. He wondered what they had been talking about before he came in. Presumably the most horrible death referred to in the letter from Cis he'd read from beginning to end before tucking it tidily onto the mantelpiece. He also wondered what lay behind Cis's reference to Newton Montagu. He knew it was one of Alyce's more remote manors, deep in Dorset, but he'd never been there.

Cecily took a long draught from her goblet. 'But enough of the Wydevilles. How are my daughter and my new grandson? No ill effects after the journey? And how is the feeding going? I hope there is no need of a wet nurse. Nothing but Neville milk is good enough for a Neville baby. Now, who might I match him to?'

The Duchess of York played the marriage market with just as much energy and acumen as Jacquetta of Bedford and Queen Elizabeth. Getting the Suffolk estates hitched to Bess seven years ago had given her huge satisfaction. Alyce, politically isolated since William's murder and King Henry's mental collapse, had been in no position to object.

'They seem well,' said Alyce. 'We rested at intervals along the way and Bess's breasts are bountiful. Little Ned is adorable. And Farhang came with us in case she or the baby ailed.'

'At what hour of the clock and on what day was he born?' demanded Cecily. 'I must set my soothsayer to work – I want to know the shape of his future. Perhaps the Church...'

Alyce frowned. 'On Friday the thirteenth of December, at two in the morning. Not the most propitious of dates, if you set any store by such things. But surely you don't go in for such sacrilegious tittle-tattle? Remember the Duchess of Gloucester's downfall.'

'And remember that those prophecies of Henry's doom were fulfilled. The stars are older and wiser than we are, my dear. Nor does the day itself matter much: it's the conjunction of the planets that reveals all. As that charming astrologer of yours Denzil Caerleon always said. I remember him being rather a favourite of yours at Wingfield.'

Simon saw his mistress wince at the mention of Denzil – and saw Cis smile maliciously. She would have heard all about the uproar over Caerleon and Marlene Stonor last September from her network of gossips.

'I hear he is retained by the Earl of Warwick now. Living in Calais and making discreet forays into the courts of Burgundy and France to sound out treasons planned against my son the king.'

Bemused at the idea of Denzil in service to the mighty Earl of Warwick, Alyce decided to change the subject. She turned to a topic guaranteed to distract Cis.

'And how are your other sons?'

A complacent smile spread over Cis's face. 'Richard has just left for Yorkshire again: he's being trained in arms at Middleham Castle by my nephew of Warwick. I was sorry to see him go, but he is set on being a soldier now that Edward has taken the Vere lands away from him and restored them to the Earl of Oxford. A mistake, in my opinion. Vere seems meek enough at the minute, but isn't to be trusted. He was just a frightened boy when he gave his allegiance to Edward and I suspect he's still heartsick at his father's and brother's deaths. Still, the match with my niece Meg may keep him loyal.'

Simon saw Alyce start with surprise. 'Meg matched to John de Vere?'

'Yes,' said Cis. 'Hasn't she told you?'

'No,' said Alyce abruptly and subsided into silence. Simon knew why. John de Vere was notorious for his betrayal of his loyally Lancastrian father and older brother, both of whom had been tried for treason and brutally executed on Tower Hill five years ago. His mother Elizabeth, an old friend of Lady Alyce's, was so embittered that she had vowed never to speak his name again.

Cis was watching Alyce triumphantly. 'I thought you'd disapprove. That'll be why Meg hasn't let you know, no doubt.'

Simon saw Alyce recover herself with an effort.

'What of your other son, Clarence?'

'Clarence is here in London and wants to escape my rule. He

talks of an establishment of his own as soon as he is sixteen. His friends are a riotous lot, but he is fortunately somewhat checked by my brother George, now raised to the dignity of Archbishop of York. But you know George, of course; he interests himself in Oxford a good deal as he's the University's chancellor as well as England's. That reminds me: when I told him you were soon to be in London, he suggested that we all join him for a feast at his palace in Temple Bar tomorrow night.'

Simon knew that his mistress loathed such tedious ceremonial occasions. But she remained composed, nodding courteously.

'Of course. Simon, make sure that you send a man to thank His Grace. And say that you will attend me. But Cis, tell me about Vere. Is his mother still set against him?'

'Absolutely. She won't have him at Hedingham at all. Edward has done him proud, though. He made him a Knight of the Bath on the eve of Elizabeth's coronation and he's being appointed Chamberlain while Warwick is away.'

'Where is the Earl going?'

'It's a face-saving manoeuvre. As all Europe knows, Edward owes him his throne, but Queen Elizabeth and he are like cat and dog. So Edward is sending him on a diplomatic mission to treat for peace with France. For which pigs might whistle, since Edward signed a pact with Burgundy last autumn. And it's ill-advised. The king needs his strong right arm close by, especially given this Pailton business. The devil only knows what lies behind it. But tell me, how is Ewelme? It's the prettiest domain in Oxfordshire by now, I'll warrant.'

'I hate being away from it,' said Alyce, sincerity in her voice for the first time. 'The school thrives: we sent four pupils to study in Oxford in October. We've a vacancy for a bedesman in the God's House and Bishop Waynflete has an elderly scholar who needs a quiet harbour in his old age, but could still put in some time with our older boys. He'll be the fifth retired cleric there. It's becoming quite a college. And we're installing underground pipes from the Ewelme brook to bring water to the God's House vegetable gardens. It was Farhang's notion. He saw such a system in Bury St Edmund's Abbey. The bedesmen will be able to increase their stipend by sending produce to Wallingford market. The new wing of the palace is almost finished, too. There will be a fine chamber for you when you next journey to Oxfordshire. You can see all over the shire from its turret.'

But Cis was no longer listening. She had no intention of visiting Ewelme and was quickly bored by any news that didn't concern her own interests. Alyce changed the subject again.

'Cis, as we passed St Paul's I saw a broadsheet nailed on its door. It referred to the prophecy of Merlin. Which, I seem to remember from Geoffrey of Monmouth's telling, predicts the undoing of the king. Is there unrest in the city?'

Cis reddened with anger. 'These ancient romances have no bearing on modern times. Merlin was a devil's incubus. Edward is more and more loved by … by the better part of the citizenry. As he deserves to be. They couldn't have a more regal monarch. Unlike that saintly scarecrow Henry.'

Hoofs sounded in the courtyard and Cis abruptly stopped talking, heaved herself upright and swung her legs onto the floor. 'There's the horse-litter to take us home to Lombard Street. We won't rest on your hospitality further. Don't forget what we discussed. Keep me informed. And hurry. There's no time to lose.'

She gathered up her gown, got down from the bed and headed for the door, which Simon leapt forward to open for her. Then she paused.

'One other thing. You said Farhang came with you to London. Send him to me at Baynard's when he's rested. Tell him I'd like some of the excellent ointment he made up for my sister Katherine last time you brought him to London.'

She swept out of the room, calling for her maid. Her monkey snarled at Alyce, then with a hiss scampered after her. Simon was put in mind of a witch's familiar.

The Mermaid Inn

The bone-shaking pillion ride to the Mermaid shook Sukey out of the torpor induced by the drugged posset. She slipped down from the horse and Tom handed her the bundle of her own and Peter's clothes.

'God be with you, child,' he said. 'Sure you don't want me to come in with you?'

'Best not,' said Sukey. 'If you've already gone, then I can't be sent back, can I?'

'Depends on how ruffianly they are,' said Tom. 'I could wait around the corner for a bit, if you like. Just in case they throw you out straight away.'

Sukey thought quickly. 'All right, why not? Wait at the porch of St Bride's, the church we just passed.'

She raised her arm in quick salute, then disappeared into the courtyard of the old inn. Maids were busy in its upper galleries, pulling out hay mattresses, sheets and feather beds, shaking them and hanging them over the railings to air. A skinny boy was peeling rushes and throwing long lengths of pith into a shallow pan of fat to make tapers. Sukey walked over to him.

'Have you seen a lad? He's a bit smaller than you and his name is Peter. I think he must have been brought here early this morning.' The lad looked up and Sukey saw that his grimy face was tear-stained and bruised. He looked wary and shook his head. But Sukey had seen his eyes swivel towards an open door at the far end of the courtyard.

'Micky, get on with those rushes. How many times do I have to tell you not to talk to strangers?' A rangy raw-boned woman high on the upper gallery was looking down on them.

'Wasn't talking,' said the boy sullenly.

'And what do you want, missie? We don't buy from pedlars.'

'I've been sent by the Ardernes,' Sukey called up to her boldly. 'To look after the little boy. I've got some clothes for him.' She opened her bundle and held up a pair of breeches and a little doublet.

The woman looked relieved. 'Thank the Virgin and all her saints for that. Sir Gervais said a wench would be coming. The boy certainly needs somebody to look after him, poor little mite. We've tucked him well away as we were told to, so that no one could hear him crying. Micky, take her to the kitchen and tell Cook to shut her into the meat larder with the boy. Then you can relieve Abel on the spits. I need him to help me with the slop pails.'

Sukey followed the boy across the courtyard, through the small door and along a short passage that opened into a high-roofed kitchen bustling with scullions. Breakfast in an inn was always a busy time. A cauldron of pottage stood on a high trivet close to the roaring fire in the great hearth and a glistening hog was skewered on the central spit. A haunch of beef, four chickens and two rabbits were positioned below it on smaller upright spits. The great handle that turned the hog roasting spit was being wound round by an older boy, who was sweating profusely. Abel, no doubt. There was no mistaking Cook, either. He was almost as wide as he was tall, with a stained apron wrapped around his capacious middle. He cast a wary but kindly eye on her.

'Not looking for work, I hope. I don't hold with women in my kitchen. More trouble than they're worth.'

'She's come to look after that boy they brought here this morning,' said Micky. 'Nancy says she's to be locked in with him.'

'Christ's passion, about time too. The little fool won't eat or drink. Here's the key.'

The smell of roasting meat made Sukey feel desperately hungry. Cook saw her longing glance at the spits and laughed.

'Fancy some food, do you? Abel, that middle hen is about done. Take it off and put a leg on a platter for the girl. No, two legs, one for the boy as well. Put a ladleful of the ginger sauce over them. And go and check the bread oven. The rolls should be cooked. Cut a wedge of cheese too and take it all over to the larder. Perhaps she can make him eat. There's already some water in there. Micky, show her the way.'

Sukey was careful to keep her face expressionless and vacant as she followed Micky into another small courtyard. There was a well in the middle of it and several doors leading off it, one with a barred window. Micky fitted the key that Cook had given him into the lock and tried to turn it, but it was too stiff.

'Help me, can you, miss?' he said. Sukey stepped forward and saw that his thin fists were bloodied at the knuckles and swollen. She jiggled the key in the lock until it turned, then pushed the great door inwards. The room inside was smelly and dark. Tubs and barrels lined the walls and carcases hung from hooks in the ceiling. Sukey strained her eyes, but couldn't see Peter anywhere. Then a heap of blankets on the floor in one corner stirred and a small tousled head peeked out.

'Peter, it's me, Sukey,' she said. 'Don't be frightened. I'm going to stay with you.'

'Where's Mamma?' said the child, a sob choking his voice.

As Sukey bent down and put her arms round him, Abel came into the room, carrying a platter heaped with food. He put it on the larder's thick stone shelf.

'God's teeth, what a stench. Hasn't he been taught to use a pot?'

Sukey was about to snap sharply at the sneering scullion, but remembered that she needed to seem spiritless.

Not waiting on an answer, Abel grabbed Micky by the ear. 'Come on, you lazy devil. Your turn to sweat on the spit.' He dragged the boy out of the larder and turned the key in the lock.

Sukey sprang to the barred window in the door. 'Micky, stop. Could you tell Cook I need hot water and cloths and some sort of light? Peter's always been frightened of the dark.' Micky looked back and nodded, then stumbled out as Abel gave his shin a brutal kick.

Sukey crouched down beside Peter again. As well as smelling foul, he was icy cold and there was a blank look in his eyes.

'It's all right, Peterkin. I'm with you now. And we'll get you back to Mamma, I promise.' Peter said nothing, but he nestled close to her. Sukey put her arms around him and held him tight. When Micky came back he passed first a lit candle then a jug of hot water and some old linen cloths through the bars. She took them, then stretched her hand towards him.

'Take these,' she whispered. 'The penny is for you, but the ring is for a kind lady called Joan Moulton. Take it to her at the Sign of the Mole in Paternoster Row. She'll give you three more pennies when you tell her that I'm with Peter. You see, Peter's mother wants him back very, very much and Joan is helping her to look for him.'

A wail rose from Peter at the mention of his mother. A worried little frown appeared on Micky's face, but he took the penny and the ring.

'Micky! What the devil are you doing?' It was Abel, shouting across the courtyard from the kitchen door. 'I told you not to talk to that girl. Come here at once.' Micky cringed in fright and hurried away.

Praying that the boy would deliver the message, Sukey stripped off Peter's dirty breeches, rolled them up tightly and pushed them through the barred window. Then she cleaned him up and dressed him in the fresh clothes she had brought. Fingers had to serve as a hairbrush and a strong straw for his teeth. They had just started to eat when the key rattled in the lock again and Abel came in. He pulled her roughly to her feet. To her horror she saw that Joan's ring was on his grubby thumb.

'So you were planning to send word to his family, were you?' he said, giving her arm a vicious twist. 'Let's see what else you've got.' He grabbed the hanging pocket on her belt, took the purse out of it with an appreciative oath and stuffed it into the front of his jerkin.

'And it's no good thinking that anyone can rescue you. Sir Gervais is taking Peter off with him tomorrow and I doubt he'll want a little spy with him. A sound whipping is all you'll get. In fact, I might teach you an even better lesson right now.' He shook her hard and began to wrench the dress off her shoulders.

'Stop that, you churl.' An elderly man in a dark green velvet cloak shouldered his way into the larder, followed by a liveried retainer. 'What on earth is going on here? That's no way to treat a little lass. And why is my grandson being kept in a dark larder?'

Abel let Sukey go and made a sketchy bow. 'We were told that he had to be hidden away where no one would find him, your honour. This girl said that you had sent her, so we let her in. But I found out that she was sending a message to someone called Joan Moulton. She's a spy.'

'Peter should not have been put in a hole like this. Tell Nancy to get an upstairs room ready for him at once. As to the girl, I'll deal with her. Now, get out.' When Abel had left, Sir Gervais turned to the children and saw the way that Peter was huddling himself closely to Sukey.

'It looks as if my grandson knows you well enough. Who are you?'

So this was Sir Gervais Arderne, thought Sukey. He wasn't the ogre she'd imagined at all. Stooped and thin, with eyes that had a deep weariness about them but also held the hint of a twinkle. She wondered why Sir Richard had always been so against him. She decided that honesty was the safest plan. Slightly qualified.

'I've looked after him since he left his wet nurse, sir. His mother sent me to find him when the beadle told her where he had been taken. Please let me stay with him; he's so little and frightened.'

Sir Gervais looked puzzled. 'So you aren't the wench Harcourt said would be looking after Peter? Well, you're a bit young, but he seems fond enough of you. And, judging by the stink, the boy still needs your care. I thought my squire Tobias could look after him, but I hadn't realised how small he was. I can see that he'll be much happier if you're with him. I'm sure my wife will tell me I'm an old fool – she doesn't hold with spoiling children. But I remember what I felt when I had to leave my parents for service in my godfather's house. I was seven. Just Peter's age.'

He looked sadly at the little boy. 'My son never visited us after the wedding. We had a quarrel. He was as stubborn as his mother. Never resolved it. And now he's dead. Which is why I want Peter with us now, especially as my wife has discovered that his mother is an egregious trollop.'

'By the Rood sir, Mistress Kate is no such thing,' protested Sukey. But Sir Gervais was not listening, just gazing at Peter, lost in the past.

'He has his father's eyes,' he said sadly, then turned to Sukey. 'You can stay with him as long as you promise me not to escape. No more messages to Joan Moulton, whoever she is. They won't do any good, anyway. What's your name?'

'Sukey,' she stammered.

'Suits you,' he said. The twinkle was now clearly evident. 'We leave tomorrow for Warwickshire, where my wife awaits us eagerly.'

Sukey's heart sank.

'You will come, won't you Sukey?' It was Peter. He slipped a small damp hand into hers and looked up at her with huge haunted eyes.

Montagu Inn

Simon Brailles closed the door behind the king's mother and looked across at his mistress. The composure Alyce had maintained in front of Cis had gone and she had a worried frown.

'What's wrong, your grace?'

'The foulest of murders. Denis Pailton, the best scribe and limner in London, was found last week in the charnel house of St Paul's. He'd been hacked to pieces then buried under the old skulls and bones they put there when the graveyard gets full.' She paused and he saw her swallow an urge to retch.

'But whoever thought they'd left the body for the rats to dispose of didn't bargain for the kites. They flew in under the eaves and hauled out an arm. They were fighting over it when a beggar girl happened along. She told a churchwarden, and he and his henchmen searched the charnel house and found more hunks of flesh and a bundle of blood-soaked clothes. And tucked away deepest of all – a terrier sniffed it out – a severed head. The face was battered beyond recognition. But the murderers had been careless. In a concealed pocket in the cloak wrapped round the clothes there was a steel pen case with the badge of the Mystery of Stationers. They took it along to Stationers' Hall and the clerk there asked around. A stationer who was waiting for a permit for his stall took a careful look at it and said that he was sure it was Pailton's. Damascene work. He'd been very proud of it.'

Simon was puzzled. 'But what's all this got to do with us?'

'Pailton once worked in Queen Margaret's household. I remember him well. He was a Wallingford boy, one of the first pupils we had in the God's House. Had a way with his pen right from the start and he was a marvel at likenesses.

But he was always in trouble. I got him a job as an apprentice scrivener to John Doll. When Doll discovered how adept he was, he suggested that I gave him work in my own library. But two of my bedesman were excellent scribes, so I didn't need him. Truth to tell, talented as he was, I had my doubts about his honesty. Doll recommended him to Bishop Waynflete, who took him on at Mary Magdalen Hall and sent him to train in Bruges. Later he recommended him to Queen Margaret. He became her most trusted secretary, not least because he made her laugh. He was a first-rate artist by then and a fine calligrapher. I've got three of his books: a *City of Ladies* I bought from John Doll, a Boethius retold by my grandfather and my *Ars Moriendi*.'

'The one with those delicate printed plates?' asked Simon.

'Yes. For that he used the new craft of engraving on copper, which he learnt from a playing-card maker in Bruges. The detailing is quite extraordinary. He disappeared after the Lancastrians were slaughtered at Towton and hasn't been seen for the past seven years. But a fortnight ago a boy delivered a packet to Cis at Baynard's Castle. It was an octavo psalter, prettily limned. Cis recognised it instantly as Pailton's own work; she'd known him well in the old days, when she was close to Queen Margaret. She opened it and tucked deep inside was a long letter from Pailton. She thinks he sent it to her because she'd got on well with Queen Margaret – nursed her like a mother when she was so ill before her wedding, and sent her own dressmaker Margaret Chamberlayne to her when she became queen.' Alyce paused wearily. How times had changed.

'What did he say in the letter?'

'That for the past three years he'd been lying low in London, channelling funds over to Lorraine to help Queen Margaret survive in exile. But that he'd recently got involved in a new kind of treason: a war of words. Printed broadsheets prophesying Edward of York's fall are being nailed up on church and alehouse doors all over London. That was what we saw the constables tearing down on St Paul's. They must be smuggled in from presses in the Low Countries. They accuse Edward of being a bastard and a bigamist and Elizabeth of being a witch and a whore. And they call Henry a saint and miracle-worker and prophesy that he will be restored to the throne. They're the more effective because of their striking illustrations and catchy verses. Pailton must have had a hand in a good many of them.'

'Who is nailing them up? And how do they get into the country?'

'No one knows. Most are turning up in London, but they're being found as far afield as Coventry and Norwich. The Royal Council fears that if they get into Lancastrian parts of the country, they'll ignite rebellion like wildfire. People are already scrawling the initials RQFQ, *rex quondam futurusque*, the once and future king, everywhere. And the obvious time for a major uprising is the tournament Anthony Wydeville has planned in June. He's challenged the Bastard of Burgundy.

'Wouldn't Duchess Cecily be delighted if Wydeville's tournament is a fiasco?'

'Not if it means an uprising against her son.'

'Then why did she care about the danger Pailton was in?'

Alyce hesitated, then decided that she could trust Simon with Cis's secret.

'His letter claimed that a Neville close kin to her was at the heart of the treason. He said that the king's spies were closing in on him and asked for safe passage out of the country in return for not revealing the Neville's name to anyone but her. She sent the boy back with a message telling Pailton to meet her in the Lady Chapel at Paul's on St Anselm's Day, almost two weeks ago. He didn't turn up. The kites worried his bones out of the Paul's charnel house a week after that. Sacrilege in a sanctuary. You can imagine how quickly that was hushed up.'

'But didn't Pailton's death end the threat to the Nevilles?'

'Not necessarily. He could have left word of it hidden somewhere or with someone. Cis wants to find out whether he did or not. And she wants to know who the traitor Neville is and what he's up to.'

'So how did Cecily find out about his death?'

'Sheer luck. The stationer who identified the pen case was John Grafton. Do you remember him? A hen-pecked little man with a stall in Paul's Yard? When he took it to the cistern to wash off the blood before he examined it, he noticed that it was of the cunning sort with a double case. Once the top of the outer one is taken off, you can slide out an inner one. Cecily's letter to Pailton was hidden in it. The minute Grafton read it, he realised that there were higher things afoot than a chance robbery that turned to murder. He managed to pocket the letter without anyone noticing and brought it to Cecily, hoping for a generous reward for a promise to keep his mouth shut. Which she gave him. He told her he was the only person who saw the letter. But there's no guaranteeing that. He'd have shown it to his wife, for sure. She's the horse that draws the cart. So the duchess also wants to know if the Graftons can be trusted.'

'Has she told the king about all this?'

'God forfend. Edward may be half-Neville himself, but he's in thrall to Wydeville now. And Elizabeth has long been on the lookout for ways of cutting the Nevilles down to size, especially her mother-in-law, whom she loathes because Cis told Edward to make her his mistress, not his queen.'

'But why should her grace think you would help or could help?'

'As to why I would help her...' Alyce paused and her pale face coloured. 'It's complicated. A long time ago she helped me with a delicate matter. I owe her a debt for that. And she has stayed silent on a more recent threat to me.' She looked pensive and Simon remembered Cecily's Neville's scrawled reminder of Newton Montagu.

Then she rallied. 'As to why I could help, she knows that I was fascinated by my father's tales of murder cases when he was Coroner of London. He used to talk them over with me, saying I had a gift for getting to the heart of matters. She heard about last year's murders in Ewelme and was impressed that I had confounded Sir Robert Harcourt, though as you know in truth I did little enough.'

Simon saw her become lost in thought as she recalled the dramatic events of last September. He jogged her back to the present with another question.

'But wouldn't her London spies find out more?'

'Cecily wants to keep it as quiet as possible. She trusts me. And she knows that my interest in books means that I have many acquaintances in the Guild of Stationers. She also knows how close I was to Queen Margaret and she thinks I'd have ways of finding out about attempts to bring back Lancaster.'

'I doubt if that will happen,' said Simon. 'The citizens of London worship King Edward. He's made the greatest citizens knights and he wines and dines them generously and charms their wives with his flirting. And his secret marriage appealed

47

to their sense of romance. To say nothing of all his royal progresses scattering bright new coins to seed the ground with goodwill. And now this June tournament open to all comers. They say there'll be a hundred knights and more. While Henry, our rightful king, counts his beads in the Tower in a shabby blue gown.'

He wondered if he'd gone too far. But Alyce didn't reproach him. He looked at her sharply, wondering how many other secrets his mistress hid from him.

'Or am I wrong?' he ventured.

Alyce's face remained inscrutable. 'All you need to know is that we have to find out who Pailton was working for and who killed him. King Edward spends thousands a year on intelligence. His network is far more effective than Cis's clutch of gossips. I wouldn't put it past him to be spying on his own mother and nor would she. She says I'm her only hope. After that fiasco over Milo of Windsor last year, Edward is convinced I'm loyal, an ageing has-been bound to him by Jack's marriage to his sister. Which is the way I like it. I have no intention of risking Ewelme, my heartland.'

Simon had a new thought. 'Talking of gossips, Peggotty says that Duchess Cecily had that witch Agnes Quincey with her when she arrived. I saw the evil crow coming away from your inn as we were going down Paul's Wharf.'

'I saw her too,' said Alyce. 'I sent Tamsin to the kitchen to find out what she's been up to and to tell Peggotty that she's not to be let into my house again.'

There was a shy tap on the door. Brailles went over and opened it. It was Tamsin, clearly nervous that she was intruding.

'Just the person we need,' smiled Alyce. 'Any news of Agnes Quincey?' Dimpling with relief, Tamsin nodded.

'Cook said she's been calling in regularly to treat Pek's aching joints over the last three weeks, but that today she brought herbs to enrich the young duchess's milk and a poultice to ease soreness of the nipple.'

'Were they given to Bess?' asked Alyce in alarm.

'No, they're still in the kitchen. Cook said that Agnes was going to tell her how to seethe them and prepare them. But then he heard our outrider and went out to ask him how long it would be before our carriage got here. He wanted to have the spiced ale hot and ready. When he got back to the kitchen, Agnes had gone.'

'Tamsin, tell the gatekeeper not to let her in again. And see if you can find out if she went anywhere apart from the kitchen while she was here. Peggotty or Pek might know.'

After Tamsin had left the room, Alyce turned to Simon again.

'Simon, I will call on Lord Wenlock in the morning with you and Tamsin. As King's Butler, he's Coroner of London. He probably wasn't at the inquest on Pailton himself. In London that's usually a job for a deputy. But he's likely to be aware of the background to it. He's always been a knowing man.' She mused for a minute. 'Perhaps too knowing. We must tread carefully. And not a word to a soul about this disaffected Neville. We'll take a couple of grooms. Tell Hugh and Brian to be ready after terce. After that, we'll visit Joan Moulton, but not just on my own business. Cis told me that the spine of the psalter Pailton sent her had a mole imprinted on it. So it was bound in the Moulton bindery. Now, leave me in peace. I must rest. My son will no doubt come and pay his respects soon.'

Proud to be invited to accompany his mistress the next day,

Simon bowed. 'I'll go straight to the stables and let Hugh and Brian know.'

Alyce listened to his slow, deliberate footsteps descend the stairs. It was a relief to be alone at last. She needed to reflect on all that she had heard. A traitor Neville who was close kin to Cis. As Ralph Neville, first Earl of Westmorland, had had twenty-three impressively fertile children, the potential suspects were like leaves on a tree. But surely she could rule out the descendants of the Earl of Westmorland's first wife Margaret Stafford? Close kin to Cis meant that he – or she – must, like Cis herself, be descended from Ralph's second wife Joan Beaufort. Who'd had fourteen children. Then there were their children. She sighed. She needed a genealogy of the whole clan. She'd ask Joan about one tomorrow.

Wishing for the hundredth time that she still had Denzil Caerleon to help her, she wandered over to the window and looked out over the river. A cacophony of sounds drifted up to her – watermen hailing each other, fishwives crying their wares on the wharf, dogs barking. She always felt an alien in London, unable to forget the jeering cries of the citizenry in 1450 when they wanted William's blood, the battering ram at the door of the Suffolks' Manor of the Rose. She'd been glad to hand the splendid house over to Jack as soon as he came of age and to move back into Montagu Inn, which held nothing but the memory of happy hours with Thomas of Salisbury, most loved of her husbands. But she pined for Ewelme, where the world as far as it could be seen was under her sway, a secure domain of her own making.

There was a familiar rat-tat-a-tat on the door and she smiled.

'Come in, Farhang. Are you comfortably settled?'

'You can count on Mistress Peggotty for that, my lady. I

wondered if you would like a game of chess? It wants an hour to dinner.'

'Why not?'

They moved over to the chess table by the window.

'Red as ever?' asked Farhang.

Alyce smiled. 'Red as ever.'

Half an hour passed in silence.

'You are not yourself, my lady,' said Farhang, as, having given up a bishop to her knight, he moved his own knight to pin her king and queen. 'You rarely fall for such an obvious sacrifice. What's on your mind?'

Alyce sighed and knocked her king over.

'Cis Neville. I told you of her letter and my summons. She wants me to solve the murder she wrote of.'

'Was it of somebody you know?'

'Do you remember a scrivener and limner called Denis Pailton? He had asked Cis for safe passage out of the country because he knew that the king's spies were on to him.'

'Why would she help Pailton? He was no friend of York, as I remember.'

Alyce hesitated, then went on, reflecting that Farhang knew most of her secrets and guessed more. And she needed someone more subtle than dear Simon to help her think things out.

When she'd told him all she knew, Farhang scratched the back of his neck meditatively.

'What kind of treason was Pailton mixed up with?'

'Lancastrian propaganda. Making and distributing broadsheets full of prophecies and poison. They are unsettling London just when Edward wants to impress all the visitors for the Burgundian tournament with his firm hold on the throne. He may have cause for concern, as we learnt at Syon.'

'You can't believe everything the abbess says, my lady. She is York's bitterest opponent, did he but know it. She and John Langstrother.'

'The Prior-elect of the Hospitallers? I heard rumours that he was disaffected.'

'That's an understatement. Gossip has it that Queen Elizabeth seeks to have her brother Richard Wydeville succeed Prior Botyll instead of Langstrother.'

Alyce felt shocked. 'But surely Edward would not allow that. Legally, he could not. The appointment of the English Prior of the Hospitallers isn't in the royal gift. It's decided by the Grand Master in Rhodes.'

'There are other ways. Suppose Langstrother was outed as a Lancastrian?'

Alyce carefully put the chess pieces back into their opposing ranks of red and white before speaking again.

'Then perhaps you should warn Prior Botyll.'

'He is already gone to Rhodes to put the matter before the Grand Master.'

'Send to Langstrother, then. Oh, and Farhang, Agnes Quincy has left herbs for Bess. Please make sure they are destroyed.'

Farhang looked puzzled. 'Why? Mistress Quincy is very skilled in such things.'

Alyce flushed with anger. 'Don't you remember the acrid brew she gave me when I was expecting my Lord of Montagu's child? Cis sent her to me then. Our baby was born so malformed that it couldn't even be given a name.'

Farhang shook his head. 'No herbal brew could have caused that damage. It was wished on you by fate.'

Alyce looked unconvinced. 'Well, destroy them anyway. And, after that, go to Baynard's Castle. Cis wants to see you.

About some ointment of yours that her sister Katherine, the Dowager Duchess of Norfolk, values highly.'

Farhang's old face creased in amusement.

'What is it for?' asked Alyce.

'That would be telling,' he said. 'I take the oath of Hippocrates seriously, as you know. All I can say is that it seems to have done wonders for marital relations.'

Their eyes met. Alyce couldn't stifle a snort of laughter.

Soon after the midday meal, the door of Alyce's chamber swung back against the wall with a crash. Tamsin, who had been tidying the embroidery silks in Alyce's work basket, started up in surprise, strewing the contents of the basket over the floor. The short tubby young man who strode in wore skin-tight hose, one leg salmon-pink, one pale green, and the green sleeves of his doublet were slashed to reveal a pink undershirt. He had striking deep-blue eyes but his mouth had a discontented droop and as he made Alyce a cursory bow his left cheek twitched. That nervous tic had become a habit after the violent death of his adored father when he was eight years old.

'Mother. I hope I find you well.'

'Well enough, Jack,' said Alyce, putting down the tiny baby's bonnet she was making and presenting her cheek to be kissed. 'It is good to see you.'

She looked down at Tamsin, now kneeling on the carpet and picking up the upset hanks of silk, pins, needles and thimbles. 'Stop that, child, and make your curtsey. This is my son the Duke of Suffolk, lately back from Burgundy. I call him Jack, but to you he will of course be "my lord".'

She turned back to Jack. 'You'll recall Tamsin's father Roger Ormesby, I'm sure. A faithful servant of your own father, just as his father was of mine.'

Glowing with pleasure, Tamsin produced her best curtsey yet.

Duke John ran his eyes over her appraisingly. 'I remember Roger well,' he said. 'He taught me to ride and gave me my first lessons at the quintain. How does he do?' Tamsin hesitated, tears rising to her eyes.

Alyce spoke for her. 'Roger died three years ago, of the sweating sickness. So did Tamsin's mother. But in September she did me a good turn by finding my lost rosary and earned a trial in my service.'

'Has the faithful Sarah failed you then?' the young duke asked. His black hair was curled and combed into a short bob on which was set the slim gold circlet of a ducal coronet. Alyce was interested that he remembered Sarah's name. Jack looked on servants as tools, not people.

'She became pregnant at Wingfield before I left for Ewelme,' she said curtly. 'I didn't know about it and the journey to Oxford was the death of her. She had taken too much pennyroyal, Farhang thought. Tamsin was not trained as a tiring maid, but she is quick and willing and I hope to keep her by me. As I get older I find I need an extra pair of eyes and hands more and more often.'

'And a pretty pair of each they are,' said Jack. Tamsin blushed and bent down to gather up the rest of the scattered sewing things. Jack crouched down to help her. Alyce eyed him suspiciously. Stooping to servants was not Jack's habit.

'Tamsin, when you've finished picking those up, take them away and sort them out in the solar,' she said. Tamsin hastily grabbed the remaining things and left the room, blushing again as Jack sprang to open the door for her.

'Bring us up a bottle of malmsey and some comfits when you've finished, sweeting,' he said, pinching her cheek. She fled.

Watching him use his charm, Alyce thought sadly how little she understood the young man. He and she had not had much chance to be close. When he was two years old she'd gone with William to Normandy to negotiate the marriage of Margaret of Anjou and King Henry. The visit had dragged on for almost two years and nursemaids had looked after Jack at Wingfield. On their return William had kept the boy by his side in London, dressing him up as a miniature lordling, showing him off as if he was a pet monkey rather than arranging a proper education for him. Alyce had wanted him to learn Latin in the fine school she had established at Ewelme, but William insisted on keeping him at court, saying that there was time enough for book learning when the boy was older, that the priorities were for him to learn to ride, aim an arrow into the heart of a stag – and win the king's favour.

It hadn't taken much to do so. Henry doted on all children and Jack was a handsome boy. But he had quickly picked up on the rift between his parents. Since William indulged his every whim, he naturally preferred his father, seeing Alyce only as a killjoy. He'd been only seven when he was told he was to wed the precociously learned Margaret Beaufort, a year younger than he was but a head taller and much better than him at her letters. He threw a tantrum and blamed Alyce, although it was William who had negotiated the match, aware that it would clinch his political power. Margaret, the great-granddaughter of John of Gaunt, was the closest Lancastrian heir to the throne of England. If Henry remained childless, which seemed likely after four years of marriage without his French Queen conceiving, Jack's and Margaret's descendants had a good claim to the throne.

It was a step too far for their aristocratic enemies. Within months of the children's marriage, William had been indicted for treason and found guilty. His death sentence was commuted to exile by King Henry's personal intervention, but his ship was intercepted on its way to France by a warship called *Nicholas of the Tower*. The sailors who had been left on Dover beach with William's decapitated corpse said they didn't know the name of her commander, only that he had ordered one Richard Lenard to hack off the duke's head with a rusty sword 'in the name of the Commons of England', and told them to row it to shore, plant a pikestaff in the sand beside the body and stick the head on it. After having been exhaustively questioned, the sailors were deemed to have been acting under orders and released.

When Alyce had told Jack as gently as she could that his father had died on his way into exile, he'd instantly blamed her, and when stable gossip reached him of the full horror of William's death ice froze his heart. William had written his son a long letter while he was in the Tower, exhorting him to love and obey his mother and listing her many virtues, but Jack had torn it to pieces, accusing her of forging it. He had loathed his new orderly life at Ewelme, loathed the old-fashioned strictness of his tutor John Clifford, and loathed his haughty little bride, pinching her arms black and blue when he discovered she was too proud to tell on him. To his delight, he was relieved of her three years later, when Henry, despairing of a son of his own, insisted that Jack's marriage be annulled so that Margaret Beaufort could wed his own half-brother Edmund Tudor. Edmund wasted no time seeding Margaret's young womb. If Margaret of Anjou had not so unexpectedly conceived and given birth to a son a year later, Margaret and Edmund's child Henry would have been the heir to the throne.

It had been a relief to everyone at Ewelme, including Alyce, when Richard Duke of York, Protector of the Realm during King Henry's mental collapse after the loss of Aquitaine, had happened to visit Ewelme when Jack, now thirteen, was in the tiltyard riding at the quintain. Taking a fancy to the lad's undoubted fire and courage, he had suggested that he join his own boys at Fotheringay for more advanced training. Alyce had let him go. She couldn't afford to offend the man who seemed ever more likely to be England's next king. What she didn't foresee was that York's daughter Bess and Jack would fall in love. Though in her heart she hated the idea of an alliance with York, she had had to accept their marriage three years later. It would, ironically, prove the saving of her estates. After the death of the Duke of York, his oldest son Edward seized the throne from the enfeebled King Henry. Three years later, to do his sister honour, he re-endowed Jack with the title of Duke of Suffolk.

The dramatic events at Ewelme last autumn had mended the rift with her daughter-in-law, who was now a loyal ally. But Jack remained distant, baiting her when they met, keeping dubious company in London and Suffolk. The trouble was, Alyce reflected sadly, that he was still furious that she had not done more to bring his father's murderers to account seventeen years ago. She watched him prowling around the room, picking up trinkets that took his fancy and glancing teasingly at her as he examined them. He ate incessantly and was never without a pocket full of sugared almonds or quince comfits. She knew that it rankled with him that she was far wealthier than he was. Bess's dower had still not been fully paid and Jack was too awed by Edward to request the lucrative court sinecures customary to his rank. The Yorks were Janus-faced; they could switch from easy warmth to stony frost in seconds. Edward had soon seen through the veneer of charm that had captivated Bess to Jack's true nature: a confused, rash young man who could never quite be counted upon.

'How was Burgundy?' she asked. His face darkened.

'Frustrating. There we were in the most splendid court in Europe for two months and those has-beens Astley and Norreys wouldn't let me join in the tournament held to honour us. They said Anthony Wydeville was the English champion and that they couldn't risk our standing being damaged by my getting knocked off my horse. As if I'm not a match for Anthony himself.'

'Perhaps King Edward told them to make sure his sister's husband stayed in one piece.'

'It would have been far better to have allowed me to do Bess honour by competing. Which brings me to another matter.'

She braced herself for a new demand for money and was not disappointed.

'I have urgent need for a new suit of armour for the June tournament against Burgundy's finest knights. I must keep up the state that befits a duke and the Suffolk name.'

Her heart sank. Tournaments were chancy affairs and, though she knew Jack to be a ferocious fighter when roused, he could easily have some accident that would mean the loss of everything she had fought for since his father's death.

'You could do more honour to the Suffolk name by winning worship locally,' she said sharply. 'I had another letter from Dame Paston before I left Ewelme. She says that your men have seized Hellesdon, killed a tenant and razed the haystacks.'

'But Hellesdon was part of my father's inheritance. That old fox Judge Paston tricked him out of it for a tenth of its worth.'

'It wasn't worth that when he took it over. Your father hadn't been there in six years and the house was occupied by a band of tinkers, who fired it when they left. The Pastons improved it beyond recognition and, as far as I'm concerned, they are welcome to it. I don't know why Dame Paston thought I was involved in its seizure. But enough of argument. The tournament will be a great occasion and I'm proud of your prowess in the lists. I hear that you bested John Paston at Eltham in March and impressed your royal brother-in-law mightily. You may have your new armour willingly. Tell the armourer to send me the bill.'

Jack's face had tensed when she was talking about Hellesdon, but now it lightened and was transformed. He reminded Alyce painfully of his father when she first met him, the handsomest man in Rouen. It was a shame that Jack hadn't inherited William's height. And that self-indulgence had made him chubby.

Entering with a tray of wine and sweetmeats, Tamsin saw him bow low in front of Alyce and kiss her hand.

'Thank you, mother,' he said as he rose. 'And thank you too for looking after Bess so well. She has borne me another fine son. We asked Queen Elizabeth and the Earl of Oxford to stand godparents at his christening.'

'Choosing Elizabeth will please the king. And the Earl of Oxford seems in favour at court,' said Alyce. 'I'm impressed.'

'All Bess's idea, actually. I was for having Lady Scales and Clarence.'

Alyce inwardly thanked heaven for her daughter-in-law's acumen. It was hard to imagine two flightier sponsors than the flirtatious Lady Scales and Edward's younger brother George, Duke of Clarence. She certainly was a most capable wife and mother. And having her at Ewelme for the birth of her child had brought them even closer. Which put her in mind of their exhausting journey to London.

'By the way, has *Lyonesse* been refitted? I miss her sadly. We would have made a much pleasanter passage by river.'

Jack hesitated for a fraction of a second before replying. 'No, she's still in the yard. Horner found a bad outbreak of rot in her stem. Why don't you have another barge built? It is absurd for a family of our rank not to have a presentable barge in London as well as at Wallingford. I am constantly waiting on the king and queen in Greenwich or in Sheen and using hired craft is demeaning. When my father was alive, we had a veritable fleet.'

Alyce considered. He had a point. She could certainly afford a new barge. But a habit of thrift had been drilled into her by her parents and reinforced by William's fall. Although, she thought a little guiltily, she had spent enough on books in the last few years to pay for the most lavish of barges.

'Perhaps we should,' she heard herself saying. 'I'll talk to Ben about it. If wool sales are as good this year as they were last, I'll set the Wallingford shipwrights to work.'

'Thank you, mother. And I'll be able to take over the cost of manning it soon. I haven't told you. I have a position at court at last. I am to serve with Lord Tiptoft. I am due to wait on him now, at Pembroke Inn. He sent to say that he had a commission for me already.'

Alyce's heart sank. Earl of Worcester and Constable of England Sir John Tiptoft was also head of the royal intelligencers, dedicated to hunting down anyone with Lancastrian sympathies. She remembered his brooding, unreadable presence during the crisis that had come close to destroying the little community of Ewelme last September. She did her best to smile.

'Congratulations, Jack. And how does Bess do? She was complaining of cramps all the way from Syon.'

'She is greatly recovered. Sitting in her chamber playing cards with her boon companion Lady Anne Neville, with the babe sucking lustily at her paps.'

'I'm glad to hear it. Go to her after you have seen Tiptoft and send her my good wishes. Tamsin, show his lordship out.'

He flashed another brilliant smile at her and swirled out of the room, humming a catchy tune. Alyce looked after him sadly. He had been easily pleased by a gift ever since he was a boy and as easily incensed by having a whim denied. When he was a child she had tried hard to teach him the virtues of self-denial, of thrift, of thought for others. But all her efforts had been nullified by William's spoiling. Now, if she was honest with herself, Jack frightened her a little. She feared he saw her merely as an obstacle between himself and the rest of his inheritance, the kind of rich old lady so often mocked and jeered at in the Southwark theatres. Dowagers whose death was a matter for rejoicing rather than mourning. Whose death might so easily be engineered. Particularly when they were once high in Lancastrian favour.

Speed was of the essence, but nourishment was, to Joan's mind, even more essential. Her stepson escorted them back to Moulton Inn, where they dined on cold ham and slabs of cheese between freshly baked bannocks, finishing with raisins and dates, washed down with red Bordeaux wine. Or rather Joan did. Kate could only toy with her food. Half an hour later, when Joan woke from the nap that she regarded as essential for good digestion, she summoned foot litters to carry herself, Kate and Amice to Wenlock's house. The chairmen were burly, jocular men who delivered a non-stop commentary on the passing scene, the weight of one of their passengers and the desirability of the other two. Kate was too fraught to notice, Amice sniffed haughtily and Joan gave as good as she got, accusing them of being lily-livered blaggards with no tools between their legs. They chuckled appreciatively and Joan, aware that nobody was better informed than chairmen and watermen of the comings and goings of the gentry, followed up her insults by asking them who'd come to town lately. She was interested to hear that the newest arrivals were the old and the young duchesses of Suffolk.

'Likely they'll be up for the tournament against Burgundy,' suggested the oldest of the chairmen. 'The young duke is already here. And his wife, her as is the king's own sister, will be waving his colours, for certain.'

'Naah,' said another. 'In pod, ain't she?'

'Not any more,' called a third. 'But will she be churched by then?'

'Long gone,' said the first. 'Babe was born over four months ago. Fine little chap, I was told at the Manor of the Rose's

New Year feast. Wonder why they've come this early. Babes are better off in the country than in this plaguey city of ours.'

So they are, thought Joan. She wouldn't have expected Alyce to leave Ewelme any sooner than she needed to, without good reason. No doubt she'd tell her when she called in at Moulton Inn to collect her *Tales of the Canterbury Pilgrims*. Joan looked forward to handing it over and seeing her friend's delight in the intricate workmanship of its new binding. There had been trouble over that. She had found a mistake in the symmetry of the cover design and an entirely new cover had had to be made. Joan was a perfectionist when it came to her craft. But she kept the flawed cover. Only an expert eye would notice that mistake and many a book lover would happily settle for such a bargain.

Soon they were in sight of the Royal, a tower house so ancient that it was rumoured to have been built by Brutus himself when he founded London and declared it a second Troy. It had been a crumbling ruin fifteen years earlier when Lord Wenlock had offered to take it in lieu of money owed to him by the cash-strapped Henry VI. Now the quadrangle of buildings around it had been restored and raised by another storey, jutting out over the narrow lanes around. Stained-glass coats of arms glinted in the windowpanes, and the woodwork of their casements was riotous with carved foliage and gilded mythical beasts. The tower itself had been made higher, and from its roof there was a breathtaking view over the city. The gatehouse was a forest of pennants and blazons, for when Wenlock was in residence so too were his wards, mainly the wives and children of wealthy Lancastrians killed at the terrible battle of Towton seven years ago, or who had fled with Queen Margaret into exile later on.

The chairmen set down the litters and waited for their fare. As Joan was counting pennies into the hand of the oldest, he leant forward and muttered a warning.

'Mind your backs when you leave the Royal, Mistress Joan. We were followed from Broome Place. Two hooded men, no badges on their cloaks.' Joan pressed an extra penny into his hand to thank him. No badges. Not, then, the beadle's minions. Perhaps, however, more to be feared. As Amice and Kate were handed out of their chairs, she glanced around, but could see no sign of watchers.

The porter on the gate bowed when he saw them and hauled open one of its double doors so they could enter. A handsome young man with a sullen mouth escorted them into the great hall and a cheerful small boy raced away up a staircase to announce their arrival to Lord Wenlock.

'We're honoured, Kate,' said Joan. 'Both those lads are likely to be the heirs to great estates. Most of Lord Wenlock's wards are. He had Harry Stafford, heir to the Duke of Buckingham, and Thomas Fitzalan, heir to the Earl of Arundel, here until they married two of the queen's sisters a year ago.'

A tall, distinguished-looking man in a dark red gown trimmed with black fur was standing at a lectern reading to a group of richly dressed ladies, some matronly, some little more than children. Perched on stools, they were industriously hemming the edges of a sumptuously embroidered coverlet, their high conical headdresses nodding and waving as they worked and whispered. Far too impractical for Joan's taste. She preferred Kate's butterfly wings. Or the new horned style that was all the rage in Bruges. Gave a woman a redoubtable air. Also listening was a thin stick of a man dressed in black. He stood up as they entered.

'Mistress Moulton. Sir John is with his barber. Can you wait?'

'Good day to you, Master Thynne. I fear not – this is a matter of great urgency. We'll go straight up. Amice, you wait here. Take a needle and join the sewing circle.' Kate was already climbing the winding spiral stairs. Joan followed more slowly. Waiting for her on a half landing, Kate looked out of its small window. She could see over the smaller houses huddled round the Royal to the great bulk of Paul's. Its steeple dwarfed those of the lesser churches but was challenged by the soaring spire of Greyfriars a few hundred yards to the north of it. Tears welled in her eyes. Greyfriars. Where Richard had been buried.

Breathing heavily, Joan caught her up, just as the boy they'd seen in the courtyard came down the stairs. Joan smiled at him.

'How goes it, Walter? How you've grown. You're going to be the image of your father, God rest his soul. Your mother must be proud of you. How are you getting on with the *Stans Puer ad Mensam* Thynne chose for you when you came to my shop?'

'Well enough, Mistress Moulton,' said Walter Hungerford, dimpling with pleasure at being remembered. 'But I like the riddle book you gave me better. Sir John says you are to wait beside the fire down in the hall, that I should order you a glass of Rhenish and that he will be with you in a trice.'

'We'll be with him sooner than that. Tell Thynne to bring the wine upstairs. Off with you, now.' Walter hesitated, then went on down the stairs.

They could hear music now, the clear notes of a flute and a boy's voice singing a ballad. It was on everyone's lips at the minute, brought down from the north by the Nevilles.

'Sith it is so that you will go,
I will not leave behind,
Shall ne'er be said the nut-brown maid
Was to her love unkind.
Make you ready, for so am I,
Although it were a-noon;
For in my mind, of all mankind,
I love but you alone.'

Joan opened the door at the top of the stairs and the pretty treble quavered and stopped. They were in a huge room, wainscoted below and painted above with glowing frescoes of Arthurian legends. Sir John Wenlock was seated on a chair by the window, staring dreamily at his own reflection in a polished silver mirror. His eyes swivelled to the reflected door when he heard the real one open and a smile twitched at his lips. His barber, a slim, raven-haired Italian in his twenties, had sheared the back of his grey hair into an even bob and was now trimming the neat beard that emphasised the squareness of a determined jaw. Wenlock waved him away, stood up and bowed.

'Always so headlong, Joan. A moment and Giorgio will be done, if you will excuse me. Sing on, Adam.' He sat down again. Giorgio resumed his snipping, the flautist piped a bar or two and the small boy perched on a stool beside the chimney place cleared his throat and headed bravely into the next verse of the interminable ballad. Joan wandered over to some books lying on a table and began to turn the pages of the topmost volume. It was Vegetius' *De Re Militari*, generously illustrated with scenes of battles and details of siege weapons. Effete Wenlock might choose to seem, but she knew he was a daring soldier, with a long military career to his credit.

After a few minutes spent trimming stray whiskers, the barber took away the cape of linen crash that he had placed around his client's shoulders to reveal a midnight blue doublet with white silk puffing through slashes in its sleeves. Wenlock nodded his satisfaction and sniffed appreciatively at the sandalwood-scented salve that Giorgio was smoothing over his face and neck.

The barber put salve, shears and razors into a worn leather bag, took out a handglass and held it up behind Sir John's back so that he could see his reflection. Wenlock moved his head from profile to profile.

'Excellent. See Thynne for your guerdon.' Giorgio backed out with a bow, one hand twirling in the exaggerated Italian manner. Wenlock then turned to the small boy, still pluckily singing away.

'Thank you, Adam. You may go.' Joan looked at the retreating back of the heir to the Moleyns inheritance as the boy scuttled away.

'How busy you keep them all, John. The lads waiting on you hand and foot and the ladies making your wife fine coverlets. And all from the kindness of your heart, of course.'

Unperturbed, Wenlock nodded, looking at Kate with unconcealed admiration.

'But who is this?'

'This is my goddaughter Lady Katherine Arderne, sole heiress of Gregory Browne, the mercer. She's lately widowed and the Ardernes have falsely accused her of adultery so that they can keep her dower – and her son, the heir. I was with her today when that fetid bag of lard Sewardby came and told us that she was under arrest, that all her lands and chattels were forfeit and that her son – who's but seven years old – was to be made a ward of the queen. I bawled him out and rustled up two thousand marks bail, but they'd kidnapped little Peter in the night.'

Wenlock frowned. 'How so? Was the house not locked up?'

'One of the servants must have let them in – or taken the boy out. His nursemaid was drugged. If Sewardby is to be believed, he's now at the Mermaid Inn in Candlewick Street with his grandfather Gervais Arderne and is to be taken north to Warwickshire to stay with his grandmother.'

'That would be somewhat previous if he's not yet officially a ward of the queen. I've only lately arrived in London from Calais and I haven't been to Greenwich yet, so I don't know what's been going on. If Lady Katherine stands accused of adultery, it is acceptable for her son to remain with the queen, or with whoever buys his wardship from her. But he should not be taken out of London and there must be no forfeiture of goods and chattels until the case is proven against her. Which, from what you say, it won't be. And there are ways of speeding up process in the church courts, if you know the right pockets to line. She'll need a lawyer, of course.'

'Can you recommend one?' said Joan. 'Cost is no object. Kate is very dear to me.'

'I suggest James Danvers. One of the cleverest young men in the Inns. And it's just possible that I could acquire wardship of the boy for myself – though it would cost a pretty penny. Our gracious queen likes to tuck away gold against a rainy day. Wisely, I suspect, given her husband's wandering eye.'

'If that can be arranged, we would be eternally in your debt,' said Joan. 'As I said, any monies needed will be found. But first I have another favour to ask of you. Our chairman told me that we were followed here. My happening to be at Broome Place

68

will have set the Ardernes' plans awry. I wouldn't put it past them to abduct Lady Katherine, or even to do away with her, if they got the chance. Could she and her maid shelter under your roof for a few days until I can find a safer place for her? Paternoster Row is no place for her at the minute. Saturday is the day of our annual sale of unwanted stock and I'm laying on a feast in my hall for all my customers.'

Wenlock looked across at Kate. She met his gaze trustingly, clearly feeling complete confidence in him. Joan saw him give a regretful grimace as he realised that Kate saw him only as a father figure.

'I don't see why not, Lady Arderne. There's a large chamber in the south wing next to Lady Moleyns and young Adam that should be adequate for your needs. I'll also send a messenger to Lincoln's Inn to see if James would be prepared to act for you and to invite him to meet you here tomorrow if he agrees.'

'You are a true friend in need, Sir John. I thank you,' said Kate. The exhaustion she'd been fighting off for the last two hours suddenly overwhelmed her. Wenlock noticed her pallor and the way she was half-leaning on the table. Just then the door opened and Francis Thynne came in, carrying a jug of wine and some silver-gilt goblets.

'Fine timing, Francis. Quick, pour wine for Lady Arderne. Then please escort her and her maid to the chamber next to Lady Moleyns.'

In a daze, Kate drained the goblet and turned to the door. Joan put her ample arms around the pale girl in a farewell hug, whispering into her ear. 'The Royal is the best port for you in this storm, my dear. But unless you have a mind for a frolic, stick with the ladies and keep Amice by your side at night.' She flashed a meaningful glance towards Wenlock.

Looking even paler, Kate followed Thynne downstairs and Joan turned back to Wenlock. He had overheard her warning and was grinning broadly as he filled a goblet for each of them.

'Spoil my hope of sport, would you?' he said as he handed one to her. Joan took a generous swallow and looked at him reprovingly.

'Have a heart, Sir John. She's much too young for you, newly widowed and has had her only son grabbed from his cot but twelve hours since.'

'All the more need for comfort. I seem to remember that you weren't averse to such things yourself. Incidentally, it's far too long since we last – er – comforted each other. Every time I look at the pictures in that Ovid you procured for me, I think of you.'

Joan pursed her lips in mock disapproval, then subsided into a reminiscent chuckle and tweaked Wenlock's cheek fondly. 'You remember too much too well, my lord.'

He slipped an arm around her ample waist and pulled her towards him. She allowed him a nuzzle at her neck, then pushed him away.

'Enough. We both have business to attend to. Are you coming to my book sale tomorrow?'

'Is there anything that would interest me? Along the lines of that Ovid. I know you have a sideline in such things.'

'It'd be more than my charter is worth to admit that, my lord, as you know. Nor will they ever go cheap. For those, you'll have to come by in a few days' time. But your industrious Mr Thynne might find some useful schoolbooks. I've also got some blank books sewn up from odds and ends of paper that would suit his grammar lessons well. If he'd like to have a foresight of them, he could come there with me now. I'd welcome a bodyguard in case those men are still around. Although I doubt if it's me they're interested in.'

'I'll send two other men with Thynne, who will, I'm sure, be pleased to renew his acquaintance with Madame de Chinon. And if Lady Katherine's maid went as well, she and Thynne could collect Lady Arderne's necessaries and bring them back here.'

'A thousand thanks, John. My mind will rest easier if Kate is safe behind your high walls. Now I must get back to my shop. A fine mess they'll be making of things without me. By the way, the chairmen also told me that Princess Alyce is in town. Came with her daughter-in-law yesterday. I'm sure she'll come to Paternoster Row as soon as she can to collect the rebound *Canterbury Tales* I showed you a fortnight ago.'

'That's good news. It's months since I've seen her. Though I don't blame her for lying low after last autumn's ructions, she shouldn't lose touch with the court. You might warn her when you see her that several legal vultures have been hired to make claims on her properties. One false move and she'll lose the royal protection.'

'I will. And thank you for everything, John.'

Wenlock listened to her footsteps descending the stair as the great bell of St Mary's tolled for terce. He crossed his chamber to a small door in the wainscot. It led along a passage to the second stair from the hall. He walked up this to the library he had arranged in the topmost room of the tower. As he opened its door, he felt the calm that always settled on him when he stepped out of clock time and into that of prayer and study. It was one of the smallest rooms in his house, but it held his greatest treasures. He turned the hourglass mounted on the wall and selected a prayer book with a heavy, bejewelled binding and moved it to the sloping desk beside the long leaded window that looked out across all London. Reading the office was a pleasure when gay vignettes frolicked around the staid, familiar words. A gilded leather bookmark showed him where he'd left off three hours ago at the end of prime. Opening it carefully, he laid two change to: two long silk cords, heavily weighted at their ends, on its margins to keep the pages flat and began to read the psalm allotted that day to terce, murmuring the words to savour their music and fingering the smooth amber beads of his rosary.

The hourglass still had a quarter to go when he said a final amen and closed the primer. What now? Pleasure before business had always been his motto. Reminded of it by Joan's visit, he took up Ovid's *Metamorphoses*. After savouring to the full the limner's imaginative rendering of animals and humans coupling, he closed it and walked over to an iron-bound chest. Pulling two keys strung on a thin black velvet ribbon from the neck of his doublet, he opened its complex Italian locks and lifted the lid. Inside were piles of notices large and small. They'd been collected for him from the doors of taverns, city churches, even the headquarters of guilds. He leafed through them. All were scurrilous, accusing notable Yorkists, ladies and lords alike, of political, financial and sexual trangressions and prophesying Lancaster's return.

Whistling softly, Wenlock searched for clues to their makers. Not so many different hands, in fact. Perhaps three or four scribes? He held each sheet of paper up to the light to examine its watermark. A unicorn, a fleur-de-lis, a rose … they were far from uniform. So made perhaps from odd ends, throwaway scraps from stationers and parchmeners. He unrolled the last, a broadsheet. Sir Robert Harcourt had sent it over from Greenwich a few weeks ago. It had been posted up on the door of the Chapel Royal just before the queen arrived for Mass. It was in verse, catchy stuff about corrupt court practices. In its margins were engravings, wickedly grotesque caricatures, including one of the queen in the shape of a magpie pecking viciously at a nest of fledglings. A tawny-coloured hound, a crown cock-eyed on its head, lay stretched on the ground below, fast asleep. Beside it, alert but looking in the other direction, was a terrier, one eyebrow anxiously raised. Recognising himself, he smiled wryly. No prizes for who had done this one. Though its maker would never engrave copper again. But where had it been printed?

He turned to the latest wallet full of broadsheets, brought to the Royal by the constables that morning, and shook his head. These were much more dangerous. The headings were enormous, easily legible from a distance. Not written by a backroom scribe but imprinted from moveable individual letters cut from boxwood and inked; there were doubtless many copies of each of them. The paper was from Nuremberg, machine-made at Stromer's great watermill. So the broadsheets were probably made in Bruges or Arras and smuggled into the country. But it was odd that there were so many different watermarks. The message was bold and simple.

The usurper York and his traitor wife oppress the people!
Look to your true anointed!
The Once and Future King, the God-given Healer!
LANCASTER ARISE!

Wenlock noted the religious overtone, making full use of the deposed King Henry's growing repute as a miracle-worker.

Edward had no time at all for the old ceremony of healing scrofula, the king's evil. People were already whispering that he couldn't cure people because he was a usurper. Notices like this, often headed 'A Prophecy of Merlin', had been appearing on church doors in Kent and villages around London for weeks. Now they had reached the door of Paul's itself. Words were weapons, especially such strong, skilfully crafted ones as these. And this devilish new German engine using moveable metal type was going to make such treasons spread even faster. He examined the watermark on the paper again, then pressed his finger on to the capital L. A black smudge of oily ink stained it. He frowned. He needed to speak to Harcourt. He put the roll back, locked the chest and went back to his chamber.

Two hours later, a soft tap sounded on the door. Wenlock closed the book he was reading and called out 'Come in'. Silent as a cat in his felt slippers, Francis Thynne sidled into the room.

'Back already, Thynne?'

'Yes, my lord. I sent Amice and the men back from Broome Place and went on to preview the book sale on Saturday.'

'Anything useful?'

'Half a dozen notebooks, a Virgil and a Catullus – both too battered to be good for anything but schoolboys. You owe me three marks.'

'Take them from my purse. What do you think of our new guests?'

'Amice is a little doxy. Lady Arderne is a rarity, a true-heart. She deserves your protection.' The reply and the slight emphasis on his last word, startled Wenlock. He had rarely heard his austere secretary praise a female. And wasn't there also a hint of a warning? Could pretty Kate Arderne have touched Thynne's flint heart?

74

'And she will get it,' he said crisply. 'But first I need to know how far the dealings over the Arderne boy's wardship have got. Go to Greenwich first thing in the morning and find out for me. And Thynne, I need to speak to Sir Robert Harcourt. You might find him at court. If not, he usually lodges at the Mermaid Inn. Ask him to wait on me tomorrow afternoon.'

Thynne nodded and vanished without another word.

The Manor of the Rose

Jack de la Pole bent over the cradle and wiggled his fingers in front of his baby son's fascinated eyes. To his delight, a tiny hand came up towards his and clenched confidingly over his forefinger.

'I will be such a father to you, my little lad. I'll teach you to ride and to hunt as my father taught me. You and your brother will be renowned masters of game.'

From the deep cushions of her bed of state, Bess of York watched him lazily, a tolerant smile playing on her lips.

'And how was your meeting with your mother yesterday?'

'Well enough. She's opened her purse strings to pay for a new suit of jousting armour for me to wear in the Burgundian tournament. I shall go to Lothbury and speak to the armourers about it tomorrow. And she says that we can have a second barge built.' He began to pull faces at little Ned, opening and shutting his eyes and making little babbling noises with his mouth. The little creature gazed up at him, fascinated. Then he blinked back, gurgling and waving his fists.

'And what did she think of your new position with Lord Tiptoft?'

Jack grimaced. 'She took it graciously enough. Though I could see that she didn't like the idea of my pursuing Lancastrians. Look, Ned's talking to me.'

'So he is,' said Bess fondly. 'But when he can really talk, he might well agree with his grandmother. After all, her family

76

and your father's family have been followers of Lancaster ever since the first Henry usurped the throne.' Thoughtfully, she tickled the neck of the kitten that lay curled up in her lap.

'Have you considered what you would do if Tiptoft's spies found evidence that your mother was still loyal to Henry?' she asked him. 'As they thought they had done last autumn.'

Jack looked round at her sharply and was silent for a long minute. 'It might suit us well enough, my love,' he said eventually. 'If she took up residence in the Tower, I would come into her property sooner than I otherwise would. In fact...' He broke off abruptly and turned back to the baby, who looked eagerly up at him and held out both tiny hands.

'What were you going to say?' Bess asked.

'Nothing. Nothing that I can talk about, that is. When he brought me news of my appointment, Sir Robert Harcourt swore me to secrecy.'

'Harcourt? He is no friend of your mother's, as we discovered last September. You didn't tell me that it was he who enrolled you.'

'You didn't ask. He has been a good friend to me. Yes, he suggested to Tiptoft that I join the intelligencers. And he thinks that my father would approve. He knew him well, you know. He tells me all sorts of stories about him.'

'Of course. He fought for Lancaster in the wars.'

'He did. But he is as loyal to Edward now as I am. And he says my father would have become so, if he hadn't been brought down by jealous churls and foully murdered by hired pirates. After all, Henry of Lancaster let my father down.'

'He had no choice, Jack. Your father was arraigned for treason by his peers. Henry did his best, sending him into exile rather than letting him risk a trial.'

'But he didn't hunt down his murderers. For good reason, Harcourt says. It was all the doing of his witchy French wife. Which is why my mother has done nothing either. She and Queen Margaret were ever close. Closer than she was to my father, says Harcourt. She's an unnatural woman, he says. She had no feeling for my father and welcomed his death. Sir Robert thinks she might even have been directly involved in it.'

Bess shook her head. 'Jack, we are both too young to know the truth about what happened so long ago. You must beware of believing mere rumours. And you owe a parent loyalty.'

'What if to be loyal to one parent I betray the other? Bess, seven years ago you lost your father as brutally as I lost mine. But now your brother has avenged that loss. Should I not want to avenge the death of mine? I cannot reach the French queen, but I can unseat my unnatural parent.'

Bess tensed at the word 'unnatural'. Surely Cecily could not have told Jack the secret of Newton Montagu? How she regretted the unguarded moment when she had told her mother-in-law the truth about Jack's birth.

'How unnatural?' she ventured, heart in mouth. 'She has always been kind to me, Jack.'

'More of her devilish policy,' he snapped back. 'Putting me in the wrong. Overriding my orders. Treating me as if I was an idiot.'

She realised with relief that Cecily had not risked telling him about his real mother. 'What's found is history, what's lost is mystery' Joan had said firmly as she threw the evidence of it into the fire. But what of the adage about secrets? 'Two can keep a secret if one of them is dead.' And now four people knew.

There was a wail from the baby, as if he sensed the troubled cross-currents running above his head. Jack picked him up and cradled him in his arms, rocking him to and fro.

'I'm going to be such a father to you, Neddy,' he crooned. 'Such a father.'

He turned back to Bess. 'My love, I am to go hunting in Epping Forest the day after tomorrow. I'll ride with John Paston.'

'On a Sunday, Jack? But I was looking forward to having you to myself.'

'It's important for my advancement, my darling. All the coming men will be there. And as to it being Sunday, since Archbishop Neville himself is our host, I'm sure God will grant a dispensation. And I'm here now, though Lord Tiptoft asked me to dine with him at Pembroke Inn. I said I was promised to you. As I am. Forever.' He walked over to the bed and lounged back beside her, putting a plump arm around her just now plump waist and cuddling close to her and the baby.

She stroked his head. 'And tomorrow? Could we both go to Greenwich? Edward is holding May revels and mother is going. We can introduce little Ned to Court.'

Jack hesitated. 'I'm not sure. I have some duties early in the morning and I don't know how long I'll be. Perhaps you had better go with your mother. I'll join you there if I can.'

He yawned, then closed his eyes contentedly.

The Royal

The bells for terce were echoing around the Royal as a young man in the sober black cloak of a lawyer, followed by a junior in a short blue and white gown, lifted the great gate's knocker

79

and gave it two resounding raps. The porter opened the picket and bowed the visitor in.

'Welcome, Master Danvers. Lord John is expecting you. You know the way to his chamber, I think.' James Danvers nodded and strode across the courtyard and into the house, followed by his clerk. He twirled the cloak off his shoulders to reveal an intricately quilted black velvet doublet with snowy white linen gleaming though its sleeve slashes. He bowed to the ladies grouped around the hearth, listening to a story as they stitched away.

> Then they brought Sir Launcelot into the tower; and when he came to the chamber thereas this lady was, the doors of iron unlocked and unbolted.

The voice was mesmerising, deep and resonant and sure. Danvers loved Arthurian tales. He paused to listen a little longer.

> And so Sir Launcelot went into the chamber that was as hot as any stew. And there Sir Launcelot took by the hand the fairest lady that ever he saw and she was naked as a needle; and by enchantment Queen Morgan le Fay and the Queen of Northgalis had put her there in that pain, because she was called the fairest lady of that country.

The reader had silver hair that curled around his neck and an aquiline nose, on which were balanced steel-framed spectacles. As James wondered who he was, one of the listening ladies turned round and looked at him, wide-eyed and hopeful. He hadn't seen her before. She had an innocent alertness that took his breath away. Another wealthy widow, by the look of her gown. Wenlock was a master at acquiring responsibility for such promising milch cows. He began a bow, but she'd already turned back to the storyteller. Clearly, it wasn't him she expected. Nudging his clerk, who seemed rooted to the spot, he indicated the spiral staircase that led to Wenlock's chamber.

'"Naked as a needle," Will. What a good way of making her bare and slender at the same time. Lovely image.'

'Yes,' said his clerk, eagerly. 'I've heard Elaine described that way before – in a telling of the tales of Arthur that I read in John Doll's Oxford bookshop. I wonder if that is Malory himself. Doll told me then that he lived in London.' His eyes took on a faraway look.

James eyed him searchingly. 'What's up, Will?' he said as they walked up the Royal's wide staircase. 'I'm betting you're thinking of a wench. Who is she? Someone special?'

Will Stonor grinned ruefully. 'You're right. She haunts me rather. I met her in Doll's bookshop and she loved the tales as much as I did. She's in the service of my godmother, the Dowager Duchess of Suffolk, and last year we' – he paused – 'we had quite an adventure together.'

James raised his eyebrows. 'Oh, did you? You told me that you were affianced to Elinor Golafre. Could be some temper tantrums over a rival. I've heard Elinor's a hot-blooded filly.'

Will shook his head. 'Not that sort of adventure. A real one. But I'm not allowed to talk about it.'

'Then I won't press you,' said James, though he was intrigued by his normally forthcoming clerk's reticence. 'Come on, we must wait on Sir John.'

Danvers knocked at Wenlock's chamber door. A page opened it and ushered them in. James looked at him in surprise.

'Waited on by a page, Sir John? Where has the faithful

Thynne gone? And who's the pretty widow listening to the tale of Sir Lancelot and Elaine? And where does that version come from? I haven't heard it before.'

'One thing at a time, James,' said Wenlock. 'The tales of Arthur are a new telling, by a knight called Malory. That's him downstairs. I first met him in France. He was captain of Gisors and led the siege of Compiègne. Used to be in demand for organising masques at court, but he's become a bit of a pariah, thanks to his tactless remarks about the new queen.'

'Does he live here?' asked James.

'No. As his uncle was Prior of the English Knights Hospitaller, he's lodged as a corrodian in their priory at Clerkenwell. He's an interesting man. He spent the 1450s in and out of Newgate, caught in a legal net spun by the late Duke of Buckingham. After Buckingham's death, I did what I could to get him freed – I was his proxy overlord once, as his family seat Newbold Revel was subject to the Duke of Norfolk and the Norfolk heir was then my ward. He's collected tales of Arthur all his life – picked up books of legends in France when he served in Normandy. Now he's writing them all up in his own words in a series of tales, which he's hoping will win him a pension from a book-loving patron. But I doubt whether he'll succeed. The truth is that he's one of the people Lord Tiptoft observes with deep suspicion.'

Well, I wish him success,' said James. 'But what of the pretty widow?' A vision of her naked as a needle flashed on his inward eye.

'She's the reason I summoned you. Lady Katherine Arderne is caught up in a nasty wardship dispute with her dead husband's family. They've snatched her seven-year-old son, applied for him to be a ward of the queen and are packing him off to their home in Warwickshire. They're also claiming rights not just to her jointure but to her inheritance as their son's widow on the grounds that she's an adulteress and no fit guardian for the young heir.'

Numerous airy castles in James's head collapsed. How could appearances lie so much? She'd looked so innocent. But then so had the pretty wench at the George who had disappeared with his purse last week. His friend Paston was right. Women couldn't be trusted.

'She's pretty enough to tempt a saint,' he said with elaborate casualness. 'Any truth in the accusation?'

Wenlock was not fooled. He studied Danvers's long thin face, deep-set hazel eyes, prominent bony nose and attractively wide mouth. It wasn't a conventionally handsome face, but he knew that many women found its owner irresistible.

'Not according to Joan Moulton. She's Kate's godmother and she'll have your balls for umbles pie if you lay a finger on her. What she does need is a good lawyer. Could you act for her without seducing her, do you think?'

James's spirits soared. 'Difficult. But I'll do my best, especially if she's a godchild of Mistress Joan. Could lead to some spicy reading from the Sign of the Mole.' Then he looked pensive.

'But it won't be easy as far as the boy's concerned. Possession is nine points of the law, especially if it's a relation who's doing the possessing. Though if he's only seven, we could try a plea of *infans proprio mater debit*. But we'll need to clear Lady Arderne's name fast.'

'I don't think that will be difficult. Joan and a good many other citizens of standing will speak for her. She's the only daughter of Gregory Browne. He was one of the most distinguished aldermen in the City and twice a mayor. Your first move should be to talk to Joan.'

'I'd much rather begin with Lady Arderne.'

'Fair enough. But remember, no flirting. And before you meet her, we need Thynne. He went to the queen's court at Greenwich this morning to find out what stage the wardship has reached. He should be back presently. While we're waiting, take a look at the Ovid Mistress Moulton acquired for me in Bruges.'

James went eagerly over to the table in the window, but Wenlock had hardly opened the book when there was a soft knock at the door and Thynne slipped silently into the room.

'Perfect timing, Thynne,' said Wenlock. 'Adam, could you go down and ask Lady Arderne to come up? And Francis, could you prepare paper and ink? James's clerk will need to take notes as you tell us about the Arderne wardship.' He turned to look at Will.

'But I know you, don't I? Didn't we meet at Ewelme Palace in the autumn?'

Will bowed. 'We did, my lord. I was lucky enough to be of service to Princess Alyce.'

'You were indeed,' said Wenlock. Their eyes met, both remembering the hectic events that had all but lost Princess Alyce her heartland. 'But how come you are in London now? I thought you an Oxford scholar.'

'I was then. But my father decided it was time for me to train in the law. He sent me to Lincoln's Inn.'

James intervened. 'To train under me, as my father has long acted as his father's lawyer.' He smiled at Will. 'And I'm very glad he did.'

'It is an honour to meet you again, my lord,' said Will. 'And also an honour to hear Sir Thomas Malory read his own tales. I have long admired his writings.'

Wenlock chuckled. 'You've acquired a dreamer in your clerk, James. I hope he also has a grasp of legal practice.'

Will blushed, but James gave him a friendly pat on the back.

'He's more than able. I fear I'll lose him as soon as my wealthier rivals realise his worth.' Will reddened even more and Wenlock and James laughed.

Francis Thynne set paper and ink down on the table, then turned to Wenlock. 'My lord,' he said in a low voice. 'I should warn you that Sir Robert Harcourt...'

James saw Will's head whip round in surprise and Wenlock give his shoulder a warning pat as he turned to Thynne.

'We won't talk of that now,' he said firmly. 'Tell me later. Now, James come and see my latest treasure.'

He led the two young men over to a reading slope.

'Turn to the tale of the Sabine women,' he said. 'There's a marker in it.'

They were soon so absorbed that they didn't hear the shy tap on the door. It was Thynne who opened it and let Adam in, followed by Kate. Wenlock quickly closed the book and slid it onto the shelf under the slope. Then he stepped forward to welcome her.

'Lady Arderne, I hope you are a little rested. This is James Danvers. He's the lawyer I promised you. And this is his clerk, Will Stonor.' Danvers dropped into a graceful bow and smiled a welcome. Kate hesitated, looking distinctly anxious.

'Don't be put off by his youth, my dear,' said Wenlock, guessing at her thoughts. 'Anyone at Lincoln's Inn will confirm that he's a most effective attorney in matters of wardship. He has one of the intricately perverse minds in the Inns of Court.'

'It is not that, my lord. I am sure that anybody you recommend could only be ideal. It is Amice. She has still not come back from Broome Place. The man who went with her says she told him to come back here with my things and that she would follow with one of our servants. But she hasn't. I fear for her safety. Perhaps she has been arrested by that beadle.'

'Worry not, Lady Arderne. Thynne can go and find her, if she is to be found.'

Adam coughed. 'My lord, the Dowager Duchess of Suffolk is below. I said that you had company and she said that she would wait in the garden until you were free.'

Wenlock raised his eyebrows. 'Princess Alyce? I am honoured, indeed. What a pleasure to have her back in London. Lady Arderne, I will leave you to instruct James in the facts of the case. Francis will take notes and tell me all about it later. Lead the way, Adam.'

'My lord!' Thynne, looking unusually flustered, put a restraining hand on Wenlock's sleeve. 'If I could have a brief word – in private.'

He gestured his head towards the closet. Wenlock waved him away.

'Not now, Thynne. Would you have me keep her grace waiting? Stay with Lady Arderne and James, in case you are needed.' He checked his reflection in a mirror, picked up a leather satchel and left the room.

Kate turned to Thynne. 'But what about Amice? She may be in danger.'

'I doubt it,' said Thynne. 'If ever I saw a wench who could take care of herself, it was her. She'll be back when it suits her, rest assured. But my guess is that it was she who gave access to your house to the Ardernes.'

86

Kate sat down on the window seat, stunned.

'But I treated her so well. I gave her dresses, money, anything she wanted.'

'Perhaps I'm wrong. Maybe she just got talking to her friends at Broome Place and lost track of the hour. As soon as I've made a record of your case for Lord Wenlock, I'll do what I can to find her.'

Kate's face crumpled. 'It seems that everything is going wrong,' she said miserably.

James ached to put a comforting arm around her, but knew he would have to be meticulously formal if he was going to win her confidence.

'We really should get down to business, Lady Arderne,' he said. 'Will, please make notes for me.' Stonor sat down at the table and picked up a quill and James turned to Kate again.

'What I'd like first from you are the names of any citizens who would be prepared to vouch for you. Joan Moulton will do for one; she's highly thought of everywhere. But are there other family friends in the city that we could call upon?'

Will jotted down the names Kate suggested, James nodding approval at each one. Sir Thomas Cook, an ex-mayor. Thomas Porthaleyn, of the mercers. Matthew Fettiplace, alderman and also a mercer. William Constantine, Master of the Guild of Skinners. Alyce Paslowe, a notable mercer and, usefully, a highly respectable widow. It would be a brave judge who turned down these affidavits.

'That's plenty,' James said. 'Now – can you tell me about the terms of your marriage contract? What was supposed to happen in the event of your husband's death?'

Tears filled Kate's eyes and she blinked rapidly. A lump in her throat strangled her voice.

James tactfully turned away from her to Thynne. 'How long is it since Sir Richard died, Francis?'

'Barely a week. Mistress Moulton told me that the family descended like vultures, bitching over trifles at the funeral. That was last Thursday. They have already applied to the queen for wardship of the heir.'

'But isn't Lord Wenlock the queen's chamberlain? Did he know nothing about it?'

'It all happened while he was in Calais, treating for the king. What I found out this morning at Greenwich Palace was that a few days ago Sir Richard's mother Lady Margery Arderne slipped a hefty douceur to the queen's older brother Anthony and he told his sister that Lady Katherine was an egregious trollop.'

'And the queen believed him?'

'It suited her well to do so. Not least because Sir Richard Arderne was retained by the Earl of Warwick. She never misses a chance to spite him. But things didn't all go the older Ardernes' way. They were expecting to be granted guardianship and to be allowed to take young Peter back to Warwickshire, but the queen kept them hanging about for an hour, then announced that she had sold the boy's wardship to Sir Robert Harcourt.'

'Harcourt?' said Kate, so surprised that she forgot her grief. 'Of the Oxfordshire family?'

'That's right. That's what I wanted to tell Lord Wenlock. Very close to both the king and the queen is Sir Robert. Master of the Royal Falcons. An enthusiast at hunting game of all kinds. Two-legged as well as furred and feathered.'

'A spy?' asked Kate.

'He prefers to call himself an intelligencer.'

'So where will he take Peter?'

'Eventually to the Ardernes in Warwickshire. He holds manors near them – that's why he's interested in the wardship, of course. But the chances are that he plans to take the boy to his principal seat, Stanton Harcourt, first.'

'But that's close to my own Oxfordshire estates.'

'That is no coincidence either. Sir Robert has a daughter – a little minx of nine or so. He is doubtless planning to spouse her with Peter. In geographical terms, there couldn't be a better match. Their lands march together.'

'But that's terrible. The Harcourts are not a family I want my son to marry into. So where is Peter now?'

'He might already be on his way to Oxfordshire, though Harcourt is still in London. He's coming here to see Lord Wenlock later today.'

Kate's face cleared. 'And Sir John will make him bring Peter back?'

'No,' said Thynne. 'Lord Wenlock summons him on a quite different matter. I haven't had a chance to tell him that he is involved in your case.'

'But if he is a friend of Lord Wenlock...'

'I cannot imagine my lord describing him as such. No, Harcourt is one of Lord Tiptoft's agents.'

James saw Kate blanch. The Earl of Worcester was nick-named 'the Butcher' because of the extreme cruelty of the executions he visited on captured Lancastrians. He also no-ticed that his clerk had stopped taking notes at the mention of Harcourt. He nudged him, and Will picked up his quill again.

'So does Wenlock work for Tiptoft too?' Kate asked. 'And where is Peter now?'

'No,' replied Thynne. 'Lord Wenlock is Coroner of London,

so all unnatural deaths come before him for examination. Which means that his business and Tiptoft's frequently overlap. And if treason is suspected, then he is duty-bound to report to him.'

'Can't we stop them leaving London with Peter?'

'I fear not,' said James. 'The first thing is to exonerate you in court. Once that's done, we can appeal the wardship. If the grounds for it are baseless, then the Consistory Court judge will declare it rescinded.' He decided not to add that it might even then prove difficult to gain possession of Peter.

'No!' Kate leapt up from the window seat. 'I must find Peter straight away. He will think I've deserted him.' She swayed, about to faint again. James stepped forward, but Thynne was quicker.

'By your leave, my lady.' He put his arm around her and led her to Wenlock's high-backed chair. Will jumped up, poured a glass of wine and handed it to her.

'You must quit yourself in court first,' James said to her. 'If you don't, you'll be an outlaw, prey for any bounty-hunter who fancies the reward. That's why Mistress Moulton has lodged you safely here, under Lord Wenlock's wing. It need not take long, with friends as eminent as yours. I will file suit straight away and with any luck we will see you clear of the accusation first thing on Monday morning. Don't worry, Lady Arderne. Peter will be well looked after. It isn't in either the Ardernes' or Harcourt's interests for him to come to harm.'

Kate rounded furiously on him. 'He's already harmed. He must have been terrified at being taken away and now he'll be wondering where on earth I am. Old Sir Gervais will be dripping poison into his ear, I am sure, though he hasn't even met me. Lady Arderne was furious when Richard announced he was going to marry me. She wanted him to marry the daughter of some titled cousin of hers. She called me a base-born slut and refused to come to the wedding. It wouldn't be so bad if Sukey has managed to get taken on, but we haven't heard from her at all.'

'Who is Sukey?' said James.

'She's the girl who normally looks after him. Joan sent her off to the Mermaid Inn. But she hasn't sent any message.'

Thynne looked up from his script. 'Where would she send a message to? Nobody at your house knows where you are. And you left Moulton Inn over an hour ago. There could be news in either place.'

Hope lit up Kate's face.

'You're right, Master Thynne. Can we find out?'

'Mistress Moulton would send word immediately if intelligence came to the Sign of the Mole. I'm going to Broome Place myself to look for Amice as soon as I am given leave by Lord John. I'll see if I can find news of Sukey too.'

Before Kate could open her mouth to thank him, he slipped out of the room like a shadow. James cursed himself for not thinking of offering to go, but then reflected that he would be much better employed going to Lambeth and arranging a Monday morning hearing in front of the clerk of the Consistory Court. He bowed to Kate.

'Can I escort you back to the other ladies?' he asked shyly. 'Then Will and I will go to Lambeth to arrange the Monday morning hearing,' he said.

'Thank you,' she replied in a toneless voice. She walked down the stairs behind him, oblivious of anything but her grief. He was, he realised, utterly unimportant to her except as a lawyer.

After he had left her with Wenlock's flock of wards, he turned to his clerk.

'You looked startled at the mention of Sir Robert, Will. Have you some quarrel with him?'

'Not personally,' Will said. 'But he is notorious in Oxfordshire for his seizing of land. And he's no friend of Princess Alyce, who's one of my family's oldest friends. I'd welcome any chance of stopping him marrying Lady Arderne's son to his daughter.'

'For in my mind, of all mankind, I love but you alone,' hummed Wenlock as he strode along the screens passage towards the garden, then chuckled at his own foolishness. Love was not quite the right word. But Alyce fascinated him. Her dry wit and great learning made her as interesting a companion now as she had been when she was a renowned beauty. He'd protected her as best he could from the predatory sharks who'd descended after the Duke of Suffolk's disgrace and terrible death, sending her the shrewdest lawyers he knew. But when he began to put his hopes in the reformists who gathered behind Richard Duke of York in the 1450s and had been suspended from his post as Queen Margaret's chamberlain, they'd lost touch. At that point he'd diplomatically disappeared abroad on pilgrimage, first to St James of Compostella and then to Jerusalem itself.

When he returned, civil war was rife. He'd fought for Henry VI at St Albans and been wounded. At that time both sides regarded him as a fair man and in 1455 he was made Speaker of the House of Commons. But the misrule and turbulence had continued. In 1459, unable to stomach the poisonous politics of the Beauforts in their mindless campaign of hate against the Yorkists and the Nevilles, he'd thrown his lot in with the mighty Earl of Warwick, accepted Edward of York as King Edward IV and fought for him at Towton in 1461. Edward probably guessed at his reservations at the ousting of an anointed king but was determined to make use of Wenlock's long experience in office. To anchor his loyalties permanently, he had lavished honours upon him.

Now Wenlock was a Garter Knight, King's Butler and Chamberlain of the Duchy of Lancaster. He'd renewed his friendship with Alyce, who was following a carefully cautious course, accepting her son's marriage to Edward's sister and pursuing a tactical friendship with Cecily Neville, a woman whom Wenlock regarded as close kin to a scorpion. The world had it that Alyce had foreseen York's victory before anyone else and decided to ensure Jack's accession to his father's dukedom. But Wenlock knew that Alyce didn't give a fig for ducal honours and that she and her son were notoriously at odds. Last autumn she had taken all her possessions from Wingfield Castle, the Suffolk ducal seat. That had triggered an unpleasant episode involving Sir Robert Harcourt and the mysterious death of a spy he had installed at Ewelme to hunt out fugitive Lancastrian traitors. But Alyce had emerged unscathed, thanks in part to some diplomatic work by Wenlock.

Now Princess Alyce was expending all her energies on making her beloved Ewelme renowned as a centre of culture. He'd heard that a succession of talented painters and sculptors had been summoned there in the past six months, embellishing palace and church. And that the God's House, once a mere almshouse, was now more like a college, home of retired Oxford scholars rather than suspect Lancastrian veterans of the French wars. There was even a small scriptorium, where scribes copied books for Alyce's library.

When he walked out into the intricately laid out parterre that filled the inner court of his ancient house, he saw Alyce examining the swelling flower buds on his medlar tree with a knowledgeable eye. The serenity of her rural existence was reflected in the calmness of her long thin face. He nodded at Simon Brailles, remembering the secretary's steadfast loyalty to his mistress in the autumn crisis at Ewelme, and at Tamsin, who was, he noticed, promising to become a striking young woman – not a beauty, but with a taut energy about her. Then he bowed low to Alyce.

'Princess Alyce, I'm honoured to welcome you. If there's anything in my garden that interests you, you only have to ask. Now, how can I entertain you? Sir Thomas Malory is telling tales of Arthur to my wards in the great hall. He's recovered respectability since the death of the Duke of Buckingham, who was determined to ruin him, and he's hoping to find a courtly patron. You might have met him when he was retained by Henry Beauchamp, the Duke of Warwick, who thought very highly of him, as everyone did until he was accused of all manner of riot by Buckingham. Shall I summon him?'

Alyce considered. 'I only met him after Duke Henry's untimely death. His heir, little Anne Beauchamp, was made our ward after the death of her father in 1446 and Malory brought her to Ewelme.' Her face darkened. 'Poor child. She died of an ague three years later. Malory attended her funeral in Reading Abbey, stayed with us in Ewelme for a few days, then took her small coffin back to Warwick Castle.' She sighed. 'Anne's death was the start of all our troubles. William meant her to marry Jack, bringing with her the Beauchamp inheritance entire.

94

Her death led to Jack's disastrous betrothal to our other ward Margaret Beaufort – and William's downfall.'

'How so?' asked Wenlock, fascinated. Suffolk's sudden fall remained one of the great mysteries of the age. He had never connected it with wardships and betrothals.

'The Beauforts were incensed by the match. King Henry and Queen Margaret had no child then and little Margaret Beaufort's issue was the best hope of a Lancastrian heir. They didn't want William pulling her strings. They dripped poison into the queen's ear and without her support William had no defence against his many enemies.'

'I see. I hadn't looked at things that way round. So do you think that it was not York but the Beauforts who arranged for the *Nicholas of the Tower* to intercept William's ship?'

Alyce felt the muscles around her heart contract. She loathed talk of William's death. She knew that she should have done much more at the time to find out who had been behind it, but she had only wanted to take little Jack away to Ewelme and shelter him from the poisonous gossip at court. She had also been overwhelmed by guilt at the fact that her husband had grown increasingly avaricious and overbearing and that she had frequently longed for his death.

'No more, John. It could have been anyone of half a dozen factions – Lord Cromwell, the Duke of Exeter, York himself.'

'Might Malory shed light on it?'

'I doubt it very much. I remember him as uninterested in the never-ending squabbles over precedence. He would have had no truck with the ruthless despatch of a helpless man. Moreover, he was mired in his own troubles a few months before William was killed. But I'd rather not meet him just now. I have an urgent matter I need to discuss with you.'

'In that case, we will go up to my private chamber. There's a fire there. Adam, bring us some hot spiced cider. We need something to warm us up. Summer isn't quite here yet.'

He led Alyce, Tamsin and Simon through a little door in the wall opposite the great hall, up a short winding stair and into a room lined with tooled leather panels. Soon Adam returned with a steaming jug and four goblets.

Alyce settled herself comfortably on one side of the fire, musing on Wenlock's mention of Malory.

'So Sir Thomas is still in London. I would have thought he would have returned to Warwickshire after offending Queen Elizabeth so mightily with his masque of the Loathly Damsel. She thought its message that what women want most is their own way was a reference to her tendency to rule the roost.'

'You heard about that, did you? I'm impressed at your intelligences. Yes, he's still here but he's lying low. Can't go back to Warwickshire, because he and his wife agreed to live separately long ago, in part to protect her from his enemies, in part because they grew apart. However, he's not well. Still not recovered from his wounds at Hexham three years ago. Happily, he's under the wing of the Hospitallers. He has a set of apartments in the priory, where he works on his magnum opus, a collection of everything that's known about King Arthur and his times. I like him. He borrows books from my library and to help him make ends meet, I pay him to spin yarns to my wards. But enough of Malory. How can I help you?'

'I was summoned to London by Cis Neville.'

Wenlock raised an eyebrow.

'So. Still dancing to her tune. Is that wise?'

'Probably not. But I have no choice.'

Alyce accepted a goblet from Adam and sipped the warm cider. Then she spoke again.

'Cis is deeply troubled, John. She has told me about a most sacrilegious murder in the precinct of Paul's. Moreover the victim was known to her – as he is to you and to me. Denis Pailton the scrivener.'

Wenlock stiffened. 'Pailton? The scribe who illustrated my *Ars Amatori* and your pretty Boethius?'

'I know nothing of your Ovid, though I blush at the thought of Pailton limning it. But yes, he did both my Boethius and a Pisan I acquired recently in Oxford.'

'Does Cis know when he died?'

'You mean you hadn't heard about it? Probably about two weeks ago. But you're Coroner of London. Doesn't your deputy keep you up to date?'

'Only at the month's end and I've been away. What a tragedy. Such a talent. I thought he had fled the country with Queen Margaret.'

'Apparently not. He was hiding in London and raising what monies he could for the exiles, but he thought that the king's spies were on to him and he decided to flee. He made contact with Cis with a story about … about knowing something that touched her nearly and asked her for a safe conduct to Calais and money to buy his passage on a ship at Sandwich in return for his silence. She wrote back, asking to meet him, but got no reply. Gobbets of his body were found in Paul's ossuary a week ago. Cis summoned me to investigate.'

'What was the matter that touched Cis nearly?'

'I promised to tell no one.'

'Why did she ask you to act for her?'

'She knew she could count on my discretion.'

Wenlock gave a dry laugh. 'I doubt if you can count on hers. So what do you want me to do?'

'Firstly, I'd like you to authorise Simon Brailles to inquire into what happened and to talk to any witnesses. Is John Laweley still your deputy?'

'He is. But he's an old curmudgeon, as you know. Simon will be better off talking to his clerk, Giles Scott. I'll write him a general warrant that covers them both. What's secondly?'

'You're closer than most to Edward's web of informers and agents. You could find out if they're involved at all, or even interested.'

Wenlock gave her a sardonic glance, then nodded. 'For you, Princess Alyce, I would do much. I can't promise results but I'll pen you a warrant.' He walked over to a high windowsill where writing materials – a stack of paper, an inkpot and a quill – were laid out. He wrote rapidly, signing off with a flourish and shook a little sand over the ink to dry it. Then he folded it up, lit a spill from a nearby brazier and warmed a black lump of sealing wax until a heap of soft drops lay across the fold. He pressed his ring seal deep into it and handed it to Alyce.

'Thank you, John, I'm beholden to you. Tomorrow I must go to Paternoster Row.'

Wenlock was puzzled. 'What for?'

'To see Joan Moulton. She was the last person Pailton is known to have worked for. And the book in which Pailton concealed the letter he sent to Cis came from her shop.'

'Did it indeed? Well, you'll find the Sign of the Mole a mill of folk. She called here yesterday about a wardship she wants me to handle. Then she rushed off to prepare for her book sale on Saturday.'

Alyce's face lit up. 'Excellent. I love bargains. I also have some books for her to repair for me – and one to collect.'

'Ah. The wonderful rebound *Tales of Canterbury*. Your grandfather's masterpiece. Joan showed it to me three weeks ago. A treasure indeed.'

'Don't tell me what it's like. Joan promised me a surprise.' Alyce was a little piqued that she was not going to be the first to see her beloved book restored to glory. She drained her glass and swept out of the room, Tamsin in her wake. Brailles bowed to Wenlock and followed them, stealing a quick backward glance just as the door swung to. He saw that Wenlock's face, wreathed in smiles when he talked of Joan and her books, had fallen. The Coroner of London was gazing out of the window still as stone, brow furrowed.

As soon as he heard the sound of their feet die away, Wenlock climbed the stairs to his tower library, unlocked the iron-bound chest again and unrolled one of the new broadsheets. It had a huge woodcut showing Edward of York kneeling in front of a bare-breasted women with a serpent's tail, a crown in his upraised hands. His own crown was drunkenly tilted and a litter of flasks and cups were strewn all around. Brilliantly rendered, he reflected. Under it, in enormous letters, ran a single sentence:

KILL THE TWICE-WED WHORE OF BABYLON
BEFORE SHE SINS AGAIN

Wenlock held it up to the light. Its watermark was the same as that on the broadsheet with the spirited copperplate engravings. He pressed his thumb hard onto the dense black of the tip of the serpent's tail, then looked at it. It too was stained with oily ink. 'Proof positive,' he murmured.

The library door opened and Sir Robert Harcourt strode in. He was heavily built and had the red-veined nose of a drinker, but he showed no sign of being winded by the steep climb; nor did he have the ghost of a paunch. He would be as formidable in a fight today as he had been in the French wars, Wenlock reflected as he bowed in greeting.

Harcourt barely stooped in response. 'This had better be good, Wenlock,' he snapped. 'I'm infernally busy. I need to leave for Oxfordshire as soon as I can. My daughter's to be wed.'

'On the contrary, it is very bad,' answered Wenlock coolly. 'Which is why I summoned you. Look at this. The latest broadsheets are printed, not written, and they're being replaced as soon as they're torn down. As you know, at first we thought they were being smuggled in from abroad, so we were searching cargoes. But I'm beginning to think that the confession the constable tortured out of that limner Denis Pailton was the truth. They're being printed in London. Look at this one. The ink on it is barely dry.'

'Did he say where the press was located?'

'Died too soon unfortunately for us, but perhaps fortunately for him. When I summoned you, I had no idea where it could be. But, happily, I may just have been given a clue that could lead us to it. Her grace the Duchess of Suffolk has just left.'

'Which one? The subtle dowager or the gormless blonde?'

'Princess Alyce.' Wenlock watched Harcourt's jaw drop.

'You mean she's involved? I would never have credited it.' An avaricious gleam came into his eye. 'This is the fall of the dice I've been waiting for. I thought I'd come in for the Chaucer lands in Oxfordshire fifteen years ago when the duke got what he'd long deserved and she was on trial too. But I hadn't bargained for Henry of Lancaster's fondness for Lady High and Mighty, damn her eyes. Last autumn I almost brought her down though, didn't I? I won't let her escape again.'

Wenlock looked at Harcourt coldly. Though he had often heard Harcourt complain that his family had been granted Bensington and Ewelme by William the Conqueror and that they ought to be his today, he had only realised how much personal animosity the arrogant, hot-tempered knight entertained for Alyce last September. It was doubly unfortunate that he was still a firm favourite with Queen Elizabeth.

'You go too fast,' he said. 'I did not say that she had anything to do with the distribution of propaganda. I said that she had just left – and, given your intemperance, it's as well that you didn't bump into her. No, the lead we've been seeking lay in the reason she came to see me. Cecily Neville has found out about Pailton's death. It seems that she had business of her own with him and she's asked Princess Alyce to find out what happened to him.'

Harcourt's face fell. 'So she isn't involved in the secret press Pailton told Tiptoft about?'

'Absolutely not. She is, as you well know, virtually a recluse at Ewelme. The point is, how did Cecily Neville find out about Pailton's death? We paid the Graftons well to keep quiet. My guess is that she learnt of it from her gossip Agnes Quincey. Agnes's daughter Bronwen was married to Pailton. Margaret Grafton said they were estranged, but perhaps they weren't after all.'

'Old Tip-Toe is ahead of you on that one,' said Harcourt. 'As soon as Mistress Grafton said that Pailton was once married to Quincey's daughter, he told us to find the witch. I sent a squad out only this morning. Led by our new recruit.'

'Young Suffolk? I'm still not convinced that he's suitable for Lord Tiptoft's service. It requires discretion and ruthlessness. He's a petty-minded boy, with no subtlety. And his mother won't like it a bit.'

'He cares nothing for her,' said Harcourt. 'Sees her as an obstacle to his ambitions.'

'Influenced by you, no doubt,' said Wenlock. He saw a smirk spread over Harcourt's face and his heart sank. Harcourt had clearly not given up hope of damning Alyce.

'As to Agnes Quincey, she isn't a witch and there's no need to hunt for her. I can tell you where she lives. She lodges at the Priory of St John's in Clerkenwell.'

Harcourt was startled. 'But that's where we caught up with Pailton. He was leaving it late at night.'

Wenlock's jaw dropped. 'Was it indeed?' He thought for a long minute, then an idea that made sense of a dozen loose ends suddenly occurred to him.

'Prior Botyll is visiting Rhodes and his deputy John Langstrother is a notorious Lancastrian. So are most of the Hospitallers. Suppose the press has been set up in Clerkenwell while Botyll is away?'

Harcourt whistled. 'The Priory of St John. But it's outside royal jurisdiction. The prior owes allegiance only to the Pope.'

'Quite so. The perfect place to hide an illegal press.'

Harcourt was elated. 'I'll arrange an audience with Tiptoft. He can sign a warrant for our latest recruit the young Duke of Suffolk to search it tomorrow before the prior can appeal to the Pope. I know you don't think much of Roly-Poly but having a peer of the first rank officially in charge of us will be most useful in winning us entrance. After that, it depends what we find. Treason trumps Rome. If the press is there, the king will overrule Langstrother's objections and put him in the Tower. He knows his queen has no fondness for him. And if we don't, the prior's wrath will fall on Suffolk's head, not ours.'

'The press itself is not everything. We still need to track down the traitors who set it up. And the paper suppliers. Once you've been to see Tiptoft, I want you to go to Joan Moulton's bookshop in Paternoster Row again. She's having one of her sales of surplus stock on Saturday, and you could make that your excuse. The place will be crawling with stationers and scriveners. We need to find the source of the paper used by the press. And who buys large quantities of it. Ask around.'

Harcourt pursed his lips. 'Won't the fat besom get suspicious? She knows I don't give a tinker's curse for books.'

'Find some excuse. And talk to that loose-tongued servant of hers you told me about. I don't think Joan is involved – she doesn't mind who's on the throne as long as they buy her books. But one of her journeymen might be. Here's a purse for your expenses. And, Harcourt – Princess Alyce is likely to be at Joan Moulton's. Be civil. As well as being someone I personally respect, she is, unless proved otherwise, as loyal a servant of King Edward as you and I.'

Harcourt raised a shaggy eyebrow.

'We'll see about that, Wenlock. Personally, I doubt it very much. You're a fool to trust her. Her father and that notorious rhymester her grandfather were Lancastrian to the marrow. I'll prove she is too very soon and profit well from it. As to civility, I'll get none from her.' He strode to the door and went down the stairs.

No sooner had he disappeared than Thynne materialised from a narrow door in the wall. Wenlock lifted an eyebrow.

'Have you been eavesdropping from the closet, Francis?'

'I did hear a little of what you were saying, my lord. But I thought it better to wait until Sir Robert had gone. There is a complication. What I wanted to say to you before you withdrew from the great chamber was that Harcourt has bought the wardship of the Arderne boy from the queen. He is planning to marry him to his daughter straight away. He was packing to take Sir Gervais Arderne and the child to Stanton Harcourt when I delivered your message. No doubt they'll set off as soon as whatever business you have with him is done.'

'A complication indeed.' Wenlock thought for a moment. 'He did speak of an espousal for his daughter that required him to return to Oxfordshire. This won't please Joan. If she hears about it while Harcourt is at the Sign of the Mole, she'll be at his throat in a trice. I hope he's got the sense not to mention it.'

'I said to Lady Arderne that I would go to Broome Place to see if the boy's nursemaid has managed to send word. Would you like me to catch Harcourt up and warn him not to boast to Mistress Moulton about his wardship?'

'An excellent idea.' He was silent for a few seconds, then spoke a little tentatively.

'Thynne, do you think that I should warn Duchess Alyce that her son is become quite an acolyte of Sir Robert Harcourt?'

Thynne thought a long minute before answering. 'I suspect she will discover it for herself soon enough, my lord. But it would do no harm to go to Moulton Inn yourself tomorrow and, if needs be, exert your diplomatic skill.'

The Mermaid Inn

Saturday dawned bright but cold. Sukey and Peter had finished breakfast and were playing hide-and-go-seek. It was one of the little boy's favourite games and the rambling old inn was an ideal place for it. Since Sir Gervais's visit, they had been moved out of the chilly larder and into a set of rooms on the second floor. They could be reached from both the gallery that ran right round the courtyard and a little service stair that came up from the kitchen. There were two chambers, each with a four-poster bed and a chest for clothes; each had a door to the gallery. The service staircase led into an anteroom between them with a door to each room. It was Sukey's turn to hide. Leaving Peter with his hands over his eyes trying to remember how to count up to twenty, she went into his grandfather's room and looked round for a good place. She raised the lid of the chest. It was full of blankets. Perfect. Carefully pulling a piece of one of the blankets between the top of the chest and its lid so that she'd have breathing room and a way of getting out, she climbed in and lowered the lid over herself.

After a few minutes, she heard the door open.

'She isn't in here.' It was Sir Gervais.

She was about to push up the lid of the chest, when she heard another voice, deeper and rougher.

'God forfend she hasn't already gone with word of the boy to Broome Place. What possessed you to hire her? I told you

I'd be bringing the wench who helped us kidnap Peter. She's downstairs.'

'She said she was Peter's usual maid. And the boy was much comforted by her being here. Nor do I like the look of the girl you brought with you. Eyes only for the men, and if she's betrayed her mistress she's not to be trusted. I think we should keep Sukey if she's still here. She's devoted to the boy. I doubt she's gone. The courtyard is full of your men.'

The man with the deep voice sniffed. 'A boy his age shouldn't need a nursemaid still. Time he was taught to be a man. Hope he's not the ninny he seems, or my grandsons won't be made of much. Well, we'll keep her if that's what you want.'

'Then send away the other wench.'

'I'd rather not. I'm enjoying her... ministrations. And my plans have changed. The beadle failed to arrest your son's widow because an interfering cow called Joan Moulton stumped up bail for her. We need to get your grandson out of London as quickly as possible. The Duke of Suffolk is lending me his barge to take you to Oxford by river.'

'To Oxford? But I thought we were to ride for Warwickshire.'

'That's what they'll expect us to do. So we won't. Once Peter and my daughter are espoused at Stanton Harcourt with your assent, all the lawyers in Temple Bar won't be able overturn it. You must catch the afternoon tide from Old Swan Steps. Apparently, Joan Moulton is Lady Arderne's godmother. She's also a notable bookseller and one of the richest women in London. She won't waste a minute in getting the legal wheels turning to free her.'

'*I* must catch the tide? Aren't you coming with me?'

'I'll catch you up as soon as I can. Yesterday Lord Wenlock sent for me on royal business and I have to wait on him this afternoon. And tonight I must dine at the Archbishop of York's inn. I won't be able to leave until Sunday, perhaps not even then. I'll travel by road, as I have business in Windsor. Wait for me at the White Hart in Henley. I'll join you as soon as I can. We'll ride from there to Oxford, then on to Stanton Harcourt. You'll like my place there. Every comfort imaginable. Now, how about a jug of sack? Let's go down to the fire.'

Sukey heard heavy feet leaving the room. She lay there mouselike. So it had been Amice who dosed her posset and unlocked the door for the men to take Peter away. She was wondering what to do next when she heard light footfalls and a whisper.

'Sukey, are you in here?' It was Peter. Cautiously, Sukey raised the heavy lid a little and looked out. He was alone, his little wooden sword at the ready. She clambered out and lowered the lid quietly.

'I guessed you'd be in the chest,' he said. 'But I didn't tell them. I thought they might be cross with you.'

She smiled at the anxious little face.

'You did quite right, Peter. I think they would be very cross with me if they knew I'd heard what they were saying. Let's make it our secret. Now we must go and greet them. Do you know who the man with Sir Gervais was?'

'Sir Robert something. I didn't like him. He's got an angry face.'

The door opened. It was Abel. Peter cringed into Sukey's skirts. Abel smiled unpleasantly and made a lunge towards him. Peter screamed, dropped his sword and jumped onto the bed.

Abel looked triumphant, then turned to Sukey. 'The snivelling whelp is to come down to his grandfather. And I was to find you if I could and tell you to pack his things, then join them. So where were you? They said you weren't up here.'

'I went to the jakes. I heard them go out onto the gallery as I came up the back stairs. The packing won't take any time. I'll bring Peter down.'

'Oh no you won't,' said Abel. 'I'm taking him down and I'll be back presently to bring the bags. He grabbed Peter roughly by the arm and began to drag him out onto the balcony.'

'Remember, be brave, Peter,' Sukey called after them. 'Like your father was.' She picked up his sword. The little boy took it, pressed his lips together tightly and raised his head gallantly. Sukey's heart went out to him. Then she had an idea. She tied their belongings into two bundles. Then she raced down the back stairs, bolting the door to the room behind her. She peered cautiously into the kitchen. It was empty, but she could hear a clattering from the scullery. She looked into it and saw Micky scouring a huge stewpan.

'Micky,' she whispered. He looked round and she saw that he had a large bruise over his left cheek and eye.

'Go away. You're trouble. If Abel sees us talking he'll give me another of these.' He touched his bruised cheekbone gingerly.

'But he won't. He's waiting on the grand folk in the hall. Look. I know Abel stole my ring and penny from you, but there's a chance that you could still earn a reward.'

As she spoke, she untied the empty pocket hanging from her belt and handed it to him. 'Take this and go to Moulton Inn. Ask for Lady Arderne or Mistress Moulton. Show them this pocket, then they'll know you come from me. Say that we're going upriver to Henley by barge. Then we take horse for Oxford. Oh and tell her that Sir Robert someone will join us at the White Hart at Henley. Can you remember that?' The small boy looked dully at her and her heart sank. He was an unpromising messenger. Nor, thinking of Abel's malevolent eye, could she blame him for being terrified. She made a last appeal.

'Look, Micky, if you do this, I'll ask Peter's mother Lady Arderne to take you into her service. You want to get away from here, don't you? Well, I know that she'd do anything for someone who'd helped get Peter back to her. Then you'll be with me and Peter all the time. Think what brave times we'll have.'

From upstairs she heard an angry rattling of the bolted door.

'I've got to go now. Whatever you do, don't tell Abel about this.'

She raced out of the kitchen, through the buttery, passing Cook, who gave her a friendly wink, and into the central hall of the inn. Beside the fire in two high-backed chairs, she saw Sir Gervais and the man he'd called Sir Robert, red-faced and heavily jowled. To her horror, she saw that he had Amice on his knee, one hand fondling her bodice. She looked tearstained and dishevelled. When she saw Sukey, she gasped, a guilty look on her face. Peter stood stiffly in front of them, reciting a psalm. Sir Gervais listened benignly until he finished, bowing deeply and doffing his little cap.

'You see, Harcourt, he's been well taught. He'll make a fine husband for your girl.'

Sukey's heart sank. Amice a traitor to their mistress and Peter to be wed to this stranger's daughter? But she hid her disgust behind a vacant grin as she advanced on them, bobbing a curtsey.

'Ah, Sukey,' said Sir Gervais. 'Where were you? We found

Peter all alone just now.' Sukey repeated her story about the jakes. Sir Gervais nodded absently, then gestured to the burly man, who was kneading Amice as if she were bread dough.

'This is Sir Robert Harcourt. We're going to his house in Oxfordshire.'

Sir Robert interrupted. 'No need to tell the world and his wife what we're doing, Arderne. The less anyone knows the better.'

Sir Gervais ignored him. 'And this is my squire Tobias. Ask him if there's anything you need.' Tobias, calm-faced and sturdy, gave her a friendly wink.

Just then Abel came in, carrying the bundles that Sukey had packed and a basket of food from the kitchen. He put them down beside Sir Gervais's chair, accepted the penny he was handed with a servile bow, and pinched Sukey viciously as he backed past her.

'I'll get you, one day,' he said in a sibilant whisper. Sukey pretended not to hear, which was made the easier because Nancy had come into the room.

'The horses are ready, Sir Robert. Where will you leave them? I don't want them going too far.'

Sir Robert looked evasive. 'I haven't made my mind up. I still have business in London. I'd like the use of them for a day or two, perhaps longer. And can you spare this lad of yours to act as groom while I'm in London? I'll pay you well.'

Nancy considered. 'You're welcome to Abel's services. But I'll need both him and the horses back by Tuesday. We aren't a livery stable and I'm short-staffed.'

'Of course,' said Harcourt. 'Now, come on, all of you. Or we'll be late.'

Sukey was lifted onto the saddle of the packhorse in front

of Tobias and their bundles were pushed into its paniers. Peter rode in front of Sir Gervais and Amice was swung up onto the back of Sir Robert's saddle. She wiped her nose with the now stained and tattered sleeve of her green dress and Sukey saw that her arms and neck were purple with bruises. She looked back as she went through the gatehouse. There was no sign of Micky. Would he dare to go to Mistress Joan's? She doubted it. Then Abel tugged at the rein of the packhorse and she grabbed the saddlebow to save herself from falling.

The little cavalcade trooped along St Martin's Street towards Old Swan Steps. There was no barge to be seen. Sir Robert gave a curse, swung Amice down and then dismounted himself. He tied his horse to a hitching rail, then disappeared into a nearby alehouse, pulling Amice after him. Her head drooped. Sir Gervais looked after them with distaste as he handed Peter down to Abel. Then he dismounted himself and went to help Sukey off her horse. Peter ran over to her and she put a reassuring arm around him.

'Remember your father, Peter. Make him proud of you,' Sir Gervais heard her whisper and saw his little grandson's back straighten and his chin lift. Thoughtfully, he turned to Abel.

'Tie our horses to the rail, lad, then take the luggage down to the waterside,' he said. Puzzled, Abel did as he was told, stacking their bundles beside a sturdy oak bollard, much worn by the warps of boats.

After they had waited on the wharf for twenty minutes or so, a huge barge steered out of the main navigation channel towards them. Her eight oars made a couple of sweeps, then swung into the air, erect as lances, as the helmsman steered her hull alongside the wharf with such precision that its fat round fenders of plaited hemp barely touched it. Two of the oarsmen stepped ashore. Ropes from bow and stern were thrown to them and the barge was made fast in an instant. Sukey and Peter gazed at it in awe. The hull was brilliant blue and the gunwales gilded. The prow was a snarling lion's head and the single word *Lyonesse* was painted in elaborate gilt script across the transom. The passengers' seats towards the stern were protected from the weather by a tilt, a magnificent blue awning embroidered with gold lion heads. In the stern there was a raised platform for the helmsman.

A plump young man in a deep-blue velvet cloak who had been lounging under the tilt stood up and made his way to the gangplank that had been dropped into place by one of the rowers. The man who had been at the tiller hastened to help him onto the wharf, no easy matter given the rise and fall of the boat on the choppy water of the Thames. He was followed by a thickset man wearing Harcourt livery. Arderne bowed low.

'I am honoured to meet you, my lord.'

Jack de la Pole courteously echoed his bow. 'The pleasure is mine, Sir Gervais. So this is your grandson. A fine-looking boy.'

Peter looked down and clung even closer to Sukey. Arderne frowned.

'Make your bow, sir. This is his grace the Duke of Suffolk. He does you honour.'

Peter doffed his cap and managed a shaky bow. Suffolk nodded, then turned to Arderne.

'Well, here we are, as I promised Sir Robert I would be. This is Rufus Savernake, one of Harcourt's retained men. My watermen will row you to Henley. Sir Robert and Savernake are to meet you there, I believe, then you'll continue to Oxford by road. But is Sir Robert not with you?'

'He's in the tavern over there,' said Sir Gervais, disapproval in his voice. 'I trust you will find him sober. He has a young harlot with him. She was to have looked after Peter for me, but his own nursemaid followed him to the Mermaid and is altogether better fitted to the task.'

Suffolk looked at Sukey, hair awry and skinny as a beanpole.

'There'll be no one trying to tempt her away from her charge, that's certain,' he sneered. Sukey flushed, hating him.

The young duke turned back to Sir Gervais.

'You'd best set off straight away, Arderne. Savernake tells me there's no time to be lost.' He beckoned to the brawny, weathered man who had helped him off the barge. 'This is Piers, my steersman – there's no better waterman on the river. Piers, get the men to load these bags. And when the Ardernes have disembarked at Henley, bring the barge back to London. Here's your rowing silver.'

'But what shall I do, your grace?' It was Abel. 'Shall I take the horses back to the Mermaid?'

'We'll ask Sir Robert,' said Suffolk. He looked Abel up and down, noticing his muscled forearms. 'You seem a likely enough lad. Perhaps Harcourt thought you might be useful. The squad is short of henchmen as the minute. Play your cards right and you might have a new job. Come with me.' He strode away towards the tavern and Abel followed him. Arderne sniffed.

'Young coxcomb. It's to stop our Peter turning out like him that I want to get him away from London. Though I'm not sure that my wife was wise to choose Sir Robert Harcourt as a father-in-law for him. The man seems to think he can ride roughshod over everything and everyone. Oh well. When we've got Peter safely back in Warwickshire, we can think again. Many a child spousal has been reversed.' He saw Sukey's startled face and smiled.

'Sorry, my dear. Thinking aloud. It's a bad habit of mine. Now, let's get aboard.'

The Sign of the Mole

'Sir John looked positively tranced when I glanced back as we left yesterday,' Simon said to Alyce as they rode along Cheapside towards Paternoster Row, the two Suffolk henchmen at a discreet distance behind them. 'Shaken to the core.'

'Strange. And he seemed almost amused at the idea of finding out what Edward's agents know. Perhaps he knows already. Simon, after you've escorted me to Joan's, I want you to go to the Guildhall and call on John Laweley and his clerk. Ask them if any pointers to Pailton's killers were found. Here's Lord Wenlock's warrant.'

Brailles touched his cap in assent, though regretfully. He had been looking forward to visiting Moulton Inn. Gossip had it that Joan Moulton kept a famous table that was especially generously laden on the days of her book sales. His stomach, bilious with the morning's mix of ale and wine, echoed his thoughts by rumbling. Embarrassed, he coughed to drown the unseemly sound. Alyce eyed him.

'I'm being thoughtless. Like enough Laweley and his cronies will be eating when you arrive and I doubt the stingy old fox will ask you to join them. I'm sure Joan Moulton will invite us both to her table. You can go to the Guildhall this afternoon.'

Moulton Inn had four floors, each jutting out beyond the one below, so that its highest windows were only a handshake away from those of the houses opposite. The ground-floor walls were brick, the next two were hung with tiles, and the attic storey had wattle and daub between narrow wooden struts. The huge beams supporting the floors ended in grotesque carvings and the sunshine glinted off the innumerable panes of glass in the deep bay windows. Dormer windows looked out like quizzical eyes from the tiled roof (no bookseller ever risked thatch or wooden shingles) and the lead gutters ended in ornate spouts stretching out so that they were above the deep gutter in the centre of the street. No place to be on a rainy day, thought Simon. A painted green shield showing three black moles *courant* scampering on gilded claws hung outside the entrance.

The sale was in full swing. Outside the shop to the left of the porter's lodge the upper shutters were propped outwards so that they formed a roof, and the lower ones swung out onto trestles to form a long table. A crowd of sober-gowned clerks and lawyers were elbowing each other as they grabbed at the books and bundles of parchment and paper laid out on them. Leaning out from inside the shop was a tall journeyman with a cadaverous, pock-scarred face, shouting prices and collecting coins. Clearly there were bargains to be had. Simon noticed that the journeyman had a formidable knife in a sheath on his belt and that two burly yeomen were also watching over the stock, one at each end of the table. A clerk's gown was no guarantee of honesty. He watched a wrinkled, bony hand snake towards a small leather-covered book on the edge of the middle of the table, the place furthest away from the yeomen. He only saw the movement because he was high on horseback: an eyeblink and the book was gone. He could see the stooped back of the man who must have taken it and a tell-tale bulge in the furred sleeve of his shabby mantle. The man turned towards them and Simon saw that he was an ancient, bearded and rheumy-eyed. And familiar. He looked up, caught Simon's surprised eye, gave him a broad wink and pushed his way through the throng towards them. Doffing his worn black cap, he bowed to Alyce.

'What a pleasure to see you, your grace. And you, Master Brailles. What brings you from sylvan Ewelme to this den of iniquity?'

'A pleasure to see you too, John Hardyng,' said Alyce. 'How goes your great history?'

'I thought I'd done with it, but King Edward has asked me to revise it. I'm deep in Plantagenet genealogy now. Perhaps I should hedge my bets and keep the old version, so there is one for York and one for Lancaster.' He cackled. 'But I must speak no treason. These are delicate times. Are you, like me, visiting Mistress Moulton?'

'We are. Hoping for something to eat as well as some bargains.'

'As I am myself. I'm sure Joan won't fail us.' He went ahead of them into a courtyard utterly different from that of Montagu Inn. Long raised beds, gay with gillyflowers and wallflowers, flanked its paths. Neatly trimmed nut trees shaded them at intervals and a short canal lined with marble ran down the centre. Simon looked into it and saw a great tench mouthing among watercress roots. Arbours stood invitingly in each corner, laced with sweet briar, honeysuckle and jasmine in full flower. Hardyng laughed at Alyce's astonished face.

'Of course, you haven't seen it, have you?' he said. 'It's a paradise after the Moorish style. Mistress Moulton has been working on it ever since she returned from Compostella in

February. She saw houses with gardens like this and wouldn't rest until she'd created her own private Eden. It's so sheltered from the frosts and warmed by Moulton Inn's ever hot chimneys that summer has come a month early.'

As they dismounted, two lads hurried over to take their horses into the stable. In anticipation of a manger full of sweet hay, Lady Alyce's horse promptly shat. A heap of turds steamed on the cobbles. Just then the main door to the house opened and Joan swept out like a ship in full sail, a beaming smile on her face and her impressive bosom bouncing. She was dressed in her best: a generously gathered blue gown trimmed with squirrel fur and soft red leather shoes. On her head was a blue two-horned headdress, over which stiffened lawn was draped. Behind came a tall thin woman in a simple grey gown edged with black, as elegant and poised as a heron.

'A timely gift, Larkspur, and as welcome as your own presence, Princess Alyce. My new walnut tree will relish the nourishment. Ned, get a shovel and remove this generous contribution to our flowerbeds.' Hidden until then by Joan's bulk, a skinny boy in the ink-stained jerkin of an apprentice darted away towards the stables.

'We're about to eat – as old John there must have calculated. Will you join us?'

'With pleasure. Simon too has high hopes of nourishment. But we can send Hugh and Brian to the pie shop.'

'I wouldn't hear of it. Moultons have always kept a good house for all. When they've seen to your horses, they must come and eat with my grooms. Now, come and admire my new Flemish hangings. Monique, ask Matthew to make place for her grace and Master Brailles beside me on the dais.' The heron nodded and disappeared into the buttery.

Simon watched Monique go, assured and stately. He envied her her confidence. Why did he always feel so inadequate with women? He followed Alyce and Joan into the great hall after pausing in the screens passage to allow a page to pour warm rose-scented water over their hands and another to towel them dry. There was already a hubbub of voices, as visitors and household jostled for positions at the long trestle tables. At one side, a huge chimney with an elaborately carved stone surround rose almost to the rafters. Joan's rebuilding of Moulton Inn had been much influenced by the comfortable ways of the Flemings, which she'd observed on her buying trips to Ghent and Bruges. The walls were hung with boldly striped cloths, and behind the high table on the dais there was a tapestry in the millefleur style of an enclosed garden with an apple tree flanked on one side by a coquettish Eve and on the other by a doltish-looking Adam. Twined around the trunk of the tree head downwards and looking greedily at Eve was a rainbow-hued serpent with a suavely expressive head, its scales exquisitely outlined with silver thread.

'It's magnificent, Joan. I can see why Eve was tempted,' said Alyce as she settled down on the high-backed chair at the centre of the dais. 'Spending eternity with that dullard Adam would soon pall. The serpent looks familiar...' She craned her neck to look at it more closely. 'God's wounds, it has a look of Wenlock.' Joan's eyes twinkled.

'Just what I thought when I saw it in Arras. That's why I bought it.'

Hardyng cackled in amusement, but the black-cowled friar who was sitting next to him scowled.

'Eve is not suitable as a centrepiece,' he snapped. 'She set your sex off on their downward path. The first of a long line of women who betrayed men. As Tertullian so rightly has it, a woman is the devil's gateway – a temple built over a sewer.' His English was heavily accented. Eyes as black as his habit blazed from a face yellowy with fading suntan.

'But thanks to your sermons we are learning wiser ways,' said Joan placidly. 'Although I always feel that Tertullian's views on women reflect more about his wife's behaviour than that of the sex in general. I prefer Christine de Pisan's notion that man has gained much more through Mary than he has lost through Eve.'

She turned to Alyce, who had just managed to quell a laugh into a cough. 'Your grace, may I introduce Brother Pietro of Padua? Hotfoot from the Vatican. Best hellfire preacher I've ever heard and a plantsman into the bargain. He's on his way to Oxford to sell printed pamphlets exhorting repentance and strikingly illustrated with visions of heaven and hell. They're the latest thing; there's an Austrian press in Rome which is churning them out. The Canterbury folk liked them so much that they bought them all up, so he's been lodging at the English house of his order in Blackfriars while my scriveners write him new ones. Slow work compared to printing. But we'll be setting up presses of our own before long, I don't doubt. Though not if those stick-in-the-muds at the Stationers' Guild have their way.'

'Brother Pietro will find plenty who need to consider their immortal souls in Oxfordshire,' said the irrepressible Hardyng. 'Though it's earthly forgiveness from the king they need more urgently. The county's stuffed with closet Lancastrians.'

A silence fell. Brailles, who had been at a side table collecting a plate of the carp collops that Alyce particularly liked, glanced at her as he sat down. He knew how she loathed such jibes, especially from a man whom the Chaucers had always treated generously. But her face was icily composed as she spooned a generous helping of fish onto her trencher.

'From your own tanks, Joan?' she asked.

'That they are. We keep them for at least a week in clear water to wash the taint of river mud from their flesh. Then the day before we cook them, we hang them in damp moss to keep them alive and feed them on milk-soaked bread. Try the braised fennel; it comes from our plot over the river in Southwark. It's the Italian variety. The last time Brother Pietro came, he brought me a few roots.'

'I'd welcome a piece for my Ewelme garden.'

'Nothing could be easier. I have some roots in the coaxing hut by the bakehouse that are doing nicely. And some other unusual things. I'll show you after you've eaten your fill.'

The awkwardness eased and soon the clatter of spoons and chatter of voices all but drowned the viols, pipes and timbrels of the musicians in the gallery of the hall. The meal was almost over when there was a flurry of excitement by the screens as the musicians summoned up a ragged fanfare. A tall young man dressed in black velvet embroidered with silver stars and slashed with brilliant blue entered, followed by a burly knight in a murrey doublet trimmed with gilded cords. The steward thumped his staff on the floor for quiet and announced the names of John de Vere, Earl of Oxford, and Sir Robert Harcourt of Stanton Harcourt. The hubbub returned as Joan heaved herself to her feet with a smile of welcome as they approached the dais.

'The Sign of the Mole is honoured by your presence, Lord John, and how good to see you here again, Sir Robert. That's twice in as many months. Can it be that you are becoming a bibliophile? Come, keep us company. Here's her grace of Suffolk. Have you eaten? Boy, trenchers for their lordships. By the Nails, is all London coming to this sale of mine?'

'All London with any sense, Mistress Moulton,' said the younger man with a smile. 'Paul's Walk is echoing with tales of the bargains to be had today. I met Sir Robert there and when I said that I was on my way here, he insisted on coming too.' He bowed low to Alyce. 'Your servant, *Principessa*. It's been more than ten years since we met at Broughton Castle, but you haven't changed at all.'

Alyce inclined her head. She remembered the occasion well. Vere's mother Elizabeth had brought him and his sister to visit her kinsfolk, the Fiennes. When Alyce had heard that the Countess of Oxford, one of her oldest friends, was at Broughton, she'd ridden over without delay. Even at thirteen, their second son had been striking, with his straight black hair and wide-set grey eyes. Now he was full-grown, handsome as a knight out of Arthurian legend. But also, according to the last letter she had received from the countess, a coward who had forsworn his father to save his own skin. Cis had said he was to marry her favourite godchild and here he was with Harcourt, her most ruthless rival for power and influence in Oxfordshire and the man rumoured to be foremost among King Edward's intelligencers. Her face was rigid with disapproval.

Joan was by contrast all smiles. She tugged at Simon's sleeve. 'Master Brailles, would you mind making place for the Earl of Oxford and Sir Robert?' He stood up obediently.

'Thank you,' said Vere. 'But where will Master Brailles sit?'

Joan turned and looked down the room. An arm waved from a place halfway down the left-hand table. She waved back and turned to Simon.

'There's room down there beside Matthew, my head book-man. He's very keen to hear about Princess Alyce's library. And you'll have the fire to warm your back.' Simon bowed and headed down the hall. Although he knew he was much lower in rank than the new arrivals, he felt obscurely resentful. At Ewelme he had a respected position; here in London he was just another servant.

He negotiated his way through the throng of serving boys to the empty place Joan had indicated. The man she had called Matthew half-rose.

'Master Brailles, I am honoured. I'm Matthew Cobham, chief binder at the Sign of the Mole. Mistress Joan told me that her grace had brought her secretary with her. You must have seen many treasures in her famous library. Tell me what you've brought for repair today.' Mollified, Simon was soon deep in discussion as to the respective merits of leather, parchment and wooden bindings. After twenty minutes or so, he remembered what Alyce had said about the book that Pailton had sent to the Duchess of York.

'I believe you once made a small psalter limned by Denis Pailton?'

Matthew looked puzzled. 'I'd need to ask Guy of Yarnton, our chief journeyman. He's a better memory than I have for these things. It must have been a while ago, though. We haven't bound a psalter limned by Pailton for over a year. The last one was ordered by Sir Richard Roos, the court poet. It was bound as a girdle book, as Sir Richard said he wanted to take it on his travels. It had two silver clasps and the leather of its binding tapered into a knot he could hook over his belt. Ready to read as he rode. Not that Roos is likely to be riding for a while. He fled with the late queen to Scotland, but was captured. He's kicking his heels in a dungeon at Windsor now, hoping for mercy from King Edward and thinking hard about his immortal soul. The psalter before that was commissioned by Sir Anthony Wydeville, the queen's oldest brother. But that was a full folio. The gayest and grandest we've ever done, for he intended it as a gift for his sister. He knew that her star was rising before any of the rest of us. She's rewarded him well, so he can indulge his two great loves, books and tournaments. He's waiting impatiently to tourney with the Bastard of Burgundy, they say. Boasts he's unbeatable.'

'Less canny than his father, though,' said Matthew's neighbour. 'Did you see the feint old Rivers made against Lord Hastings at the Yuletide tournament at Smithfield?'

They began to argue about the respective merits of the Wydeville menfolk and of other noted jousters – Paston, Parr, Sellenger and Montgomery. After a few minutes, the thin, pockmarked man who had been overseeing the street stall joined them.

'Ah, Guy, I have a question for you,' said Cobham. 'Do you remember us binding an octavo psalter limned by Pailton a few years ago. Not the girdle book we did for Roos. Earlier than that.'

Guy considered. 'Five years ago or so Pailton brought us one to bind. It was to be for his own use. He asked if he could earn the cost by illustrating another book for us.'

Cobham turned to Simon. 'Would that be the one?'

'I suspect it is. So does Pailton work regularly for you?'

He saw Guy tense. It was Cobham who answered.

'He used to until recently. But the word is that he's gone abroad. Now, about the Burgundy tournament. Who's your money on, Guy? I'd risk mine on young Paston.'

'Not young Suffolk, for sure,' said Guy. They all guffawed. Simon bristled and to his own surprise heard himself saying 'What makes you say that? After all, he trained at Fotheringay.' The printers were silent for a beat, then Matthew clapped Simon on the back and refilled his ale beaker.

'Well said, Master Brailles. Loyalty's respected here at the Mole. Guy – Master Brailles is secretary to the duke's mother, Princess Alyce. Whose *Tales of Canterbury* we've clad in the handsomest binding in England.'

'Then I spoke out of turn and I'm sorry for it,' said Guy.

'Apology accepted,' said Simon magnanimously and they returned to talking of books.

Meanwhile on the dais, Joan moved onto the chair Simon had given up. She motioned to Vere to sit beside her and to Harcourt to sit opposite, next to Hardyng. Alyce remained stony-faced, annoyed that Joan was tolerating Harcourt's presence and angry that Simon should have been relegated in favour of men she distrusted. Joan seemed impervious to her displeasure and asked Vere how his mother did. His face grew serious.

'She is more than happy to be back at Hedingham, though the churls who occupied it after the Lancastrian defeat at Towton left it in a sorry state. Still, housekeeping keeps her mind from greater torments. I – er – I haven't been there for some months, however.'

'And what of Aubrey's wife?' put in Alyce. 'I hear that like you she has been restored to favour and is one of the queen's favourite ladies.'

She was interested to see Vere's eyes flash with anger at mention of his sister. 'Aye, so she is,' he answered coldly. 'As she was of the last queen – a reflection of her versatility.'

'And your own new position proves yours, my lord,' Hardyng put in snidely. 'My spies tell me that you are to act as Queen's Chamberlain in a fortnight's time, since Sir John Wenlock is to be away on the king's business in Burgundy with the Earl of Warwick.'

Alyce frowned. Wenlock had not told her that he was going abroad so soon. And Vere's promotion confirmed the rumours that he betrayed his father and brother. She turned to Harcourt. Much as she disliked him, they could at least talk of Oxfordshire matters now that Hardyng was boasting to Vere about the popularity of the new version of his chronicle.

'Would you like one, my lord?' Hardyng was saying. 'Joan has made twelve copies for me. Everyone of consequence at court should have one. They say that Edward notices who doesn't buy it as well as who does. His eyes are everywhere. I've never known a man with a better memory for men. And their estates.'

But then the word 'Oxfordshire', spoken not by Harcourt but by Vere, caught Alyce's attention. She turned her head. The young earl was talking to Joan.

'It has long seemed to me absurd that the earls of Oxford had no seat in the city of their title. So I've purchased one. And Sir Robert Harcourt told me as we walked along that the refurbishment of the property I've bought from him is complete. Which means I can load my barge with furnishings for it tomorrow and leave London on Monday.'

'Where is this property?' Alyce asked him.

'In Cornmarket Street. When I bought it, it was a coaching inn called the Golden Cross. But Sir Robert assured me that until a year ago it was used by his own family and could easily be converted back into a fine townhouse.'

'So it could. I know it well,' she replied, remembering that three years ago she had herself asked Harcourt if she could buy the freehold for just that purpose, only to be refused it on the grounds that he was planning to occupy it again himself. She turned back to Sir Robert, who was deep in whispered conversation with Hardyng and gave his sleeve a peremptory tug to get his attention.

'Sir Robert, Vere tells me that you have sold him the Golden Cross. Doesn't that leave your own family short of city lodgings?' A complacent smile appeared on Harcourt's face.

'Not now. As I expect you know, last summer I became Steward of the University and a fine stone house in New College Lane is one of the perquisites of the position. I've already renamed it Stanton Place.'

To hide her annoyance, Alyce took refuge in taking skewers of clove-spiced lamb from the platter that Ned was now offering by her shoulder. Like predatory spiders, the Harcourts were stretching a web of influence over the city and the county.

Food and wine flowed freely and the hubbub increased. Joan beamed over them all approvingly. There was nothing like a feast for promoting good fellowship – and sales. She leant towards Vere.

'And what of that pretty little partridge Meg Neville, my lord? The word is that you're to wed her before the tournament so that she can have a front-row seat. Or is there another reason for such a hurried match?' She winked knowingly.

'Absolutely not,' said Vere, visibly taken aback. He glanced nervously at Alyce. 'Yes, we're to be married by her brother George, the archbishop, in Windsor on Thursday week on St Peter's Day. But it's nothing to do with...' Blushing, he broke off and began again. 'It's been brought forward so that her older brother, the Earl of Warwick, can be there. As John Hardyng just said, he leaves for Burgundy a fortnight today. That's why I'm setting off by river on Monday. I'll stop at Windsor, but my barge and our furnishings will go on to Oxford. The Golden Cross is to be my wedding present to Meg. She and the earl will leave Warwick Inn for Windsor next Friday. The king and queen are honouring us by allowing our wedding to be part of the celebration to be held there to mark the anniversary of their own marriage.'

'Warwick will be relieved to have her safely wed,' said Joan. 'The word is that the queen had her lined up for her youngest brother Richard, a limp flannel if ever there was one. But when he proposed to her with a hand to her breast, Meg slapped his face hard and he retreated with what little there is of his tail between his legs.'

Vere grinned. 'That's my Meg. And you've hit the nail on the head as you always do, Mistress Moulton. Marrying while Warwick is still here has prevented another husband being foisted on Meg while he is away.'

'Surely no one would risk the mighty Earl of Warwick's enmity?' said Hardyng, who was listening with close interest.

Harcourt guffawed. 'Not so mighty as he likes to think himself these days.'

'What do you mean, Sir Robert?' asked Alyce sharply.

'"Answer no questions and you'll tell no lies" is my motto, your grace,' said Harcourt, noisily sucking marrow out of a beef rib. 'But there are straws in the wind, for sure.'

And, according to Cis, a traitor Neville on the horizon, thought Alyce. But surely not Warwick himself. Especially if Vere, who now seemed a firm favourite at court, was marrying his sister. She realised that she had been more out of touch than she knew. She was also hurt. Meg Neville's mother had been the daughter by his first marriage of Thomas Montagu, her best-loved husband, and was until she died two years ago one of her dearest friends. She thought of herself as Meg's grandmother as well as being her godmother. Meg herself was comically like Thomas in character, impetuous and courageous to a fault. But why hadn't she sent her word of her planned marriage to Vere? Inwardly seething now, she turned back to the young earl.

'What does your mother think of your marrying Meg?' she said in a low whisper. 'Is she happy at you bedding the sister of Lancaster's greatest enemy?' She made no attempt to veil her contempt. He looked at her with flushed cheeks, naked misery in his eyes.

'I hope... I hope that she will come round to it. When she meets Meg. She's refused to have the wedding at Hedingham and she won't be at Windsor. But when she gets to know Meg for the clever loving person she is, I think she'll love her as much as I do.'

He paused, then said with a lift of his chin, 'And you, your grace? How does the king's sister, your noble daughter-in-law? I hear that she continues to endow the dukedom of Suffolk with Plantagenet babies and is now returned to London.'

There was no doubting his meaning. The pot was calling the kettle black. She too had abandoned the Lancastrian cause. Alyce felt her cheeks burning.

A serving boy bent between them with a salver of stewed capon spiced with aniseed and fennel. From across the table, Hardyng leant forward and asked Vere if he would be interested in a new genealogical roll of his family.

'Just the thing now you're getting married,' said the old man with a salacious leer. 'We'll leave plenty of space for the next generation. Not many left of the last one, I fear.'

He cackled at his own cruel wit and helped himself liberally to the capon. Vere scowled.

Alyce was reminded that she needed a family tree to sort out the Neville clan. She leaned towards the old man.

'Master Hardyng, do you have such a thing as a Neville roll?'

His rheumy eyes turned towards her speculatively.

'And what would you be wanting such a thing for, my lady? Are you planning to marry again?'

Alyce grimaced. 'I think not. I've had quite enough of matrimony. I want to give one to the Duchess of York. She's finding her family's marital intricacies hard to keep track of and the only one she has is at Fotheringay. I know that you made that one for her and I wondered if you'd kept a copy. It need only be the descendants of Ralph of Westmorland and Joan Beaufort.'

'I copy everything and forget nothing,' said Hardyng. 'Yes, I do have a Neville roll. And it's right here in the Mole's workshop. Joan keeps my exemplars in her bindery strongbox for safety. I'll tell her to have a copy made straightaway. I charge four marks, usually, but for you, my lady, only three. That's on top of whatever Joan charges for her scribe, of course.'

'Two marks for a plain pedigree, four for coloured,' said Joan, who had overheard both Alyce's conversation with Vere and her request to Hardyng.

'Plain will do,' said Alyce. 'Could it be done immediately?'

Joan looked around and saw Guy beside Simon and

Matthew. She called and he came over. She handed him her bunch of keys.

'Guy, could you make a quick copy of the Neville roll, just the Beaufort line, for Lady Alyce? For use, not show. You can get the second key from Matthew. Ask Master Hardyng to check it as soon as you've finished it. There'll be an extra groat for you if it's ready today.'

Guy nodded and walked off towards the screens. Joan rose to her feet, smiling benignly at Harcourt and Vere.

'My lords, you will excuse us. Her grace and I must withdraw. We have women's affairs to talk about. I will leave you to Sir Thomas Cook and William Constantine. Wealthiest merchants in London, so if you need a loan talk to them nicely. They're obliging and very discreet.'

Nodding a farewell, Joan ushered Alyce through a gap in the arras behind them. At their passing, Eve's slender frame quivered and the serpent leered.

St Paul's Yard

Left alone at Montagu Inn, Tamsin was enjoying herself. She'd explored the ancient house from cellar to turret with the help of Ellen, the bold-eyed kitchen maid whom she'd helped peg out the washing. Then she sat cleaning quantities of parsnips and carrots while the girl gossiped about everyone in the household. Tamsin soon knew all about Ellen's liaison with Dan the groom, Cook's tendency to tuck a bit of this and a bit of that away to sell, and Peggotty Lambourn's wastrel son who kept turning up like a bad penny.

The only fly in the ointment was an unpleasant little scene

she'd had with the young duke after they had left Alyce's chamber yesterday afternoon. He had tugged her into an alcove halfway down the stairs. Startled, she had pulled away. He'd laughed at her, then winked.

'Come, come, Tamsin Ormesby. No need to fear me. I just want to ask you a favour. In Suffolk my mother's maid Sarah used to let me know what my mother's plans were and show me her letters when she could, and I rewarded her generously. I'm hoping that you'll be just as useful to me. I'll make it worth your while. Think it over.' He'd chucked her under her chin, and gone on down the stairs, whistling cheerfully.

The bell for the midday meal sounded and she followed Ellen into the hall, where trenchers of bread were being loaded with sliced meat from last night's roasts. She watched Ellen souse hers with savoury-smelling gravy from an iron pot. Her mouth watered as she did the same.

'Do you want to come out with me?' Ellen said when they had eaten their fill. 'Cook's asked me to see if there are any vegetables for sale at Puddle Dock and to match some knitting yarn for her from her favourite Cheapside stall.'

Tamsin was wondering whether this would be allowable when Pek, who was sitting opposite them, leant forward.

'You go with Ellen,' he said. 'She knows London well and she'll take good care of you. But be back before vespers.'

They donned cloaks, found baskets and set off. They walked along Thames Street and down to the river to watch the watermen landing their cargoes at Puddle Dock. A barge had just come from the market gardens across the river in Southwark and Ellen picked out the freshest of its bunches of spinach, garlic and leeks and put them in her basket. There was a brisk westerly wind and the river was turbulent, far wider and wilder than it was in Oxfordshire. Sailing barges surged downstream, cautiously reefed. Some were heavily laden with freight, others carried passengers under canvas shelters. Small rowboats criss-crossed from bank to bank like water beetles. Ellen pointed out the banners waving from the tall flagpoles around the circular enclosures of the bear- and bull-baiting pits on the river's south bank and the high spire of St Mary Overy at the far end of London Bridge.

'Keep away from that side of the river unless you've got a couple of Suffolk men at your side,' said Ellen. 'You'll be snatched to join the Winchester geese otherwise.'

'The what?' Tamsin had asked.

'The Winchester geese. That's what they call the doxies. They aren't allowed in the city after the curfew bell, so they live in Southwark – it's part of the diocese of Winchester. See the great house across the river next to the church? That belongs to William Waynflete, the bishop. Looks grand, but they say it's tiny compared to Waltham Palace, his Winchester home. Or, when it's finished, his fine new college in Oxford. If you're still here the next time there's a feast day, we could go over to the Southwark Fair with Dan and a couple of his friends. Now, how about seeing St Paul's? It's the greatest church in all England. And it's on the way to Cheapside.'

'I'd love to. We came past it. Its steeple looked like to reach the sky.'

'Wait until you get inside it. All London meets there on a Saturday and there's lots to buy on the stalls in the churchyard. Have you got any money?' Tamsin hesitated. Her grandmother had given her a purse full of small coins but had also warned her to lace it tightly into her bodice and deny its existence.

'No,' she said.

'Never mind. I can lend you a penny or two if we find anything you fancy. You can pay me back when you get your wage. There's some very pretty trinkets on Widow Chancey the silk weaver's stall.'

Feeling a little mean at her cautious untruth in the face of Ellen's open-handedness, Tamsin followed her new friend up Puddle Dock Hill and into a labyrinth of small, crowded alleys. The afternoon crowds jostled against the two girls and she was glad that she'd got her purse safely tucked away. When they came out through a tunnel-like gateway into the open ground around St Paul's, she caught her breath. Close to, it was like a mountain range: arched windows soaring up to the steep roofs, buttresses leaping over them, frivolously decorated turrets and ranks of pinnacles and gargoyles etched against the sky. Immediately in front of them was a great octagonal outcrop with an intricate stone lantern on top of its slated roof.

'That's the chapter house,' said Ellen. 'Where the church court sits of a Wednesday.'

All around the walls of Paul's Yard were stalls under lean-to roofs. Most sold books, paper and parchment. Tamsin longed to linger, but Ellen tugged at her arm. 'It's only boring stationers on this side of Paul's. And the letter writers and lawyers. We need to go right through the church to the other side. That's the way to the Cheapside haberdashers.' She pointed to the great portal of the south door.

Inside the church felt tomb-cold, despite the brilliant colours seeping through the stained-glass windows and a blaze of candles which would have warmed any smaller space. Sprouting from its pillars like ferns, slim stone ribs disappeared into dusky space. Ellen walked to the centre point of the transepts. She pointed to the left down the nave.

'That's Paul's Walk.' As she'd promised, it was crowded with opulently dressed merchants and their wives and fashionable young men about town. Lawyers stood beside the pillars, greeting old clients, hopefully eyeing up new ones. In the shadows beyond the pillars lurked women with painted faces and dead eyes.

'They're no better than they should be,' whispered Ellen. 'They're banned from touting for custom here, but nothing stops them.'

She turned to the right, where a magnificent screen cut the choir off from view. Behind it, a Mass was being sung and the air was full of the scent of sandalwood and frankincense. Ellen crossed herself.

'They're celebrating the second flowering of the Thorn today. The tree that grew from the staff brought by Joseph of Arimathea to Glastonbury. A budded branch is sent to London from Somerset every year at Christmas and in May. But only aldermen are invited to the feast after the Mass. Last week it was St Zita's day and all the maids in the ward lit a candle for her and went to the merrymaking in Bunhill Fields. Pity you missed it. Come on, I'm chilled to the bone. I need to get Cook's yarn and we'll have to be getting back soon.'

They came out of the other side of the church and walked down a short alley to Cheapside, where trestle tables heaped with silks and wools, lace, fur tippets and balls of thread lined the north wall of the churchyard. Ellen found her favourite stall and was soon happily bargaining over the brightly coloured kerchiefs, caps and woven silk purses.

Tamsin tugged at her arm. 'I'm going back to the bookstalls on the other side of St Paul's – I promised Simon that I'd get him some things.'

Ellen nodded absently and went on rummaging.

Tamsin went back through the church and came out on the other side. The biggest stall was resplendent with colourful block-stamped paper folders, sheets of paper with gilded borders and little notebooks made up from odd trimmings of paper. These were bound in different coloured leathers and had thin leather ties around them. She picked one up and leafed through it, stroking the creamy, slightly ridged pages, wondering if her money would stretch to one. Above the stall was a painted sign: 'John and Margaret Grafton, Stationers'. Beside the counter a middle-aged woman was sitting and behind it a stooped, bespectacled figure was standing, talking to a tubby young man in a feathered hat who had his back to Tamsin. A wealthy customer who had been invited round to the back, out of the press of the crowd, presumably. Tamsin could see from the ermine trim on his blue velvet cloak that he was a nobleman.

The seated woman eyed her shrewdly as she fingered the notebooks.

'Interested are you, dear? It's the new Italian style – imported from the Rialto. That's in Venice. Some of them are a little travel-soiled and I'm selling them off cheaply, if you're short of pennies. Not a London girl, are you? Where are you from?'

'No, I'm from Ewelme, in Oxfordshire,' said Tamsin. 'I arrived this morning with her grace the Dowager Duchess of Suffolk.' The woman raised her eyebrows.

'Princess Alyce? Why, she's a most valued customer. I'd be grateful if you'd remember Margaret Grafton to her. I can give you a special price if you're in her service. No doubt his grace here will vouch for you.'

The man who had been talking behind the counter turned

round and Tamsin recognised him with dismay. The young duke's face creased into a teasing smile.

'Why, if it isn't my mama's new maid from Ewelme. What a lucky chance. Let me buy you that notebook in memory of your father. He was the closest thing I had to a friend in that dreary Oxfordshire hole. And it will celebrate the little arrangement we came to yesterday.'

Confused, Tamsin made a clumsy attempt at a curtsey. Determined not to accept anything from him, let alone betray her mistress, she shook her head to protest as she rose. But she lost her balance and if Suffolk had not stepped forward and grasped her, she would have tumbled to the ground. For a moment he held her tight, hard fingers probing her ribs, straying higher. She went rigid and he stepped back, a sneer on his lips.

'I can see that you are not made in Sarah's mould. But by gainsaying your master, you risk causing offence. Bear in mind that I can make or break you.'

Tamsin thought quickly. It was vital that she avoided offending him. She managed a self-deprecating smile. 'My lord, the notebook was not for myself,' she said. 'I was just looking at them to tell her grace's secretary Simon Brailles about them.'

But Duke John was no longer listening. His eyes were focused somewhere over Tamsin's shoulder. He shouldered his way past the Graftons and strode towards the north door of St Paul's. He was immediately followed by two other men, one evidently a gentleman, the other a rough-looking young servant. They must have been waiting on him at a discreet distance from the Graftons' stall, Tamsin realised.

'Would you like to see some of the cheaper notebooks, dear?' Margaret Grafton bent down and lifted the fustian cloth over the stall's counter and pulled out a bundle. She unrolled it and Tamsin was soon absorbed in its contents.

Suddenly she felt a heavy weight hit her from behind and she staggered forward onto the stall, knocking several of the little books onto the ground. She turned angrily and saw the back of a woman in a dark green cloak. The heavy basket hoisted high on her right shoulder had sent Tamsin flying. Margaret Grafton shouted indignantly after the hurrying figure, but the woman didn't look back.

'Curse that witch Quincey,' said the stationer, stooping to pick up the scattered notebooks. 'Never a thought for anyone else. She was in a fine temper this morning because she wanted to sell her plague remedies on the empty stall at the end of the row. But the market warden wouldn't let her. She's no right to be there, either. We've all paid for our licences.'

'Plague?' said Tamsin, alarmed. Margaret chuckled.

'Don't worry, my duck. It was terrible last year and there is a rumour that there's a case in Southwark. I wouldn't be surprised if it was Agnes who spread it so that she could sell more potions and talismans. There's been nothing in the city yet, but she's known to have the sight and folk listen to her.'

'The sight? You mean she can read the future?'

'She's learned in astrology and stirrings in water and signs in flames. But not above lying about what she sees for her own gain, if you ask me.' Just then Ellen joined them, nodding a greeting to Margaret.

'I saw what happened, Tamsin. Are you all right? That was Agnes Quincey, wasn't it? Second time I've seen her today. She was in our kitchen this morning, creeping around like a boggart.'

'Do you know what she was doing there?' asked Tamsin,

remembering Alyce's anger at hearing Agnes had been to Montagu Inn.

'Snooping I'll bet. Later on she passed me coming downstairs when I was taking warm water to the solar for Dame Cecily to wash with.'

'Ellen, have we got time to see where she's going now? Princess Alyce asked me to keep an eye out for her.'

Ellen looked at the sun. 'We ought to get back with the vegetables fairly soon, but I haven't heard the bells for vespers yet. We could follow her for a bit. Are you going to buy anything? I bought this bracelet.'

Tamsin looked at the notebooks, then at Agnes, who was already almost out of sight. Margaret Grafton patted her arm reassuringly.

'You go, dear. You can come to the stall another time. And don't forget, servants of the Dowager of Suffolk and her son get special treatment from me. As to Agnes, she has lodgings in Clerkenwell Priory with the Hospitallers. But don't get too close to her. She's a contrary hag.'

The two girls followed Agnes at a cautious distance as she scuttled with remarkable speed through lanes and alleys, finally coming out onto a broad street running from east to west.

'Newgate Street,' said Ellen. 'She's heading out of the city. Looks as if she's going to the priory. Look out – there's some nobs on horseback coming. There was a clatter of hoofs and the swirl of cloaks as three grim-faced horsemen rode up behind them.

'Why, it's his grace the Duke!' exclaimed Ellen. 'Get back into the alleyway, Tamsin, or you'll be under their horses.' But it was too late. Tamsin had tripped on an uneven cobblestone and lay sprawling in front of the men. The oldest of them lifted his whip to slash at her, but Suffolk's curt voice rang out in protest.

'Stop that, Savernake. She's my mother's new maid, not some slut from the streets.'

Tamsin scrambled up, panting. The men dismounted. The young duke handed his reins to the third man.

'Little Tamsin Ormesby again!' said Duke John, with the mocking smile she was beginning to hate. 'You have quite a knack of falling at my feet. But you may be able to make up for it. We're looking for a local woman called Agnes Quincey. I saw her going into St Paul's when I was talking to you, but she'd gone by the time we got into the church. Did you see her? In a green cloak with a big basket on her shoulder?' Tamsin hesitated, wondering why he was so interested in Agnes. It was Ellen who answered, bobbing a curtsey as she did so.

'We were following her too, your grace. Tamsin wanted to find out where she was going. We think she was heading for the Priory of Clerkenwell.'

Suffolk turned to her, taking in her pretty figure and bright eager eyes. 'And you are?'

'Ellen, m'lord. From her grace's kitchens at Montagu Inn, if it please you.' Tamsin was shocked to see Ellen's little pink tongue flicker along her lips.

'It might please my friends here very much, my dear,' said the duke. Then he cocked his head, as the great bell in the clock tower in front of St Paul's struck the hour.

'But I must leave you to tell them why you were following Mistress Quincey. I need to visit the armourer before he closes.' He nodded to Savernake. 'I'll be back presently. The redhead is a maid of my mother's so don't be rough with her. As to the other... Maybe young Abel here would appreciate her charms. But don't neglect our business for too long.' He remounted and rode away towards Cheapside. Savernake turned to the trembling girls.

'So you were following Agnes as well, were you?' Let's find an alehouse and you can tell us why.'

'The Clapping Bell is over there, down Tinker's Alley, my lord,' said Abel, putting an arm round Ellen. She slapped his cheek, only to receive a stinging blow on her own. To Tamsin's horror, Savernake put an equally familiar arm around her own waist and hustled her towards the alley.

The Sign of the Mole

Joan led Alyce down a passage to the innermost courtyard of the house. Monique followed like a shadow. Alyce knew the way well. Since meeting Joan last September and finding her a stalwart ally during the murderous crisis that beset the God's House, she had made several visits to Moulton Inn and discovered that she and Joan shared a passionate love of plants as well as of books. With Joan's help, Alyce had added considerably to a library that now held more fine books than most Oxford colleges. Joan frequently toured Flanders to seek new texts. Her personal collection included over twenty French romances, which her first husband Walter Caerleon had acquired through Monique from Queen Margaret. English translations of such stirring French tales as *Perceforest* and *Roland*, the *Sainte Grail* and *Lancelot* were now one of the mainstays of Joan's prosperity. Once her stable of scribes had made enough copies of a text, she kept one especially fine one for herself and sold on the original and the copies. All her personal bindings were the same: black and gold, embossed with her crest on the front cover and a scurrying mole on the spine.

They passed the scriptorium, where half a dozen clerks were bent over manuscripts, each writing down a text being read aloud in a clear voice by Joan's stepson William. At the back of the room, Alyce was glad to see that Guy was already cutting a large sheet of paper in half for her copy of the Neville Roll. Next door was the showroom, a lofty hall with long windows and a high raftered roof with a central lantern to allow light to flood in. It was warmed by charcoal braziers on the windowsills, each with a bucket of water beside it in case of fire. Curtained shelves for books lined the walls and four double-seated chairs with reading slopes were arranged in a square in the centre of the room. Alyce's books had been unpacked and were spread out on a long table. Joan and Alyce both burrowed in the pockets hanging at their girdles for their spectacles. Soon they were immersed in plans for leathers and gildings, clasps and page markers.

Once they'd finished looking at the books Alyce had brought to be rebound, Joan crossed to one of the reading slopes and opened the folio volume that lay on it.

'Here's one I have to thank you for, Alyce. Lydgate's *Pilgrimage of the Life of Man*, taken from the copy you left here to be rebound in red leather. My favourite limner had a bit of fun with the frontispiece. It's for my own library.'

Alyce opened the book at its title page. On the left-hand side was a beautifully detailed drawing of a bookroom very like the one in which they sat. A plump female figure with a pen case and a pair of hinged lenses dangling from her girdle stood proudly in front of its shelves, on which books lay open to display their contents. Alyce chuckled.

'It's you to the life, Joan – spectacles and all. Who drew it?'

'Denis Pailton, the deftest illustrator in London and a fine scrivener to boot. He's an adept at this new craft of engraving. As book-printing presses are banned in London, I used to take his work to Bruges with me to be printed. I'd suggest you meet him, but since the battle of Towton he's been a marked man and he's been in hiding for the last few years. He earns his living working for me, but I never see him these days. He uses a messenger, a mute Ethiopian called Cabal.'

Alyce put down the book and looked up in surprise. 'Sweet Jesu! That means you haven't heard either. How was it hushed up so? Pailton's dead, Joan. I was going to ask you if you could tell me anything about the way of his murder.'

Joan's face paled in shock. She sat down heavily on the seat of the desk.

'Was it some roughhouse in the Southwark stews? That's where he was living, I know.'

'No – he was found in the charnel house of Paul's. According to Cis Neville, he was mixed up in a new plot against Edward. Pailton wanted a safe conduct abroad and was trying to get one in exchange for some secret knowledge he had that closely concerned Cis. She agreed and sent him a message a fortnight ago but he was murdered before they could meet. They found his body hacked into pieces in the ossuary in Paul's Yard. She's desperate to find out what he knew in case there's a chance that the Wydevilles catch a sniff of his secret, and she's relying on me to find out. Could Cabal show us where Pailton was living?'

'So what was his secret knowledge?'

'I'm not at liberty to tell you,' said Alyce abruptly.

Joan raised a sardonic eyebrow. 'Fine. None of my business. I understand. But why should you help the old besom. Tell her to go to hell.'

'I can't do that. My daughter-in-law has told her of Newton Montagu.'

Joan swore softly under her breath, remembering her own part last autumn in preserving the secret of Jack's true parentage. Then she shrugged her shoulders. 'Well, it isn't in Cis's interest to spread that story any further. You should call her bluff.'

'I dare not. What I need to do is put her under an obligation to me, which discovering what he knew will.'

Joan shook her head dubiously. 'That won't be easy now. Cabal will take some finding. Brother Pietro hired him to go ahead of him to Oxford with the first bundle of pamphlets. He collected them from here last Wednesday.'

'So he was still in London when Pailton was murdered. He could know something. We need to find him as soon as possible. Do you know where he was going to stay?'

'Brother Pietro gave him a billet addressed to John Doll, the bookseller.'

Alyce pondered. She was tempted to go back to Ewelme and enquire in Oxford for Cabal. She had already had enough of the city and longed for the peace of her home. But was it really the best way of finding out who killed Pailton? Or did the answer lie in London, perhaps even in Moulton Inn itself? If Wenlock knew more than he'd admitted, perhaps Joan did as well. She made a decision.

'If he walked to Oxford, he could still be on the road, unless he got a lift on a cart. And once he's there, it'll take him a fortnight or so to sell the pamphlets. I'll send letters by a fast rider, one to Doll, asking him to send a message to Ben Bilton in Ewelme when Cabal gets to Oxford, and one to Ben bidding him to seek Cabal out when Doll contacts him.'

Outside a bell tolled for nones. 'Three o'clock already!' she exclaimed. 'Simon should be off to the mortuary.'

'Monique can take a message to him,' said Joan.

Monique nodded and left the room. Joan turned to Alyce.

'I have a present for you, my dear. From one of your oldest admirers.' She raised the curtain from one of the cloaked shelves and lifted out a slim book bound exquisitely simply in blue-dyed velvet, with two silver clasps. Alyce opened it. She stared at the title page in disbelief.

'Where in heaven's name did this come from?' she said, as she leafed through the little book. 'Does it mean…? Is he…?'

Joan put her hand on her arm. 'He is dead. But on his deathbed he commissioned his most trusted steward to bring this to you.'

Alyce's brain spun. Charles of Orleans, brother of the king of France and most eminent of all the French nobles captured at Agincourt. She remembered his arrival at Ewelme soon after her marriage to William and how for the first time in her life she had found a mind perfectly matched to her own. William grew jealous and arranged for Charles to be entrusted to another guardian. It was another five years before Charles was freed and during them he had secretly sent her poem after poem. These poems. She had met him again when she went to France to bring Margaret of Anjou back to marry King Henry. By then Charles had remarried. But one day they had ridden together into the great forest that surrounded the Château d'Angers and felt again their kinship of spirit. She gripped the little book tightly, turning away as tears came to her eyes.

Joan watched her appraisingly, then spoke again.

'Now you're in the mood to sympathise with true lovers, Alyce, I want to talk to you about the Earl of Oxford. I sense that you disapprove of him.'

'Not as much as I do of Robert Harcourt. But you're right. I don't like the idea of Vere marrying Meg Neville. Why did you give him and Harcourt such a rapturous welcome?'

'Customers are customers, my dear, and booksellers can't be choosers any more than beggars can. But that isn't the only reason. These days no one can afford to antagonise Sir Robert. He's retained by Tiptoft, who has the king's ear. And Harcourt himself is close to the queen. As to Vere, I think you're wrong about him. He was young and terrified when his father and brother were executed, but I very much doubt that it was he who betrayed them.'

'His mother thinks he did,' said Alyce flatly.

'She should think again. Veres rightly have a reputation for truthfulness and loyalty and young John is straight as a die. Rumour has it that the traitor was his brother Aubrey's wife Anne. To save her own Stafford estates, she handed Tiptoft a casket of letters that Aubrey had been sent by Queen Margaret.'

'I never heard that. Who told you?'

'John Wenlock. It's all around court, apparently. Explains why the queen took Anne on as one of her ladies, of course.'

'Wenlock said that you were at his house yesterday. What was that about?'

'Oh, a terrible case of injustice. I have a goddaughter, Katherine Arderne, who is being persecuted by her dead husband's family. They have kidnapped her seven-year-old son and are taking him to his grandparents in Warwickshire while they negotiate his wardship with the queen.'

'Ah yes. Wenlock said it was about a wardship. And the boy is only seven? Poor girl, she must be beside herself. But if anyone can help, it's Wenlock.'

'I hope so. He's sent that strange man of his Thynne to Greenwich to find out the position on the wardship and he's recommended a lawyer. Have you heard of James Danvers?'

Alyce raised an eyebrow. 'My son Jack has used him on occasion. He's something of a young blood, I believe. Clever enough, though. And my neighbours the Stonors have sent their son Will, my godson, to train under him.'

There was a perfunctory knock at the door and Harcourt and Vere came in, followed by Pietro of Padua. Alyce drew herself up, resenting the invasion. But Joan smiled a welcome.

'Have you come to see my treasures as well? But where is Master Hardyng?'

'At Guy's elbow, checking the genealogy Princess Alyce requested,' said Sir Robert. 'Eager for his commission, the greedy old scoundrel.'

Joan picked out a book from a shelf and placed it on a nearby reading slope.

'Sir Robert, this will amuse you, I know.' She opened it up as he walked over to her. 'It's a list of cure-alls and love potions translated from Latin by an Irishman called Yonge for the Earl of Ormond. I had it made from King Edward's own copy, smuggled out to me by the Dowager Duchess of Norfolk. She's desperate to fascinate her young husband. I promised her I'd have a copy made for her in return for making a few more to sell myself. This one is being coloured, so it isn't bound yet. If you like it, I can have it made up in a week or so.'

With Harcourt at her side, Joan leafed through the densely illustrated pages, pausing at the colourful astrological diagrams.

When she came to a picture of a half-naked man vomiting copiously, she stopped, giving Alyce a conspiratorial wink. Harcourt read the text below it aloud.

Drunkenness makes for forgetting in the soul, by the reason that the great smokes go up to the brain and trouble the imagination, therefore it puts away all remembrance of things that were understood before and disturbs the knowledge of things that are to be understood.

He looked up angrily. 'What are you implying, Mistress Joan – that I can't hold my wine? I wager I could drink you under the table any night of the week.'

'But I wouldn't trust myself under it with you, Sir Robert,' Joan retorted smartly. 'Your reputation as a satyr goes before you.'

'As does yours as a mistress of the game,' replied Harcourt with a leer, stretching out an arm to encircle her waist. Joan moved deftly out of his reach to the other side of the table where Vere was standing. He was looking tense, still smarting from Alyce's disapproval. Joan turned to him.

'Sir Robert has put me in mind of another fine present for your wife, your grace. She is I know a notable huntress and I have a finely limned copy of *The Master of Game*. It is much in demand these days as it was written by King Edward's great-uncle, Edward of York.'

Vere stepped forward eagerly to look at the book and Joan looked over at Alyce hopefully.

Alyce softened. She was very fond of Meg Neville. The girl had all her grandfather's vivid, energetic character. If both she and Joan saw something in Vere, then perhaps she was wrong about him. She walked over to look at the manual of hunting, open at a picture of Diana aiming her bow at a stag, deerhounds at her heels. Joan read a few lines from the text aloud:

Deerhound: Muzzle of wolf, haunch of lion, neck of swan, eye of sparrowhawk, ear of snake, shoulder like the roe, flank like the doe, loin of stag, tail of rat, thigh of hare and foot of cat. Follows its master faithfully, sweet, clean and gracious in all its doings except towards wild beasts to whom it should be terrible, spiteful and hostile.

Alyce smiled. 'Wonderful writing. And Meg is indeed a very Artemis. I had a fine day's coursing with her when I visited Bisham last September. In fact, I applaud your choice of a bride, Vere. She is a prize any man would be proud of.'

Vere looked uncertainly at her, then gave a hesitant smile. 'Thank you, Princess Alyce. And … I hope you will honour us by coming to our wedding.'

Alyce hesitated. Then, on a sudden impulse, found herself saying, 'With the greatest of pleasure,' and smiling in return.

Not wanting to give their new but perhaps still fragile amity a chance to splinter, Joan turned to Pietro.

'Brother Pietro, perhaps you could take Princess Alyce to my garden and show her the exquisite plants that you brought with you from Padua.'

Alyce followed the Dominican out of the room, relieved to have an excuse to get away from Harcourt. How adroitly Joan could handle people of all kinds, from a lecherous knight to a nervous young apprentice. The buxom bookseller was like a chameleon, showing different sides of herself to different customers. But, she wondered, as she entered the sheltered second court of Moulton Inn, were there sides of Joan that she did not know about?

Raised beds lay along the courtyard walls, so that the scents of the flowers that filled them were intensified. Huge tubs containing orange and lemon trees in blossom stood in the centre. Kneeling in front of one of the borders was Ned, evidently Moulton Inn's boy-of-all-work. He had a leather apron round his waist, a trowel in his hand and a trug of limp weeds beside him.

'This way, your grace,' said Pietro. He led Alyce over to some shelves on the northern side of the courtyard on which stood five little terracotta pots. She caught her breath.

'They're beautiful – like but not like primroses. So delicate, such subtle colours. And such smooth, silky leaves.'

The stern face of the friar softened as he gently touched the flowers of two of the little plants, one with a heart of black edged with bright gold, the other one of lime green edged with creamy white.

'These five are the only ones that survived the voyage, I am afraid, though I have also brought some seeds,' he said in heavily accented English. Their Latin name is *Primula auricula*, but in Italy we call them *orecchiette*, little ears. Because of their smooth, stiffly curled leaves. They often produce unexpected colours and divide easily. Our gardeners make a science of crossing different varieties.'

'How do they do that?' asked Alyce, entranced.

'It is very difficult. They take pollen from one and apply it to the stigma of another. I wish you could have seen the red and white one edged in green that I lost: it was a flower fit for a queen. If you ever make a pilgrimage to Italy, visit me in Padua. I would love to show you my garden there. Flowers are not like people. They are luminous with perfection, whereas men and women are dark with sin.'

Just then Joan came out to join them. She was carrying a roll of parchment.

'Harcourt's going shortly, thank the Lord. I don't know why he came at all. He's not a man for books. I've left Vere to the good offices of Matthew. He's wrapping up *The Master of Game* for him to give to Meg. And here's the genealogy of the Nevilles you wanted, Alyce. Hardyng has checked it and I've paid him his commission, so you owe me seven marks.'

She bent towards the bright-faced little flowers and stroked a petal. 'What do you think of my new treasures?'

'Enchanting,' said Alyce, reaching into the hanging purse on her girdle for the right coins, then taking the roll and tucking it into a long pocket inside the front of her mantle as she looked around the courtyard. 'Everything is flowering so early, Joan. It's so sheltered here.'

Pietro turned and bent down towards a tiny blue flower. 'But what is this? I have never seen its like.'

'It's a very rare fleur-de-lis. The bulb was brought to me by a Saracen from Aleppo.' When Joan had finished a long story about the plant's acquisition, Alyce told them about her plans for glassing in a corner of her inner court at Ewelme. It was half an hour or more before she turned to Joan with a start.

'All these delights put out of my head the main reason for my visit – collecting my dear grandfather's *Tales of the Canterbury Pilgrims*. You sent word that the binding had been completed.'

Joan beamed. 'It's the loveliest casing we've ever made

– well-suited to the finest copy of good Master Chaucer's tales that I've ever seen. I can't wait for you to see it.' She turned to find a messenger and saw Ned kneeling on the path.

'Ned, run to the bindery with this key and tell Matthew to get Duchess Alyce's Chaucer out of the strongbox.' Then she turned back to Alyce.

'Why don't you take some cuttings and plants with you. We'll pack them in moss in a strong willow hamper and tie it to Larkspur's saddle. Perhaps you would like to have one of the *orecchiette* and some of their seeds.'

She turned to Pietro. 'Would you like a bulb of the little fleur-de-lis? It spreads well.'

The friar looked wistfully at the intensely blue flower. 'Perhaps when I return from Oxford. But I fear it will be a long time before I get back to Italy. *Sono in esilio dal paradiso.* Thank you for your hospitality, Mistress Moulton. Farewell, Princess Alyce. I wish I had made your acquaintance earlier and could continue it for longer.'

'As do I, Brother Pietro. If it suited you to make a halt at Ewelme, either on your way to Oxford or back to London, my steward Ben Bilton will make you welcome. Indeed, I may be there myself – I half-think of returning to Oxfordshire for a brief visit.' She wondered whether to mention that she wanted to speak to Cabal, but decided against it. It might be a mistake to warn anyone that inquiries were being made about Pailton's death.

Pietro looked searchingly into her eyes. 'I thank you, your grace. I will make a point of doing so. And I hope I find you there.' He raised a long bony hand in blessing and headed for a small postern gate that led out into Paternoster Row.

Alyce, who had learnt Italian to read Dante, looked at his

retreating back thoughtfully. Why should the friar feel that he was exiled from Eden? And how strangely his tenderness with plants contrasted with his virulence against women.

The thought of exile made her thoughts turn, as they so often did, to Denzil Caerleon. It puzzled her to think of him retained by the Earl of Warwick. Whom he had often spoken of scathingly as ruthless and untrustworthy. Surely Joan would know the truth.

'Joan, what of your brother-in-law Denzil? Has he taken over his parents' estates?'

'I doubt if he'd ever want to settle down in Gloucestershire. Too greedy to see the world. I haven't spoken to him since he came back to England, but Wenlock said he saw him in Calais last week.'

'Cecily said that he was in the service of the Earl of Warwick now. Is that true?'

Joan looked at her quizzically. She remembered Denzil's dejection at leaving Alyce's service. Was it possible that her friend also regretted his departure?

'I don't know,' she said. 'But I can ask Wenlock.'

Alyce turned back to the flower bed with a casual shrug, intended to convey unconcern. Joan smiled, not deceived.

The Guildhall

The musicians' instruments wheezed and wailed to a close and there was a ripple of applause. Matthew Cobham rose and stretched himself.

'Time to get back to work. I enjoyed meeting you, Simon.'

Flushed with ale and animated conversation, Simon looked across to the dais and realised that Joan and Alyce weren't there. Nor was anybody else at the high table. How long had they been gone? Should he follow after? There was a gentle tug at his sleeve. It was Monique.

'Her grace sent me,' she said. 'She's still with Mistress Joan, but she asks that you go to the Guildhall to see the mortuary.'

'Thank you, Monique,' said Simon. She moved away, her long grey gown whispering over the tiled floor.

Head fuzzy, he went out into the courtyard. He collected Jankin from the stable and led him past the throng fighting to get close to the book table. Once mounted, he turned eastwards along Cheapside, past Cheap Cross and north up St Lawrence Lane towards the Guildhall. Luck was with him. At the door of the Guildhall, a chubby clerk in the scarlet robe of a man of law and with Wenlock's badge on the fold of his mantle was coming out. Simon hailed him.

'Is John Laweley around? I wanted to ask him about the murder of Denis Pailton. I've a warrant here from Lord Wenlock.'

'Master Laweley is at Westminster. So the news is out, is

it? We were told it was to be kept oyster-close. I'm his clerk, Giles Scott. You can give the warrant to me.' He broke its seal and read it.

'That seems in order. I hope you'll make it worth my while. Poor Pailton's remains are in a rented coffin in the cellars, waiting the go-ahead to bury him. Did a nice job, the barber-surgeon. Soused the joints in salt, arranged them in the right order, head one end, feet the other – actually, there was only one foot and no hands – and swaddled him in his shroud like a newborn. I suppose you'll want to look at them.'

Simon paled, but nodded. Giles chuckled.

'Let's get it over with, then you can recover over a jug of ale. Tie your horse up here. The Guildhall porter will keep an eye on him. The door to the cellar's over here, at the side of the building. Convenient for the vintners as well as the mourners. I'll get a lantern.'

The low, vaulted cellars of the Guildhall were shadowy. Pailton's coffin lay on the wide stone shelf that ran along one wall, a bloodstained cloak draped over it. Plump casks of wine stood in a rank on the other side. Scott took off the cloak, folded it neatly and put it on the shelf.

'That's how we knew who he was. His killers wrapped his remains in it and bundled it into the charnel house. They didn't notice that it had a pen case inside an inner pocket. A local stationer, John Grafton, identified it as Pailton's.'

Scott ran a knife round the edge of the coffin to release the wax that had been melted along its topsides to seal it. Even before it was open, the stench was stomach-churning and Simon felt his gorge rising. With a huge effort of will, he swallowed and looked inside as Scott took off the lid, laid it alongside the wall and folded back the shroud. To his relief, the body parts were bound together with long strips of cloth, overlapping to create the shape of a body.

'Do you want to take a look at the head?' said Giles. 'That's the bit most people find of interest. Not that there's much left of his face, poor devil.'

Simon didn't want to look in the least, but, since it seemed expected of him, he nodded. Giles picked up the bulky cloth-bound lump and began to unravel it slowly, winding the strip of cloth neatly up as he went.

'I'll need to put it back just so,' he explained. 'That's what's seemly. Not that anyone else is likely to want to see him. Except his mother.'

'His mother?'

'Yes, she's on her way from Wallingford for the funeral. The Stationers' Mystery is paying for it, as everything Pailton had in his Southwark house was lost in a fire that burnt it down last week. Wouldn't be surprising if his killers had something to do with that, would it?'

He took the last of the wrappings off Pailton's head. Simon shuddered. Swallowing hard, he managed to look at the shattered face, now crawling with fat white maggots. He retched.

'If you ask me, they wanted to make him unrecognisable,' said Giles. 'Bad luck for them that they missed the pen case.'

'Where is it?'

From the side of the coffin Giles picked up a long slim object, also bound in linen. He unwrapped it.

'At least his mother will have something to remember him by. Or to sell for candles for his funeral Mass. It's fine workmanship.'

Simon ran his fingers across the delicately engraved patterns on the metal case, then opened it. He found two quill pens, a penknife, three brushes and a stiff tube of paper. Inside this was a slim steel tool with a wickedly sharp tip. He touched it gingerly. Giles saw him examining it.

'Coroner said he hadn't seen one of those before. He decided that was for making delicate corrections. Scraping very small areas of parchment, perhaps. Handy weapon, too. Like one of those Italian stilettos.'

Simon said nothing and replaced everything in the pen case. Giles wrapped it up again, placed it beside the jigsaw of body parts and crossed himself.

They emerged from the cellar into the street. Giles looked at Simon's wan face and grinned.

'I'll seal the coffin up again after you've gone. But now we need ale. Over there. The Rising Sun. Best ale in the ward.'

Simon thankfully followed him to a bench outside the tavern. A harassed-looking girl was wiping the table in front of it. Giles gave her a friendly smack on her bottom and she whirled round indignantly, then gave him a gap-toothed smile.

'What's your pleasure Master Giles?'

'If I can't have you, I'll have two pint pots of your best and oldest. And a bowl of ribs from that pig I can smell roasting. Looking at corpses is hungry work.' She grimaced and headed for the kitchen.

'So who told you to keep oyster-close about the murder?' said Simon as they sat down.

'He was a high-up, that's all I know. Only the nobs wear velvet. I didn't recognise him. Laweley knew who he was all right, but he wasn't saying, was he?'

'Was he wearing a badge?'

'He had a chain round his neck with a pendant, but it wasn't an emblem I knew.'

The barmaid came out with a large tray and put ale, pork ribs and two hunks of bread in front of them. Even though he'd lately eaten, Simon took a bite of the bread. He needed to quieten his quaking stomach.

Wiping his lips appreciatively after draining most of his pint in one draught, Scott leaned forward.

'It's a weird case, I reckon. "Vengeance is mine, says the Lord." Isn't there something in Revelations about God summoning the birds of the air and the beasts of the field to eat human flesh and drink human blood?'

'Did the beasts get involved as well, then?'

'The rats had been at him before the kites. No sign of the guts.' Simon felt his stomach churning and reached for the bread.

'Of course the churchyard and the charnel house were all purified and reconsecrated straight away,' Scott continued cheerfully. 'We got the godliest man in England up.'

'Who?' asked Simon.

'The Earl of Warwick's little brother. Lately become Archbishop of York. You can't get a better sin-cleanser than that, short of his Holiness the Pope. He was already in the precinct, fortunately. Been dining with the canons and stayed the night as he was saying Mass in Paul's in the morning. Then we were all sworn to secrecy.'

'Were there any witnesses?'

'Not really. A lame beggar girl called Bethan raised the alarm. She ran crying to Sam Fogge, one of the churchwardens, as he was opening up Paul's at sunrise for lauds, saying that the kites were pecking at a man's bloody arm on the pavement. A great flock of them, mewing like cats and swooping in and out of the eaves of the charnel house. Fogge took one look and went for the watch. They searched among the skulls and bones and found the rest of the poor sod and his cloak. Put everything into a sack and took it to the Guildhall. Then they sent a messenger to John Laweley. He told him to collect me and we both came straight over.'

'Was there an inquest?'

Scott nodded. 'Laweley invested a jury of citizens from Cripplegate and Faringdon Within and called the church-warden, the watchmen and the beggar girl to give evidence. The inquest was held in the chapter house. They'd kept the girl in the great tower at the west end of Paul's Yard as she was the first on the scene. They brought her in, crying and stuttering some gibberish about four devils in black cloaks and carrying burning brands who tried to catch her to take her to hellfire. Hallucinating from the horror of it all, I thought. Wood-witted, for sure. Laweley thought the same – he said she could go after five minutes. Ordered Pailton's body to be tidied up and salted down until his kinsfolk could be contacted. He really didn't seem to be interested. Which I thought was odd. Coroners are usually avid to find someone to fine.'

Simon shivered. A living man reduced to joints salted and bound in strips of cloth. No prayers for poor Pailton's soul, no lessening of purgatory, just the high road to hell.

A thought came to him. 'Was the body cut up with skill, or just hacked at random? Was there any sign of what was used?'

Giles thought for a moment, rubbing his short rough beard.

'It was a neatish job, now you come to mention it. Must've used a razor-sharp knife. And a hatchet. Done after death, obviously. Maybe one of the butchers from Smithfield had a hand in it. The hands and one foot were missing. We haven't found them yet. I expect the kites flew away with them. But

Laweley hazarded that they might have been bagged up for a relic-maker by his killers.'

Simon thought it only too likely. Small human bones, conveniently sized for pocket amulets, were much in demand for sale as saints' digits.

'So where did the jury think the crime took place? There must have been a good deal of blood when he was butchered.'

'That's another puzzle. The room above the charnel house is rented out as a stationer's storeroom. But there was no sign of blood up there. Must have killed him somewhere else.'

'Do you know who rents the storeroom?'

'John and Margaret Grafton. They've got lots of tenements around here – two stalls in the churchyard, a solar above the great gate and a chamber in the belfry. They kept parchment above the charnel house – it's fine and dry up there.'

'Grafton? The man who identified the pen case?'

'That's right. He knew Pailton well.'

'I suppose all this is recorded in the Coroner's Roll. Could I have a copy of the entry?'

'You could,' said Giles, 'but it'll tell you a good deal less than I have. It's just a one-liner, saying Denis Pailton was done to death by persons unknown in a place unknown and that the case was unresolvable. Doesn't even mention Paul's. How about another ale?'

'Not for me. But here's enough to buy yourself a few more. And thank you. I'll tell Lord Wenlock how helpful you've been.'

Simon stood up, straightened his doublet and went over to where Jankin was quietly grazing. Then he had a thought. He called back to the clerk, who was deep in conversation with the girl who'd served them.

'Would it be easy to find that beggar girl?'

'Bethan? I don't know. She's from St Giles Without. She's the servant of its anchoress, a pernicious beldam if there ever was one. During the day, she runs errands for her around the city. Or hops them, rather. She's got a clubfoot.'

'Poor girl. Why doesn't she get an indoor place, in a kitchen or a pie shop?'

'Why aren't all the beggars in London riding fine horses? Nobody wants to take in these waifs and strays, specially not if they bear the devil's marks and are half-touched. But I don't envy her her mistress. Quicker to curse a man than bless him.'

Simon remounted and headed Jankin north again towards Cripplegate, traditional home of the maimed, but more recently something of an artists' quarter, thanks to the fame of Gilbert Prince, court painter to Richard II, who'd lived here all his life and been buried in St Giles. He nodded to the gatekeepers, crossed the city ditch and turned into the square around the church. There was a new conduit house in front of it, crowded with women waiting their turn to fill pots and jerrikins with water. He asked one of them where the anchoress lived. She was a handsome woman with black hair and a tilt to her eyebrows that made him think of the Spanish girls he'd found so unsettling on his pilgrimage to Compostella. She pointed to the north side of the square. Built neatly under the eaves of the eastern end of the church was a stone lean-to with two narrow windows, each curtained with black cloth marked with a white cross. Around it was a low wall, enclosing a small yard that was full of herbs and worts. In one corner of this there was a roughly made wooden shelter, again curtained with black cloth. Bethan's hovel, no doubt. He called her name, but there was no reply.

'She won't be back till curfew,' called a voice. It was the Spanish-looking woman, now laden with a yoke across her shoulders holding two brimming pots of water. But the lilt in her voice told him that she was not Spanish, but Welsh. Curfew. That was four hours away. As if reading his thoughts, the woman went on speaking.

'If you can't wait that long, you could ask the anchoress herself if she knows where she is. There's a squint to her cell inside the church. Tap a penny on its sill and if she's in a good mood, she'll tell you. If she isn't, you won't have lost anything.' She flashed him a warm smile.

Flustered, Simon thanked her. Had that smile been an invitation? he wondered. Might she? Could he? Cursing his inadequacy in such situations, he walked Jankin to the west end of the church. As he tied Jankin to a rail, half a dozen small boys rushed up, offering to guard him. He shook his head and headed for the church porch where two old men in the fustian gowns of churchwardens were sitting.

'A farthing apiece for you when I come out if you'll keep an eye on my horse,' he said. They nodded placidly.

He entered the church and dipped his fingers in the holy water stoup just inside the door. Making a sketchy sign of the cross, he looked around him. It was an incense-scented cave of colour; its stained-glass windows filled with images from the Old and New Testaments flanked by the meekly kneeling figures of the families who paid for their making. Behind the font a scribe sat on a folding stool writing a letter for a young apprentice, and over to the north side of the nave a sergeant-at-law sat on one of the new benches that were beginning to be introduced for the benefit of frail parishioners. He was dozing over a roll of parchment. A couple of messengers were squatting on the south side of the nave, playing dice until someone summoned them to take a letter. The pillars of the aisle were painted as if they were trees, with gilded trunks and green-leaved capitals, with carvings of musicians poking their heads and instruments out from the foliage. Above the central arch was Gilbert Prince's notoriously lurid Doom. Demons thrust malefactors into the jaws of monsters and angels welcomed those who had won their place in heaven. Above them, Christ, enthroned in all his glory, looked calmly down.

Simon walked up the aisle a little anxiously. Was it legitimate to ask the anchoress about a godless crime rather than the prospects for his immortal soul? In the side chapels candles blazed before the shrines of London's favourite saints: St Paul; St Alphage, killed by the Danes at Greenwich; St Bartholomew and St Dunstan. From a chantry on the south side of the church came the sound of a Mass being sung. As Simon walked past it, he saw St Giles's greatest treasure: an exquisite diptych showing a golden-haired boy wearing a delicate crown of gold kneeling before a blue-robed Virgin Mary and a crowd of angels with blue-tipped wings. A scattering of supplicants knelt in front of it, mainly hooded women. A Dominican friar knelt in front of them, leading the prayers. No doubt they were for the soul of Richard II, who had donated the diptych to the church. Unvisited by the prudent for decades of Lancastrian rule, Edward's accession had made it once more a popular place to pray.

He walked across to the north side of the chancel. In a chapel to the left of the altar was a carving of St Giles, painted, gilded and bejewelled. In the north wall he saw what he was looking for: a trefoil-shaped hole with a worn cushion on the floor in front of it. He felt in his pocket for a penny but could only find a silver groat. He tapped it on the stone sill, worn smooth from a century of offerings and pushed it over it. There was a clink as it landed on other coins. He knelt down on the cushion, murmuring a paternoster and waited.

At first he heard nothing at all. Then there was a soft shuffling and a scrabbling sound. He imagined fingers feeling for the coin. The shuffling retreated. Simon wondered if he should call through the window, but then he heard the shuffling again. And a voice, cracked with age.

'You are a seeker, my son and a generous one. What is it that you want?'

'Blessings on you, holy mother. I am sent by my mistress to find out what I can about the murder in Paul's Yard two weeks ago. Word is that your servant Bethan discovered the crime. I wondered if she had told you what she knew of it.'

'She did. Who is it who wants to know what she was told to hide?'

Simon decided that simple truth would be the best policy. 'My mistress is her grace Alyce de la Pole, Dowager Duchess of Suffolk.'

'Ah. Ever a brave and generous spirit. Great danger threatens her. Tell her to be wary of those closest to her.' The old voice was silent for a moment, then began again, almost chanting. 'It was the heaven-sent birds of the air that would not let malefactors hide their misdoings. "Thus says the Lord God: speak to the birds of every kind." Though the devils tried to catch Bethan to stop her telling what she saw, the Lord watched over her and brought out the churchwarden early to unlock Paul's door.'

'Did she talk of these black devils to you?'

'She did. Hooded and with tails and burning brands, she said.'

'Tails? The clerk didn't mention those.'

'No, because Bethan didn't tell of them. It was only when I asked her to paint what she saw for my mind's eye – I'm blind, you see – that she said they dangled from their waists. Which was why she talked of tails. But it put me in mind of the Black Friars' rope girdles.'

Or men dressed as Black Friars. Who could have disappeared into the Dominican house down by the river in a few minutes – and be in sanctuary into the bargain? Simon's mind clicked back to the Dominican he had seen at Joan's. His watchful eyes, the thin mouth. The anchoress began to mutter a blessing and then an Ave Maria. Gradually her voice dropped to a whisper. 'Beware, my son. Unseen eyes are on you.' Then it swelled out loud into a blessing. 'The Lord bless you and keep you and make his face to shine upon you. Amen.'

Simon slid another coin across the sill, stood up and turned in one smooth movement. He saw the edge of a black gown frisk behind the rood screen and walked as rapidly as he decently could after it. By the time he was back in the nave, there was no sign of its wearer. The Mass in Richard II's chantry had ended and it was empty. Otherwise, no one seemed to have moved. The lawyer studied his texts, the scribe sat bored on his stool. He went back outside. The wardens were gossiping together.

'Did you see anyone leave in the last few minutes?' he asked. They glanced at each other, then shook their heads. Simon burrowed in his pocket and pulled out two coins. 'Here's a farthing for the man who didn't and a groat for the man who did.' They glanced at each other again and shrugged. Neither spoke. Nor did they reach out for his coins. Simon looked past them to where he'd left his horse. Jankin had gone. Stolen no doubt by a man in black who'd paid handsomely to have his anonymity preserved.

He picked up his farthings and walked angrily back towards Cripplegate. Once he turned out of view from the church, one of the urchins who'd offered to hold Jankin stepped out from an alleyway.

'I saw what happened, your worship. I can show you which way the man who took your horse went.' He was an honest-looking lad, as dark and Welsh-looking as the woman at the conduit.

Simon sighed. 'Lead on, then. I wish I'd let you and your friends look after him. He's too old to be stolen.'

'Not stolen, borrowed. The man who took him isn't a thief. He just wanted to get away and to stop you catching up with him. He told me where your horse would be.'

Mystified, Simon followed the boy across the churchyard and along a lane into a great expanse of green. Most of it was garden plots, but one section was full of the exotically lettered headstones of Jews and Moors who had died in London. St Giles, outside the city walls, was one of the few places where they were allowed to bury their dead. They came into Aldersgate Street, where the boy turned left for twenty yards or so before ducking into another narrow lane that led into the close of St Bartholomew's Priory. Without hesitating, he led Simon through the close and out of it on its far side, then turned north beside the great open grazing meadows of Smithfield, noisy with lowing cattle and bleating sheep awaiting the butchers. Now they were in St John Street, still heading north. The boy took a left fork and Simon saw a long straight lane leading to a massive fortified gatehouse. Beyond it was a substantial castellated palace with gardens and orchards all around it and a high surrounding wall. Jankin was tied to a hitching rail just inside the gate, his head deep in a bag of hay. As they approached, a porter came out of the gatehouse.

'There you are. I was told someone'd be looking for 'im before long. One of the corrodians found him straying. Brought him here for safekeeping.'

Simon dug in his waist pouch and handed another groat to the porter. 'What place is this?'

'The Priory of Clerkenwell. Headquarters of English Langue of the Knights Hospitaller.'

Simon instantly understood why the wardens had been so clam-mouthed. The Hospitallers wielded immense influence. An ancient crusading order financed by a network of estates all over Europe, they were a close-knit society with huge wealth and high connections. They were also universally popular, providing as they did schools for poor boys and girls, and hospices for the old and the sick. Simon walked into the courtyard and looked around. It was deserted, except for a cloaked woman with a basket on her shoulder, who was walking rapidly towards a door at the far end. He frowned. How odd. She looked uncannily like Agnes Quincey. He went back to the porter.

'Who was that woman? And where does that door lead to?'

'I didn't see her, your honour. Perhaps she was the washer-woman delivering the prior's linen. Bit old for you sir,' he added with a leer. Embarrassed, Simon turned to the boy who'd guided him.

'Thank you, lad. I'm indebted to you.' He handed him the rest of the change in his hand. 'What's your name, by the way?'

'Owen, your worship. You asked my mother about the anchoress. She told me to watch out for you. And to tell you that we live in the priest's house on the corner of Fore Street and Whitecross Lane if you need to know more. Her name's Bronwen ap Gryffydd.'

Simon patted Jankin's head to hide the blush that was rising up his neck. Was the woman a witch? Had she known that he had been mentally undressing her as she talked to him? Or rather guessing at what he would find if he did, not having ever seen a woman naked. Had she even known that? Had there been a touch of amused pity in her smile? He swung himself into the saddle, gave Owen a stiff nod and set off back down Cheapside.

Halfway down the street, a voice hailed him.

'Master Brailles, I give you good day. I heard that Princess Alyce was in London.'

It was Will Stonor, dressed as a lawyer's clerk, riding beside a handsome young man in the black gown of a lawyer.

Simon reined in his horse and waited for them. 'It's good to see you again, Will. Princess Alyce told me that you were apprenticed to an Inn of Court. Is this your master? And how did you hear that we were in the city?'

'My master James Danvers of Lincoln's Inn was lately summoned on a matter of wardship by Lord Wenlock and while we were taking details he was told of Princess Alyce's arrival. He disappeared to talk to her. Perhaps you were with her?'

'I was. The Duchess of York has asked her to investigate rumours of...' He broke off, then continued with a sense of self-importance. 'But it is a secret matter.'

Danvers studied him with narrowed eyes. 'Seems to have left you whey-faced, whatever it was.'

Simon's gorge rose again at the memory of the pathetic remains of Pailton. He swallowed hard and gave a feeble smile.

He was spared further questions by an exclamation from Will. 'Surely that is Tamsin!' he said, pointing to four people at the entrance to an alley.

Simon saw two men trying to pull two wenches towards the tavern at its end. One of the girls was indeed Tamsin, struggling in the arms of a man in the Harcourt livery. The other, a kitchen maid, was clutching a basket of vegetables which a shabby servant lad was trying to tug from her grasp.

Will dismounted and advanced on the group, calling to Danvers as he did so. 'To me, James, I know that girl. She's in Princess Alyce's service.' James promptly dismounted too and followed him. Quaking, Simon did the same. There seemed no end to the day's unpleasant surprises.

'What's going on?' Will shouted. 'Let those girls go. They clearly don't want your company.'

'What business is that of yours,' said the liveried man, drawing his sword. 'Go find your own whores.' The shabby lad pulled out a knife.

'I should warn you that threatening with a blade is an offence against the peace,' said James. 'Except in self-defence.' He drew his own sword, as did Will.

'What is your name? And whose service are you in?'

The man glared at him. 'Rufus Savernake. Retained by Sir Robert Harcourt. These wenches are needed for questioning. Not that it's any business of yours.'

The sound of hoofs made them all turn their heads. Savernake gave a triumphant smile as a small troop of horsemen joined them. He sheathed his sword, doffed his hat and bowed.

'A timely return, your grace. These young fools were meddling in our business.'

Simon recognised Jack de la Pole. He bowed, as did James and Will. The young duke took in the weeping girls and the young lawyers' naked blades and frowned.

'What's going on, Savernake? Master Danvers is a friend of mine and that man is my mother's secretary.'

'They were stopping us taking the wenches into the tavern for questioning,' the henchman said sulkily.

'It looked more like abduction to our eyes,' snapped James.

'The wenches deserve punishment,' said Jack. 'The young fools have been interfering in our business. But Master Brailles here can make sure my mother sees to that. Take them back to Montagu Inn, Simon.'

'Yes, your grace,' said Simon, avoiding meeting Tamsin's tear-filled eyes.

Jack bent down to Tamsin and whispered something. Then he turned to Savernake.

'Let's to horse, Rufus. We're already behind time.'

Once they had left, Will put his arm around the shivering Tamsin. Simon saw her clutch him in a most unseemly way. He glared at her.

'Tamsin – what by the Rood were you doing with such ruffians?'

Still clinging to Will, Tamsin answered in a small, defeated voice.

'Ellen and I went shopping for Cook and she offered to show me St Paul's. Then I saw Agnes Quincey and we tried to follow her. My lady wanted to know what she was up to, didn't she? And then his grace the duke and those men...' Her voice faltered.

Simon turned to James and Will. 'Lady Alyce will be most grateful to you. The girls have been most foolish. Tamsin is country-bred, but Ellen should certainly have known better. I will escort them back myself.'

Bells suddenly pealed out, different voices repeating from all over the city.

'Vespers!' said Ellen in consternation. 'I hadn't realised how late it was getting. Cook'll lambast me properly. She wants these vegetables for supper.'

'We must go too, Will,' said James. 'There's still much to settle.'

'Of course,' said Will. He turned away from Tamsin and remounted. Looking down to her, he smiled. 'Stay safe until we meet again.' Then they trotted away.

Tamsin looked after Will with evident regret, which made Simon, feeling foolish at his undistinguished part in her rescue, even crosser.

'Come on now,' he said. 'Walk ahead of me, so that I can keep an eye on you.' But the girls had only gone a few paces when Tamsin stumbled again and clung to Ellen for support.

'What is it now?' said Simon impatiently.

'She fell over earlier,' said Ellen. 'I think she's twisted her ankle.'

Simon heaved a sigh. 'Well, she'd better ride Jankin.' He dismounted and picked Tamsin up bodily. As he lifted her on to the horse's broad back, he was intensely aware of her warmth, her birdlike lightness, the scent of rosemary in her hair. He settled her carefully and rearranged her skirts. She looked at him anxiously.

'Thank you very much, Simon. I'm sorry we've been such a trouble. But please, please, don't tell Lady Alyce. She will send me back to Ewelme, I am sure. And I so want to please her and stay in her service.'

Simon sniffed. 'Well, this is hardly the way to go about it.' Then he gave her a little smile.

'Don't worry, sparrow. We Ewelme folk must stick together.'

She looked down gratefully at him. Then he saw her wipe a tear from her eye and felt a lump rising in his own throat. Unsure what to do, he turned away and walked to the horse's head. Ellen hurried along by his side in unaccustomed silence.

The Sign of the Mole

'What do you mean, gone?' Alyce stared at Matthew Cobham in disbelief. 'What in the name of Lucifer and all his devils has happened to my *Tales*?'

'I fear your book has been stolen, your grace,' he said, quaking at her fury. 'We finished it early in April and it was locked up securely in the shop's strongbox. The only people who have keys to its two locks are myself and Mistress Joan; one each, so we both know exactly when and why it's opened.'

'And when was it opened?'

Matthew scratched his head and thought hard. 'I borrowed my mistress's key soon after it was finished to show it to Denis Pailton. We'd asked him to copy the miniature of your grandfather that you wanted enlarged on the title page and to create flourishes around it. He'd done the job beautifully and wanted to see the finished book in its binding. And he'd arranged for John Hardyng and the Earl of Oxford to join us. Hardyng was hoping to persuade young Oxford to commission a copy of his chronicle illustrated by Pailton. And my mistress borrowed my key to show it to Lord Wenlock a couple of days later. Apparently Hardyng had told him about it. His man Thynne was with him and so was Sir Robert Harcourt.'

'Christ in Heaven. Any of them could have contrived to steal it. What were you thinking of?'

'We were so proud of it, my lady. And we always made sure it was safely put away.'

Pallid with worry, Joan came hurrying out into the courtyard, Monique close behind her.

'I've just heard. I don't understand it. Neither of us took our eyes off the book for a moment. We locked it up afterwards both times.'

'What about the keys?' said Alyce. 'I saw you hand your own to Guy so that he and Matthew could open the strongbox to get the Neville Roll. And then to Ned to give to Matthew to get my *Tales*. If you make a habit of handing your keys over to messengers, what's to stop them putting a lump of soft wax into his pocket and making an impression of it?'

'They'd still need the other one.'

'But do you and Matthew always keep your keys close before and after unlocking the strongbox? Or do you put one down while you use the other? If so, it would be the work of a moment to imprint it. For that matter, a visitor could take imprints of both of them while your backs were turned.'

Joan looked abashed, her mouth opening and shutting like one of her own plump carp.

Alyce turned to Matthew. 'If someone had duplicate keys, could he have got into the bindery to open the strongbox at another time? Presumably you have a guard on the gate all night?'

'In theory, yes. But I wouldn't be surprised if whoever was

on duty retreated into the kitchen to keep himself warm by the fire in the small hours. Then there's young Ned – he sleeps on a mattress in the bindery. But he's the devil to wake in the mornings, so I dare say a subtle thief could creep past him at night. The locks would be noisy work, though. Unless...' He paused. 'Come to think of it, they were uncommon easy when I opened it just now. I remember thinking that perhaps my mistress had greased them.'

Joan shook her head miserably.

Alyce pushed doggedly on with her interrogation. 'What about during the day?'

Matthew considered. 'There are usually journeymen or apprentices at work there, except at mealtimes. We've had paper go missing recently and I've told the men to keep an extra sharp lookout. Visitors often call in to look at the exemplars of our bindings, but they're escorted.' He shook his head in wonderment. 'Why should anyone steal your grace's famous *Tales*? It's far too recognisable.'

Joan shook her head. 'There are many collectors who like to gloat in privacy over stolen treasures,' she said. 'In the recent troubled times, a great many fine volumes have gone astray. I know for certain that Lord Wenlock has books he wouldn't show to anybody, but I doubt he'd spirit away one of yours. Thynne was with him of course. A mystery man, that, though Monique thinks a lot of him. I've often seen them together, jabbering in French. As for Pailton, why would he steal his own work? Hardyng might have stolen it out of mischief if he could think of a buyer, but I doubt if Harcourt was involved. He'd rather burn books than collect them. He sees all writings as subversive. In fact, it's odd that he came at all. Sent to snoop, I suspect. All stationers are suspect at the minute, because of the anti-Yorkist bills that are being stuck up faster than they can be taken down and Sir Robert is one of Tiptoft's henchmen.'

'What about Vere?'

'I can't imagine him stealing. He's the soul of honour.'

Alyce wasn't so sure. She remembered the tension she'd seen in Vere's eyes when he'd seen her beside Joan at the feast. Had it been guilt, knowing that the loss of her book was about to be discovered? And he had looked positively haggard when he had followed Harcourt into the showroom. Just then Wenlock himself came out into the little garden. He was holding several books.

'How about a discount for quantity, Joan?' he asked cheerfully. 'Thynne said that your sale was so good that I decided I'd let the queen's affairs be and come bargain-hunting. I've found a Tully, a Hoccleve and a *Legend of Good Women*. Not many of those about these days, I fear. And, in truth, I'd prefer a *Legend of Bad Women*.' He chuckled at his own joke, then noticed their worried faces. 'What's wrong?'

Matthew explained. Wenlock looked thunderstruck.

'You mean the wonderful book Joan showed me and Harcourt a fortnight ago? But it was locked up. Was the strongbox broken open?'

'No. Whoever took it had the keys – or copies of them,' said Joan. 'Nor did many people know it was there. Apart from yourself, Harcourt and Thynne, the only other people outside the shop who did were old John Hardyng and the Earl of Oxford. And Pailton, of course, but Alyce has just told me that he has been murdered.'

'Perhaps the theft of the book had something to do with his death,' said Wenlock. 'If he stole it for someone, or was party to the theft, they wouldn't want him alive to tell the tale.'

Joan frowned thoughtfully. 'But he was so proud of his title page. It seems very unlikely that he'd arrange for it to be stolen.'

'Unless he was planning to sell it abroad,' said Alyce. 'He intended to flee the country, after all.'

'Could an insider have stolen it?' said Wenlock. 'Some of your own people were in the room when you got the book out for me and Harcourt. I remember a tall lanky fellow brought Matthew's key to you. Very quiet.'

Joan bridled with indignation. 'That was Guy. I can vouch for him. As I can for all my men and women. They owe me too much to think of stealing.'

'Wait a minute.' It was Matthew. 'I've just remembered. When Pailton showed it to Vere and Hardyng, the Paul's bookstall keeper Margaret Grafton was in the bindery as well. She buys odd ends of paper from us and has them made up into notebooks by a Lambeth glover from Italy. And I think Pailton's man Cabal was probably around somewhere too. He always came with Pailton when he crossed the river. He was his bodyguard as well as his messenger.'

'So we have two more suspects,' said Alyce. 'But when, I wonder, could the theft have taken place? Could Cabal have slipped into the bindery with a counterfeit set of keys when he came to collect Brother Pietro's pamphlets from you, Joan?'

Joan considered. 'He did come at noon and that's always a quiet time. We were all at lunch.' She coloured, embarrassed at the realisation that her security had been so lax. 'And Matthew told him to fetch the pamphlets himself from the storeroom off the shop. That's next door to the bindery. But it seems so unlikely. Cabal's been a true friend to Pailton for a year or more. Pailton told me about him. He used to act as a messenger for Queen Margaret, but he was caught and tortured by Constable Tiptoft's men. When he wouldn't talk, they cut his tongue out. He was thin as pauper's pottage when Pailton befriended him. He owed him everything.'

'But why did Pailton employ him?' asked Alyce.

'He needed a discreet messenger who could double as a bodyguard. After he regained weight, Cabal was very well set up,' said Joan. 'He was once a royal tumbler, a brilliant acrobat and he knew lots of strange Eastern wrestling holds. He used to take on all comers at the Southwark wrestling ring. That's where Pailton noticed him.'

'What about Margaret Grafton?' said Wenlock. 'I know her stall. She's always seemed a sharpish piece of work to me. And she'd certainly know who to sell your book to.'

'And it was John Grafton who identified Pailton's body, according to Cis,' said Alyce, thoughtfully.

Joan shook her head. 'It would be difficult for the Graftons to creep round the Sign of the Mole unnoticed.'

'I can't help thinking that John Hardyng is the most likely culprit,' said Alyce. 'He'd sell his own daughter for money. Simon saw him pocketing a book from your outside table as we were coming in. But we shouldn't rule out other possibilities. We know the book was here until Matthew showed it to Wenlock and Harcourt. John, can you remember what day that was exactly?'

Wenlock thought for a moment. 'I think it was the Thursday after Easter. We went on to Greenwich afterwards. The queen was holding a masque.'

Alyce turned to her friend. Seeing her stricken face, she felt a stab of sympathy.

'Joan, can you question your workmen and find out if

anyone noticed anything amiss or saw anybody acting suspiciously between that Thursday and today? I know you trust all your household, but who knows what pressures may have been brought to bear on one of them.'

'We've never had such a theft at the Sign of the Mole,' said Joan, her plump cheeks sagging. 'I don't know what the world is coming to.' Alyce patted her arm.

'I know I can count on you to search Moulton Inn. But now I must get back to Montagu Inn. I'm inclined to return to Oxford as soon as possible. This makes it doubly important to find Cabal. He could have intelligence both of Pailton's death and of the theft of my *Tales*. And if my grandfather's book has found its way to Oxford by his agency, there are half a dozen bibliophiles there who'd stop at nothing to tuck it away in an inner sanctum. But first I must speak to Simon. He has been scouting for me on this business of Cis's. I hope to goodness he's found something out. She'll be expecting me to have news for her when we meet tonight at Temple Place.'

'I have urgent business too,' said Wenlock. 'Joan, thank you for your hospitality. And I hope you recover Princess Alyce's precious *Tales*.'

He and Alyce walked out into the courtyard. Joan's grooms hurried to get their horses out of the stable, and Hugh and Brian, who'd been lounging with Wenlock's groom beside the fish tanks throwing small lumps of bread into the water and betting on which of the obese fish would get to them first, scrambled to their feet.

'The Dominican packed your plants into this hamper, my lady,' said Hugh as he held out clenched hands for her to use as a mounting step. 'I'll strap it to my pillion, shall I?'

'Thank you, Hugh. And goodbye, my lord. May our next

meeting be more auspicious.' Her men mounted their horses and fell in behind her as she clapped her heels to Larkspur's flank and rode out of the courtyard. Wenlock watched her go thoughtfully before mounting his own horse and turning its head towards the Royal.

Back in the bindery, Monique cleared her throat. 'Might I say a word, madame?'

'Speak on,' said Joan. 'You're a woman of few words, but they tend to be valuable ones.'

'I did not want to speak in front of your visitors. I have been worried for some little time about Guy. He has been – how do you say in English, *préoccupé*. I know he is anxious about his mother's health, but I think there is more to it than that. And I saw him whispering to Cabal on the occasion that Monsieur Pailton and Milord Oxford were here. And I think Madame Grafton, she was listening with all her ears. Also, I think that Guy was frightened of *le vieux* Hardyng. When I went to give the message of Princess Alyce to her man, Guy was sitting beside him. And he was staring at Hardyng like a rabbit regarding a *belette*.'

'You mean a weasel,' said Joan absently. She had to admit that for the last few days Guy had barely made an appearance unless summoned. It was beginning to look as if he was deeply embroiled in either the Pailton affair or the theft of the *Tales*. Or both.

'Where is he now?'

'He left as soon as he had completed the roll for Princess Alyce. I think he was going to see his mother. He had a bag with him.'

'Where does his mother live?'

'She used to have lodgings in Barking-by-the-Tower. But

recently he moved her to somewhere new. I asked him where it was, but he wouldn't say. Just that it was outside the city. It was as if he was afraid for her.'

'How strange,' said Joan. 'Send him to me as soon as he returns.'

Montagu Inn

As Simon, Ellen and the wilting Tamsin turned down Paul's Wharf Hill towards Montagu Inn, they saw Farhang's unmistakeable silver halo of wiry hair ahead of them. One of the stable lads was with him, his arms full of packages.

'Looks as if you've had rich pickings, Master Farhang.'

'I have, I have.' His deep brown eyes gleamed in excitement. 'And a truly fortunate encounter. I went to Baynard's Castle, in answer to a summons from the Duchess of York – Lady Alyce had told her I was arrived from Ewelme. Coming back along Knightrider Street, I turned off to Spurrier Row to visit Malachi Fryse the apothecary. The duchess had paid me well for several – er – necessaries for herself and her sister Katherine, and I bought so much that I sent the lad who'd been guiding me back to Montagu Inn with half of them. And while I was waiting for him to return, a most interesting man came in. A friar called Pietro of Padua, who has studied both medicine and surgery. He'd brought in a splendid Italian herbal that he urgently needed to sell and I bought it.'

He produced a book from under his arm and opened it.

'Look at these pictures. You could almost pick the flowers from its pages. It explains their uses in medicine and there's a short treatise on common surgical operations bound in at the end. I invited him to dine with us tomorrow, but he said he was leaving for Oxford. He was selling the book because he needed money for the journey. He'd expected to be travelling in a friend's wagon, but the friend never turned up. Clearly he didn't want to part with it. So I told him that I'd sell it back to him on his return, if he had come into funds by then. I'll get it translated and copied first and leave the original in the Priory of St John's in Clerkenwell. Brother Pietro has been lodging with the Hospitallers and will be returning there before he leaves for Italy.'

He turned over the leaves of the book, humming content-edly. Then he held it out to Simon.

'Look at these splendid illustrations of how to cure *anulum fistulum*, Simon.'

High above them in Jankin's saddle, Tamsin craned her head to see as well, but Farhang closed it with a snap. 'Not seemly for you, child. Men's business. All too often, unfortunately. But what are you doing upon Simon's horse? You look very pale.'

'I... I twisted my ankle.'

Farhang handed the herbal to Simon and felt her foot with expert fingers.

'Mmm. A nasty sprain, but it won't take long to heal. The great Galen recommends a poultice of narcissus bulbs grated in honey for such wrenches. When we get back, I'll prepare one and bandage it up. And you can help me unpack my other new treasures.'

They came to the gate of the inn, which was wide open. Farhang headed towards his room and Tamsin limped after him, grateful to get away from Simon's disapproval.

Ellen raced to the kitchen and Simon walked across the courtyard on his way to the hall, noticing that Larkspur was being led into the stable by Joseph Pek. The old groom stopped when he saw him.

'My lady wants to see you, Master Simon. She's in her chamber. She's had bad news. Her grandfather's *Tales* have been stolen away from the Sign of the Mole.'

Simon's jaw dropped. Stolen? He hurried into the hall and up the stairs. His mistress was sitting on a window seat in her solar, looking out across London, threading her rosary through her fingers. She looked up at him, giving a weary smile when she saw his anxious frown. Her pale, austere face was strangely calm.

'Pek has told you, I see. Riddle on riddle, Simon. Where I wonder is all this leading us? First Pailton, now my *Tales*. It seems unlikely that the two are connected and yet...' She looked away into the distance for a long minute and then spoke again.

'If, as is just possible, Pailton arranged for my book to be stolen, then his client might well have thought it a wise precaution to shut his mouth. But why in such a brutal way? And where does this business of Cis Neville's come in? What did you find out from the deputy coroner?'

Simon told her about Pailton's corpse and Giles Scott's testimony, his interview with the anchoress and the taking of his horse. When Alyce heard that Jankin had been found safe at Clerkenwell, she chuckled.

'The Knights of St John are famed for their hospitality, but I hadn't realised that it extended to hungry-looking horses. So the point was just to slow you up?'

'Yes – to prevent me catching up with whoever had been spying on me in St Giles.'

'And perhaps to distract you from chasing after the

anchoress's servant. Wasn't that what you were planning to do next?'

'So it was. I'd forgotten. Shall I go back again tomorrow?'

Alyce shook her head. 'I doubt a scared chit of a girl could tell us anything useful. Did you have any other adventures?'

Simon hesitated, weighing truth and tact before he spoke.

'Well, I met up with Tamsin and Ellen the kitchen maid in Cheapside. They were in some distress, as two of Harcourt's men had been – er – manhandling them.'

There was a crash as the door flew open and banged against the wainscot. Tamsin, ankle bandaged, limped in, leaning on a staff. Hearing Simon's last words, she dropped to her knees.

'I'm sorry, my lady, I didn't mean to do wrong. But I saw Agnes Quincey and I knew you wanted to know what she was up to. So we followed her. And then his grace the duke's horse knocked me over. But he didn't mean to.'

Alyce pursed her lips. 'I suspect that my son was riding with his usual reckless abandon. But you and Ellen had no business to be so far from home without a manservant with you. You were very lucky that Simon came along. Were you hurt?'

Tamsin looked down, expecting Simon to describe the scene he had happened upon, but to her surprise and huge relief he said nothing at all. So she spoke up again.

'No,' she answered. 'Just a sprained ankle. But I think I know where Agnes Quincey was going. I was talking to a stationer, Margaret Grafton – she said she knew you well – and she said Agnes lodged in Clerkenwell.'

Simon gasped, remembering the woman he'd seen in the courtyard.

'Then it was her! When I was collecting Jankin. I saw a woman in a green cloak with a big basket hurrying off towards the prior's lodging. But the porter said she was a washerwoman.'

'Perhaps she was,' said Alyce. 'There must be a good many cloaked women with baskets in the city.' Her brain was spinning. Too much had happened too fast. And so many puzzles. She needed to be alone to think things out. She sighed, then stood up.

'Simon, we will start for Ewelme on Monday. The best hope we have of finding out what happened to Pailton is to seek out his man Cabal in Oxford. And there's just a chance that he has my *Tales* with him. Instruct the household accordingly. Then dress yourself suitably for the feast at Temple Place tonight. Tamsin; lay out my court dress. I'll call you when I need you.'

She walked towards the door to her private chamber. Simon, accustomed to such exits and his mistress's sudden acute need to be alone, stood back to let her pass. Tamsin, less experienced, followed her, still talking.

'I'm sure it was Agnes. And I think that Duke John might have been chasing after her when he knocked me down. Oh and Mistress Grafton the stationer told me to greet you from her. And I'm sorry, really really sorry, about your book being stolen.'

Alyce's patience, ever in short supply, was exhausted. She turned on Tamsin. 'Words tumble from you like water from a tap,' she snapped. 'My mother's motto was *Tac aut fac*: keep quiet or do something about it. I've adapted it a little: *Tac et fac*: keep quiet and do something about it. You'd be wise to think on it.'

She nodded dismissively and disappeared into her inner room.

Tamsin stood rigid, her cheeks burning. Simon felt a mean

sense of triumph, though as he stepped towards her he planned to say something comforting. But she spun on her good heel and limped out of the room.

❧

Alyce settled herself at the reading desk by the window so that she could make the most of the light. She could see the spires of Westminster Abbey and the turrets of the old palace that surrounded it etched in black against the sun. She needed to study the roll, but first she would indulge herself. She felt in her pocket for the little blue volume of Charles's poems that Joan had given her.

Half an hour later she tucked the book away with a sigh and spread out the Neville family tree that Guy had copied for her. It was dense with names. At the very top was Ralph, first Earl of Westmorland, who had died in 1425. Alyce remembered meeting him at court just after she had married Thomas Montagu. A tall man with a Roman nose and eyes fierce as a falcon's, he had come south again for the coronation of Henry V's French bride, Queen Catherine. With him had been his second wife, Joan Beaufort, John of Gaunt's exquisitely beautiful daughter by his mistress Katherine Swinford, her own grandmother's sister. It had been Joan who had persuaded Ralph to back her half-brother Henry, Duke of Lancaster, against Richard II, a move that had made them pre-eminent among all other lords of the north when he was crowned Henry IV.

It was, Alyce reflected, important to remember that loyalty to Lancaster ran far deeper in the Nevilles than loyalty to York. All Ralph's children by his first wife, Margaret Stafford, remained true to Lancaster. As she had requested, Hardyng had left out details of their descendants; just noting that they had eight surviving children. They were rarely seen south of the Trent and some at least were with Queen Margaret in Koeur.

But the world and his wife knew of the Lancastrian sympathies of the Stafford Nevilles. What Pailton had claimed was that a member of Cis Neville's side of the family was now a traitor to her son the king. Alyce studied the names of Ralph's children by Joan Beaufort. Cis herself could of course be ruled out. Her oldest brother the Earl of Salisbury was dead and his oldest son Richard, Earl of Warwick, had masterminded Edward's seizure of the throne. Surely Salisbury's other sons could also be discounted. John, now Earl of Northumberland, was commander of Edward's army in the north. George, Lord Chancellor and Archbishop of York, was high in Edward's favour and a bosom friend of the king's younger brother Clarence.

What about Salisbury's daughters? She knew better than to underestimate the discreet but often immense power wielded by women. But none of them seemed a likely traitor. Joan, Countess of Arundel, was knee-deep in toddlers down in Sussex. Katherine was expecting her second child by William, Lord Hastings, Edward's favourite companion. And Meg was busy planning her wedding. The idea of a chit of her age as a dangerous subversive was absurd.

Next, she considered Cis's other siblings and their children. Here matters were less cut and dried. Alyce remembered the second oldest, William of Fauconberg, with deep affection. Short, stocky and tough as yew, he had been a brilliant soldier who had fought beside Henry V and all three of her husbands in Normandy. He'd died four years ago, but his only son Tom, a handsome bastard born of his French mistress, had a swift and well-disciplined fleet based in the Channel Islands. It preyed ruthlessly upon merchant ships of all nationalities, in defiance of repeated royal commands to return to Southampton. It was hardly the action of a loyal subject. But nor was it news to Cis.

Cis's brother, George, Baron Latimer, was crippled with palsy and rarely left his bed. His son Henry ran the family estates in Gloucestershire and the marches. He had young sons of his own. Would he risk all for Lancaster? Doubtful, but possible. Cis's only other brother Edward was married to the sister of the Duke of Norfolk, but his first wife had been Elizabeth, oldest daughter of the legendary Sir Richard Beauchamp, champion jouster and boon companion of Henry V. He might well incline to Lancaster and still prided himself on his prowess in the field. She put lines under both their names. What of Cis's sisters? Katherine of Norfolk would hardly have married young John Wydeville if she was planning to overthrow his sister the queen. And, from what Farhang and Cis said, the lively dowager was more than happy in the marriage. Then there was Anne, whose husband the Duke of Buckingham had died fighting for Lancaster at Northampton and whose son was now destined to marry one of the queen's sisters. She might well want to do York down. She lived in Essex, but she had a house in Bread Street. Alyce put a line under her name.

She sat back and watched the last of the light fade from the sky. The truth was that any one of these Nevilles could secretly hold to Lancaster – as she did herself in her heart of hearts. It was only Margaret of Anjou's visceral dislike of the Earl of Salisbury and his son the Earl of Warwick that had driven them, the mightiest men in the Neville family, into supporting the Duke of York against the queen and her counsellors. But Edward of York's choice of a Lancastrian widow as his queen had blurred the traditional lines of loyalty. It was now less York and Lancaster and more Neville and Wydeville who were at each other's throats. She looked at the family tree once again. Finally and unwillingly, she made a hesitant mark under the name of Meg Neville. She might be about to get married, but where, Alyce wondered, did young Vere's allegiance lie?

There was a knock at the door. 'Come in,' she called. Simon Brailles entered, a tray held before him. On it was a dish of cinnamon cakes and a steaming jug of mulled wine.

'I've brought you sustenance, my lady.'

Alyce's face lit up.

'How well you know me, Simon. I didn't have much appetite at Moulton Inn. How's Tamsin? Did I bite her head off unfairly?'

Brailles hesitated. How much to tell of what he had seen?

'She meant well, my lady. And it was made hard for her...' He stopped.

'By my son's behaviour?'

'Well, he left her with Harcourt's men, who were nasty pieces of work. And I think she was right about Duke John wanting to find Agnes Quincey.'

Alyce raised her eyebrows. 'I wonder why. No doubt Jack will have a plausible explanation. Though not necessarily a true one. It was well that you happened on them.'

She sighed and turned back to the roll spread out on her reading desk. 'Look at this, Simon. I have marked the possibilities, I think. To narrow it down, we need to find out what Pailton was up to. We know it was something to do with the making and distribution of these scurrilous broadsheets. So which Nevilles might be involved in the circulation of printed propaganda?'

Simon looked at the names she had underlined. 'In truth, my lady, I do not know the Nevilles well enough to help you. Best perhaps you could consult the Duchess of York about them tonight at Temple Place.'

Alyce nodded. 'You're right. Little as I trust her, Cis is a discerning judge of character.'

'There is one other thing, my lady,' Simon said. 'The coroner's clerk showed me Pailton's pen case. There was a steel engraving burin in it. Suppose Pailton was engraving illustrations on copper plates for treasonous broadsheets being printed in secret in London. And the king's intelligencers caught up with him.'

'Surely Joan or the Graftons would know of it?'

'Presses are illegal in England. Joan might know something, but she would be likely to deny all knowledge of it. And I can imagine the Graftons staying mum if their pockets were being well lined.'

Alyce grimaced. 'They would indeed. I think I'll go to Paul's Yard tomorrow and question them. I wouldn't be surprised if the pair of them were in this up to the hilt.'

Clerkenwell

The Priory of Clerkenwell was in uproar. Jack was reminded of a disturbed antheap as he strolled into the inner courtyard after Harcourt. Savernake had arrived an hour earlier with two companies of the constable's men and a search warrant that Tiptoft had signed. The priory was being turned inside out from cellars to attics. As they stood watching, Savernake, smeared with dust and cobwebs, emerged from the great church to the north of the courtyard. He was looking baffled.

'Have you found anything?' called Jack, thrilled to be in the thick of high polity at last. No force in the country was more feared than Tiptoft's intelligencers. And here he was leading a team of them, a royal chain of office around his neck. 'What were we looking for, anyway?'

'It was in the crypt of the church once, I'm sure of it,' Savernake said to Harcourt, ignoring Jack's question. 'But there's nothing we can prove. There's no law against keeping stores of paper and ink for the scriptorium, though the quantities we found in the attic above the dormitory are unusually large. The press itself has been spirited away.'

'The press? A printing press? But they're banned in England,' said Jack.

'Quite so,' said Harcourt. 'Which hasn't stopped these Lancastrian scum from setting one up.'

'But who would dare do that?'

'We have our suspicions, but until we find the press and its operatives and force confessions out of them, we can't prove anything. Our men overdid their ministrations to one of them and he died without telling us very much.'

The slow beat of a drum sounded and they looked round. A squad of Hospitallers formally dressed in black tabards embroidered with a white St John's cross and with long swords at their sides was marching towards them. It opened out into a line and Sir John Langstrother was revealed, dressed for the occasion in Robert Botyll's scarlet robes. The English Grand Prior of the Knights of St John of Jerusalem was a position so distinguished that the holder sat on a special throne in the king's Great Council to signify his unique independence. He looked at them coldly.

'Call off your men. You have no authority here. The royal writ does not run within these walls.' Seeing Jack, he bowed.

'My lord of Suffolk. I am surprised to see you in company with these dogs. Your lady mother will be disappointed in you.'

'She's always disappointed in me,' said Jack defiantly. 'But I am here on the king's business. He fingered his chain of office. 'The search for treason knows no boundaries in his realm or beyond it.'

'No treason has been committed here,' said Langstrother. 'Harcourt, call off the constable's men and leave.'

Grimly, Harcourt turned on his heel and strode away, gesturing to Savernake to do the same. The search party fell in behind them, leaving Jack alone with the deputy prior. He had been made humiliatingly aware that Langstrother knew that Harcourt, not himself, was in charge. He tried to think of a dignified way of taking his leave, but only managed a haughty nod as he turned on his heel and followed his companions. He realised that he was in deeper waters than he had bargained for.

As he caught them up, Harcourt broke off from his conversation with Savernake and turned to him with a warm smile.

'Well done, Jack. Your father would have been proud of the way you bore yourself back there. Every inch a peer of the realm. Just as I told Lord Tiptoft you would be.'

'But I thought everything had gone wrong. There was no printing press there.'

'Not now, no. They must have got word of our raid and taken it away. But we've got them on the run. It's only a matter of time until we find out what they've done with it. And we still have my other plan. The one we hatched when I dined with you two weeks ago. Come to the Mermaid with us and we'll down some sack before we go to Temple Place.'

Jack hesitated. In truth, he would have preferred to go back to the Manor of the Rose and play with his children. But he could hardly admit as much.

The Mermaid was crowded with customers. Abel, who had been sitting at a table near the fire, stood up as they came in and they sat down beside him.

'Savernake, go and get that girl down from our room,' said Sir Robert. 'And Abel, order a jug of ale.' When both were out of earshot, Harcourt gave Jack a conspiratorial smile.

'He's a good man, Savernake, but the fewer people who know about our other scheme the better. Now listen, Jack. If we're to make it work, we need to make quite sure that your mother doesn't get in our way. She's already stirred things up so much that the traitors knew to get the press out of the priory. We need to stop her interference. And the best way of doing that is to have her removed.'

'Removed?' said Jack in alarm. You don't mean... I don't want her to come to any harm. I just want...'

'What's rightfully your own,' Harcourt finished for him. 'You needn't fear. I'm just planning for her and the Earl of Oxford to be arrested for conspiracy. He's the one we think is behind the printing press. We've been keeping a close eye on him for a year now. What's brought things to a head is his hurrying forward his marriage to the Earl of Warwick's sister. We need to prevent that at all costs, or Warwick will gain a powerful ally. Vere will go to the block, of course, especially when we find proof that he's been running the secret press. But your mother's an old lady. And Edward is fond of her. She'll be placed under house arrest in Wallingford Castle. Under your wardenship. And you'll be duke in truth, instead of a puppet dancing to tugged strings.'

Just then, Savernake returned, pulling Amice after him. She was pale, her cheeks tear-stained. She wore a red cloak over her green dress.

'There you are, sweetheart,' exclaimed Harcourt. 'And Nancy has found you a cloak to cover up that flimsy gown. The right colour too. Doxies should proclaim their wares. Come and sit on my knee. Savernake, go and help Abel bring over our ale and we can toss for who's the first to enjoy Amice's favours tonight. Or shall we let Jack lead the way? If you turn tricks prettily my girl, I'll get Nancy to find you a new gown as well.'

Summoning up all his courage, Jack stood up.

'No ale for me, Savernake. Sir Robert, I'm going back to the Manor of the Rose. I need to change for the archbishop's feast.'

Harcourt grinned. 'I'm going to that myself. There's time enough for pleasure first.'

Jack shook his head and headed for the door, feeling sick at heart.

'Well, if you must,' Harcourt called after him. 'But remember, not a word.'

Montagu Inn

Tamsin wandered disconsolately into the hall of Montagu Inn and saw Farhang had pulled a chair up to the fire and was placidly toasting his toes while he sipped at a tankard of ale. She dropped into the chair opposite him. He looked up and saw a tear rolling down her cheek.

'Bit your head off, did she? Simon told me. That's her way when she's worried herself. She has ever been of a melancholic humour: stiff in opinion, wracked with fearful dreams when she is fretting. Least said, soonest mended. She'll soften.'

'But I'm afraid that she might end my service with her. I need to do something to prove I'm useful. Something splendid and clever and brave.'

He looked at her appraisingly, liking her youthful fire and honesty. And, he reflected, she could in fact be useful.

'Chasing somebody through the London streets was fool-hardy rather than brave; nor was it very clever. Anyway, there's no harm in Agnes Quincey. I've known her a long time. People whisper that she's a witch, but she isn't. She's a healer and a good one.'

Tamsin was taken aback. 'Simon says she's an ill-wisher. And my lady asked what she was doing creeping round Montagu Inn. I could tell she didn't trust her.'

'It's her own son that Princess Alyce shouldn't trust and I've told her so. But when has her grace ever taken advice from anybody?'

'Can't I do something to help?'

'There will be opportunities. One thing leads to another. I wonder why young Jack was trying to catch up with Agnes? I will have to think on it.'

'Master Farhang, the man with Duke John said something about finding Agnes to see what she knew about Pailton. And he said he was going to see Lord Tiptoft. And when we got back my lady said to Simon that they needed to go to Oxford to find out what Cabal knew about him. Who is Pailton? And who is Cabal? And why is Lord Tiptoft involved?'

Farhang hesitated. 'Knowing too much can be dangerous,

my child. But I think knowing a little more would make you safer. As you know, Lord Tiptoft is Earl of Worcester, Constable of England and head of the royal intelligence service, dedicated to arresting Lancastrian traitors. Pailton is the reason we are in London. He was a very able scrivener and limner and he was murdered. The Duchess of York summoned Lady Alyce to find out why, for reasons that I don't want to go into now. When the time is right, I'll tell you. But if Jack de la Pole knows about Pailton and Tiptoft is involved, then it looks very much as if Denis had Lancastrian sympathies and that the king's intelligencers were behind his death. Cabal's an Ethiopian mute. He was Pailton's bodyguard, but he'd been sent to Oxford – maybe by chance, maybe to get something out of the way.'

'But isn't Duke John on the same side as his mother?'

'I fear not. But that's enough disclosures.' He gestured towards a table where a large book lay. 'How about reading to me from the herbal I've just bought. My eyes are tired and I can think better when I'm listening.'

Tamsin sat down at the table and turned the book's pages until she found an entry that seemed useful.

VALERIAN infused with hops will ensure sound sleep...

As she read on, a low snore arose from Farhang. Deep in thought, no doubt. No need for valerian just now. She smiled to herself and went on browsing the herbal, fascinated.

MARIGOLD is sometimes called jackanapes on horseback. It hath pleasant, bright and shining yellow flowers, the which do close at the setting downe of the sunne, and do spread and open againe at the sunne rising. Some make their hair yellow with the flower of this herb, not being content with the natural colours God gives them.

PERIWINKLE stays bleeding in the mouth and nose. It is good in nervous disorders. The young tops made into a conserve is good for the nightmare. When it is beaten into a powder with earthworms and houseleek it induceth love between man and woman if it be introduced in their meals.

Soon she was fast asleep herself, slumped over the table. She didn't see Alyce and Simon wrapped in dark cloaks hurry past and out of the door without a backward glance. Or the hooded old woman who came silently into the room five minutes later. But Farhang, who had the ears of a hare for all his feeble eyesight, missed nothing. When Agnes Quincey beckoned, he rose silently and followed her out of the room.

Agnes led him into a small antechamber and closed the door. She pushed back her hood. Her face was brown and wrinkled, her eyes beady as a robin's.

'There is black work afoot, Master Farhang,' she whispered. 'Your mistress is in danger, and she won't listen to me, I know. She still blames me for the death of that babe of hers forty years ago, though there was nothing in heaven or earth that could have saved him. But there must be something you can do. Lord Tiptoft and Sir Robert Harcourt are planning to demand a royal warrant for her arrest. And young Vere's. How they know he's involved in the press I have no idea. I suspect they're guessing. Vere's lands would be a juicy reward if they can prove his guilt and Harcourt covets Ewelme. They have arranged an audience with King Edward tomorrow at noon.'

'How do you know of this?'

'Francis Thynne told me about it. Tiptoft sent a note to Wenlock, telling him to meet him at White Hall. And her grace's own heir is working for them, thinking to feather his nest. He doesn't know what he is about. Never has done, the poor little orphan.'

'Why call him that, Agnes? He has a perfectly good mother in Princess Alyce. Much too good for him, in truth. What are the grounds for this warrant?'

'It will claim that Princess Alyce and John Vere, Earl of Oxford, are traitors. Joint organisers of a secret printing press that is flooding the country with propaganda. Harcourt and the young duke raided the Priory of St John after vespers, but they found nothing. They'll say that they need to take Princess Alyce and Vere into custody so that they cannot destroy evidence. When Thynne took Wenlock's reply back to Tiptoft, Harcourt was there. Francis hung around and overheard them discussing the best way to get a warrant issued directly by the king. Old Tip-Toe said that the first thing was to speak to the queen – and to ensure that she was at the audience. Edward is loth to condemn without cause; he seeks always to reconcile. But Elizabeth can bend him to her will.'

Farhang pursed his lips in thought.

'But Lady Alyce knows nothing of a secret press.'

'Aye, but Lord Oxford knows a good deal. And Harcourt has something else up his sleeve. We don't know what it is, but it links Lady Alyce and Vere in treason conclusively, apparently. The press has been safely hidden now, but the other evidence will incriminate both Lady Alyce and Vere beyond dispute.'

'What is it?'

'I told you. We don't know.'

'Did you say they were going to see the king tomorrow at noon? That gives us no time at all. But I can call in some favours.' He scrabbled in the writing pouch that hung from his belt and found paper and a stick of charcoal. Agnes watched as he wrote two notes, folded and sealed them and handed them to her.

'Could you drop this in at the Cheapside Tavern on your way home? And take the other to Cis Neville in the morning.'

Agnes looked at the name on the first note and was puzzled.

'Dickon Green?'

Farhang chuckled. 'Trust me. It will answer. But Agnes, I need to know the truth about the press. Where is it now? Who else is involved?'

Agnes hesitated. 'The less you know, the safer we are. Meet me at Malachi the apothecary's shop in Spurrier Row tomorrow morning. By then we will know whether Lady Alyce and Vere are to be arrested and I can tell you more – if the others agree.'

'So Malachi is involved?'

Agnes nodded. 'He makes the inks. And his shop is a fine place to hide both paper and people.'

Farhang remembered his encounter there with the ascetic Dominican friar. 'Agnes, what do you know about Brother Pietro, the Dominican pardoner from Rome?'

'He is no lover of York, that is for certain. And he came to London by way of Lorraine.'

Farhang's rheumy eyes widened. 'You mean he visited Queen Margaret?'

Agnes nodded. 'He stays with John Langstrother when he is in London. I heard him talking about her and the court at Koeur. Sir John Fortescue is there and Sir Edmund Mountfort and the Beauforts. They are desperately short of money, but they are in good heart.'

'When did you last see Pietro?'

'He called in to the priory this afternoon on his way to Oxford. He'd been collecting some pamphlets that Joan Moulton had copied for him. He was worried about John Hardyng. Said he was supposed to meet him at Paul's Cross, but he hadn't turned up. But that he'd got money for his journey by pawning a fine herbal to a very clever doctor that he'd met at Malachi's shop.' She stopped. Farhang was smiling complacently.

'That was you, wasn't it?'

'It was. So I've done your cause a good turn without realising it. How ironic. I will only have myself to blame if I'm taken for high treason.'

'No more today, Farhang. I hope I'll be able to speak more freely tomorrow.'

Montagu Inn

The bells of Paul's woke Alyce at eight. Her head ached and her throat was furred. She'd drunk far too much sweet Bayonne wine at Temple Place last night, thanks to her host's convivial presence beside her. Plump and jovial, George Neville had his finger in innumerable diplomatic pies. He was Chancellor of England and of Oxford University and Archbishop of York. He loved books as much as she did. When she told him about the theft of her *Tales* from Joan's strongbox, he was full of sympathy and offered to lend her his own Chaucer to have copied. He hadn't understood how important her own book was to her. Nobody now alive could, she reflected sadly. It had been given to her by her parents on her first marriage and illustrated by Gerard Vespilian, her grandfather's secretary. She'd then asked George about his reconsecration of Paul's Yard after Pailton's death. He'd looked startled.

'Was that his name?' he'd said. 'I wasn't told who he was. There was little enough left of him. And how did you hear about it? Lord Tiptoft was adamant that it was to be kept secret.'

Lord Tiptoft. Alyce shivered at the memory of his visit to Ewelme last autumn. One of the cleverest men in England. And the most ruthless. If he was behind Pailton's death, then it was doubtful that Cis's disloyal relative could be saved from discovery.

Her head throbbed again. Fragments of the passage that

Joan had teasingly read out to Harcourt yesterday came to her. 'Drunkenness makes for forgetting in the soul ... great smokes go up to the brain. It disturbs the knowledge of things that are to be understood.' It had certainly disturbed the knowledge of something that had been said last night, something that she'd half-noticed and needed to think over. Something about hunting boars and falling stars. Something that jarred. Who had been talking?

She stretched her hand out gratefully for the tankard of water on her bedside chest, a cloth draped over it to keep it clean. Tamsin must have put it there. Thoughtful child. She looked over at the low truckle bed beside the door and saw that it was already empty, the sheets and the rough blanket neatly folded. She'd been too curt with her yesterday. But so much had gone wrong so fast and the idea of Tamsin skittering around London with no companion but a kitchen girl had appalled her.

The door opened slowly and Peggotty Lambourn put her head round it. When she saw that Alyce was awake, she came in with a tray loaded with a steaming infusion of purslane and nutmeg and two slices of soft white bread spread with butter and honey.

'Ready to break your fast, my lady?' Alyce pulled herself up on her pillows, looked at the tray and smiled at her. 'A welcome sight, Peggotty. But where is Tamsin? She should be doing these chores, not you.'

'She's already been busy this morning helping me out. And she made this infusion for you from an old book that Master Farhang showed to her and she spread your bread with honey. She's gone with him now on his rounds as he said he needed young eyes. I said that I could help you dress. I've got little enough to do this morning as you're leaving tomorrow. Master Simon's still asleep.'

Peggotty looked at Alyce's bleary eyes and tousled hair and shook her head. 'If you don't mind my saying so, my lady, you're too old to take so much wine. When my old mistress was your age, she always halved it with water – and didn't pick up her glass over much, either.'

'She didn't have George Neville at her elbow.'

A muffled chuckle came from Peggotty, who had disappeared into the closet where Alyce's dresses hung. She came out, carrying a lightweight gown suited to the warm spring sunshine outside and a silver and grey overdress.

'He's a notable toper, to be sure. But carries it well, they say. Was the Duke of Clarence there too?'

'Yes, he was. What made you think he might be?'

'Likes his drink too. And the word is that they're thick as thieves. And that your grace's son is often in their company, cockfighting and gaming for more than he can afford. Was he there last night?'

The half-forgotten knowledge stirred again. Did it have something to do with Jack? At table, he'd been some distance away from her, seated between Clarence and Harcourt. She remembered his flushed young face and the sly glance he had given her. And Harcourt's ribald laughter. Then George Neville had started boasting about officiating at his sister's marriage to Vere at Windsor next week and she'd been distracted from what they were saying. Later she had heard Clarence say that Roly-Poly, which was she knew Jack's demeaning nickname around court, was to join them on a boar hunt tomorrow at the royal hunting lodge at Epping. But that couldn't be right. Today was Sunday. Hunting was against the law of the Church.

He must have meant Monday. She'd meant to ask Jack, but he hadn't come near her. In fact he had ostentatiously kept his distance after his formal bow when she arrived at Temple Place.

'Oh, I nearly forgot.' Peggotty felt inside her pocket and pulled out a folded and sealed piece of paper. 'This came for you. From the Duchess of York.'

More memories stirred. After the feast was over, she had withdrawn with Cis and her sister Katherine of Norfolk to the jakes tower. The chamber of easement maid attended on each of them in turn as they entered it and sat on the circular wooden seat above the shaft down to the midden. She held their skirts clear of the rush-strewn floor, handed them rags and checked that their many layers were adjusted correctly after they had relieved themselves. While Katherine was inside, Cis asked Alyce if she had made any progress. As she described the developments so far, Alyce hoped she'd made Simon's discoveries at the Guildhall and St Giles sound more significant than she'd thought them herself. Cis frowned when Alyce mentioned Tiptoft and frowned again when she said that she planned to return to Ewelme. 'To find your *Tales* or to discover the traitor? Or just to scuttle home?'

'How did you know about my *Tales*?'

'George told me. A bitter blow. I know how much that book means to you.'

'Cabal, who is probably in Oxford by now, is the best lead we have where Pailton is concerned. And I need to get to him before Lord Tiptoft does. If he knows anything about my *Tales*, that will be a bonus, but I think it unlikely. But I need to know more about your relations. I've got a copy of Hardyng's Neville family roll at Montagu Inn. When can we meet?'

Just then Katherine and the maid came out of the jakes.

'I'll send,' Cis had hissed, disappearing inside.

Alyce and Katherine had walked through a couple of crowded rooms to a quieter one, where they'd sat by the fire and talked about days long gone. When they had been in their twenties, living in Rouen and not knowing if their husbands would return from the latest siege in one piece. And one day Thomas hadn't. He had lost half his face at Orléans after a chance shot from a French gun hit him when he was peering out of a siege tower, and died in her arms a few days later. Katherine had been luckier, returning to England with her husband, who died in his bed. Now married for the fourth time to the queen's brother John Wydeville, young enough to be her grandson, she was determined to retain his affections. Her thinning grey hair was stained with walnut juice and she had woven a few bought swatches of auburn tresses into the cauls on each side of her elaborate horned headdress. Her face was unnaturally white, as if enamelled, and her lips a slash of puce.

'Young John is very ardent, my dears,' she had whispered to them. 'But I am ready for him day or night. Your Master Farhang has provided me with a lotion that smooths his path.'

Alyce had turned away in disgust, at which Katherine had cackled coarsely. 'And his sister has plans for both Cis and you, you know. Your dowers are tempting prizes, even if your bodies aren't. Do as I did: choose for yourselves before you're chosen for is my advice.'

Half-amused, half-appalled, Alyce had made her excuses and gone in search of Simon, whom she had found drinking sack with a man in Harcourt's livery. He was hardly able to totter to his feet. As their carriage rattled over the cobbles of the gateway into Montagu Inn, she had heard the great bell of St

Nicholas' strike midnight. But Pek had been in the courtyard to hand her down and escort her into the house, steady as a rock.

Her head throbbed and she drained the infusion gratefully. She opened Cis's note. It told her to bring the roll to Baynard's Castle later that afternoon. Then she remembered her plan for the morning.

'Peggotty, after I've dressed and said my office, I'm going to call on the Graftons. The stationers in Paul's Yard. But I don't want to attract attention. Find my old brown cloak with the hood and tell Pek to ready himself to come with me, will you? We can walk – it isn't far and it's a fine day. We'll leave Simon to sleep.'

Peggotty shook her head. She disapproved of her mistress's fondness for disguising herself so that she could walk the streets seeing and listening unobserved, but she knew it was no use saying so. She went off to fetch the cloak.

Paul's precinct was quiet when Alyce and Pek reached it. Not many stalls were open, only a few selling foodstuffs. The stationers had put away their gay leather bindings and pretty papers; they only offered psalters, primers and religious tracts on a Sunday. Pek wandered off to sun himself on a bench beside the cathedral porch. From inside came the sound of singing. John Grafton was arranging the wares, but there was no sign of Margaret. When Alyce pushed back her hood, a welcoming smile spread across his face and he made her a deep bow.

'We are honoured, your grace. My wife told me that you were in London. Did the little maid remember us to you?'

Alyce suddenly thought of a way of reassuring Tamsin of

204

her favour. 'She did, John. And prattled away to my secretary about your delectable Italian papers. She mentioned some little leather notebooks too. Do you have any left?'

He looked cautiously around to see if a churchwarden was in sight.

'I'm not supposed to sell them today. But I've got some in this bag, if you want to have a look. Course, if I gave it to you and you happened to pay me on another occasion, they'd be no harm in that, would there?' His rat-like face puckered into a toothless grin. 'In here – all the colours of the rainbow. A groat apiece.'

Alyce stooped down to look into the bag. The yellow appealed most to her, but it was far from practical. The purple was too sombre and she liked to reserve red for her own books. 'I'll take that apple-green one,' she said. It wasn't very practical either, but who wants to be practical when they are young?

'A fine Maytime colour,' said Grafton as he wrapped the little book up in a scrap of sackcloth. 'She's a sharp little miss, my wife says. Fast as a fox after Agnes Quincey. The evil beldam had sent her flying with the corner of that great basket she carries on her shoulder. In a terrible hurry, she was. Looked as if she was trying to get away from someone.'

'John, do you still rent the upper storey of the charnel house to store your books in?'

Taken by surprise by the sudden change of subject, Grafton looked up sharply, to be confronted by gimlet grey eyes. His mouth gaped. Alyce was glad that Margaret wasn't there; she was much quicker witted than her husband.

'You do, don't you? And you were letting it to Pailton, weren't you? And you don't want the bridge wardens to know.'

'How did you... who told you? I mean, I don't know what

205

you're talking about.' John's face had reddened in panic and he looked wildly around him.

In what must have seemed an answer to his unspoken prayer, Margaret was walking across the churchyard towards them. As soon as she was close enough to recognise Alyce, she bobbed a curtsey, a welcome on her lips. Before she could utter it, Alyce continued her offensive.

'John tells me that Pailton rented the upper storey of the charnel house from you, Margaret.'

Margaret glared at John.

'You fool. You'll have us clapped in Newgate. Why did you tell her?'

'He didn't. You just did,' said Alyce coolly. 'Now, shall we talk here, or up in your storeroom?'

Margaret glanced nervously around the precinct, which was now becoming crowded as worshippers poured from the cathedral and more stalls opened up.

'In the storeroom. And alone. I don't want anyone hearing us. John, you stay by the stall with the duchess's man.' She headed towards the charnel house and up the outside staircase that led to its upper storey. Unlocking the iron-bound door, she walked inside and waited for Alyce to follow. It was a spacious room, full of bales of paper and bundles of leather and well lit by mullioned windows. Under one of them was a table with some neat stacks of paper on it, a few stone jars of ink and a chair. Alyce waited expectantly.

'Denis used to work here sometimes,' said Margaret sullenly.

'When did he start renting it?'

'He took it over three months ago. Said he wanted some-where peaceful for a special job and somewhere safer to store his things than his lodging in Southwark.'

'I imagine you had a good look at what he was doing. What was it?'

'Couldn't say,' said Margaret sourly. 'He always locked himself in, and when he left he locked everything in chests.'

'Where are his chests now?'

'The coroner asked that. They've disappeared. Taken by whoever killed him, I'd hazard a guess. Unless he had enough warning of his danger to get them away himself.'

'I also want to know about your visit to the Sign of the Mole with Pailton three weeks ago. I hear you saw my rebound *Tales of Canterbury.*'

Margaret looked truculent. 'And what of that? Denis had arranged to show it to John Hardyng and the Earl of Oxford. He was that proud of his work on its title page. Told me to come with him and have a look. I don't often get a chance to visit the Sign of the Mole, so I did. Thought I might be able to get some offcuts. They have the best papers in the city.'

'Did you notice anybody fiddling with the keys that Matthew used to open the strongbox?'

'I noticed he'd left them on the table. I thought how careless that was of him. But I didn't see anyone touch them. I was busy sorting through the snippets of waste that Guy got out for me.'

She stopped speaking and raised her eyebrows in shock. 'It's never been stolen?'

Alyce nodded, wondering if her expression was assumed or real.

'That beautiful book? It must be worth a fortune, with a binding like that. Who do you think took it? Was it Pailton? He was a fly one, you know.'

'It's a possibility. But your group weren't the only people who saw it. Mistress Moulton showed it to Lord Wenlock and

Sir Robert Harcourt about a week later.' Wariness had replaced the shock on Margaret's face and Alyce wondered what had caused it. Mention of Wenlock? Or of Harcourt? Or a dawning realisation about something she'd seen during her own visit?

'The best person to talk to about Pailton would be his mother,' Margaret said suddenly. 'She's just arrived from Wallingford. She's staying with her sister, the landlady of the George Tavern in Southwark, near Pailton's burnt-out lodgings. Shall I tell her to call at Montagu Inn?'

'Tell her I'll send a man for her,' said Alyce. 'She'll likely need a guide. But first I'd like to know more about the pen case that John identified. Simon tells me that it had an engraver's burin in it as well as pens and brushes. Do you know what Pailton was engraving?'

'I've no idea,' Margaret said flatly. 'And I need to get back to the stall.'

'One more thing. I hear that John also found a letter in an inner part of the pen case from the Duchess of York.'

Margaret gave her a measured look.

'If you know about that, then you know that he took it straight to the duchess. Who rewarded him well. As great ladies ought to do, when their good names are at stake.' She nodded slowly, smiling meaningfully at Alyce.

Alyce tensed. 'Was anything else hidden in that compartment?'

The stationer looked sly. 'Might have been. What's it worth to you if there was, your grace?'

'That depends. Have you still got it?'

Margaret stayed silent. Sighing, Alyce fumbled in her pocket and felt for a groat.

'Worth more'n that to you, I'll stake my life on it.'

Alyce took out two marks. Margaret pocketed them promptly and crossed the room to a shelf on which stood a small chest. She took a key on a chain from around her neck, unlocked it and groped inside. Then she turned to Alyce and handed her a scrap of paper containing a single word.

Alyce

Alyce swallowed. It was written in her own hand. Torn from some document that she must have signed. Stolen, then, by someone close to her. Or to whom she had written. Secreted in a scrivener's pen case for the purpose of using it as a forgery. Perhaps for many forgeries. She remembered the angry letter from Margery Paston and Jack's sullen face when she had talked of the mayhem Suffolk retainers had caused at Hellesdon. She looked up at Margaret, whose sour face was suffused with mean triumph. Then she turned on her heel and went down the stairs, her brain racing.

Peggotty was up to her elbows in soapsuds washing napery and small clothes in a sunny corner of the courtyard when Alyce returned, deep in conversation with Pek. Once he had bowed her into the house, he turned on his heel and walked briskly out of the inn. A man with a mission, thought Peggotty. She wondered what her mistress was up to. Pek didn't come back until she and Ellen were hanging the washing out to dry. He was followed by a countrywoman in a patched cloak with a mud-stained hem, who looked shyly around the courtyard.

'Hasn't seen the like before, I daresay,' Peggotty whispered to Ellen. 'Famished, by the look of her, too.' She hung a last shift on the line, dried her hands on her apron and went to welcome the newcomer.

'This is Mistress Pailton, Peggotty,' said Pek. 'Come from Oxford for the funeral of her son. It's to take place in St Asphage's this afternoon. I've brought her to talk to Princess Alyce.'

'You're very welcome, Mistress Pailton,' said Peggotty. 'The funeral will be an ordeal; you'll need a full belly. Come into the kitchen and take some food. Her grace is upstairs in the chapel. Ellen will let her know you're here.'

'I don't know what she wants of me,' said Mistress Pailton as she sat down at the kitchen table, watching eagerly as Peggotty ladled a stew of beans into a wooden bowl and poured her a beaker of hot ginger cordial. 'Nor do I know what Denis was up to. He was too clever, that was his trouble. Always thought he could put one over on the rest of the world.'

She had almost finished eating when the door of the kitchen opened and Alyce swept in. She nodded to Peggotty, then turned to the visitor.

'Mistress Pailton, I thank you for sparing me a few moments on this saddest of days for you. I want to assure you that I won't rest until I find out who murdered your son and bring them to justice.'

The woman at the table stared at her with burning eyes. 'So you say, my lady, but I doubt it. Wolves eat the sheep, great fish swallow the small, petty thieves die and the great scoundrels who put them up to their crimes walk away.'

Alyce was puzzled. 'Are you saying that your son was a thief?'

'I wouldn't be surprised. All that book learning. He was up to no good, for sure. He never visited me unless he needed something. The last time he came he had that cocksure look that he always had when he was deep in mischief. He boasted that a great lord had offered him a chance to make his fortune, but that it meant he must go into hiding for a while, so I wouldn't be seeing him again until the king came...' She stopped abruptly, looking uncertainly at Alyce.

'Until the king came into his own again?' Alyce finished for her. 'So Denis was a Lancastrian?'

The woman hesitated for a moment, tears welling in her eyes. Then a torrent of words burst from her lips.

'Yes. He was. Died in the wool. Led on by that Welsh witch his wife and her mother. I knew they'd be the ruin of him. He told me it had to be kept a secret. But he's dead now, so it doesn't matter if I tell anyone, though I didn't say a word while he was alive. Denis told me that there was a scheme afoot that would rock Edward off his throne. And that his skills would make it all happen.'

'And did he tell you who was behind it?'

'No. Just that it was the cleverest engine he had ever seen. "It will bring all old England back to its proper loyalty," he said. And now he's dead and hellbound for sure.' Mistress Pailton's face was working in agony. 'And all because he believed in Lancaster, the poor mazed idiot.'

'Engine? What did he mean by that?'

'I don't know. Some newfangled invention or other.'

'When did Denis tell you all this?'

'When he visited me at Candlemas, in February.'

'Did you know that he was planning to leave the country?'

Mistress Pailton nodded her head. 'He didn't want to. Something went wrong. Two weeks ago, just before St George's Day, the carrier brought me a cartload of bundles and a message from him. I was to put them in a safe place until he could get home again. Someone had found out what he was up to and he was trying to find a way of going abroad.'

'Did he say how he was going to manage that?'

'He said that a great lady was going to arrange things for him because she owed him a favour.' Mistress Pailton looked accusingly at Alyce. 'It was you, wasn't it? He was always talking about you and your accursed books. If only you'd given him that job in your library he'd never have gone to this city of sin and he'd still be alive.' Her mouth worked furiously and suddenly she spat a glob of saliva at Alyce, who looked down, shocked into immobility at the sight of the ugly wet patch on the front of her exquisitely embroidered overdress. Then the half-demented woman lunged forwards, fingers arced like talons. But before she could reach Alyce, Peggotty leapt forward and dragged her away, pinioning her arms behind her back with deft strength. Alyce shook her head.

'Let her go, Peggotty. She is beside herself with grief. No, Mistress Pailton, it was not me, though I do know who it was.'

'Tell me her name.'

'I can't do that. But I can assure you that she had nothing to do with Denis's death. Indeed, she is shocked by it. It was she who asked me to find out why he had been murdered.'

Peggotty touched Alyce's arm. 'Ask her what was in the bundles that the messenger brought.'

'That's a shrewd thought,' said Alyce. 'Mistress Pailton, what did Denis send to you?'

The woman had sunk back onto the bench by the table. She looked up with a hint of cunning.

'Books, I don't doubt. They were all Denis cared about. He said I was to hide them well; that he'd got buyers for them.

Weren't safe in London, he said. And rightly. Burnt out, his lodgings were.'

'Did you know what books they were? Or the buyers' names?'

She shook her head. 'All he said was that if he didn't return, a messenger with a token from him would contact me and arrange for them to be collected. Now I must go. The funeral Mass is to start at two o'clock.'

As she gathered her shabby cloak around her, Alyce took a purse of coins out of her pocket and handed it to her.

'There should be enough here for prayers for Denis's soul for a year. Your son's work will live on to the glory of the Lord as long as men read and pray. I am sure our most merciful Redeemer will find it in his heart to forgive him. If the books are of value to me, I'll pay you generously for them. Where are they stored? In your house in Wallingford?'

Peggotty saw a curious look of triumph cross the old woman's face as she shook her head.

'No. I knew that would be the first place anyone after them would look. I took them to Job Smith. He's a good friend of mine. He'll have put them up in the loft above his smithy.' She paused and looked into the purse. At the sight of the glinting coins it contained, tears welled into her eyes again. She looked up at Alyce and this time there was only a great weariness in her face.

'I'm sorry, your grace. I spoke brainsick. I thank you for this. And as for the books, if they're of any interest to you, you can have them. They've done nothing but cause my family trouble and I wouldn't be surprised if whoever wanted to buy them was the death of Denis. I was going to tell Job to use them to light his forge when I got back, but you gave my boy his first

chance, after all. And I know of your great love of learning.'
She felt inside the pocket that hung from her girdle, took out
a piece of dark wood and held it out to Alyce. 'Here you are.
You'll likely get to Wallingford before I do. I'm planning to stay
with my sister in Southwark for a few days after the funeral.
Take this token to Job. He'll know it for mine. He gave it to
me many years ago when he came back from Hailes Abbey.
Tell him to keep it safe for me until I get back.'

She handed Alyce a small holding cross made of boxwood
and inlaid with a silver scallop shell. It was the kind pilgrims
carried with them, much worn, doubtless much kissed. Alyce
inclined her head with respect, then looked across at Peggotty.

'Peggotty, go and get that brown cloak of mine, the one I
wore this morning. It's hanging in the porch. It'll keep Mistress
Pailton warmer than her own during the funeral. Then tell
Pek to set her on her road.'

When they'd both left the room, Alyce sat down on
Peggotty's fireside stool and gazed into the glowing embers.
Matters seemed ever more complicated. Was Pailton serving
two masters, one planning to foment rebellion, one merely
interested in acquiring her *Tales*? What had been in the chests
in the charnel house storeroom? And why did he have a
specimen of her signature in his pen case? Suddenly a thought
struck her. Was the theft of the *Tales* a mistake? Had other
things been stolen from Moulton Inn? She must ask Joan
what else was kept in that strongbox. She looked round the
comfortingly orderly kitchen. Fresh bread lay cooling on racks
on the kitchen windowsill. It felt a long time since she'd eaten.
She hacked off a thick crust with her girdle knife and was
just spreading it with dripping from the fat jar that stood in a
hearthside niche when Peggotty came back and glared at her.

'Loaves baked today are not wholesome, my lady. Nor is dripping until it's been clarified. If you want a morsel to eat, you only have to ask. Now, out of my kitchen. I'll bring you across a tray of more suitable fare.'

Westminster

There was silence in the king's chamber. Gold stars studded the painted blue ceiling and sunlight flooded in through long windows. The huge young man shifted wearily on his throne and stretched his long legs out impatiently. He lifted his right arm to run his fingers through his hair, only to find them impeded by a crown. He pulled it off and dangled it from his fingers, staring angrily at the printed broadsheet he was holding in his other hand. Elegant in black, Lord Tiptoft stood beside his king. In front of them knelt Lord Wenlock and Sir Robert Harcourt. Edward sighed and motioned them to stand. Replacing the circlet of gold on his head, he ran his eyes once again down the notice that Tiptoft had just handed him.

'So you believe that the Earl of Oxford is behind the treasonable and pernicious propaganda that is being hammered on church doors through the land?'

'We do, your grace,' said Tiptoft.

'Do you have proof? You have already caused me considerable embarrassment and the threat of excommunication by your invasion of the Priory of St John. Hospitallers are not subject to the king's writ except in cases of manifest treason and you have failed to prove any such thing.'

'It is only a matter of time, your grace. A suspect confessed that Vere has a printing press at work in London, which explained why we never found this scurrilous stuff when we searched ships from the Low Countries. We haven't found the press yet, but we will. Now that Vere knows we are looking for it, he will be trying to get it away from the city.'

'But what proof do you have that Vere is involved? He is to be married at Windsor in four days' time to the Earl of Warwick's youngest sister. In front of myself and my queen and all the Nevilles, on the day after the celebration of the anniversary of our own marriage. I will do nothing without proof.'

'And proof you shall have, your highness,' Harcourt interposed emphatically. 'Proof that shows beyond doubt that Oxford is a traitor – and that the Dowager Duchess of Suffolk is close allied to him in his treasons.'

'Alyce de la Pole? Not more accusations? Your vendetta against her last autumn caused me considerable embarrassment, Harcourt. She is the mother of my sister's husband and all but a recluse. About to become a vowess, too, much to my wife's disgust. She had a husband in mind for her.'

'She and Vere are in league,' insisted Harcourt. 'The great castle at Wallingford is to be at the hub of a rebellion. Foul murder has been done to cover up their activities, but I have proof positive of their guilt, even if we can't find the infernal engine that makes these broadsheets.'

'And where is this proof?'

Harcourt paused a moment before speaking.

'It is in Windsor. Hidden safely. But Princess Alyce and Lord Oxford could yet destroy it. Which is why we seek warrants for their arrest under the privy seal.'

Edward looked at Wenlock, who was ashen pale. 'Wenlock, you look ill. Has this been a shock to you too?'

Wenlock swallowed. 'It has, my liege.' He mustered his dignity and added, 'And I, like you, hesitate to believe such treason of Princess Alyce or Lord Vere without proof.'

There was a flurry at the entrance to the council chamber and the regal figure of Cecily Neville swept past the protesting guards.

'The Duchess of York,' an usher called out belatedly.

Edward rose to his feet and motioned his mother to the second of the two thrones that dominated the chamber. Cis nodded graciously and settled herself onto it. Edward sat down again and turned to her.

'Well, mother, your arrival is timely. My lord of Worcester accuses the Earl of Oxford of sundry treasons and Sir Robert Harcourt says that his companion in dishonour is your own confidante, Alyce de la Pole.'

'Arrant nonsense,' said Cis. 'What proof do they have?'

'It is to be shown to us at Windsor.'

'Moonshine!' Cis snapped. 'Harcourt's zealousness in pursuit of traitors whose lands abut on his own is well known. You will recall that fiasco last year. No doubt he is already demanding warrants for their arrest. Then he can plant what lies he chooses. But consider the ramifications of this if no proof is forthcoming, Edward. The public insult to Warwick's sister Meg, to the Veres, who stand high in popular acclaim, and to Princess Alyce, whose son is married to your own sister.'

Edward held up his hands in surrender and smiled. 'On this occasion, mother, I need no persuading.' He turned to Tiptoft.

'Constable, there will be no warrants until proof of this unlikely plot is forthcoming. I have been put to enough embarrassment by your raid on the Hospitallers. Fortunately Langstrother has been magnanimous. Plans for John de Vere's marriage to Meg Neville will go ahead unimpeded. I cannot afford to antagonise her brother any further. Vere and Princess Alyce will remain at liberty until evidence of their guilt is shown to us. If it is, they will of course be arrested. And if it is not...' The lazy eyes lingered on Harcourt, but Edward left the sentence unfinished. 'We are weary. Withdraw, my lords, if you please.'

'How was it that the king's mother joined us, instead of his wife?' asked Tiptoft icily, as he and Harcourt strode down the long gallery towards the stairs that led to Westminster's great hall.

Harcourt shook his head, bemused. 'I don't know. The queen said that she would be there without fail.'

'Well, I hope that you are secure in your proofs, Harcourt. If Vere and Princess Alyce still have their freedom, they could yet discover your plan. You will look a consummate fool if you have nothing to show at Windsor. Why did Wenlock speak so doubtfully? And why did he hurry away? Is he with us, or against us?'

'Who knows where Wenlock's loyalties lie?' growled Harcourt. 'He's fond of Warwick's little sister and fonder still of Duchess Alyce. But would he dare flout you? Or risk the king's displeasure?'

'Perhaps he knew he had to do one or the other. Have him followed.'

'Yes, my lord.'

'And track down that infernal printing press.'

'My men are even now scouring the city.'

They entered the great hall and stopped dead, astonished

at the tableau in front of them. A crowd of courtiers milled about, laughing and joking as they watched a group of dancing men in beribboned costumes and jingling bells on their shins cavorting around Queen Elizabeth, who was seated on a chair of state, dressed in a ravishing spring-green and white gown, her hair loose and woven with a rainbow of ribbons. With a final whoop of triumph the dancers raised the chair and its occupant shoulder high and then gently lowered it to a skirl of the pipes and a rat-a-tat of drums.

'Bravo!' The cry came from the gallery. King Edward looked down at the bride he had elected to marry against all advice, feeling as much in love with her now as he had been when he first met her four years ago. Elizabeth looked up at him, her cheeks rosy, her eyes bright.

'There's your answer,' said Tiptoft wearily. 'Her grace could never resist a chance to dance. Slowed her up enough to miss our audience. Find out who summoned the Moorish dancers and you'll know who's fouled things up for us.'

'Leave it to me, my lord.'

Harcourt advanced on the dancers purposefully, only to hear a rattle of bells and find himself thwacked hard with a bladder tied to a stick. It promptly exploded, drenching him in a cloud of flour. Blinded for a moment, he spun round, reaching out furiously. But the entire troupe were racing away, hooting with laughter. Tiptoft, ever careful of his dignity, had disappeared. The courtiers were tittering and the queen raised her perfectly arched eyebrows.

'How now, Sir Robert? Is it snowing where you are? Here we have been celebrating spring with Master Green and his merry men.' He backed away with as much dignity as he could muster, inwardly incandescent with anger.

Montagu Inn

Simon didn't stir from his slumbers until the bells of sext sounded. He started up guiltily, wondering how he'd come to sleep so long – then remembered last night's revels at Temple Place. Savernake had plied him with an ale so heavy that his head had spun after a single tankard. And he'd plied him with questions, too. About Alyce and about Ewelme. Did his mistress confide in him? He remembered uneasily that he'd boasted of knowing all her secrets. And then Savernake had asked about Pailton. Why was Simon asking about his death? But how had Savernake known about his visit to the Guildhall? Giles Scott must have told him. Then he realised that it was not just the bells that had woken him. There was a hubbub of voices in the courtyard. He looked out of the window. Joan Moulton, resplendent in scarlet, was dismounting from a fat gelding while her groom steadied its head. The elegant young lawyer that Will Stonor had introduced to him as James Danvers and a pale young woman had already handed their horses over to Hugh and Brian. Will himself was dismounting. He dressed quickly and hurried down to the hall.

'Wonderful news, Alyce,' Joan was saying, as she munched a square of lardy cake from a tray that was being handed round by Tamsin.

'Young James here appealed the case against Kate yesterday. He produced half a dozen utterly respectable witnesses to her virtue and the Consistory Court dismissed the Ardernes' trumped-up accusations as pernicious and perjured. She's free, but she still needs protection. I wouldn't put it past the Ardernes to mount some new cause against her. Now we've got to get Peter back. But it's going to be more difficult than

I thought. He's been made the ward of Sir Robert Harcourt. We will be able to rescind the wardship, but it has to be done through the Court of Wards and the boy may already have left London. Harcourt plans to marry him to his daughter before anyone can stop the match.'

'So we share an enemy,' said Alyce. 'And if Harcourt's busy kidnapping children, it makes it unlikely that he is involved in the theft of my *Tales*. But he hasn't left London yet. He was at York Place last night, putting back more wine than I'd have thought any man could hold. I dare say he slept even more soundly than Simon here.' She gave Simon a curt nod, then turned back to Joan.

'I do recall that he was saying something to Clarence about having business in Henley. I remember thinking that there was something odd about it. He looked even more wolfish than usual.'

'Perhaps Peter and his grandfather have gone ahead of him to Oxfordshire,' said Joan with a frown. 'If only we knew. We sent Sukey, the child's nurse, to see if she could get taken on to look after him. She was going to send a message if she did, but we haven't heard from her.'

'I hope she's all right,' said Kate. 'She's much too young to be alone in London. If they didn't take her in, she could have got abducted herself.'

'Tom said he waited nearby for a whole hour. She must have had some success,' said Joan. 'But they know they are chancing their arms in acting before the legal formalities have been completed. They may be watching her closely to prevent her from telling anyone what their plans are.'

Simon saw a way of redeeming himself. 'Would you like me to go to the Mermaid to see what I can find out?' he said.

'If the Ardernes are gone, it's possible that one of the servants will know something.'

'Good idea, Simon,' said Alyce. 'Be as quick as you can. We need to prepare to depart for Ewelme tomorrow.'

As she watched Simon ride away, a thought struck Alyce. 'Joan, if you and Lady Arderne find you need to go to Oxfordshire, we could travel in company. I've another clue to follow up. I was talking to the Graftons in their storeroom above the charnel house. Pailton used to work there, apparently. Though it's strictly against the rules of the close.'

Joan looked startled. 'Is that so?' she said. 'Did you see what he'd been working on?'

'There was nothing to see. Either it was taken by his murderers or he removed it himself before his death. I've just spoken to his mother. A week ago a carrier came to her house in Wallingford with several bulky packages. He said they belonged to her son and that she was to hide them well until he could get to Wallingford himself. She's told me where they're hidden, which makes it even more urgent that I leave for Ewelme as soon as possible. My *Tales* could be among them.'

'It would be well worth knowing what he sent so far away,' said Joan. 'It might give us a clue as to who he was working for. And if he rather than Cabal was involved in the theft of your book, it could easily have gone with his stuff. Unless, God forbid, it went up in the fire at his lodgings.' She paused, thinking hard, then spoke again.

'Wallingford's on the Thames close to Ewelme, isn't it? I've had an idea. Didn't Vere say that he was setting off on Monday morning for Windsor on his barge and that the barge itself would go all the way to Oxford with furnishings for his new house there? Shall I ask him if he'd have room for us to travel as far as Wallingford on it? If the wind keeps blowing from the east like this, it will be almost as quick as by road and much safer.'

Alyce was filled with longing. Nothing was pleasanter than river travel, especially in Vere's famously swift barge *Silver Star*. Then she remembered her tart words to him at Moulton Inn.

'I'm not so sure that he'd want to take me, Joan. I wasn't exactly civil yesterday.'

'I think he will,' said Joan. 'He knows how fond of you Meg is. He was delighted that you said you'd attend their wedding and he's eager to win your favour. I'll send word to him. You get yourselves packed up. The Monday morning tide turns around seven o'clock. He won't leave before that.'

Alyce nodded slowly, still unsure that she was doing the right thing. She saw Joan turn to the young lawyer, who was guiding Kate through the convoluted legal language of her acquittal document.

'What about you, James? Will you travel with us? Lady Arderne will need a lawyer when she gets to Oxford.' James looked uncertainly at Kate.

'I'd like you to,' she said. 'Just in case they throw some other legal impediment in our way.'

He hesitated. 'I won't be able to come on Monday. The Court of Wards is to hear your case in the afternoon. A miracle of speed, much assisted by Lord Wenlock's open-handed generosity. I have an appointment with him this afternoon to go over the case. But Will and I could catch you up by road on Tuesday. Mercury, my horse, is famously fleet-footed and the Stonors have mounted their son well.' He looked round for his clerk, but there was no sign of him.

'Where's Will gone?'

'He said something about seeing to his saddle girth,' said Joan's groom.

'Could you go and get him?' As the man disappeared, James turned to Joan.

'It just struck me that I will pass Lord Oxford's inn on the way to the Royal. Shall I pass him your message?'

'An excellent idea,' said Joan, walking over to her desk. 'I'll give you an impress of my seal as a token.'

She lit a stick of wax, dripped a few drops on a square of paper, pressed her signet ring into it and handed it to James. He bowed to her and Lady Alyce, then strode over to where his handsome black gelding was tied up. Hugh hastened to offer his linked hands as a mounting step and the young lawyer swung up into the saddle, then looked around for Will. There was still no sign of him.

'Curse the boy,' said James. 'He'll just have to catch me up. I need to get to Lincoln's Inn as soon as possible.'

He was about to ride away when Kate called out. 'Wait a minute.'

She walked over to him and they saw her looking up at him and speaking urgently. He nodded, then clattered away. Kate walked to the gate and watched him ride off. Then she disappeared into the house.

Alyce saw Joan looking pensively after her. She touched her arm. 'Thinking of marrying them off, are you? Well don't. It's much too soon. Not that it wouldn't be a fine match for both of them.'

'It would indeed – in time, as you say. Although the most promising marriages go awry. As we both know.'

The two women were silent for a long beat, Alyce recalling Thomas Montagu's ghastly death; Joan Walter Caerleon's womanising. Then Alyce decided to ask a question put into her mind by something Margaret Grafton had said.

'Before Kate returns, Joan, can I ask you something. Was anything apart from my *Tales* stolen from your strongbox?'

She saw Joan looking distinctly shifty as she answered. 'In truth, I never thought of checking. Why do you ask?'

'I'm just wondering if the theft of my *Tales*, which seems so pointless, was an accident. Part of a bigger theft of things that had more market value. Books for the bedroom, perhaps?'

She saw a blush redden Joan's cheeks. It was as she thought. Her friend had secrets that she wasn't privy to. Nothing to do with the treasonous propaganda that John Wenlock was so exercised about, but everything to do with his sly smile as he mentioned Pailton's Ovid and Margaret Grafton's snide remark about Pailton. And if Joan had a sideline in what was known in the polite world as *litterae eroticae*, it would explain why Wenlock himself had turned up to the book sale.

Joan had recovered herself. She gave Alyce a conspiratorial wink. 'I do occasionally have such things for sale, and of course they are carefully locked up. I will look in the chest when I get back to Paternoster Row and see if anything else is missing.'

Kate was coming towards them, her face thoughtful.

'Well, Kate, I hope you were thanking Master Danvers,' said Joan. 'He's devoting himself to your cause like a knight out of legend.'

'I know,' said Kate. 'And I am grateful. But what I was telling him was that if he does bring us a letter cancelling the wardship, he must be careful. I fear Sir Robert will stop at nothing. And he may have left men here in London to watch us. You said you thought we were followed on our way to Lord Wenlock.'

'Quite so. Which is why the sooner we are all safely on Vere's barge with a dozen men to defend us the better. Your safety is the most important thing.' She turned to Alyce. 'Could she stay here, your grace, until we are ready to leave for Oxfordshire?'

'Of course,' said Alyce, absently. She was looking at Farhang, who was coming towards them carrying a large book-shaped object wrapped in a piece of sacking. Her heart leapt.

'What have you there, Farhang? Is it my *Tales*?'

The old physician shook his head. 'Sadly not. Just a piece of work for the Sign of the Mole.' He turned to Joan.

'A word in your ear in private, Mistress Moulton,' he said, leading her out of Alyce's hearing.

What was he up to? wondered Alyce, watching them walk away towards the gatehouse. She looked around for Tamsin. Where had she gone to? And where on earth was Will? She walked towards the stables. His horse was still munching hay from a nosebag and Hugh was gently coaxing tangles out of Larkspur's silky mane.

'Have you seen Master Stonor, Hugh?' she asked.

He nodded towards the well at the far end of the little yard. Tamsin and Will were sitting side by side on its stone rim. Tamsin jumped up guiltily as Alyce appeared. Blew the wind in that quarter? She remembered their adventures together last autumn and the way Will's eyes had lit up at the sight of Tamsin when he and James arrived. Had they had other meetings? She hoped not. Nothing could be more impossible than a match between them. Will was his father's heir and was to marry an heiress, one of his own station. And she still treasured the idea of a match between Tamsin and Ben. But she knew that it would be a mistake to confront them. Nothing lends tinder to a spark more than forbidding a friendship. For the moment she just smiled.

'There you are. Will, you're to follow Master Danvers to Lincoln's Inn. And Tamsin, fetch my psalter and bring it to the chapel. It's time we said a prayer for a good outcome for Kate Arderne.'

Spurrier's Row

After the chaplain had finished prayers, Tamsin followed Alyce back to the great hall. Joan had returned to the Sign of the Mole and Peggotty had taken Kate upstairs for a much-needed rest. Farhang was dozing in a chair beside the hearth. He opened his eyes when they entered and stood up.

'Lady Alyce, I wonder if you could spare Tamsin to be my eyes again this afternoon? I have some business to settle and, as you know, I need to be guided when I am abroad. I can see close, but the distance is fogged.'

'Of course,' said Alyce. 'I'm in sore need of some solitude. Take your cloak, Tamsin, and a basket, in case Farhang makes more purchases.'

Ten minutes later, Farhang was stumping down Cordwainers Street, Tamsin at his side.

'Where are we going?' she asked.

'To Malachi, the apothecary. I need him to make up a medicine for me. You'll like his shop. And it's time you met Agnes Quincy properly. Tamsin, anything you hear you must keep secret. But I promise you that what we are doing will help our mistress, not harm her.'

Tamsin felt uneasy, but excited. She was beginning to

understand the two worlds that she had to negotiate: that of the great men and women who wore fine clothes and spoke fair words that rarely revealed their true thoughts, and that of the lesser men and women who protected their patrons loyally but could also be threats when they had ambitions of their own. And she was still elated by her brief meeting with Will – and his whispered promise as he left that he would engineer another as soon as he could.

When they reached the apothecary's door, they found it was locked, a sensible precaution for any shop selling precious goods. Inside they could see bald-headed Fryse, an obese bullfrog of a man, grinding a pestle in a mortar. He looked up warily when the bell jangled, smiled a welcome when he saw Farhang and ambled over to open the door. Tamsin followed Farhang in and looked round. It was full of wonders. Rows of blue and white jars with cryptic gold lettering stood on shelves above ranks of small drawers. Plump, wide-necked bottles were filled with curiosities – a writhing forked root that Tamsin guessed to be a mandrake, a curled salamander with bulging, desperate eyes and claws pushed against the enclosing glass.

Farhang introduced her, then handed the apothecary a folded paper. After he had read it, Fryse pulled out drawers and measured out this and that into a tiny stone mortar, pounded them with a pestle and rolled them into pills using a little spittle. Then he prodded them into small pouches and pulled their drawstrings tight.

A sharp rap on the windowpane made them look up. Agnes Quincey stood outside, gesturing urgently. Fryse unlocked the door again and she hurried in.

'Lock it, quickly. And close the shutters. Then into the back room.' She hustled Farhang and Tamsin ahead of her. With agonising slowness, humming under his breath, Fryse closed shutters across the window and followed them into the rear of the shop.

He was just in time. They heard heavy feet jogging past the shop, the clink of spurs and the rattle of a sword.

'Liveried men, evidently,' said Fryse. 'Even so, they should not be carrying arms in the city of a Sunday.'

'They're Harcourt's men,' said Agnes. 'I was on my way back from the Royal to Clerkenwell and his henchman Savernake was waiting for me in Paternoster Row. I had to leave my basket behind so that I could get away from them more quickly. It's got the last of the broadsheets in it. It's all up with us if they find it.'

'Where did you leave it?' asked Farhang.

'I ducked through St Paul's, so they'd have to get off their horses to follow me. I pushed it behind a tomb, then I came out the other side. It worked the other day. But this time Savernake was expecting it. He and his men had just ridden round the church. I only just got away.'

'It'll be safe enough, surely?' said Malachi.

'That depends whether any of them noticed that I wasn't carrying anything when I came out.'

'One of us must go back to Paul's. Not you, Agnes.'

There was a staccato rap on the door. They froze. Fryse quietly opened the door into the shop and put his eye to a crack in the shutters. Then he unlocked the door, letting in a tall, stooped man in a dark-red velvet cloak, walking with the aid of a long yew-wood staff tipped with a curious silver device. With him was a dark-haired boy with the olive skin of a Spaniard. He was carrying a bulky sack.

'Sir Thomas! And Owen!' exclaimed Agnes. 'What are you doing here?'

'I thought you might hide with Malachi,' said the new-comer. 'Owen saw you fleeing through Paul's as if the hounds of heaven were after you. He also saw you push your basket behind a tomb and guessed its contents needed protection. So he emptied them into his scavenging sack and brought them to me.'

Agnes gave a sigh of relief. 'You have saved the day for us again, Owen bach.'

The lad answered with a torrent of unfamiliar words and a wide smile.

'Is he Spanish?' Tamsin asked Farhang.

He smiled. 'No, child. He's Welsh. Or half of him is. Agnes is his grandmother. She came over with Henry V's wife Catherine of Valois. After Henry's death, Catherine married Owen Tudor and Agnes married a Welshman in his service. Both he and Tudor were killed five years ago, at Mortimer's Cross. Agnes is a corrodian in Clerkenwell now, like Sir Thomas here. Her daughter Bronwen married Denis Pailton.'

'Pailton?' exclaimed Tamsin. 'The man whose body was found in the charnel house?'

'That's right. Owen here is his son. Bronwen and he live in the priest's house at St Giles Without. Pailton decorated the church's pillars many years ago and after he went into hiding the priest felt that the least he could do was to give Bronwen a job as his housekeeper and educate the boy.'

'And who is Sir Thomas?'

'The greatest tale-teller of our age,' said Malachi. 'One day I predict that his history of King Arthur will be read all over the world. But at the moment he is in disgrace for offending the queen with his masque of *The Wedding of Sir Gawain and Dame Ragnelle.* Saints, but it was funny. Though her high and mightiness didn't think so. Called it much too bawdy.'

'Sir Thomas Malory,' breathed Tamsin, remembering the story that Will had given her to read last September in Doll's bookshop. She looked towards the back of the room, but could not make out what Agnes and Malory were talking about. Meanwhile, Fryse had gone to the front of the shop and was cautiously opening the shutters. Outside, the street was empty.

'Time for us to return to Montagu Inn, my dear,' said Farhang.

But as he spoke there was a clattering on the cobbles. Horses drew up outside the shop.

'This was where we lost her. She must have ducked down that alley.' It was a harsh, nasal voice. Tamsin shivered, recognising it instantly as Savernake's, the man who had been with Lady Alyce's son in Paul's Yard.

A younger voice replied. 'Let's go to the priory and tickle up that traitor knight until he tells us where she is.'

Agnes frowned, then whispered, 'That's the new lad. The cruel boy who twisted Brother James's arm so brutally when they were searching the priory. A born bully.'

Savernake spoke again. 'Won't answer, Abel. Malory is a favourite of Edward's. He won't hear a word against him. Likes his stories too much. Only banished him from court because the queen insisted on it. And Clerkenwell is outside the royal jurisdiction. We're already in trouble for invading it yesterday. And we're late for the hunt. We must ride for Epping straight away.'

The troop of men rode away. Peeping cautiously through a crack in the shutters, Fryse watched them disappear.

Malory turned to Agnes. 'It's as well they didn't find the broadsheets, my dear.'

'And that the press is long gone,' said Agnes.

'What press?' asked Tamsin.

'Better you don't know, my child,' said Sir Thomas, frowning at Agnes.

'Is Pailton's death connected to whatever you're up to?' asked Farhang.

Malory hesitated.

'Tell him, Sir Thomas,' said Agnes. 'We can trust him. And he might be able to help.'

Malory looked at Tamsin. 'But what about the girl?'

'I can vouch for little Tamsin,' said Farhang. 'She comes from a long line of trustworthiness. Her father was Roger Ormesby.'

The old knight's eyes softened. 'A loyal line indeed. I remember Roger at Bayonne. Yes, Pailton was working for us. Tiptoft's men had been watching him for some time because of word sent by the Graftons, the people whose storeroom he used, and after he sent Cabal to Oxford he had no one to protect him. They tortured him to find out his suppliers. But Savernake overdid things and he died. Francis Thynne overheard Harcourt telling Wenlock that they should torture Agnes next, because Margaret Grafton told him that she was close to Pailton. But then Wenlock realised how recently the broadsheets had been printed and guessed that there was a press in London. Which is why they raided the priory. If it hadn't been for Thynne sending a warning, they'd have found it.'

'Does Mistress Joan know about all this?'

'She knew about the press, but not about the broadsheets. She has a quite different interest in printing in secret. She thinks it's entirely for what she calls her specials. Books like *Speculum al Foderi*, *Le Jardin de Plaisir* and Aretino's *Modi* – all illustrated with Pailton's engravings. It was Monique's idea. She has been helping us from the beginning. She's as loyal to Lancaster now as she was when she was the toast of Queen Margaret's court. She thought, rightly, that selling such books was a way of making enough money from the press to pay for the paper we needed for printing the broadsheets and she persuaded Joan that they were a good business proposition. The books were shared between Joan, ourselves and Pailton, who squirrelled away his share of the copies to sell later. We used to buy paper from the Graftons, but I could see they were getting suspicious. Then we struck lucky; an Italian stationer sold up and we bought the whole of his paper stock. A fine hotchpotch of stuff, old and new. Very hard to trace. We also saved a few sheets of paper from each consignment imported for the books, so that the batches of broadsheets are impossible to identify from their watermarks.'

'But where does Master Thynne fit in?' asked Tamsin. 'Why would he spy on his master?'

Malory smiled. '*Amor vincit omnia*, as old Chaucer's Madame Eglantine boasted. He's become very close to Monique. He also knows that Wenlock is far from fond of Harcourt. And very fond of Lady Alyce – and Mistress Moulton's specials. So he feels he is not really disloyal.'

'We must return to Montagu Inn, Tamsin,' said Farhang. 'Lady Alyce needs to know of this.'

The Mermaid Inn

Simon dismounted in the busy courtyard of the Mermaid Inn and handed Jankin to the stable boy, who had run over to take his bridle. The landlady came forward with a welcoming smile.

'Can I help you, master? A room for tonight? Or just a meal? There's a fine stew simmering in the kitchen.'

'I'm looking for Sir Gervais Arderne,' said Simon. Her face closed.

'Then you've missed him,' she snapped. 'He left yesterday.'

'With the children?' risked Simon.

'Children? He only had the boy. Oh, you mean the shrimp of a girl who came to look after the lad? Yes, all of them, thank goodness. Nothing but trouble, they were. And took one of my kitchen lads with them. Not that he's much of a loss. A nasty piece of work.'

'I've got an important message for Sir Gervais,' Simon said. 'Do you know where they were going?'

'I do not,' she said. 'Very secretive, Sir Robert was. Said they would send back our horses from their first halt, but when I offered to have them collected, he said no, he'd send Abel back with them. But there's no sign of them yet and I'm beginning to wonder if there ever will be.'

'That's a shame,' said Simon, noticing that the small boy who was scouring a pan near the scullery door was covertly watching them. He raised his voice a fraction. 'There are some grand folk who would pay well to know which way they went. But I'd welcome a bowl of your stew. I'll eat it out here in the sunshine.' The landlady was cheered by the prospect of custom.

'I'd tell if I could,' she said. 'But you won't regret my stew.

Best meal you'll ever eat for tuppence.' She turned to the scullion. 'Micky, you come with me.'

They disappeared inside and the stable boy took Jankin to a nearby tethering rail. Simon sat down at the long table under the eaves of the inn. After a few minutes Micky brought out his stew. As he put it down on the table, he spoke in a whisper, carefully turning his back to the kitchen door.

'D'you know Mistress Moulton?' Sensing the need for caution, Simon gave a barely perceptible nod. The boy dropped a spoon and whispered again as he stooped to pick it up and place it on the table.

'After you've finished, I'll meet you outside.' With a scared look towards the kitchen, he walked away towards the well near the entrance to the inn and began winding down a bucket for water.

Simon ate the stew, which was as good as it had smelt, rich with beef marrow and juniper. Then he stood up casually, put two pennies on the table and walked over to Jankin. He examined one of his hoofs, tutted under his breath, then led him out of the courtyard.

'Loose shoe, by Our Lady,' he said to the stable boy, who had come up to help him mount. 'I'll have to walk him to the smith. Is there one nearby?'

'Turn right, then left down Eastcheap. Only a hundred paces or so. Thank you, sir.' He bent down for the penny that Simon tossed towards his feet. As he did so, Micky put down the brimming jug he had just filled from the well bucket and skittered off through the gatehouse like a rat.

Leading Jankin, Simon followed at a leisurely pace, turning first right and then left. Round the corner he saw Micky cowering in a doorway. The boy stepped out.

'I know where they went, sir. I wanted to help the girl. She was kind. She gave me a message for her friends, but Nancy wouldn't let me go out. I was to go to the Sign of the Mole with this pocket and say that Sukey sent me. Did Lady Arderne send you?'

'As good as,' said Simon.

'And will Lady Arderne take me into her service? Sukey said she would if I gave her the message. I can't go back to the inn now.'

'I'm sure she will,' said Simon. 'She'd do anything for someone who helps to get Peter back. What's the message?'

'Sukey said only to give it to Lady Arderne.'

'Then I'll take you to her.' Running feet sounded behind them. There was a hoarse shout. 'Micky!'

The boy paled. Simon picked him up bodily, set him on the front of Jankin's saddle, mounted behind him and clapped his heels into the horse's sides. As Jankin lumbered into a trot, passersby threw themselves out of their path, cursing them roundly. They turned a corner into the broad expanse of Cheapside, then another into Friday Street. Soon they were dismounting in the courtyard of Montagu Inn. Peggotty hurried out, wimple fluttering.

'Master Simon, such goings on there's been. Another murder! Monique brought us word from Moulton Inn half an hour ago. Old John Hardyng. Joan wanted Lady Alyce to go there straight away. You're to follow as soon as you get back, taking word about the Ardernes, if you have news.'

'I will have soon. Where's Lady Arderne?'

'She's upstairs, praying for news of Peter.'

'Take this boy up to her. He's got a message for her from Sukey. Then get him something to eat and a decent shirt and

236

breeches.' He put his hands round Micky's pitifully thin waist and lifted him down into Peggotty's waiting arms.

'Little scrap,' said Peggotty, as she set Micky onto the ground. 'There's nothing of you. I'll bring you up some bread and milk.' She eyed Simon shrewdly.

'Go into the kitchen. There's tansy water in the jug. Drink plenty of it. And eat a saffron bun. Nothing like tansy and saffron for overindulgence.'

She took the dumbstruck Micky and led him into the house. Simon dismounted and walked into the kitchen. When he sat down on the bench by the fire, he realised how tired and hung-over he was. His brain raced. Who would want to kill John Hardyng? Then his throbbing head drooped.

Someone shook his shoulder and he groaned. It was Peggotty.

'No more snoring, Master Brailles. Get something to eat from the kitchen. Then go to the Sign of the Mole and tell Mistress Moulton that Sir Gervais is taking Peter to Oxfordshire, and Sukey too. They're travelling by barge and will wait for Sir Robert Harcourt at the White Hart at Henley.'

Simon staggered to his feet and went into the courtyard to find Jankin.

The Sign of the Mole

Alyce and Joan looked at the pathetically thin corpse, stinking of excrement, that lay stretched out on the long table in Joan's scriptorium. Matthew stood beside it, his face grey with misery.

'Where did you find him?' asked Alyce.

'Ned was taking a bucket of slops out to the midden,' said Matthew. 'The poor lad lent over with the bucket and got the shock of his life. Hardyng's face was leering up at him. Thought he was still alive. Ran back for help. We fished him out, but he's dead, as you can see.'

Alyce stared at the old man's mouth gaping in a ghastly rictus of surprise. He looked horribly like the *memento mori* cadaver Massingham had sketched for the undercroft of her tomb. His yellowed eyes glared, wide with shock. She felt in her pocket for two pennies, pulled his eyelids down and placed the coins on them.

'But he's just an old man,' said Joan. 'Who would do such a thing? And why?'

'What killed him?' asked Alyce.

'We'll have to wait for the coroner's deputy to tell us officially. I told Monique to fetch him after she'd called on you. But there's no doubt about what happened. He's been stabbed in the back. Right behind his heart. Whoever did it knew his business.'

'When was he last seen?'

Matthew thought for a minute. 'He checked that roll you asked to be copied, then asked for my scraper and pen to alter something. Cackling, he was. Then he rolled it up and handed it back to me with an evil grin. I paid him off and took it to my mistress. I didn't see him after that. I assumed he'd gone to find Brother Pietro.'

'When did Pietro leave?'

'I heard him tell Hardyng that he was going back to Clerkenwell to fetch his travelling pack and that he'd meet him at Paul's Cross. They were going to travel to Oxford together. Hardyng was hoping to sell copies of his revised chronicle there.'

'Presumably when Hardyng didn't turn up, Pietro left without him,' said Joan. 'It hadn't been his idea to travel with Hardyng, anyway. His face looked like a sour lemon when Hardyng suggested that they travel in company. But when Hardyng said he'd got places on a wagon, he agreed.'

'Do you know which way he was going?'

'The Uxbridge road, I would think. It's the king's highway, so it's well kept. He'll be given rides fast enough, what with friar's gown and his pilgrim badges.'

There were footsteps at the door and Simon came in, looking worried. 'I came as quickly as I could, my lady. Poor old Hardyng. What happened?'

'He was stabbed in the back, then pushed into the midden,' said Alyce. 'We don't know who by.'

Joan remembered his errand. 'Simon – how did you get on at the Mermaid? Is there any news of Sukey and Peter?'

'Yes. Sukey left a message with a kitchen boy, but he said he was only to deliver it to Lady Arderne. So I scooped him up and took him to Montagu Inn to see her. Sukey's message was

239

that Sir Gervais was taking her and Peter by barge to Henley to meet Sir Robert Harcourt.'

'Then we can go after them with Lord Oxford,' said Joan. 'You as well, Alyce. And Tamsin. Where is your little shadow, by the way?'

'She's Farhang's shadow today. They were both out when I got your message. I've only brought Pek with me. So have you heard from Vere?'

'He sent an answer to my note straight away. Said he'd be delighted to have our company. But not to bring too much with us. The barge is taking some chantry fittings to Syon Abbey and collecting furnishings for his new Oxford house. He's expecting us at Blackfriars Wharf at the turn of the morning tide.'

She contemplated Hardyng's corpse again. 'Shall we search him, Matthew?'

'Coroner won't be best pleased, but what's done can't be undone,' Matthew replied. He patted the front of the corpse, then beckoned to two journeymen who were standing nearby.

'Help me turn him over.' Together they lifted the body and turned it over, wiping their hands on their breeches afterwards. Alyce winced at the sight of the bloodstained wound. Matthew lifted first one arm, then the other, searching for a hidden pocket. And pocket there was. He felt into it, pulled out a bulging purse and poured its glittering contents out on to the table.

Joan raised her eyebrows. 'Where did Hardyng get that kind of money?'

'A reward?' suggested Alyce, poking through the coins thoughtfully. 'If he arranged for my *Tales* to be stolen, then this could have been his guerdon.'

'So Pailton's murder may not be connected with Hardyng's,' said Joan.

There was a commotion in the courtyard, a gabble of voices. Alyce stopped talking.

The door swung open and Wenlock entered, with two men in city livery at his heels.

He wrinkled his nose. 'Christ's bones, what a stench.' He walked over to the pathetic heap on the table. 'Who's this poor wretch?'

Matthew beckoned the journeymen again and, noses wrinkling, they turned the corpse over again.

'Jesus and all the archangels,' Wenlock exclaimed. 'John Hardyng, the chronicler.'

Joan snorted. 'The lying reprobate, rather. But God assoil his unquiet soul. I don't suppose he ever put much towards his time in purgatory. You don't usually attend a death, John. What brings you here?'

Wenlock's face was shuttered and unreadable. 'I was in the Guildhall when Monique brought the news, so I thought I would come myself, as we are friends. I'm sure that corpses are not good for your business. You'll want this settled right away. Who was first finder?'

'Ned, one of my apprentices.'

'Fetch him,' said Wenlock to Matthew, who bowed and disappeared. Wenlock stepped up to the corpse and looked at the ugly stab wound in Hardyng's back.

'No mistaking the cause of death. The blade is worked in most expertly. It isn't that easy to kill with a single stab. And I can guess from the smell where the body was found.'

He turned to his men. 'Search him.'

'We have already found something on him, John,' said Joan.

'Matthew, give Lord Wenlock the purse.' Wenlock took it, peered inside and raised a quizzical eyebrow.

'A fat reward for something, evidently. And yet the murderer can't have known of it, or he'd have taken it. Now, where's that apprentice?'

Matthew pushed a cowering Ned forward. He was quivering with fright.

With an effort, Wenlock smiled reassuringly. 'Come now, boy. No need to fear. You don't look like a murderer to me. Tell us how you discovered the body.' After looking around nervously, Ned managed to stutter a reply.

'I... I was emptying the night-soil pail from the journeymen's attic.'

'Wasn't it somewhat late to be doing that?' said Joan. 'It's a dawn task, isn't it?'

'Yes, but I forgot. I didn't remember until the maid who'd gone up to clean complained that it was still full. So I went up and carried the turds down and out to the foulings court and tossed it in. And then I saw him.' His voice trailed away and he shrunk back. If ever a boy wanted to make himself invisible, it was Ned. Speaking of shit in front of one of the highest ladies in the land, not to mention the exquisite Lord Wenlock, was excruciatingly embarrassing.

'And what time was this? Straight after you ate?'

'Yes. I was clearing the tables when the maid told me to go up to the attic.'

'And when you found him, who did you tell first?'

'I told Matthew.'

Wenlock turned to Matthew. 'Is anybody missing from the Sign of the Mole? One of the servants? Or the bookshop people?'

Matthew hesitated. 'Only Guy of Yarnton. He said that his mother was close to death and he needed to find nurses for her. So I told him to come back when he'd settled things. He doesn't often ask for time off and he looked as if he needed it. White as a sheet.'

'Guilt, perhaps,' said Wenlock. 'He could have just killed the old man.'

'Rubbish,' said Joan indignantly. 'Guy has been here since he was twelve. His mother is an old friend of mine who fell on hard times. She asked me to take him on and I've never regretted it. He's one of my most skilled workers and I would trust him with my life.'

Ignoring her, Wenlock turned to his men.

'When you've recorded the state of the body, take it to the Guildhall. And send out the watch to find this journeyman Guy. We'll hold the inquest on Tuesday morning. Master Cobham, Mistress Moulton, please be there at ten of the clock, with Ned.'

'But I'm leaving for Oxford on the early tide tomorrow,' Joan protested. Wenlock stared at her blankly.

'Well, you won't be able to,' he snapped. Then, with a bow to Alyce, he left the room. A few moments later, there was a clatter of hoofs, then the courtyard fell quiet.

Joan and Alyce looked at each other.

'I've never seen John in such taking,' said Joan. 'He looked at me as if he didn't know me. I wonder what's up.'

'I can guess,' said Alyce. 'I think he knew about Pailton's death all the time and fears that Hardyng's murder is linked to it somehow. Joan, did you check to see if there were any other books missing from the strongbox?'

Joan gave an embarrassed laugh. 'You were right to tell me

to have a look. There were. All Pailton's exemplars and his copies of my specials. What we call French books in the trade. Though they're in Latin as well. The pictures are – er – lively. You know, the sort of thing husbands tuck out of sight when their wives and daughters come in. Many men are hot for them. And quite a lot of women too, truth be told.'

'So perhaps whoever took my *Tales* was really after these "French" books?'

'That could well be,' said Joan. 'Bawdy books are worth a fortune if you know the market for them and keep them out of sight. They're risky stuff to handle, though. King Edward winks at them, as you'd expect, and isn't past accepting one, but Elizabeth is determined to prove herself a model of propriety. Anyone found with one is brought before the Consistory Court and imprisoned. Or given a humiliating penance and heavily fined.'

'Joan,' said Alyce, 'suppose, just suppose, that Guy took them for some reason and Hardyng saw him. Do you think that Guy would kill him to silence him? You said yourself that you thought his whole world would fall apart if he had to leave the Sign of the Mole.'

Joan shook her head resolutely. 'I would stake my life on Guy's honesty. If he killed Hardyng, why would he leave his body where it was sure to be discovered? My guess is that he's either in pursuit of whoever did kill Hardyng – or being pursued by them. Which means his own life could well be in danger. If he isn't dead already.'

Alyce pondered for a few seconds, weighing up the situation. She desperately wanted to return to her home. To Leo and the God's House and her own people. And, God willing, her beloved *Tales*, tucked away in Job Smith's Wallingford smithy. She'd done as much as she could for Cis Neville. Time now to put her own interests and those of her friend Joan to the fore.

'I suggest that Lady Arderne and I go with Vere tomorrow morning as we planned,' she said at last. 'She will be safe with us. You need to track Guy down and young James is appearing in the Court of Wards to plead Kate's case tomorrow afternoon. If we find Sir Gervais and Peter when we reach Henley, I should be able to make the old man see reason, even if we haven't had news of the Court's decision. Kate's sweet nature will speak for itself. Failing that, I will take her to Ewelme.'

'But what about your *Tales* and my lost books?' said Joan. 'The main reason for coming with you on the barge was to support Kate, but of course I also wanted to see if they were either with the stuff Pailton sent to Wallingford or with Cabal in Oxford.'

Alyce gave a wry smile. 'You can count on me to find them if I can. Bilton and I will visit Job Smith in Wallingford and then track down Cabal and Pietro in Oxford.'

Joan heaved a sigh. 'There's nothing else for it, I suppose.' She sat down heavily. 'Matthew, go and find Monique. I need to ask her if she knows anything about all this. She's closer to Guy than anyone else except his mother.' Matthew nodded and disappeared.

'I must go back to Montagu Inn to prepare for the journey,' said Alyce. 'And I've been summoned to see Cis Neville at Baynard's Castle after vespers. Joan, I'm sorry to leave you to cope with all this on your own. God willing, Lord Wenlock will let you follow us after the inquest. I'll leave Simon and Farhang in London to ride west with you.'

Joan glanced at Simon, saw his face fall and thought quickly.

'That's an excellent idea, Alyce. I couldn't have better allies,' she said with a warm smile which went a little way to lessen Simon's disappointment.

Alyce went over to Joan's desk and seized pen and paper. 'By your leave, Joan, I need to pen a couple of notes.' She wrote hastily, then sanded, folded and sealed two letters. She handed one to Pek.

'Joseph, this is for Duke John to tell him that I am returning to Ewelme on the Earl of Oxford's barge. You'll have to take it to Epping Lodge; he's hunting in the royal forest with friends.'

Then she turned to Simon. 'Please take this to Lord Vere at Oxford Place. It's in Lime Street ward, near Bishopsgate. When you've delivered it, come back to Montagu Inn. I want you to come with me to Baynard's Castle. A second pair of ears and eyes might be useful.'

Epping Forest

Jack de la Pole, internally quailing, outwardly resolute, stood with his spear at the ready. Bagot, the Epping Lodge huntsman, was, he knew, driving a boar towards him. A horn sounded in the distance and he heard the baying of a pack of hounds giving tongue. They were coming down a broad ride through the forest. And ahead of them came a snorting fiend from hell, small red eyes rolling in rage, snarling mouth open showing savage tusks. When the beast was a mere twenty yards away, Jack took a deep breath, stepped out from the sheltering trunk of a great oak tree and stood one foot forward, the other back, as he had been taught by the Fotheringay huntsman. He held his spear at waist height with its base firmly in the ground and the short cross piece on its shaft just in front of him. As the boar veered towards him, he thrust the spear deep into its gaping maw, keeping it there by bracing the cross piece against his armpit and continuing the thrust with his shoulder. It squealed in agony, then whirled back and round, whipping the spear away from Jack and hurtling at him again without a second's hesitation, oblivious of the spearhead deep in its jaws.

Forgetting all he'd been taught about dodging sideways, Jack turned and ran, but after a mere ten paces he caught his foot in a root and fell flat on his face. He felt the boar's tusks tearing at his buttocks and screeched in terror. His voice was drowned in the ferocious snarls of the mastiffs, largest and most powerful of hunting dogs. The boar turned away from Jack and began tossing them with its tusks, but sheer weight of numbers soon saw it downed. Through the mists of his pain, Jack saw the rest of the hunt approaching, most of them holding back cautiously. But one all too familiar figure, burly in his padded leather hunting jerkin, strode forward spear in hand and ministered the *coup de grâce*. He'll claim the credit of the kill, thought Jack bitterly. Clarence and Archbishop Neville, who had been hurrahing on the hunt from a safe distance, came up and watched as Sir Robert Harcourt slit the boar's belly, yanked out its guts and threw them to the salivating hounds.

'Are you able to stand, your grace?' It was Bagot. 'Looks as if your buskins saved your life. His tusks glanced off them. From what I can see, you only have a flesh wound. You'll think twice before sitting down for a while, but you'll live to finish off your next kill yourself. It was featly done, my lord. Your stance and timing were perfect. But next time step sideways

247

briskly as he charges again, drawing your dagger as you do and get in behind the ear. It's just a matter of timing.'

A little comforted, Jack struggled to his feet. Clarence turned to him.

'Like you to botch it, Roly-Poly,' he sneered.

'That's not fair,' protested George Neville. 'I've never seen such a monster. Much fiercer than the one that did John Paston such damage this morning before it was downed. Jack deserves credit for spearing him. The beast would have done the hounds and Harcourt a lot more damage if he hadn't had his maw full.'

'It was nothing to the one I killed at Windsor last week,' said Harcourt, turning away.

Clarence followed him back towards the copse where the horses had been concealed.

Archbishop Neville shrugged. 'Don't mind Harcourt, Jack. He's a churl, for all his boasted ancestors. And in an almighty bad temper for some reason. Lean on me. We'll find somewhere to rest you. You can't ride like that.' He turned towards the group of men butchering the boar.

'Bagot, get one of your men to run to the house and return with a litter.' He led Jack towards a fallen tree and helped him to lie back against it. Then he pulled out a leather flask and removed its stopper.

'Have a swallow of this. I think we better get you to the Manor of the Rose as soon as we can. Bess will see to your wounds. John Paston is returning to London to have his torn arm treated. You can share a cart. Looks as if you'll have a black eye from the tumble you took. Lucky your lady mother is to leave town.'

'Leave town?'

'Yes. That one-armed veteran of hers brought word to the

lodge a couple of hours after you and Bagot left to track the boar. She is setting out for Ewelme early tomorrow. The Earl of Oxford is taking her by water as far as Henley.'

Jack paled. 'Does Harcourt know?'

'Yes. He didn't seem best pleased. Swore like a bargee himself and went into a huddle with that henchman of his.'

'Savernake?'

'That's the one. Not a man I'd like to meet in a dark wood. He'd only lately arrived, but Harcourt sent him off again at the double. Then he told that silly young whore of his to pack her things and tell his squire to get his own bagged up as well. Told me he had to ride for Windsor as soon as the hunt was over. Does he have business with your lady mother, then?'

Jack hesitated, then muttered, 'I don't know.'

'What's worrying you, then?'

'I owed him a hundred marks. He offered to cancel the debt if I would lend him the Suffolk barge to take his new ward to Oxfordshire. But when my mother came to London, she asked about the barge. I lied. I told her that it was in Horner's boatyard. If she comes across it on the river, she'll be furious. Do you know why she left? Where is Pek?'

'He left the note for you and went back to London.'

'For me? Where is it?'

Neville had the grace to blush. 'Clarence broke the seal and read the letter out to us. Then he threw it in the fire. It just said that she was leaving on the first tide tomorrow morning for Ewelme and sent her blessing for the hunt. Which she clearly assumed was tomorrow. As well she might. Heaven certainly punished us. Not a hart to be seen, Paston's arm ripped open and that nasty wound to your buttock. You should have a physician look at it as soon as you can.'

'Pray God it doesn't prevent me competing in the Burgundy tournament,' said Jack with a grimace of pain. 'I've just ordered the finest of jousting armours. You're right, Neville. I will send for Farhang when I get back to Lombard Street.'

'Farhang Amiri? You couldn't have a better doctor. But I thought he'd retired to the God's House at Ewelme. Isn't he all but blind?'

'Not yet, though he takes a guide with him if he's out and about. Close up, he sees as sharply as ever. He came up to London with my mother and my wife in case Bess or the baby needed him.'

'Did he indeed?' said Neville. 'Is there any chance of persuading him to stay in London, do you think? I'd make it worth his while.'

'I doubt it,' said Jack. 'It isn't a matter of money. He likes the way things are at Ewelme. Lots of clever young Oxford men visiting and more and more retired scholars living in the God's House. He and my mother both think of nothing but books. She spends a fortune on them. My fortune. Roll on the day she meets her maker and I can start living in earnest. She's managed the estates by herself for as long as I can remember. Even when my father was alive, he was busy with politics in London and left country matters to her. Five years ago, when I came of age, she did say that she wanted me to do more, but whenever I used my initiative she complained that I've got it wrong. Anyway, I'd rather be at court than down in Suffolk or Oxfordshire. She'll die soon, hopefully.'

Neville shook his head.

'You are too adamant against your mother, Jack. She is a most excellent lady, who has your best interests at heart. Remember the letter that your father wrote to you before he went into exile. He told you that she was your best and truest adviser. He didn't want you to make the mistakes that he did, trusting in treacherous friends instead of in her.'

'But she keeps me short the whole time. I can barely maintain the dignity of a duke.'

'You barely deserve the title, my lad. From what little I know of your affairs, when Alyce dies and the jointures from her two previous marriages revert, the Suffolk dukedom will have no better financial basis than an earldom.'

Jack looked startled. 'What do you mean?'

Neville stared at him. 'You surely know that your father's personal wealth was almost entirely based on offices granted to him by Henry VI. They all resumed to the Crown after his disgrace. It was only Henry's fondness for your mother that saved your dukedom.'

The young duke looked sullen. 'But Harcourt said I'd be a wealthy man if she was...' He broke off, biting his lip.

'If she was what?'

'If she was disgraced.'

'What can you mean, Jack?' said Neville. 'Don't tell me you're conniving in your mother's downfall! You won't gain a penny if you do. Everything she has will go into Edward's coffers. He'll probably put Harcourt in charge of administering her personal estates until they revert to the Philips and the Montagues when she dies. You'll have nothing but the Suffolk lands and no money to run them. You're a fool to trust Harcourt, Jack. He's had his eye on Ewelme since before you were born.'

Two men carrying a stretcher made from ash staves and leather lacings came into view, trotting in quick time.

'But I'm married to the king's sister,' Jack protested. 'And if I've helped to unearth treasons, surely Edward will reward me.'

'Not if his wife has a say in it. And she will have. As you know all too well, the king hasn't even paid your wife's dowry in full. Get on the stretcher. And then get back to the Manor of the Rose. And when you've recovered enough, see if you can't mend the damage you've done.'

Baynard's Castle

When they arrived at Baynard's Castle, Alyce and Simon were escorted up to the Duchess of York's private chamber. Cis sat on a chair of state, a trestle table in front of her and her monkey ensconced in its specially made highchair at her side. Her once-beautiful eyes had a fatigued, faraway look and Alyce felt a surge of pity for the indomitable woman who had been England's first lady until Edward married Elizabeth. Now she was fighting desperately to maintain her influence with her son.

'Sit down beside me, my dear. And Master Brailles, pull up a stool. Is that the roll? Spread it out and let's have a look at your opinion of my relations' loyalties. Would you like some refreshment?'

Alyce was suddenly aware that she had not eaten dinner.

'A glass of wine would be welcome. And some bread.'

'Cook will insist on finer fare than bread.' Cis nodded to the footman who had brought Alyce upstairs and he left the room. Then she watched as Alyce spread the roll out in front of her, anchoring its corners with four heavy candlesticks. She looked at the underlined names and nodded.

'Shrewdly chosen. But it would come as no surprise to anybody if Bastard Fauconberg sortied from Sark flying the red rose. He has long been a law unto himself. As for Henry and Edward, they are both past caring what happens in this world. Nor can I credit it that Katherine has a mind for anything but that young husband of hers. Which leaves Buckingham's widow and Warwick's little sister. Surely they can't be involved. Anne is too old, Meg too young. Pailton must have been bluffing.'

Alyce opened her mouth to answer, but stopped at the sound of the door opening. The footman and a page entered, each carrying a loaded tray.

'Put them on the sideboard, Giles, then leave us,' said Cis. 'Master Brailles will serve us.' Once they had disappeared, Simon stood up and brought goblets of wine and a dish of prettily iced sweetmeats over to them.

'Does the duchess know about Hardyng?' he whispered as he presented a goblet to Alyce.

'What's that he's saying?' snapped Cis. 'There should be no secrets between us.'

Alyce took a deep draught of the wine before replying.

'I was called to Moulton Inn this afternoon because another body has been found. It was old John Hardyng, the chronicler. Stabbed. His body had been stuffed in the midden.'

'I can't say I'm surprised,' said Cis. 'He was a master of vitriol and dealt in lies. But do you think his murder has a link to Pailton?'

'I don't know,' said Alyce. 'It could equally well be connected to the theft of my *Tales*.'

'Your *Tales of Canterbury* that Moulton's were rebinding? Stolen? But how?'

'I wish I knew. But Hardyng could have had something to do with it.'

'Did anyone see him arrive at Moulton Inn this morning?'

'He may never have left after the book sale yesterday. The house was thronged with customers. Anyone of them could have killed him and hidden the body until there was a chance to pull it into the midden.'

Simon had a sudden vision of the gaunt Dominican who had been sitting next to Hardyng at dinner. 'What about Brother Pietro?' he said. 'Weren't he and Hardyng supposed to be heading to Oxford together? But when Farhang met him in the apothecary's shop, he was trying to raise money to travel alone.'

'That's right,' said Alyce. 'They were going to meet at Paul's Cross. But what motive could he have had?'

Cis had been staring at the roll as she drank her wine. 'That's curious. Hardyng has not added John Vere as little Meg's husband. But he knew they planned to wed next week.'

Alyce leant over and gazed at the far end of the long line of the descendants of Richard Neville, Earl of Salisbury, headed by his oldest son Richard Neville, Earl of Warwick, and ending with that of his youngest daughter.

'Actually, it looks as if he did and then scraped it out. How curious. Matthew did say that he made a correction. Perhaps he miswrote it and then got distracted and forgot to write it in again.'

'Or perhaps he thought it too soon to record it,' said Simon. 'After all, Vere isn't her husband yet.'

Suddenly Cis stood up, pushed the candlesticks off the corners of the family tree and rolled it up.

'Alyce, thank you for all that you've done. Now I want you

to forget all this. Go back to Ewelme and your old scholars and your books and your dreams by the fire. Never mind the loss of your *Tales*. You can have an even finer copy made. And beware. You have powerful enemies, as you discovered last year. Fortunately, you also have loyal friends.' She drained her goblet, walked over to the sideboard and refilled it.

Simon was reminded of the words of the anchoress. 'Tell her to be wary of those she trusts most.' He saw his mistress's puzzled frown.

'But why have you changed your mind, Cis? Has Hardyng's death got anything to do with it?'

'No,' said Cis. 'I invited you here to tell you to stop investigating.'

Alyce frowned. 'But there have been two unexplained deaths.'

'Quite so. And I'd rather there were no more.'

'But what about the traitor Neville you were so concerned about?'

'As I said, I think Pailton was lying. He was desperate to leave the country. Anyway, his secret, if he had one, seems to have died with him. Now, go. Harcourt has some damning evidence against you, it seems. I know not what. Leave London as speedily as you may. The wolves are running. And Alyce, I hate to tell you, but your own cub runs with them.' She handed the roll to Simon and swept out of the room.

Alyce stared after her mystified. What could the evidence be? And how was it linked to the murders of two of the most unwarlike men imaginable and the theft of her *Tales*? 'And your own cub runs with them.' She remembered the fragment of parchment with her signature that Margaret Grafton had found in Pailton's pen case. Her heart sank and a great weariness swept over her. She remembered Jack's discontented face at George Neville's feast, the sly way he had looked at her. How distant he had been.

Simon saw her expression and stepped towards her nervously. She waved him away. Her puzzlement had changed to grim determination.

'Don't worry, Simon. I have no intention of leaving Joan in the lurch. We'll go back to Ewelme, but not to give up.'

Montagu Inn

Alyce had settled herself down by the hearth of her chamber when the door opened and Tamsin came in, carrying a tray of food that Peggotty had prepared. Farhang was with her, munching on a drumstick he'd removed from it.

Alyce raised her eyebrows. 'Have you no respect, Farhang?'

'You won't grudge me provender when you hear how fully I have earnt it, my lady. Tamsin and I have been ferreting around to great purpose. We know who killed Pailton and why.'

Alyce glanced sharply at Tamsin, then back at Farhang. 'You should not have got Tamsin involved in this. She's only a child. And from what the Duchess of York has just told me, it seems that I am now the hunted, not the huntress.'

'Tamsin's got a more sensible head on her shoulders than many twice her age, your grace,' said Farhang firmly. 'Anyway, involved she is. Now, don't you want to know about Pailton?'

'I've been told to stop investigating his death and to leave London or risk downfall. But, yes, I do want to know the truth. Tell me all.'

'Pailton was deeply involved in spreading propaganda to

discredit Edward and Elizabeth using a printing press with moveable type here in London.'

Alyce opened her eyes wide in astonishment. 'A press like the ones Joan told me she saw in Cologne? In London? But where?'

'It was hidden in the Hospitallers' Priory at Clerkenwell. Pailton was taken by Tiptoft's men and tortured until he told them about the press, but they overdid things and he died without revealing its whereabouts or who was responsible for it. They hid his broken body in the charnel house, but the girl who found the kites scavenging for his flesh told local people – among them Owen, Agnes's grandson. Agnes is at the heart of things. Her daughter Bronwen was Pailton's wife and they were all in on the secret. When you told Lord Wenlock that Cis Neville knew about his death, he thought, wrongly, that Agnes had told her. She'd been under suspicion for some time. Then he made the connection with Clerkenwell, where she lives, and told Lord Tiptoft and Harcourt of his suspicions. It is all over town that the constable's men raided the priory yesterday evening. But they found nothing. The press had been spirited away in time.'

'Who by? And where is it now? And how do you know all this?'

'Entirely by chance. Tamsin came with me on my morning rounds, then I took her to Malachi Fryse's shop in Spurrier Row to restock. I've been so busy in London that my supplies were running low. Agnes banged on the door in search of a hiding place. She was being chased by Sir Robert Harcourt's henchman Savernake and his men. After they'd gone, Sir Thomas Malory came in with Agnes's grandson Owen.'

'Malory? He was at the Royal when I visited Wenlock. What has he got to do with all this?'

'A great deal. Sir Thomas was in charge of the press.'

'Jesu and St John! Wenlock told me that he was a corrodian in Clerkenwell Priory. But I thought he'd gone over to York. He fought with Warwick at Dunstanborough.'

'Although he bowed his knee to Edward, covertly he's been doing everything he can to rock his throne. When he got word of the planned raid, he and Agnes engineered the dismantling of the press and its removal from the priory. Through the watergate, I presume. It was taken up the Thames on a barge.'

Alyce considered. 'John Langstrother must have known about it, but neither he nor Sir Thomas seem likely organisers of such an enterprise. The mastermind must of course be the Neville that Pailton claimed was a traitor to York. Do you have any idea who he is? Or where the press is?'

'They told us nothing of a Neville. They said it was safer for us to know as little as possible. But they did say that Joan was involved. Though she didn't know that the press was used for politicking. As a cover for its real purpose, it was also printing bawdy books. For which Joan has many keen customers.' Farhang paused and chuckled. 'Among them Sir John Wenlock. Who thought that Joan smuggled the books into the country and was happy to turn a blind eye to such a trade. He had no idea that they were being printed in Clerkenwell.'

Alyce helped herself absentmindedly to a marzipan tart. 'We all have hidden sides. What a tangle of deceits.'

Farhang cleared his throat. 'It gets worse, my lady. The constable and Sir Robert have told the king that you and the Earl of Oxford are involved with the press. They went to the king this morning to demand warrants to arrest both of you. Fortunately, I managed to create a distraction. The king's mother invaded the audience and persuaded Edward it was absurd. Actually, to do the king credit, I think he would have refused anyway. He's fond of both you and my lord of Oxford. But Harcourt is not deterred. He swore he would offer proof at Windsor that you and Vere are traitors.'

Alyce was silent for a minute. 'Which is why Cis told me to stop looking into Pailton's death. But why do they think Vere is part of the treason? Is he?'

'I don't know.'

'Why didn't you tell me all this earlier?'

'You've been out all day, my lady. And then I got called out to Lombard Street. Your son was injured hunting boar this afternoon in Epping Forest.'

'This afternoon? On Sunday? The godless fool. I assumed the hunt was to be on Monday. Was he badly hurt?'

'Fortunately not, though he'll have cause to remember it every time he sits down for a few weeks.'

Alyce's face grew sombre, remembering Cis's warning. 'Farhang, Cis didn't say much, but she did hint that… that Jack was less than loyal to me. I know that he's proud of working for Lord Tiptoft, but surely he wouldn't involve himself in anything that would harm me. Surely, too, he would warn me if he came to hear of it.'

'Whatever he may have been up to, he repents of it now. Leave him to me, my lady. I said I would visit him again in the morning.'

'Thank you, Farhang. He is not a bad man at heart, just a weak one. A child deprived of his father often is. I wonder if he knows anything about Hardyng's death. Perhaps Tiptoft and Harcourt are involved in that as well. Though I can't imagine why.'

Farhang frowned. 'Hardyng? Dead?'

'I'm forgetting. You can't have heard. His body was found in the midden at Moulton Inn today.'

'Was he drunk? When did it happen?'

'He may have been drunk, but it was a knife in his back that killed him. He also had a fat purse under his cloak. Wenlock himself came when Joan called for the coroner. It looks as if Guy of Yarnton was responsible, though Joan won't hear of it. Wenlock sent the watch to search for him. The inquest is to be held tomorrow.' She hesitated, mind racing. 'He was in the devil of a temper, come to think of it. Told Joan that she couldn't go with me and Lady Arderne on Vere's barge tomorrow. Perhaps he's in deeper water than he likes.'

'He was ever one to trim to the wind,' said Farhang. 'Are you going to go to Oxfordshire with Vere? If you and he are jointly suspected of treason, then is it wise to travel together?'

Alyce walked over to the window and looked out. She imagined the broad reaches of the Thames, the peace and calm of the water. And her own home, wrapping her round in an all-embracing quilt of possessions freighted with memories. Then she turned back to Farhang.

'Perhaps not. But I love the river and I long to get back. Here I feel like a rabbit in a trap.'

'Can I speak, Lady Alyce?'

They both turned at the sound of Tamsin's voice.

'I'd quite forgotten you were there, child,' said Alyce. 'What is it?'

'Wouldn't it look more innocent if you *did* travel together?

To change your plans, which Lord Wenlock knows of, might look as if you had something to hide.'

Farhang nodded thoughtfully. 'She's quite right. I told you she had a good deal of nous, my lady. Go boldly and openly. And God speed you both. Simon and I will see what we can do here in London.'

The Thames

Vere was immensely proud of his barge. Sleek and black-hulled, it had a scattering of silver stars on the great black sail. This was furled around a mighty spar, fastened amidships to the mast and ready to be hoisted when there was a favourable wind. Hubert the bosun led Alyce and Kate to two of the ornate chairs in the curtained tilt at its stern and put a stool for Tamsin beside them. Vere, who prided himself on his steering, stood behind the tilt at the tiller, a silver-grey hound at his side.

'Are you warm enough, Lady Alyce?' he called forward. 'We have more fur rugs in the hold.'

'This one is keeping both me and Lady Arderne warm, thank you Sir John. Who built your barge, by the by? I like her lines.'

'Horner of Sheen,' said Vere. 'She's won the barge race from there to Kingston several times. She's light for her length and has two extra oarsmen.'

'Horner's is where my own barge is lying up,' said Alyce. 'She has some rot in her stem, apparently. She's being repaired, but I'm thinking of having another one built. Something smaller and fleeter to keep by me at Ewelme.'

As they neared Westminster, the hound whined, shivering in the wind. Vere glanced at him.

'Would you mind Wraith joining you in the tilt?' he asked Alyce.

'I'd welcome her. I miss my own Leo, but London is no place for him. He's used to running free.'

Vere handed the tiller to Hubert and clicked his fingers. Wraith followed him into the tilt and curled up at his feet when he sat down opposite Alyce and Kate.

'What kind of dog is Leo?'

'A tawny gold hound with a brave tail which he waves like a banner. Gifted in finding birds my falcons kill. And gentle with babes, fortunately. My third grandson was born at Ewelme at Christmas time.'

'Wraith is a rache. Lightning quick and excellent at following a scent. But not good with children. She'll live in the kennels when we're lucky enough to have family.'

They talked happily of the dogs best suited to different kinds of hunting as they passed Fulham Palace, where Alyce remembered King Henry holding court a decade earlier. Alyce was steadily revising her opinion of Vere. Especially when he led the conversation around to Meg, which he did often. He clearly adored her.

Soon Syon Abbey came into sight. In a smoothly synchronised movement, the oarsmen dipped the edges of their blades into the water to slow the barge. Vere stood up. 'We've time for you and Lady Arderne and your maid to refresh yourselves while we unload the fittings for the lady chapel that I've brought for the convent. We're picking up panelling, stained glass and some other furnishings for my new Oxford house.'

Once they were moored, Alyce, Kate and Tamsin disembarked and walked across a flower-filled meadow to the abbey. Abbess Elizabeth was delighted to see them again and they sat at a table on the convent's terrace dipping twists of soft white bread into their wine while numerous irregularly shaped bundles were taken out of the hold and put on the riverbank. Then the abbess and Vere disappeared into the abbey. It was almost half an hour before a heavily laden wagon trundled across the meadow to bring the furnishings for Oxford to the barge and take the bundles from the barge back to the abbey, and it took another hour for Vere to come back.

Once they had left Syon, the easterly breeze blew to such good effect that they hoisted the great square sail and the oarsmen rested while Hubert steered. They passed the royal palace of Sheen and Horner's boatyard. Alyce looked along the boats pulled up along its foreshore, but couldn't see *Lyonesse*. Perhaps she was being worked on in a boatshed. The tide had only just begun to slacken when they reached the limit of its reach at Teddington. Runners had been sent ahead to arrange for a team of horses to draw them through its awkward shallows. It made a welcome break when, to make the barge lighter, everyone got out and waited in the Tide's End Tavern.

'Never rains but it pours,' remarked the hosteller when he brought out ale for the crew of the barge. 'You're the second great barge this week.'

'Who was on the other?' asked Tamsin.

'I don't rightly know. They didn't do us the favour of stopping. Rowing like the clappers, they were.'

An hour later, they lowered sail as they neared Kingston. Hubert swung the great hourglass fixed on the barge's centre-post over to begin its fourth filling.

'Do you want to stop here, your grace?' called Vere as Kingston Bridge came into sight. 'We could do with getting food and water.'

'How long until Windsor?' asked Alyce.

'Another five hours. Stopping at Syon took longer than I

had planned. We won't be there before nightfall. But we can travel by night if you wish. There's a full moon and Hubert knows the river like the back of his hand.'

Just then the barge was hailed by a skiff rowed by two men. In its stern were barrels and baskets.

'Water-O!' one of them called out. 'Fresh eels! Pork pies! Lardy cakes! Everything you need for your journey, masters!'

'Let's get what we need from these fellows and keep going,' said Alyce.

'Rest your oars, men,' commanded Vere. The skiff threw a rope up to the barge and the bosun lent over the gunwale and began to bargain.

After the supplies had been loaded, the *Silver Swan* pulled away. The bosun made his way to the stern cabin and bowed to Vere.

'My lord, the boatman said that we needed to take great care as we go under the bridge. A coal barge sank trying to negotiate it last week and its heaped load has damaged the bottoms of several passing barges already. Last Saturday a state barge like your own had to pull in at the boatyard for repair. He thinks our keel should clear it, but he says to keep well to the starboard side of the channel.'

They approached the massive wooden structure of the bridge cautiously, Hubert beating a drum so that they kept a slow, measured rhythm. When they had just enough speed to glide through, he gave the command to ship oars and they began an eerily silent progress between the stone piers that supported its central span. The men on the starboard side knelt beside the gunwale and used the bridge's heavy supporting timbers to keep the barge moving. Once through, the great sail was hoisted again and they made good speed, passing several small islands edged with fish traps. Near Desborough the lookout in the bow called a warning and they saw that there was a net, held up by inflated pig's bladders stretched right across the river at the point where it narrowed near a large island.

'Ship oars!' Vere called and the barge slowed. Two men sitting on the bank jumped to their feet and began to haul at the net. But it had clearly snagged on something underwater and they tugged in vain.

'Cut through it,' the bosun called to the lookout. 'They're poachers. No man is allowed to impede boats passing on the king's water highways.' The lookout drew a long-bladed knife and was beginning to saw away at the net when Alyce gave an imperious command.

'Stop that. It'll take forever and it wastes a good net, which they probably stole. Just pierce the bladders until there's room for us to pass over.' Startled, the lookout looked back at Vere for approval. Vere nodded and he began stabbing at the bladders on each side of the boat until enough of the net sank down for them to pass through.

'We're fortunate to have this easterly wind countering the flow of the river,' said Alyce.

'I fear it's dropping,' said Vere. 'That last weir was Daylop Hill. Barringer's Inn is just round the next bend. I suggest we stop there for an hour and eat. It's only three hours to Windsor from here and there are no more weirs.'

Alyce, Kate, Tamsin and Vere went inside as soon as they tied up at the tavern's wharf, but the crew sat in front of Barringer's Inn watching the last rays of the sun disappear behind the hill opposite as they waited for the innkeeper to bring out supper. The dark silhouette of a great barge, its oarsmen pulling with all their might, came into view.

'They're in a hurry, right enough,' said Herbert to his mate. 'Must be paying the oarsmen double rates. Maybe it's the one that was damaged last Saturday.'

'It's a state barge, not a hire one, right enough,' said the mate. 'What's its ensign?' But as they strained their eyes to see the motif on the flag, it crumpled and disappeared. Minutes afterwards, a great lantern was carried to the bow of the barge and hung from its prow.

'Quite right too. Standards should be downed at sunset and navigation lights lit. Pity the poor night fishermen otherwise. But I can't help wondering who's racing upstream as if the hounds of hell were after them.'

'Up to no good, if you ask me.'

'You might as well say that about us.'

'True enough. I expect they're hoping to find beds in Windsor too.'

'Likely they are. It's well that my Lord Oxford sent to the Waterman's Arms Inn to keep rooms for us. We'll be needing our beds by the end of the day.'

Four hours later, the formidable bulk of Windsor Castle appeared above the south bank of the river.

'Where to, my lord?' shouted Herbert from behind them.

'Head for the wharf this side of the bridge,' Vere called back.

'There's already a barge tied up there. The one that passed us back at Barringer's, I expect.'

'There's room for us too. We can't risk the bridge in the dark and our inn, the Waterman's Arms, is on this side.'

'Let's hope that they've kept our rooms. Lady Alyce, let me help you ashore. I have a lantern to light the way.'

But Alyce had already stepped nimbly off *Silver Star* and onto the wharf.

Tamsin followed her to see her mistress staring at the other barge's transom in consternation.

'But that's *Lyonesse*. My barge. Jack said she was at Horner's boatyard, being repaired.'

'Are you sure?' said Vere, who had followed them onto the wharf with Herbert.

'God's wounds, of course I'm sure,' snapped Alyce. 'I'd know her anywhere.' Seeing Herbert's shocked face, she added a mumbled apology.

'Perhaps his grace told the boatyard to take it down to Ewelme as soon as it was ready,' said Kate.

Alyce nodded slowly, unconvinced.

'Or perhaps he's bringing it down to you himself. For a surprise.' It was Tamsin.

Alyce couldn't help smiling. 'Dear Tamsin. Always hopeful. But Jack is in London, recovering from his injury. He must have lent the barge to someone.'

'Let's go to the inn and find out who's aboard,' said Vere.

'Good idea,' said Alyce, heart heavy and mind racing. Jack had lied to her about the barge. And, it was beginning to appear, about much else.

The courtyard of the great inn was quiet. A lantern hung over the main porch. A sleepy watchman fussed with a bundle of keys and opened the door to the hall. The logs on the great hearth were still glowing red, and Alyce, Kate and Tamsin walked thankfully over to it to warm themselves. The watchman poked a bundle of blankets on one of the wide benches that flanked the hearth and there was a startled grunt. The tousled head of a little chambermaid poked out of the blankets, startled at the sight of great folks. She scrambled to her feet, yawning and flustered.

'But you've already arrived,' she said.

'What on earth do you mean, child?' said Alyce. 'Take us to our rooms at once. I trust you've aired the beds and put warming bricks in them.'

'I did,' the girl answered. But you're already in them.'

They looked at each other, puzzled. Then light dawned for Kate. 'The other barge. She's put the people from it into our beds.'

'Then she can turf them out of them,' said Alyce.

The chambermaid gasped. 'But... but...'

Vere intervened. 'With respect, your grace, we are much later than the inn expected us to be. We'll find out who arrived on your barge in the morning. They will surely be men and women of rank, perhaps friends of your son. And I suspect we will be quite comfortable down here. We can put bedding on the benches in the chimney breast for you and Lady Arderne. Tamsin can have a truckle beside you, and Hubert and I will quarter ourselves in the kitchen, on the other side of the chimney. We'll probably be a good deal warmer down here than upstairs. The crew can sleep in the loft above the stables.'

Alyce considered. Vere was right. They might well be better off down here than in some flea-infested chamber upstairs. She turned to the quaking girl. 'Who are your guests?'

'There's an old gentleman and two children in one room and oarsmen in the other.'

Kate gasped. 'Children? It must be Peter and Sukey. And the old gentleman must be Sir Gervais. We've found them. I must go up.' She made for the stairs, but Alyce grabbed her arm.

'Kate, listen. Waking them in the middle of the night is the wrong way to go about things, especially if it isn't the Ardernes at all.' She turned to the maid. 'Can you bring us bedding?'

The maid shook her head. 'The men took everything we had.'

'No matter,' said Vere. 'We'll bring the seat mattresses, cushions and rugs in from the barge. See to it, Herbert.'

The bosun nodded and went out with two of the men.

The maid looked relieved.

'Can you warm us up possets?' Tamsin asked. 'Milk, with an egg, honey and a little nutmeg.'

The girl nodded and disappeared. Tamsin piled more logs onto the fire.

Half an hour later, everything was arranged and Alyce, Kate and Tamsin were cosily tucked up by the now cheerfully blazing fire, sipping their drinks.

'This reminds me of the time I went to the Midsummer Bonfire when I was a young girl,' Alyce said sleepily. 'William Stonor, God rest his soul, the grandfather of the Will you know, was a playmate of mine and he had dared me to it. I never refused a dare. I crept out of bed after my parents were asleep and he was by the postern gate with two ponies. We headed for Ivinghoe Beacon with a mind to see the mid-summer fires blazing all across the valley. Both of us were too young to realise how far it was and what danger we were in. William's pony put her hoof into a pothole and fell, so he climbed up on mine. She went slower and slower and it got darker and darker. We weren't even halfway to the Beacon when some men came out of the woods beside the highway, as shocked to see us as we were to see them. They'd got rabbits slung over their shoulders, so I realised they were poachers. Then I recognised one of them. It was Ewan from our own Ewelme stables. We stared at each other and I could see that he was even more frightened than I was. I blurted out, "I won't tell if you won't." They went into a huddle for a bit, then they all went off, leaving Ewan with us. "I'm taking you to the Fox and Hounds Inn at Christmas Common; you'll be safe there," he said. "But pray you, keep your word, my lady." "A Chaucer always keeps her word," I said. And I did. The inn folk tucked us up for the night by the hearth and sent a messenger to Ewelme in the morning. William and I both got a whipping, just as we deserved.' She winced at the memory, then chuckled. 'Ewan never went poaching again, I suspect. He's a great-grandfather now, living out Bensington way. He and I never meet without him giving me a wink.'

She heard a gentle snore from Tamsin and looked across the fire to Kate. Also asleep. She wondered how much of the story either of them had heard before they fell asleep. Reaching out, she took the handle of the hooded iron curfew and placed it over the glowing embers to preserve them for the morning. Then she snuggled down under the furred rugs from the barge, with a hot brick wrapped in flannel between her feet.

Upstairs in the inn, Sukey stirred in her bed and opened her eyes. It was deep dark in the room. Peter, curled up beside her for warmth, was fast asleep. Sir Gervais snored loudly in the great bed on the other side of the room and Tobias echoed him in the truckle bed beside it. She could hear people's voices in the room underneath them. She went over to the window and looked out into the inn yard. A gang of men, one carrying a lantern, the rest with long poles, were trooping across it to the stable. The man with the lantern put it down and opened the door, and the men laid down the poles and went inside.

'Plenty of straw in the loft. Ladder's on your right.'

She recognised the voice as that of the porter. And when he closed the door and picked up the lantern, she saw that the long poles were actually oars. Only fools left oars in their boats at night. So it was another barge. Perhaps a means of escape back to London. She tiptoed back to her bed and felt for the cloaks that they had spread over it to keep them warm and for their shoes, the only items of clothing that they had taken off. She rolled them up into a bundle and hefted it under one arm. Then she poked Peter. He stirred and gave a little moan. She put her hand gently over his mouth and hissed in his ear.

'Peter, don't make a noise. Just get up and take my hand. We're going to get you back to your mamma.' Obediently, the little boy clambered out of bed. Just as they were nearing the door, Sir Gervais gave a snore so loud that he woke himself up. He sat up and felt for the beaker of water that he'd put on his bedside table and took three loud gulps. The children froze. Could he see them? There was a yawning sigh, then the sound of his body sinking back and a rustle as he pulled blankets and coverlet back up over himself. Sukey waited a full minute, then led Peter across to the door, lifting its heavy wooden latch as slowly and quietly as she could. Once it was open enough for them to slip out onto the gallery that gave access to the inn's two upstairs chambers, she pushed it to behind them, without risking the latch again.

'Careful on the steps, Peter. We mustn't make a sound.'

At the bottom of the steps, she took Peter's hand and crept around the edge of the courtyard, keeping in the shadows. When they reached the gatehouse, she saw to her horror that a huge iron bar, far too heavy for her to lift, had been locked down across its great double doors. Worse, there was a light in the porter's room and the deep sound of men's voices. An argument of some kind was going on.

'Well, I say you are a cheating braggart.'

'Pay up, Grady. The dice fell badly for you, that's all. You promised Mark your drinking horn.'

'I'll give it to you in the morning. My pack is still on the barge.'

'I'll have none of that. Go and get it now.'

There was the scrape of something hard and a man staggered out of the porter's lodge. Sukey and Peter shrank into the shadows. He lifted the iron bar across the little door in the great gate and disappeared through it, leaving it open.

'Come on, Peter,' said Sukey. 'This is our chance.' They followed the man at a distance and watched from behind a tree as he stepped onto the barge behind the one that they had travelled in.

He stepped on board, hailing its watchman as he disappeared below. 'At ease, Stephen. I'm just getting something from my pack.' He re-emerged and wove his way drunkenly back towards the inn.

Sukey watched thoughtfully, then whispered to Peter. 'We must get on that barge, Peter, and hide ourselves. But we must be quiet as mice.'

Sukey helped Peter over the gunwale, then the two children crept carefully along the deck to the cuddy at the far end of the barge. Inside was a jumble of anchor chain and sailcloth. Sukey pushed it aside to make room for herself and Peter and they wriggled as far inside as they could. She wrapped their cloaks around them and they huddled together, hearts beating. Had anyone seen them? But all was silence. Peter's breathing slowed as he slept again. Sukey stared through a knothole in the planking at the sweeping arc of stars above them until sleep claimed her too.

The Sign of the Mole

Joan tossed and turned in her great feather bed in the upper chamber of Moulton Inn. From St Paul's, a sonorous bell tolled for matins. She began to think about Hardyng. What on earth had he done to cause someone to kill him? He wasn't a brave man; nor would he ever have risked himself for a cause. Though he would for gain. Or, she reflected, out of spite. She remembered the malevolent gleam in his eye when he had been talking to Alyce at her feast. So what was that about? A thought struck her. Thoroughly awake now, she hauled herself out of bed, put on a fur-lined dressing gown and slipped her feet into cloth-soled house shoes. Soundlessly, she went down the stairs into her bookroom. She looked along the shelves until she came to her copy of Hardyng's new chronicle. Her memory was that he had praised Suffolk, who had been a generous patron to him. Had that altered? She opened it up and leafed through it until she reached the year of the duke's downfall. She read with fascinated horror what Hardyng had now written of William de la Pole.

> Not contented with the friendship of his own countrymen, he did win and procure the love of foreign and strange princes and made them to be of kindred with him.

So Hardyng was no friend of Alyce. And he and Harcourt had been so deep in talk at the book-sale dinner that neither had even glanced upwards as she and Alyce left.

A rumble from her stomach put her in mind of food. Dawn was lightening the sky. She locked the bookroom and walked down the passage to the kitchen. There was an ambrosial scent of fresh-baked bread. Cook looked up from his kneading table.

'You'll be wanting a manchet, no doubt, mistress. Buttered or as it comes?'

'Buttered, thank you, Cook. Don't stop, I know you're busy. I'll do it myself.' She went into the cool larder off the main kitchen, found the earthenware butter dish on a slate shelf and went back into the kitchen. Once she'd spread the roll of bread with generous curls of butter, she settled down by the range to eat it.

'Bad business, this death of Master Hardyng,' she said conversationally. Cook grunted.

'Deserved everything he got, the old humbug.'

'What makes you say that?' she asked, surprised. Cook was a silent, imperturbable man who rarely said a word against anybody.

'Came in here at the end of the sale asking for Guy, who I know for a fact didn't want to see him. Disappeared upstairs. And now Guy's gone altogether.'

'What? Surely not. He's just visiting his mother, isn't he? He said she was ill.'

'I doubt it,' said Cook. 'If you ask me, Guy's done a runner. And he's a good man. Something must have pushed him to it.'

'Pushed him to what?' asked Joan impatiently.

Cook looked up in amazement.

'Killing Hardyng, of course. Who else could have done it?'

Joan was aghast. Her mind replayed the last few days, then she shook her head. 'I know Guy had been absent-minded and crotchety lately. But I can't imagine him murdering Hardyng.'

275

'Perhaps he witnessed his murder and feared he would be a suspect.'

'Why couldn't he have simply told me? He knows I'd stand by him through thick and thin.' Even as she spoke the answer came to her. Because there was something about Hardyng's death that incriminated him. She stood up, strode out to the kitchen court and opened the heavy door of the latrines. The whole place stank. She walked along the long line of holes to the cesspit at the far end and peered into it. It was too dark to see anything but vague lumps floating in the thick swill of excrement. She went back to the kitchen.

'Light me a torch, Cook, and bring it out to the latrines.'

Cook looked appalled.

'But Mistress Joan, I'm making bread. I'll call for Ned.'

'No. He's had enough horror for one day. You come.'

He followed her unwillingly, a blazing pitch torch in his hand. Joan took it from him as they reached the edge of the cesspit and held it high. Its light shone down into the brick-lined pit. She saw the glint of a knife blade.

'There, Cook. Reach down for it.'

Cook gulped, but did as he was ordered, retching as he bent close enough to the excrement to reach the knife. He offered it to Joan, who drew back rapidly.

'Wash it first, you fool.'

Chuckling, Cook took it over to the spout of water that washed the channel under the latrine holes and rinsed it thoroughly.

'And now wipe it dry,' she commanded, half in denial about what they could both clearly see. It was, quite unmistakeably, Guy's knife. The one that he treasured as a gift from his father. The one that never left his side.

Cook said nothing, but reached for a piece of rag paper from the pile by the door and rubbed at the knife until it was bright and clean. Then he handed it to Joan.

'Do you still believe he's innocent, Mistress?'

'I do. Tell no one about this.'

She turned around, the knife in her hand. She hadn't heard Ned come in, carrying the bucket of nightsoil from upstairs. His eyes fixed on the knife. 'That's Guy's. What's it doing here?'

Joan was lost for words. But a voice sounded behind her.

'Ned, if you value your place here, you will speak no word of this at the inquest tomorrow.'

It was Matthew Cobham. He put his hand heavily on Ned's shoulder. 'And I'm sure there will be a penny in it for you if you show yourself a loyal friend of the Sign of the Mole.'

Ned's eyes darted from Joan to Cook and back to Matthew. Slowly he nodded.

'And when you've emptied the bucket, wash your hands and come to the bindery. I've a mind to teach you how to sew cords this morning.'

Ned brightened. 'As long as it isn't gardening,' he risked, giving Joan a cheeky glance.

She cuffed his head. 'Be off with you, rascal.'

St Giles, Cripplegate

Simon sighed. Montagu Inn felt empty without Duchess Alyce. And, to his surprise, he was missing Tamsin. He thought again of how she had felt when he lifted her on to Jankin's back; then he remembered how she had looked at Will Stonor and cursed himself for being a fool. He decided to ride over to

Paternoster Row and see if Joan had got any use for him. But first he would go to St Giles Without and see if he could find Bethan. And Bronwen. Going out into the courtyard, he saw Pek on a bench by the wall, enjoying the early May sunshine.

'I'd like to take Jankin out, Pek,' he said. 'I can saddle him up myself.'

'No need for that, Master Brailles,' said Pek. He rose stiffly and disappeared into the stables. A few minutes later, a lad led Jankin out. Pek followed them, patting the horse's stout rump as Simon mounted.

'Where are you off to this fine morning?' he asked. 'You'll be missing that lively little Ormesby lass, I warrant. She's got all the spirit of her father, for all she's a wench.'

Simon sniffed. 'Not at all. She's more trouble than she's worth.' He clicked his tongue and clapped his knees to Jankin's sides so that the old horse ambled towards the gatehouse.

'His grace doesn't think so,' Pek called after him. Simon tugged at Jankin's bit and turned back towards him.

'What do you mean?'

'Just the gossip from the Manor of the Rose. Their head groom told Hugh that when Duke John was saddling up a horse in the stables a few days ago he said to a henchman of Harcourt's that he had plans for her. But she's safe for a while. His grace tore his arse in the boar hunt on Sunday and he's laid flat, whimpering like a moppet.'

'What was Hugh doing at Lombard Street?'

'He went with Master Farhang last night. Summoned by the Duchess Elizabeth to repair said arse. Master Farhang's to go again this afternoon, apparently.'

Simon went on his way, frowning. He remembered the young duke whispering to Tamsin on Saturday. And Will

Stonor's evident interest in her. He hadn't thought of her as more than a nuisance up until now, a rival for Lady Alyce's favour. It was a shock to realise that to other men she might be a desirable woman, not the annoying chit he had known since she was a schoolgirl. He was, he reflected, only twelve years older than she was. A world away when she was ten and he was twenty-two, but less now. Images of her flashed on his inward eye. Teasing the kittens with Lady Bess. Listening round-eyed to Farhang describing the magical powers of bezoars. Watching Alyce with adoring eyes. He sighed. But she had no time for him, he knew. He was just her old schoolmaster, a constant critic and a harsh judge. No women seemed to have time for him. Except that dark-eyed lovely Bronwen. She'd smiled as if she knew just what he wanted.

St Giles was quiet. There were no women around the conduit house in the churchyard. Feeling both disappointed and relieved, Simon made his way round to the anchoress's cell. A waif of a girl was sitting cross-legged in its yard, weaving rushes into a mat. A thin cat lay curled beside her.

'Bethan?'

She looked up, startled. 'Yes, sir. How do you know my name?'

'I wondered if you could tell me about the morning when you found the remains of the murdered man in Paul's Yard?'

The girl looked wary. 'What's it to you? I told all I knew to the coroner.'

'I spoke to your mistress and she said that the men in black that you saw might have been friars.'

She shook her head. 'They couldn't have been holy men. I'm sure on that.'

'How many of them were there?'

'Four, at least. They came down the stairs of the charnel house and shouted at me to come, but I didn't. I saw their red hands and I ran. And they chased me. But I ducked into the yard of Lovell's Inn. I knew the kitchen boy there would be up. He's my friend. I crawled into the pile of kindling for the bread oven and when they put their heads into the yard and asked if he'd seen me, he said "Seen who?" Clever, weren't it? If he'd just said no, he might as well have said yes. I waited until they'd disappeared, then I ran back to find the churchwarden. I knew he'd be opening up Paul's for prime.'

Simon was impressed by her sharpness. It made him inclined to believe her. So the murderers had still been around the charnel house. Maybe Pailton had been tortured and killed somewhere else, then his remains brought there to be, as they thought, concealed. Perhaps they had gone upstairs into the Graftons' storeroom to remove his possessions, but when they heard Bethan's screams they'd come downstairs and tried to catch her.

'What's the name of your friend at Lovell's Inn?'

Bethan looked wary again. 'You won't get him into trouble, will you?'

'Trust me,' he said.

'Owen. He's Welsh, you see. Like me.'

'Owen? Why, I met him. He found my horse for me. Tell me, do you know Agnes Quincey of Clerkenwell?'

Bethan's face brightened. 'Owen's grandmother? Yes, we all do. Lives in the Priory of the Knights of St John. Her daughter Bronwen, Owen's mother, keeps house for the priest of St Giles.'

Loose ends linked up in Simon's mind. He remembered Wenlock's talk of propaganda being circulated all over the country by a network of couriers. Who better equipped to spread it than the Hospitallers, with their preceptories in every county? Aided by Welsh Londoners, lowest of the low but deeply loyal to Lancaster since Henry V's widow married Owen Tudor. Doubtless they'd been keeping a watchful eye on anyone who came asking about Pailton's murder. He remembered the man in black who had taken his horse from St Giles. And Agnes Quincey disappearing into the priory, a huge basket across her shoulders. And Pailton's bundles in the charnel house storeroom. And Cabal's packs. But how did Brother Pietro and that arch-snoop Hardyng's murder fit in? Was Joan Moulton also involved? She employed plenty of travelling chapmen. Or was someone else at the Sign of the Mole part of the conspiracy without her knowledge?

'Thank you. Bethan. Here's a penny for your help.'

He remounted Jankin and let the old horse amble towards Montagu Inn. Tomorrow he would go to Paternoster Row and seek out Joan. As he passed the St Giles presbytery, he glanced up at its windows, hoping to see Bronwen. He saw a face – not hers, but one he recognised. He reined Jankin in and looked up again. No one was there. He frowned. Although he'd only glimpsed it briefly, there was no doubt in his mind. Guy, the pockmarked journeyman he had met at Joan's book sale, was for some reason lurking upstairs in the priest's house.

He had almost reached Montagu Inn when a small troop of immaculately liveried horsemen came out of a side street and surrounded him. Their leader nodded. 'We meet again, Master Brailles.'

Simon instantly recognised the soft, mocking voice of Lord Tiptoft. He had last heard it in September, when the constable had visited Ewelme to investigate Harcourt's assertion that Lady Alyce was a traitor.

'Rufus Savernake tells me that you are very close to the Dowager Duchess of Suffolk. That when he was drinking with you at the archbishop's feast, you claimed to know all her secrets. Tell me, what are they? Meetings with Lancastrian sympathisers, perhaps?'

'I... I... I was drunk, that night, my lord... In truth, I know only that Princess Alyce is a loyal subject of King Edward and would have no truck with treason.'

Tiptoft's pale eyes met his with icy disdain. He turned to his men. 'Take this man to the Tower and prepare him for questioning. I will join you anon.'

Windsor

Kate woke with a light heart. Who else could the other barge's passengers be but Sir Gervais and the children? There was already a clattering of pans in the kitchen and the scent of freshly baked bread wafted through the inn's parlour. Would they be awake yet? She straightened her crumpled dress and tidied her hair as best she could without a looking glass. Then she opened the door into the hall and tiptoed up the stairs. Behind a door on the right she could hear men's voices – the crew of the Suffolk barge, no doubt. Behind the door on the left all was silence. She lifted the latch as gently as she could and pushed the door open. Inside was a four-poster bed with its curtains still drawn. Two truckle beds had been made up in the other half of the room. Gargantuan snores came from one of them. Under the coverlet of the other she could make out two small humped shapes. She crept forward and lifted a corner of the coverlet – then dragged it off with a cry of alarm. The humps were just pillows. The bed was empty. The four-poster's curtain twitched and a thin, bearded face looked out.

'What on earth are you doing in here, girl? We didn't ask to be woken.'

'But where is Peter?'

'How do you know of him? And who are you?'

'I'm his mother. Are you Sir Gervais? I thought Peter was with you.'

'He is. Though that is no business of yours.' Then his eyes fell on the empty truckle bed.

'Dammit. I hope to God they haven't run away again. They tried it on in the Kingston boatyard, when a hole in our hull had to be patched up. But we kept a close watch on them after that. I admire their spirit, actually. Boy's an Arderne to the backbone. And the girl's a plucky little wench. We'll find them soon enough. They can't have got far. But what are you doing here? Harcourt told me that you were under arrest. As you richly deserve, according to my wife. Your misdoings are all over court.'

'You wrong me, sir,' protested Kate hotly. 'Sir Robert spread a pack of lies to blacken my name. Which you and your wife were only too happy to believe.'

Sir Gervais grunted. 'We've no time to waste arguing.' He clambered out of bed and shook the snoring form on the other truckle bed. There was a groan from his squire.

'Get up, Tobias. We've got to find those damn children again.' He turned to Kate.

'And you, get out of my room. Whore or no whore, I don't choose to strip in front of you. I'll see you downstairs.'

He began taking off his nightclothes and Kate had no option but to withdraw, quivering with anger and chill with fear. This was altogether too like the dreadful morning when Peter had gone missing.

Downstairs, Alyce was sitting at the table wrapped in a blanket and reading while Tamsin arranged her hair in the embroidered snood she wore when travelling. She looked up and smiled.

'Good morning, Kate. Vere is already up and about. He's going to Windsor to check on the arrangements for his wedding. I told him that he could send his barge on to Oxford. We will of course take mine. I've spoken to Piers. He was amazed to see me. Jack told him I was at Ewelme.' Then she saw that Kate's face was crumpled in misery.

'Saints in Heaven. Are the children not here?'

'They were, but they've disappeared again. Sir Gervais says they kept trying to escape during the journey. And he called me a whore.'

Alyce bristled. 'He's an ignorant old fool. Leave him to me.'

The door opened and Vere came in, dressed for riding. Wraith was at his heels as usual. He bowed. 'Good morning, your grace. Lady Arderne, I trust you have found your son. Where is he? I'd like to meet him before I leave for Windsor.'

'Must you go so soon?' said Alyce. 'We need your help. The children have crept off in the night. Heaven knows where they are.'

'I have to wait on the king, so I can't delay for long,' said Vere. 'They're probably along the riverbank fishing for sticklebacks. Rouse your men to look for them. I've just seen off my own crew for Oxford, I'm afraid, or they could have helped. But two small children can't have gone far.'

'That's what I said.' Sir Gervais came down the stairs, followed by his still sleepy squire. 'Unless my son's wife is lying. I wouldn't put it past her to have spirited them away herself. She was up with the lark.'

'As any mother eager to see her son again would be,' said Alyce crisply.

He turned to her and Vere angrily. 'And who might you be?'

Alyce glared at him. It was Vere who answered.

'Mind your manners, sir. This is Princess Alyce, Dowager Duchess of Suffolk and aunt by marriage to the king. And I am Sir John Vere, Earl of Oxford.'

Dumbfounded, Sir Gervais bowed.

'I can assure you, Sir Gervais, that Lady Arderne would not stoop to such action,' Alyce said firmly. 'Nor has she any need to. She was declared innocent of all the charges against her.'

The old knight was shaken, but still dubious. 'And what proof do I have of any of this? Peter was made a ward of the queen herself. She thinks highly of Harcourt and gave permission for the match.'

'But once Lady Arderne was declared innocent, the queen rescinded her permission.'

The voice was young, crisp and authoritative. James Danvers, travel-stained and weary, approached them from the hythe, Will Stonor close behind him. He held out a sealed roll of parchment. Sir Gervais took it wonderingly, broke open the seal and read for several long minutes. Then he looked across at Kate.

'It seems I have done you an injustice, Lady Arderne. In truth, I am relieved. The more I saw of Harcourt, the less I liked him. Now, we must find those children.'

'I have an idea,' said Alyce. 'You were saying that Wraith

can trace anything, Vere. Perhaps Sir Gervais's squire can find a garment that belongs to one of them. We can give her the scent. She will surely nose them out.'

Vere dismounted and put Wraith on a leash. Offered a shirt of Peter's, she sniffed, wagged her tail and set off purposefully, nose to the ground, pulling her master behind her. She paused close to the inn's open gate, then went through it and down to the riverbank. There she nosed up and down beside the water, sniffing, evidently puzzled. Then she raised her head and pointed her muzzle upstream, barking loudly. Alyce realised what must have happened.

'Your barge, Vere. They must have stowed away on it. We must follow them in *Lyonesse* as quickly as possible.'

'I trust I can come with you, Princess Alyce,' said Sir Gervais. 'I don't want to lose touch with my grandson again. I must apologise for my rudeness.'

Alyce looked at the anxious old man, struggling to make sense of events. 'Of course, Sir Gervais. It will be a good opportunity for you to get to know his mother better.'

'Good luck, my lady,' said Vere. 'For my part, I will keep both eyes open for them in Windsor, just in case Wraith is mistaken. And if you don't catch them up before Oxford and it would help to stay in my new house there, don't hesitate to do so. Danvers, take this token and show it to my steward if need arises. His name is Jamie Arblaster.'

'Thank you, Sir John,' said Alyce. 'God willing, when we meet on your wedding day Kate will have Peter safe again. And our conversations over the last few days have given me an idea for a wedding gift for you.'

'No need for gifts. With Meg as my wife, I have all I need.' He smiled the same radiant smile that he had given Joan at

Moulton Inn. Then Alyce had found it arrogant; now she knew Vere better, she recognized in it a rare zest for life.

Snuggled in the cuddy of the *Silver Star*, Sukey and Peter had heard men tramp aboard early in the morning and settle themselves at their oars on the rowing benches. Sukey turned to Peter and put her finger to her lips. He nodded and pressed his own together. They heard a drum begin to beat, then felt the oarsmen drive the barge forwards in time to it. Gently rocked by the long, steady strokes and warmed by their closeness, they fell fast asleep, exhausted after their night escape. They didn't wake until there was a harsh bellow from the helmsman.

'Ship oars. Nets ahead.'

The barge slowed. Sukey risked a peep out. The rowers were all staring out over the water and the helmsman was leaning on the tiller with all his strength, willing the heavy craft to miss the bobbing string of bladders that signalled the underwater net. They were veering towards the bank, when the helmsman pulled the tiller back towards him with a curse. Too late. The bow of the barge grounded on shallows, then thrust itself inexorably further and further into thick mud.

'What's happening, Sukey? Where's mamma?' At the sound of the shrill little voice, the men's heads turned towards the cuddy as one and saw a skinny girl and a much smaller boy staring back at them open-mouthed. Sukey ducked back inside, dragging Peter with her, but it was too late.

'Christ's bones, they must be the children you told me about, the ones the gentry thought were upstairs in the inn,' said the man at the helm to Hubert. 'What in the name of Jesus and St John are we to do with them?'

Hubert considered. 'We'll have to stop at Henley and send word back to Windsor. And my lord particularly told us not to dally. He wants our cargo unloaded in Oxford and taken to his new house as quickly and discreetly as possible. Then we're to return to Windsor in time for the wedding.'

'We needn't hang about at Henley,' said the helmsman. 'We can leave the children in the care of the landlady at the White Hart.'

'That might answer,' said Hubert. He walked over to the cuddy, pulled away the cloaks and looked at the two frightened faces. Then he smiled reassuringly.

'Don't be feared, littl'uns. Come out. You'll come to no harm.'

Holding Peter's hand tightly, Sukey emerged, trying as best she could to tidy her tousled hair. She looked at the water swirling downstream past the barge in amazement.

'But we're going the wrong way. London's down river, not upstream. I thought you'd be going to London. That's why we got on board.'

'We're going the right way for us, child,' said Hubert good-humouredly. 'And I don't think you really want to go back to London. You're Peter and Sukey, aren't you? You missed the boy's mother Lady Arderne back there at Windsor. But when we get to Henley, we'll send to her and she'll come for you as quickly as she can, I know.'

He beckoned them forward. 'Come and sit here in the tilt. You'll get a much better view there than from inside the cuddy. Are you hungry? Thirsty?' They both nodded. He turned to a nearby sailor.

'Johan, get them something to eat and drink. The rest of you, go to the stern to lighten the bow. And Brian, pole us off.'

Peter was looking puzzled. 'I don't understand, Sukey. Why did we run away from mamma?'

'It's all right, Peter. That was a mistake. But these are kind men. They're going to send someone to tell your mamma where we are. And she'll come and get us straight away.'

'Straight away,' he repeated hopefully. 'Straight away.'

※

If it hadn't been for her anxiety about Peter, Kate would have enjoyed the voyage from Windsor to Henley in *Lyonesse*. The sharpness of spring had given way to the balmy warmth of early summer. Alyce had urged James to join them so that he could explain the legal judgment to Sir Gervais, so he had sent his horse on to Henley with Will. Alyce noticed Tamsin staring regretfully after her godson as he disappeared and sighed. It was time she had a word with her.

Once James had explained everything to Sir Gervais, Alyce sat beside the old knight in the shelter of the tilt, exchanging memories of the court in happier times. Kate and James sat opposite each other in the bow of the barge, enjoying the sights and sounds of river life. A heron stood still as a statue near the trunk of a willow tree, then rose lazily on huge grey wings and coasted to the other bank of the river.

'I love herons,' he said. 'Ghosts made visible.'

'They remind me of my godmother's companion Monique de Chinon,' said Kate.

'You're right,' said James. 'Both her elegance and that sense of mystery about her. But look!' He pointed out the blue flash of a kingfisher and they both smiled at the sight of its mate emerging from a tiny hole in the steep clay bank. Relaxed for the first time since Peter had disappeared, Kate realised how contented she felt in his company. She had at first dismissed him as just another of the dandified young men about town who led her poor Richard into gambling dens, but he was revealing himself as thoughtful and sensitive and as much in love with country things as she was herself.

But of *Silver Star* there was no sign at all.

'They must be rowing double time,' said Sir Gervais. 'Can we go any faster?'

'I'll ask Piers to hoist the sail,' said Alyce. 'I fear our crew are not as young and fit as Vere's. I like to linger on the river, not to race on it. But the wind is getting up and they will surely pause at Henley. They have to eat, after all. I wonder if they have discovered the children.'

But when they reached Henley, there was no sign of the *Silver Star* among the craft crowded at the staithe below the bridge.

'Go under the bridge, Piers. There's room to tie up at the Angel,' said Alyce. 'And Bogo, the landlord, knows me well. We can ask if they saw the *Silver Star* pass.'

As Piers guided *Lyonesse* to the jetty by the Angel, several watermen hurried to help make her fast. A huge young man with a shiny bald head and tattooed arms came out of the Angel, beaming a welcome.

'Your grace! You are most welcome.'

'It's good to see you, Bogo. I can see you are thriving.'

'Our cook is much too good, Lady Alyce, as you'll see if you break your fast with us. What is it about the river this morning? We don't often see two barges of the quality in a single day.'

'Was the other called *Silver Star*?' called Alyce.

'Didn't see her name. But her hangings were covered with

290

stars, sure enough. They tied up at the White Hart. Only stayed a few minutes, though. Then they were on their way with a fine wind behind their sail.'

'When was that?' asked Sir Gervais.

'About two hours ago,' said Bogo.

Kate gave a little cry. 'We've missed them. We must leave straight away.'

'Wait a moment,' said James. 'Let me run along to the White Hart and see if they saw children with them.'

'An excellent notion, James,' said Alyce. 'Meanwhile, we do need to break our fast. The rowers can't go any further on empty stomachs. Bogo, can you prepare some food for us on the instant?'

'Gladly, your grace,' said Bogo. 'There are birds on the spit already roasted to a turn.'

'And ale all round for the men,' Alyce added.

A cheer rose from the oarsmen's pit. Bogo disappeared inside the Angel and they heard him shouting at the scullions. Sir Gervais stepped out and courteously held out an arm so that Alyce could steady herself. She was about to say that she didn't need it, then decided it would be discourteous to refuse and took it, nodding her thanks. Tamsin, reading her mind perfectly, smiled to herself as she followed them ashore.

Kate stayed on board, eyes fixed on James as he hurried along the riverbank to the steps that led up to the bridge. Only when he was out of sight did she follow Sir Gervais and Alyce into the Angel. Her hopes had been dashed. Her head ached and she felt faintly sick. It had been almost a week since Peter had disappeared. And although Sir Gervais had assured her that Sukey had managed to cheer the boy up sufficiently for them to have been playing all manner of games on the barge as they rowed upriver, she was racked with guilt at having failed him. When platters of rich stew were placed in front of them, she felt her gorge rise.

She went outside and sat in the sunshine, shivering despite its warmth. Then she saw James's slim dark figure descend the steps from the bridge and walk despondently towards them. Her heart sank.

When he reached her, he looked at her in silence for a moment before speaking. 'Lady Arderne, I fear there is bad news.'

'Weren't they on the barge then? Don't say they are still at Windsor?'

James looked grim. 'It's worse than that. They were on the barge. Stowaways who'd run away from their mother and friends, Lord Oxford's men told the landlady. They said they were in a hurry to get to Oxford and asked if they could leave them with her. Paid her to send a rider back to Windsor with a note one of them wrote. She fed them, gave them a couple of fishing nets to catch tiddlers with and told them not to stray far. They went down to the riverbank. An hour later, a party came in on the London road. A knight and his squire and a groom and a wench. They were about to order food when the groom saw the children at the water's edge and spoke to the knight, who leapt up with an oath and told him and the squire to get them. The landlady asked if they'd come in answer to the rider she'd sent to Windsor, though she wondered how they'd appeared so quickly. The knight said, yes, they'd met her rider on the road and gave her a guerdon for looking after them. So she was happy enough and when she saw the children running away from them like rabbits, she just thought they were being naughty. The knight said that they wouldn't stop for breakfast now; they needed to be on their way now they'd found the children. Bought two loaves from her and filled his flask, then he was off after them. The landlady commented on how wretched the girl with them looked. Wore a red cloak over a green dress that had been fine enough once but was sadly bedraggled.'

'Amice!' exclaimed Kate. 'The empty-headed little fool. This means that Sir Robert has them again. Oh James, what shall we do?'

'We must tell Lady Alyce and Sir Gervais,' said James, intensely aware that Kate had called him by his Christian name for the first time.

They hurried into the smoky, food-scented interior of the Angel. Alyce looked up. 'Any news, James?'

'Nothing good,' said James. He repeated the landlady's story. Sir Gervais swore eloquently, then considered.

'But perhaps we wrong Sir Robert. After all, he doesn't know about the judgment. I was to wait his arrival here.'

'He was sent a message from the Court of Wards on Monday,' said James. 'So he knows full well that he has no right to Peter.'

'But he can pretend that he left London before the message reached him,' said Alyce. 'That he found them at Henley as he had expected, albeit without Sir Gervais. My guess is that he is riding for Oxford as fast as he can in order to complete the spousal.'

'Which I will upturn at the first opportunity,' said Sir Gervais.

'If you can find Peter,' said Alyce. 'He wouldn't be the first young heir to be spirited away.'

James looked at Kate, who sat slumped in despair. His heart

went out to her, and when she raised her swimming eyes to his he made up his mind.

'Will should be here any minute with Mercury. We'll have a good chance of catching up with them. They can only be an hour ahead.'

He was rewarded by a look of gratitude that transformed Kate's face.

'Will you, James? Then can I come with you? I can hire a good horse from the inn and I am used to hard riding. Richard and I always rode together.'

She moved forward, but Alyce put up a restraining arm. 'Kate, stop. It would not be wise for you to go. Sir Robert doesn't know Master Danvers is involved in the case. He and Will can catch them up and see where they are going. Then he can send word to us and Sir Gervais can confront him. I know you are desperate to see Peter as soon as possible, but consider the risk. Who knows what Sir Robert would do if he had you in his power?'

Kate said nothing, turning away sadly. As she did, hoofs sounded on the planks of the bridge and James jumped up and looked out of the window.

'It's Will with Mercury on a leading rein. We can leave straight away. Lady Arderne, can you give me a token, so that I can if need be show Peter and Sukey that you sent me?'

Kate hesitated, then groped in her pocket. She pulled out a dented brass brooch. Sir Gervais started in surprise.

'The Arderne wyvern! But that's Richard's. Why is it dented?'

'He always called it his luck. A ball from a handgun hit it instead of his heart at the battle of St Albans. Peter knows it well and loves it. It will give him courage too. Take it, Master Danvers and God speed you.'

Sir Gervais nodded approvingly. 'I wish I was young enough to go with you. But I'd only slow you down.'

James went over to where Will was waiting and mounted Mercury. Then he turned to say goodbye.

Alyce stepped forward. 'Do be careful, James. It's my experience that Harcourt will stop at nothing. And if they suspect you are connected to Kate, you could be in danger.'

'I'll risk that.'

'And so will I', added Will.

Alyce slowly nodded her head. 'You will certainly travel much faster than we can. I'll take Kate to Ewelme and we'll wait there for news. But do nothing on your own.'

Just as they rode away, Tamsin came back from the barge with Alyce's cloak. Alyce turned to her.

'You missed James and Will, Tamsin. But it's not too late to say a prayer for them.'

She saw her maid gaze longingly down the Oxford road and knew she had to destroy her dreams. But not in front of the Ardernes.

'Tamsin, I want to take a walk before we board the barge again,' she said. 'There's a shrine on the other side of the bridge where we can leave an offering and say a prayer.'

She led her away from the Angel and across the river. Just before they reached the little shrine, she stopped and looked her straight in the face.

'Child, it's no good looking sheeps-eyed after Will Stonor. He's far above you in rank. Nothing honest can come of anything more than friendship between you. His parents have long had a wife in mind for him. Her name escapes me, but she's the daughter of landed friends of theirs.'

Tears started in Tamsin's eyes and Alyce's heart went out to her. But then she saw the mutinous set of her maid's lips. She knelt at the shrine, praying that the girl would heed her words – but uncomfortably aware that they had come too late.

The Sign of the Mole

As Joan came out into the courtyard of Moulton Inn, followed by Monique, Matthew and Ned, Simon rode through the gate.

'Master Brailles, you are welcome,' said Joan. 'We are on our way to the inquest of John Hardyng. Will you come with us? It is to be held at the Amen Tavern, only a step along the lane.'

'Willingly, Mistress Joan,' said Simon, dismounting with care and limping as he tied his horse to a rail. 'But first I have news. I think I saw your journeyman Guy in the priest's house by St Giles Without. Is that where his mother lies sick?'

Joan's face paled. She looked round to see if anyone had heard what Simon had said, but Monique and Matthew had taken Ned over to the well for an unaccustomed wash and his yelps had drowned Simon's words. She turned back to Simon, taking his arm in an urgent grip. He winced and she noticed a bruise on one side of his face.

'What's the matter?'

'I... I fell from my horse. But I'll be fine.'

She nodded abstractedly. 'Say nothing more about Guy until after the inquest. I'll explain later.'

She turned as Monique advanced on them. 'Have you made Ned respectable?'

'As much as he ever will be,' said Monique. '*Sal petit cochon.*'

A few minutes later they trooped into the Amen Tavern. Joan had dressed to impress in a dark gold fur-lined houppelande over a mulberry velvet gown. Monique was in her customary grey, save for a flash of white lace at her throat. Matthew wore his Sunday doublet, and Ned, quaking with fear, had a clean shirt under his leather jerkin. Twelve local men had been summoned as jury, but of Wenlock there was no sign. Instead, the proceedings were run under the bored eye of John Laweley. Giles Scott sat beside him on the bench, quill at the ready. When he saw Simon, he gave him a broad wink.

'Call the first finder,' said Laweley. Matthew thrust Ned forward. As he stuttered out what he had seen in the midden, his eyes kept darting to Matthew for reassurance. When he had finished, Laweley gave a sniff.

'A well-coached witness, I perceive.' He picked up a document from the table in front of him.

'This is Lord Wenlock's report. The victim was stabbed in the back. He had a purse full of money under his cloak. Perpetrator unknown, but the watch was instructed to search for one Guy of Yarnton, journeyman, who has disappeared. Does anyone else have anything to say?'

Joan rose and Laweley shook his head wearily. 'When did you *not* have something to say, Mistress Moulton. But speak on.'

'Guy didn't disappear, your honour. Matthew Cobham will testify to the fact that he had arranged to visit his mother after the book sale ended on Saturday. She is very ill.'

'And when do you expect him to return?'

Joan looked at Matthew, who stood up and answered.

'As soon as she can safely be left. Or when she has made a good end.' He crossed himself.

'And where does she live?'

'None of us knows exactly, your honour,' said Matthew. 'I believe it's Deptford way.'

The bells of St Paul's tolled the hour. Laweley looked across at Scott.

'I've noted all that, your honour,' Giles said.

'Then add, "Inquest adjourned pending the return and questioning of Guy of Yarnton."'

He stood up and everyone rose, standing solemn and still until he and Scott had gone out of the tavern. Joan and her party followed them, ignoring the excited chatter that broke out behind them.

'Bravely done, lad,' said Matthew to Ned as they walked back to Moulton Inn. 'We'll make a journeyman of you yet.'

'Where's my penny?' said Ned.

'You'll get it soon enough,' said Matthew, giving Ned's ear a tug. 'And don't forget that if you say a word to anyone, I'll have it back from you.'

'That's just what Sir Robert said,' giggled Ned, then clapped his hand to his mouth.

Joan stared at him. 'What was that, Ned? What did Sir Robert give you a penny for?'

Panic-stricken, Ned turned to run, but Matthew was too quick for him. He seized him and gave him a shake.

'What have you been up to, you rascal?' The people coming out of the tavern stared at them curiously.

'Gently, Matthew,' said Joan. 'We'll question him in Moulton Inn.'

Once back at the Sign of the Mole, Joan turned to Ned, who shrank away from her, expecting a blow.

'Come, lad,' she said. 'It isn't too late to mend any damage you may have done. Tell us when Sir Robert gave you a penny? What was it for?'

'It was about a month ago. He... he wanted me to take a

sheet of paper from each new batch that arrived at the shop,' he stuttered. 'Just one from each, and save them up for him. I thought it wouldn't matter. The bundles often arrive a leaf or two short. He said he'd send someone to collect them.'

Joan looked at Matthew. 'They would have been checking them against the printed broadsheets,' he said. 'It's lucky we were using the load of unicorn you bought up for your specials when old Fenucci closed his shop.' He turned back to Ned. 'And was anybody else bribing you?'

Ned coloured. 'Three weeks ago Mistress Grafton gave me a lump of wax and told me to press the keys of the strongbox into it if I got a chance. But she didn't give me money. She said she'd tell you I'd been stealing for Sir Robert. So I had to. And a night or two afterwards, she came tapping on the door and made me let her in.'

Joan swore colourfully. 'The tricksy besom. And did you?'

The boy nodded glumly. Simon gasped.

'So Margaret Grafton was responsible for the theft of Lady Alyce's *Tales*.'

Joan frowned. 'It seems so. But I doubt she was acting alone. She may have thought up how to steal it, but she must have a customer she could sell it to. And what about the other things that were taken? My specials.'

'They could have been taken by Hardyng,' said Matthew. 'Perhaps that was why he was murdered?'

'Suppose he was her accomplice,' said Simon. 'And she needed to silence him.'

'But I can't see Margaret committing murder,' said Joan. 'Little as I like her.'

'Which takes us back to her customer,' said Matthew. 'Whoever he was.'

'And what about Guy? How does he fit in?' said Simon. He looked a query at Joan, who shrugged her shoulders and nodded. 'As I told Joan, I saw him in the priest's house at St Giles.'

'But I thought he had gone to Deptford to look after his mother,' said Matthew.

'I'm sure he's innocent,' said Joan. 'And I didn't want him arrested. He's our best hope of finding out what's happened.' She walked to the window, deep in thought. Then she turned back to Cobham.

'Matthew, could you ride over there now and persuade him to return.'

'No need for that.' A cloaked figure slipped silently out of the screens passage and into the room.

'Guy!' cried Joan.

'I'm sorry, mistress. I should have told you what was happening before. But they were threatening to kill my mother. Bar the door, Matthew. I may have been followed.'

'By whom?'

'The constable's intelligencers. A man called Rufus Savernake grabbed me a fortnight ago when I was leaving my mother's house and said that if I didn't co-operate she'd have an accident.'

'What did they want you to do?'

'Not very much. Told me to keep my eyes and ears open at the Sign of the Mole and tell them if there was anything suspicious.' He chuckled. 'Ironic, really. Considering I was the one they were looking for. I told Monique that we must on no account use more of the paper from Moulton Inn for the...' He hesitated.

'Broadsheets?' Joan guessed shrewdly, who had been turning

over in her mind what Matthew had meant when he referred to the Fenucci paper.

'You know about them now? That's a relief. But then came that dreadful day. The sale.'

'What happened?'

Guy swallowed. 'I was copying the Neville roll for Lady Alyce. I glanced round to see what Hardyng was up to and I saw him taking books out of the chest and putting them into a sack. I asked him what on earth he was doing and he told me to get back to work or it would be the worse for my mother. "And not a word to anyone after I've gone," he said. I guessed he was removing the specials.'

He glanced at Joan. 'And, to be honest, I've never liked handling those. It was a relief when Pailton told me he was planning to flee to France and sell them.'

'So that explains who took them,' said Cobham. 'What happened next?'

'Hardyng disappeared with the sack, then came back to the showroom to get the roll to give Joan. I decided the only thing to do was to go and find my mother and fetch her away to somewhere safe. I'd packed up my things and was slipping outpast the privy when Hardyng came stumbling in. Savernake was chasing after him. Hardyng ran to me for help, but Savernake leapt after him and stabbed him in the back. Then he pointed his knife at me and snatched mine from my belt. He smeared it with Hardyng's blood, then threw it into the cesspit and shoved Hardyng after it. He said "Not a word. For your mother's sake. And make yourself scarce." Then he went out again, taking Hardyng's sack with him.'

'Savernake?' said Joan. 'But I didn't see him on Saturday.'

'I doubt you'd have known him. He was dressed as a

Dominican, in a black gown with his hood up. There were a deal of friars at the sale. But my guess is that he came later on. To silence Hardyng.'

'But why?'

'Perhaps the old rascal got greedy,' said Simon. 'He'd got a fat purse from somebody who must have wanted to stay nameless.'

'That was mine,' said Guy. My life savings. Hardyng forced me to give them to him, or he'd tell Savernake where I'd taken my mother to.'

'Savernake is Harcourt's man, is he not?' said Joan.

'He is equally close to Tiptoft,' said Monique. 'They are all the three *main à gant.*'

'And where does Lord Wenlock fit in?' said Simon.

'Monique, you said that Sir John looked distraught at the audience with King Edward,' said Joan. 'I wonder if he was beginning to fear that Tiptoft's investigations were going to lead to him. He's been buying specials from me for months now and turning a blind eye to where they came from.'

'It was I think more that he did not approve the arrest of Princess Alyce,' said Monique. 'He has a *tendresse* for her. His secretary Francis told me.'

'Has Thynne told you anything about Margaret Grafton, Monique?'

'She is being paid by *le chevalier Harcourt.* And I believe she has a little business on the side with *le petit duc.*'

'Do you mean Jack de la Pole?'

'Yes. He was paying the Graftons to forge his mother's signature on documents. Francis says he is completely under the thumb of Harcourt.'

'The young fool,' said Joan.

303

'But Guy, what about your mother? Is she safe now?'

'I went straight to her lodgings and hired a litter to take her to St Giles Without. She's safe in the priest's house now. With Bronwen to tend her.'

'Bronwen?' said Simon.

'Who better?' said Guy. 'We've long been fond of each other. Pailton had not been a husband to her for years. And now he's dead, we hope to marry – if we survive this mess.'

The castles in the air that Simon had been building ever since his eyes had met Bronwen's inviting ones collapsed. What a fool he was. Fit for nothing but cataloguing and caring for Lady Alyce's books. And, rather than suffer more than a taste of torture, he had given up the only secret of hers that he knew of and undertaken to seek evidence to blacken her name.

There was a sharp rap at the door and Guy tensed.

'Pray God Tiptoft's men did not follow me here. Where can I hide?' He looked round desperately, then crawled under the great central table.

'Since when do bolts and bars meet old friends at the Sign of the Mole?' At the familiar sound of Farhang's voice, they all relaxed. Abashed, Guy clambered to his feet again and Matthew unbarred the door and opened it. Farhang limped in, leaning heavily on his staff. Behind him, also limping and leaning on a staff in bizarre parody, came Jack de la Pole. Out in the courtyard, two grooms in the Suffolk livery stood beside a horse litter. Farhang grinned at their amazed faces.

'Well. Aren't we going to get a welcome, Mistress Joan? What of your famed hospitality?'

'You are welcome as ever, Farhang, but from what I've been hearing my lord of Suffolk is no friend of mine, ingrate son that he is.'

Jack de la Pole coloured. 'You are right, Mistress Moulton. I've been a fool. But I hope it is not too late to make amends.'

Simon stepped forward, 'Are you wounded, my lord?' he asked.

'Simon!' Jack exclaimed. 'I thought you would have gone to Ewelme with my lady mother.' He turned to Farhang. 'Here is the answer to our problem, Farhang. I will give Simon a letter authorising him to...'

'Hush, my lord,' said Farhang, looking nervously round the room at the mystified faces. 'We are I hope among friends, but even so the less said the better. And we still need Lord Wenlock to co-operate.'

'I'm not sure what you have in mind, Farhang,' said Joan. 'But you can leave Lord Wenlock to me. Come, let's to my closet. I want to hear what you've been up to.'

St Paul's Yard

Margaret Grafton was packing up her stall. John had gone back to their tenement with the takings of the day and would soon return to help her take the four hampers of stock up the steep stairs of the charnel house to their storeroom. She was, truth be told, a little worried at the turn events were taking. News of John Hardyng's murder had spread like wildfire through the bookselling community. No one had liked the old man much, but to get a knife in your back and be pitched into a shitpit was a ghastly death.

A movement behind her made her jump. She whipped round, then sighed with relief. It was only Rufus Savernake.

'You made me start, Rufus. What can I do for you?'

'I was just passing by. But it looks as if I could do something for you. Do you want those hampers taken to your storeroom above the charnel house?'

'That's very good of you. I don't know where John's got to.'

'I saw him with a tankard of ale in the Rising Sun a few minutes ago.'

'If that's true, he'll live to regret it,' said Margaret fiercely. 'Well, they're very heavy. If you could give me a hand...'

'Willingly,' said Rufus and slung the largest of the hampers on his shoulders. Margaret followed him across Paul's Yard with a smaller one, pulling the key of the charnel house out of her pocket as she went. Once they were at the top of the stairs, she unlocked the door. Inside Rufus put the hamper he'd been carrying down with a thud.

'I can manage the other two myself, if you want to start putting things in order up here,' he said.

'I'm beholden to you, Rufus,' said Margaret. 'And I'll stand treat at the tavern once we're done.'

He disappeared down the stairs. After a few minutes she heard heavy footsteps coming slowly up the stairs and the door opened. There was a pause, then the scrape of a key. She stood stock still. That had been the sound of the lock. She looked round. The key that she had put on the shelf by the door had disappeared. Rufus stood there, one hamper slung over his shoulder, the other in his arms.

'There you are,' he said, putting them down with a smile. And for a minute she thought everything was all right.

From the shadows of the great north porch of St Paul's two hooded figures were watching the charnel house. They saw Margaret and Savernake go up the stairs and they saw Savernake re-emerge, collect two more hampers from the

Graftons' stall and go back to the to the room above the charnel house. A few long minutes later they heard the beginning of a scream, quickly stifled. They looked at each other.

'Should we try to help her?'

'Too late, I fear. And what could we do against Savernake? He's got twice the strength of us both put together. Look, there he is.'

The door of the charnel house storeroom swung open and Savernake emerged, a sack over his shoulder. He glanced round Paul's Yard, empty now of hustling crowds, its stalls bare. Then he locked the door, descended the stone stairs and walked quickly towards Cheapside. In the shadows of the church porch, Agnes Quincey shivered.

'Where are you going to go to?' said Sir Thomas.

'The sisters of Syon. I shall take my vows. That will make me safe enough. What about you?'

'I still have work to do. Word has come from Koeur. *Rex quondam futurusque*. The prophecies of Merlin are going to be fulfilled. Margaret of Anjou has a powerful new ally. There are plans for the king to come into his own again. I ride for Dover tonight.'

'And your great book of Arthur? And your history of Britain? I still have them.'

'Will you keep them safe for me at Syon? Who knows what will become of John Langstrother in the next little while? Lord Tiptoft will be watching him like a hawk.'

'I will. Until next time.'

'Until next time,' he repeated. Their eyes met in the quiet understanding of trusted friends.

Ewelme

Alyce led the way as they rode from Wallingford to Ewelme. When she reached the top of Rabbit Hill, she looked down over her little kingdom. Straight ahead the church stood sentinel, the courtyard of the God's House below it and the school below that. The orchards were pink with blossom and the fields sloping downwards to the heart of the valley brilliant with grass. The foaming lace of cow parsley and creamy yellow cowslips lined the track and the hedges were bright with young hawthorn leaves. Tamsin saw her smiling happily. The harbingers had ridden ahead and outside the school stood its pupils, some waving pennants, some beating little drums, some blowing lustily on pipes. Alyce saluted them as she turned her horse's head left and led the Ardernes past the tranquil pool that lay at the heart of the village. The great gates of the palace were thrown open in anticipation of their arrival, and Martha Purbeck and Ben Bilton waited in the courtyard with an ecstatic Leo beside them.

'Well come home, my lady,' said Martha. 'We hadn't looked to see you back so soon and I fear much is in disarray. I was using your absence to turn out your great chamber. But I've lit a fire in the solar. And I have prepared rooms for Lady Arderne and Sir Gervais.'

'Thank you, Martha. We'll manage. Ben, it's good to see you. Have the men unload the packhorses and take my baggage upstairs. But take the little hamper on my pannier to the kitchen garden. It's full of plants from Moulton Inn. Much in need of my attention. And wait for me there. I want to hear what's been going on.' She bent down to pet Leo.

Ben beamed, delighted to have his mistress home again. Alyce saw him look at Tamsin with surprise. She was wearing a new dress and her hair was done in London fashion. He nodded his approval. But she gave him only a brief glance, then looked away. He scowled at the snub and walked over to help the footmen with the packs.

Alyce sighed and turned back to her chamberlain. 'Tell John Cook supper need not be a grand affair.'

'He put half a dozen hens on the spit the moment the harbinger announced your coming. And there's rabbit stew aplenty,' said Martha.

'Excellent. Thank him from me.'

'She turned to Kate and Sir Gervais. 'Martha will help you make yourselves comfortable. Tamsin, come with me.' She swept inside.

Tamsin hung back.

'Martha, how is Wat doing?'

'Right well, my dear. Led the kitchen boys hunting coneys last night. He knows the warrens like nobody else.'

Tamsin went back up the winding stair to Alyce's apartments, tucking herself into a window niche as Bilton's men clattered down past her. She went into the solar and saw her mistress examining the documents laid out on the table. Alyce looked up and smiled.

'It's so good to be home. I won't be needing you for a while, my dear. Once I've looked over these papers Ben's put out for me, he's going to tell me what's been happening while I pot up my pretty little treasures. They'll get both light and warmth under the glass frames that John Carpenter made for me while we were away. Please tell Lady Arderne and Sir Gervais that I will join them for supper. Then why don't you go and see your grandmother and Wat?'

Tamsin retreated, touched that Lady Alyce had been so thoughtful. She went to the kitchen, begged a newly made cream cheese and some bread rolls still warm from the oven, then hurried along the lane to the rambling outbuildings of the God's House. Memories flooded her mind as she stepped under its entrance arch and into the narrow tunnel that led to its central courtyard. Nan Ormesby was stooping at the well, struggling to wind up its heavy wooden bucket. Although a new winch had been fitted after the death of Milo last year, it was still hard work. At the sound of her footsteps, Nan turned her head and her face creased into a web of smiles. Tamsin put down the bread and cheese and went to help turn the handle of the windlass. Once the bucket was safely up and unhooked, Nan opened her arms and Tamsin went gratefully into them. Tears came to her eyes. It was, she realised the first loving physical contact she had enjoyed since she left Ewelme. Except when Will had let his hand slide over hers as they sat on the rim of the well at Montagu Inn. Where was he now? she wondered.

Nan drew back, but still gripped Tamsin's upper arms as she looked searchingly at her granddaughter.

'You're looking bonny. Lady Alyce must be treating you right. I like the hair and a fine kirtle, too. But what are these tears?'

'Just happiness at seeing you again, Nan. I've missed Ewelme sadly. London is so big. And everyone is a stranger.

Well, nearly everyone. I did make a few friends. And Farhang was very kind to me.'

'So have you got an admirer up there in Montagu Inn? Plenty of likely lads eyeing you, I'm sure. What with you high in her grace's favour.'

Tamsin coloured. 'You know I don't seek a likely lad, Nan. Not yet at least.'

Nan hadn't missed the flush on her cheeks.

'But you've taken someone's fancy, I'll be bound. Be careful, Tamsin. There's more than one who'd not take no for an answer if he had the chance.'

Tamsin lowered her eyes, remembering Abel's rough grasp. And Lady Alyce's warning that Will was unattainable honestly. Then she rallied.

'But how are things here, Nan? I hear Wat is doing well. Mistress Purbeck said he was leading the lads on coney hunts.'

'He's a great help to me, though not as much as you were, of course. Not enough between his ears. Still, what there is, is willing. He's out in the God's House garden feeding the lambs whose mothers rejected them. He has a rare touch with helpless little creatures.'

Giving Nan a final hug, Tamsin picked up the bread and cheese and went through to the garden on the south side of the God's House. High-pitched bleats from a wattle enclosure in one corner led her to Wat, sitting on an upturned bucket holding a feeding bottle capped with a teat contrived from a piece of pig's intestine. A tiny black lamb was sucking at it thirstily, At the sight of her, he sprang up and gave her an adoring, gap-toothed grin.

Alyce donned her linen gardening apron and inspected the plants that Ben was taking out of the willow hamper and placing carefully on the shelf of the potting shed. None seemed damaged.

'What are they?' he asked.

'Those are auriculas; the Italians call them *orecchiette* – little ears. They sprout side shoots that we can pull away and repot. And the colours of the flowers are often a surprise. It all depends on where the bee sucks. The tiny blue fleurs-de-lis come from Persia. Farhang will be delighted by them. We can divide the bulbs in the autumn.'

She turned to take the last tray of seedlings out of the hamper. When she picked it up, she saw that there was a damp-stained folded piece of paper underneath it. She opened it up and read.

Principessa, beware your enemies. Pailton's books may prove your undoing. Trust no one. *PP*

She stared at the letter and read it through again, frowning. PP. Pietro of Padua. But what could the fierce Dominican pardoner know of her enemies? Or of Pailton's books? She crumpled the letter up and stuffed it into the pocket of her apron.

'Something wrong, my lady?' said Ben, seeing her set face.

'I fear so,' said Alyce. 'I wish I knew what.'

The Royal

Wenlock was in a black mood. Since the fiasco of the audience with King Edward, Tiptoft had treated him with cold disdain. Harcourt and Savernake had left for Oxfordshire, as had Alyce, and he had an uneasy feeling that trouble lay ahead for her. But what could he do? He looked out from his tower room over the smoking chimneys of the city. There was a chill wind from the east, but it was a brilliantly sunny day. Red kites swooped boldly down into the streets from rooftop eyries to grab scraps, and he could hear their chicks mewing greedily from the nest a pair had built between two of the Royal's chimney stacks. The warmth meant that the brood had hatched early. He remembered his boyhood in the Malvern hills, wandering with his kestrel in search of small game, rough-haired hounds at his heels. How much simpler life had been then.

'My lord.' It was Thynne. 'Giles Scott is below. Shall I show him up?'

Wenlock nodded. 'I suppose so. He'll have news of the inquest, no doubt. Bring some ale up for him. And wine for me.' He went back to the window and gazed out again, wishing himself anywhere but in this pestilential city with its double-dealing and betrayals.

When Scott followed Thynne into the room, Wenlock waved him to a chair and sat down on another.

'Well, Giles. How did the inquest go?'

'Much as you thought it would, Sir John. Adjourned until Guy of Yarnton is found. But I haven't come about that. There's been another murder in the charnel house. Or, rather, above it.'

'A murder? Who?'

'Margaret Grafton, the stationer. She had a stall in Paul's Yard.'

'I know she did, you fool. Do we know who killed her? Was it her husband? Couldn't blame him if he did. She was an infuriating scold of a woman.'

'No, he was drinking in the Rising Sun when it happened.

He said Rufus Savernake treated him to a quart pot and then said that he'd help Margaret with the hampers from the stall.'

'So was it Savernake?'

'There are no witnesses to that, my lord. At least, none that will testify. Folk tend not to see old Tip-Toe's men going about their business.'

'Where's Savernake now? He'll need to testify at the inquest, even if we can't nail her death on him.'

'His landlady at the Mermaid said he packed up and went last night. Following Sir Robert to Oxfordshire, he told her.'

Wenlock sighed. 'Tell Laweley he'll have to deal with this as best he can. Just like Hardyng's death. Adjourned for lack of the main witness. And he should set king's officers on Savernake's trail. Show Giles out, Thynne.'

Alone once again, he felt in his pocket for his rosary and went to kneel at his prie-dieu. Saying the familiar prayers, four paternosters and three Hail Marys, soothed him a little. But his brain was whirling. This chain of murders had to be halted. Could it be true that Tiptoft had authorised the deaths of Hardyng and Margaret Grafton? Or had Harcourt become a rogue force, acting in his own interests under the official mantle of the much-feared royal intelligencers?

Thynne returned to the room. 'Joan Moulton has arrived, my lord. Shall I show her up?'

Wenlock groaned. 'I suppose so. She sent word that she would be calling. I expect she wants permission to leave for Oxfordshire. Is she alone?'

'She has the Dowager Duchess of Suffolk's man Simon Brailles with her. And Farhang Amiri.'

Wenlock raised his eyebrows in surprise. 'Didn't they return to Ewelme with Lady Alyce?'

'Evidently not,' said Thynne. 'I should warn you, my lord: Mistress Joan has battle in her eye.'

Wenlock heaved a sigh and walked over to his mirror and checked his appearance. He tidied his beard with a small ivory comb, rubbed at the frown lines between his brows and licked his lips to make them look less dry. He was dabbing a clove-scented pomade onto his wrists when Thynne showed in Joan and her companions.

'Ever the fop, John,' she said, sniffing. 'But seeming fine is not the same as behaving fine. You have a deal to explain. Monique tells me that you and Tiptoft lately tried to have Lady Alyce arrested.'

Wenlock held up a protesting hand. 'It was none of my doing, Joan. Harcourt was determined to damn her and is still intent on finding – or planting – evidence that she is implicated in these treasons.'

'You could have spoken up for her.'

'I did what I could,' said Wenlock, aware of how feeble his words sounded. 'And in truth I do believe that Edward will stand her friend. And not only for his sister's sake.'

'You're a coward and a turncoat.'

'It may seem that way, Joan. But you know full well that I can do more for Lancaster if I wield power at court than if I were cowering in some Welsh castle. If there is anything at all I can do to help Lady Alyce now...'

Joan turned to Farhang. 'Tell Sir John what you have discovered.' Farhang fixed Wenlock with a scornful look that made him feel like an errant schoolboy.

'My lord, you know who was responsible for Denis Pailton's murder.' Sir John nodded nervously.

'You condoned his torture.'

315

'No,' Wenlock protested. 'I was helpless to prevent it. Left to myself, I would have used other means to persuade him to tell us who was behind the printed treasons. Savernake is a cruel devil. We still don't know for certain who set up the press, or where it is now.'

'Nor can I enlighten you,' said Farhang. 'But I can tell you that the press was not only used for what you call treasons. It also made a number of the most prized books and prints in your collection.'

'In *my* collection?'

'Your Ovid, for a start. And whatever other "specials" you bought from the Sign of the Mole. Suppose your political masters and your royal mistress were to find that out?'

Wenlock turned angrily to Joan. 'But you said that you acquired them in Bruges, Joan.'

'Well I didn't,' said Joan. 'Simmer down, John. There is more to come. Farhang has been talking to young Jack de la Pole. Harcourt has played him like a fish. You know how obsessed he is about the death of his father. Sir Robert told him that Sir Richard Roos might be able to help him find out who was responsible for killing him.'

'The Lancastrian poet?' said Wenlock. 'But isn't he cooped up in the keep of Windsor Castle? He'd have been executed long ago for his treasonous ditties if it wasn't for the queen's mother Jacquetta, who has a fondness for him.'

'Harcourt told the duke to go and ask him about his father's death. He went to Windsor last week.'

'And could Roos enlighten him?'

'All he did was reel off half a dozen possibilities, all canvassed already. Nothing of moment. No proof. But Harcourt also asked Jack to deliver a parcel and a letter to Roos. Inside the parcel was Lady Alyce's rebound *Canterbury Tales*. Stolen by Margaret Grafton using copies of the strongbox keys made for her by Ned. The letter asked Roos to write a poetic dedication in it praising Lord Oxford for fighting the cause of Lancaster and urging him to greater efforts. Then he was to give the book to the castle chamberlain, saying that it was a wedding gift for the Earl of Oxford and Meg Neville from Princess Alyce.'

'Surely Roos would not do that without Alyce's personal authorisation? Remote as he is from court affairs, he knows what a popinjay Jack de la Pole is.'

'The letter looked as if it was from Alyce herself. But it was the work of Margaret Grafton. For some time now Jack had been getting her to employ scriveners to forge his mother's signature on documents so he could get money from her Suffolk estates. He gave her a copy of it cut off from a letter Lady Alyce sent him. And he also assured Roos that he'd changed his ways. Claimed that he was now as loyal to Lancaster as his mother secretly is.'

'So where is the book now?'

'It will be placed on display in the great hall at Windsor. In pride of place among the wedding gifts. Presents that will be admired by the king and queen. Elizabeth has been primed by Sir Robert to tell the king to pay special attention to Princess Alyce's gift. You know how she hates her because of her closeness to Queen Margaret. Harcourt told Jack that after the king had read the dedication, Vere would be arrested for treason and Alyce cooped up for life like the poor Duchess of Gloucester. Leaving Jack to take over the running of her estates.'

Wenlock sat bolt upright. 'If I know the queen, the dedication will cost Alyce her head. Last Sunday I heard Harcourt tell the king that he would prove both Princess Alyce and Vere to be traitors. He said that the evidence would be shown at Windsor.'

'Then we have to get the book and cut out the dedication. Or destroy the whole book if need be,' said Joan. 'John, I want a pass to visit Sir Richard Roos from you. Simon can ride for Windsor and persuade him to give it to him.'

'That won't answer,' said Wenlock. 'The royal party set off today in a veritable fleet of barges. They're staying two nights at Hampton Court and plan to reach Windsor on Tuesday, in good time for the wedding on Thursday. And by now the book will be with the rest of the wedding presents, numbered and accounted for and in the care of the castle chamberlain.'

Joan frowned. 'I hadn't thought of that. What if Lady Alyce herself was to go to Windsor and tell the steward that she wanted to replace the gift with a better one?'

'There's no time for that. She's well on her way to Ewelme.'

Farhang had been sitting with his eyes closed. Suddenly he gave a grunt. 'I think I can see a solution. Joan, we must return to Moulton Inn immediately. Matthew Cobham has work to do.'

'But first we must tell Sir John what we now know about Hardyng's murder,' said Joan. She turned to Wenlock. 'Guy came back to the Sign of the Mole last night. But he didn't kill Hardyng. He fled because he saw Savernake kill him.'

'Savernake?' said Wenlock, bemused. 'But I've just been told that he murdered Margaret Grafton. When did he kill Hardyng?'

'He came to Moulton Inn after the sale on Saturday, disguised as a Dominican. Hardyng was putting Joan's specials into a sack. Guy caught him at it, but Hardyng said Harcourt would have his mother killed if he told Joan. So Guy decided that he'd better get his mother to a safe place as soon as possible. Then he could let Joan know what was going on. He collected his things together, but just as he was slipping out Hardyng came running in, crying for help and chased by Savernake. Before Guy could do anything, Savernake stabbed him – then forced Guy to hand over his knife, bloodied it from Hardyng's wound and shoved it and the old man's body into the midden. Then he ran away, taking the books with him. Guy thought he'd be arrested if he stayed and he needed to get his mother to a safe place. So he ran away as well.'

'And are Guy and his mother safe now?' asked Wenlock.

'Yes. So you must send out a warrant for the arrest of Rufus Savernake.'

'Willingly. Especially as we have a witness. Guy is lucky. Savernake prefers to leave none.'

Farhang rose to his feet and picked up his staff. 'Joan, we have no time to lose. We must get back to Moulton Inn.' He headed for the stairs, followed by Simon.

Joan hung back. She beamed at Wenlock. 'I knew you'd see us right, John. When you've sent out that warrant, perhaps you'd like to ride with us to Windsor. We're planning to overnight at the Waterman's Arms. They keep a fine table there and I've heard the beds are of the best.' With a flirtatious swing of her hips and a backward glance laden with promise, she followed Farhang out of the room.

Wenlock groaned. 'What to do, Francis? Stay here and deny everything, or hazard all and ride to Windsor?'

'Consult your conscience, my lord,' said Thynne.

'And my loins, Thynne. Did you see the look Joan gave me? Hang caution. I'm for Windsor.'

Wallingford

The little troop clattered over Wallingford Bridge, then turned left along the bank. Alyce led the way, Leo keeping pace with her horse. Tamsin could see the smoke from Job's smithy drifting lazily through holes in its slate roof. When they got closer, they could see the smith bent over his forge, hammering a horseshoe, while his apprentice trod the bellows to keep the fire hot.

At the sound of their horses, the boy looked round and saw the sovereign lady of Ewelme approaching, flanked by several retainers. His feet slowed.

Deafened by his clanging hammer, Job was oblivious of his visitors. He swore roundly. 'God's teeth, Brice, you must keep that fire hot. Else this'n harden before she's shaped. Throw on a bit more of that paper. That'll help it flare. Pesky wood is damp in its heart, for all Alan said it was seasoned two years in his barn.'

To her horror, Alyce saw the apprentice take an armful of crumpled sheets of paper, evidently torn out of the book whose ruined binding lay on the ground. 'Ben, stop him.'

Bilton dismounted hurriedly and grabbed the boy's arm. He gave a cry of pain and Job swung round. His eyes widened when he saw Alyce.

'My lady. I didn't see you.' He wiped his sweaty forehead with one grimy forearm and bowed clumsily.

She glared imperiously down at him. 'What is that paper

you are burning?' Didn't Mistress Pailton give it to you to keep safe?'

His broad face creased into a smile as he shook his head. 'Nah, nah. Would I lay a finger on anything my Alison told me to care for? These be Lollard tracts parson found.'

'Thank God for that. I have something for you from your Alison.'

Dismounting, she gave her reins to Ben and felt in her hanging pocket for the little wooden cross. She handed it to Job.

He took it gently, staring at it for a long minute before closing the palm of his calloused hand tenderly over it.

'Our love token. Happen she gave you a message for me, then.'

'She did,' said Alyce. She wants you to give me all her son's bundles. The ones she sent you to store in the smithy. And she said to tell you that she'll be coming back to Wallingford soon.'

Job gave a wide smile, then frowned. 'And what of Denis? Is he safe?'

Alyce hesitated, then decided that this down-to-earth man deserved straight talking. 'No. He had a terrible death. Alison is bereft. He was laid to rest in St Mary Overy last Saturday. She is hearing Masses said for his soul for the rest of the week.'

'I wish I was by her side,' said Job. 'But perhaps now she'll have more time for me. She put heart and soul into that boy of hers. So proud of him.'

'And rightly so,' said Alyce. 'He was a master of his art.'

'And a true Lancastrian.' With the point of the forge's iron poker, he drew four letters in the ash-strewn floor. RQFQ. 'As we all are in these parts.' He gave her a shrewd glance under his shaggy eyebrows and winked. 'Eh, my lady?'

'Speak no treason, Job,' said Alyce warningly.

'I spoke none,' said the irrepressible smith. 'But you'll be wanting his bundles. Brice, take Bilton up to the loft and bring them down.'

He picked up his tongs and thrust the shoe he was making back into the heart of the fire.

An hour later, panniers stuffed with cloth-wrapped bundles, they rode into the courtyard of the palace. Kate Arderne came running to greet them. 'Lady Alyce, was there any news of Peter and Sukey at Wallingford? Or of James?'

Alyce shook her head. 'It will take James several hours to catch them up. And more to get word back to us here. You must be patient, my dear.'

She bent down and fondled Leo's ears as Kate rattled on. 'Sir Gervais has taken to his bed. I think his heart is broken. He feels it has all been his fault.'

'I'll be riding into Oxford with all the men Bilton can muster later today. We should get news of them there. But you must stay here in safety. Tamsin, look to Lady Arderne. Settle her by the fire and get her something to eat. Then go and find your grandmother and ask her to attend Sir Gervais. I'm going to examine Pailton's books.'

She went up to her solar wearily and watched the bundles from Job's smithy being emptied out onto a long trestle table. Smiling, she thanked the men and dismissed them. Every book was carefully wrapped in cloth with a twine tie.

Heart in mouth, she opened the largest package, the only one that could have contained her *Tales*. When she saw the folio inside, her face fell. 'Plain brown covers,' she murmured to herself. 'This isn't it. And I had so hoped that it would be.' She opened the book at random. Her eyes widened as she gazed at a picture of a man and woman coupling in a way she hadn't dreamt was possible. A pulse she'd almost forgotten she had beat deep inside her. She blinked. Fascinated, she turned to another page. Then she slammed the book shut and opened another. And another. There was no doubt about it. The books that Pailton had taken such care to send away were not treason but bawdry. Joan's notorious 'specials'.

She unpacked book after book, methodically jotting down its title and the number of copies on a page of her girdle book. Pailton's exemplars were rich and varied. Some were in Latin, but most were in French. One was in a flowing script that she could not read. Was it Arabic or Indian? Job's attic had held enough banned books to damn anyone who harboured them if the Church authorities got wind of them. And now they were in Ewelme, a canker in the heart of her sanctuary. They were what Pietro had warned her about.

What was she going to do?

Perhaps it was already too late. Perhaps Job's smithy had been watched. She imagined a search party even now advancing on Ewelme. And this was Jack's doing. Jack was in league with Harcourt, intent on engineering her downfall. Weak with shock, she sat down heavily on her great chair. Then she clenched her teeth in determination. No one was going to take Ewelme from her, or her from Ewelme. If she could destroy the evidence, or at least hide it, she was safe.

But how was it to be done? The only thing was to ship them out somewhere else as quickly as possible. But where? Who could she count upon utterly? Instantly, the answer came to mind. Thomas and Jeanne Stonor. They had saved her skin last autumn by concealing the fugitive Cornish scapegrace Sir John Trevelyan in Stonor Park. A plan began to form in her head. She wrapped the books up again, then she took paper and pen, wrote a letter and sealed it. She rang a bell for a footman and told him to bring men to put the sacks of books in a cart and then to take her letter to Stonor Park.

Then she climbed the winding stair to her turret closet, sat down in front of her portable altar and wearily began to tell the beads of her rosary. Before she had said more than half a dozen prayers she was fast asleep.

An hour later, an urgent tap at the door jolted her into wakefulness.

'Come in,' she said sleepily.

Martha Purbeck entered, her face grave.

'Your grace, Lady Arderne and Tamsin went out and I'm fearing for them. They asked Jem for two horses. Tamsin said that Lady Arderne wanted to explore the park. But they've been gone for two hours now.'

'Didn't they take a groom with them?'

'Only Wat. And Lady Arderne didn't even want him. But you know what he's like. He worships Tamsin. He set up such a clamour that she said he could run behind them until he was tired. I didn't see the harm in it. I thought they'd all be back before now.'

Alyce remembered Kate begging to be allowed to follow Danvers and her agonised face when there had been no news in Wallingford. Could she have been foolish enough to ride to Oxford herself with only Tamsin and a halfwit for company? There was nothing for it but to ride after them as quickly as possible with as many men as she could muster.

'Fetch Bilton, Martha. Then return to help me dress.'

Oxford

Tamsin was bitterly regretting allowing Lady Arderne to go riding in the park. When they had reached the great west gate that gave on to the Dorchester road, Kate had turned her horse's head towards it.

'I'm going to Oxford. I've got to find Peter,' she had said, whipping the rump of her horse and cantering off. Tamsin had no option but to ride after her. Wat loped cheerfully at her side, always content when he was with her.

'Lady Arderne, this is madness,' she had called breathlessly. 'It won't do Peter any good if you come to grief.'

Kate, her mouth set obstinately, had ignored her and in truth the busy highway full of folk did not seem over-perilous. Accompanied by a maid and a footboy, Kate was certainly safer than she would be alone. Perhaps she would see someone she knew in Dorchester to take a message to Lady Alyce. But when she asked if they could stop at the White Hart Inn, Kate refused.

'You'll send word to Ewelme. And we'll be stopped before we find James and his clerk.'

'But what if we ride into Sir Robert's arms?'

Kate glared at her, eyes blazing. 'I don't care. I just know I must prove to Peter that I haven't abandoned him.'

As she trotted unwillingly behind Kate, Tamsin's only comfort was the prospect of seeing Will again. She remembered the precious minutes by the Montagu Inn well, his hand on hers, the look in his eyes. Then she remembered Lady Alyce's curt warning and cursed herself for being a romantic fool.

To avoid the flooded marshland to the south of Oxford, they skirted Dorchester and kept to the high ground east of the Thames until they reached the little hamlet of Iffley. Now they were trotting down a steep hill into the city itself. The setting sun glinted off the gilded pinnacles of its spires, turrets and towers. Wat jogged beside them, holding onto Tamsin's stirrup and apparently tireless. When they reached Pettypont, the bridge that took traffic across the Cherwell river to the east gate of the city, Kate reined in her horse and turned to Tamsin.

'I remember Joan Moulton saying that John Doll, the Oxford bookseller, was a good friend of hers. Suppose we ask him to help us?'

Tamsin was impressed by the idea. 'At least we know that we can trust him. Let's ask the gate warden where we can find him.'

The warden demanded a toll of three pennies from them and directed them to John Doll's shop. They were riding slowly along the High Street through the bustle of people, carts and other riders, with Wat looking wonderingly about him, when a familiar voice called to them.

'Lady Arderne, Tamsin, what on earth are you doing here on your own? Isn't Lady Alyce with you?'

It was James, with Will at his side.

'James!' gasped Kate. 'I'm so glad we've found you. Have you seen Peter?'

'No, but I think I know where he is. The gate warden told us that Sir Robert Harcourt arrived at around noon with two men, two wenches and a boy. He has a house here, apparently – Stanton Place, in New College Lane.' He gestured to a narrow alley. 'It's down there. But alone we can do nothing. Where is Princess Alyce and her company?'

'Coming later, she said. She had to see to some business in Wallingford. But I couldn't bear to wait any longer. Peter must be desperate by now. Let's go straight to the house and tell Sir Robert that his wardship has been countermanded.'

'That would be too risky, Lady Arderne,' said Tamsin. 'We must wait until Princess Alyce and the men from Ewelme arrive. Let's find Master Doll. He's a very good friend of my lady.'

'She's right,' said Will. 'Doll's would be safe. It's just along the High.' He gave Tamsin a wink and she knew he was thinking about their first meeting.

A mulish look came into Kate's eyes, but she said nothing. They rode on until they came to a bookseller's window. Above it hung a carving of a huge open book, with the name 'John Doll' on it in faded gilt. A table in front of the window was piled high with books, parchment and paper. Several students in shabby black gowns were turning them over under the watchful eye of a huge dark-skinned man seated on a stool at the door of the shop. His muscular arms were a network of blue and green tattoos and dull white scars and his fingers were busily weaving coloured silk threads into a long, intricate plait.

'Where is Master Doll?' asked Will.

The man gazed at him, then tapped his mouth, shaking his head.

'I think he is mute,' said Tamsin. She pointed up to the sign and raised her eyebrows interrogatively. 'Is Master Doll inside?'

The man's face creased into a smile. He nodded, never taking his eyes off the students.

'What a strange man,' said Kate, as they entered the shop. 'An African. Did you see his arms? All those scars. And his tattoos.'

Tamsin gasped. 'Perhaps he is Pailton's bodyguard, Cabal.'

'Pailton?' James frowned. 'Who is he?'

'He was the reason we came to London last week,' said Tamsin. 'My mistress was asked to investigate his death by the king's mother, the Duchess of York. And she was coming back to Ewelme to search Oxford for Cabal, the Ethiopian mute who worked for him.'

Suddenly she realised that Wat, who usually stayed as close to her as a shadow, was not in the shop. She rushed back outside, heart in mouth. To her surprise, Wat was sitting cross-legged at the feet of the man on the stool, watching him weave with fascinated eyes.

'There you are, Wat,' she said with relief. 'Don't go away, will you?' Wat shook his head. The tattooed man looked up at her and nodded reassuringly.

On an impulse, she pointed to him and said 'Cabal?' He looked wary, then nodded slowly.

'My mistress wants to meet you,' said Tamsin. 'To ask you about Denis Pailton.'

Cabal crossed himself.

'So you know he's dead?'

He nodded sombrely.

'Cabal, my mistress has lost a great book. She wondered if Pailton gave it to you to take to Oxford.'

Cabal made a face that seemed to say he didn't know. Then he mimed the action of writing and pointed into the shop again.

'Oh, I see,' said Tamsin. 'You need something to write with.' He nodded and smiled again. A warm smile that breathed an inner calm. How odd it was, she thought, that some folk instantly made you jittery and others, like this tattooed stranger and Will, made you feel just as quickly that you could trust them with your life.

She went back inside the shop. James and Kate were talking to its owner. Kate turned to her.

'Tamsin, we've told Master Doll all about Peter. He'll do what he can to help us for Princess Alyce's sake. He says that he saw Sir Robert Harcourt riding towards the west gate with two men a few hours ago. I fear he has gone to Stanton Harcourt to bring his daughter to Oxford and marry her to Peter without delay.'

She turned back to the bookseller. 'How far away is it?'

Doll pursed his lips and calculated. 'Riding fast on that courser of his, Sir Robert will be there in little more than an hour. But it'll take him longer to return if he has womenfolk with him.'

Kate looked beseechingly at James. 'If we could trick our way into the house now, we could rescue Sukey and Peter while Sir Robert is away.'

'I think we should wait for the duchess and her men,' James protested. 'Sir Robert may be planning to overnight at his manor and bring his daughter to Oxford in the morning. Lady Alyce can speak to the sheriff when she gets here. We mustn't transgress the law.'

'Who knows how long she'll be?' said Kate. 'Harcourt will know that he'll be pursued. If he returns today, Peter could be spoused before she arrives, and taken off to goodness knows where. This might be our only chance.'

'Couldn't we go and tell the sheriff what he's done?' asked Tamsin.

'Speaking to the sheriff won't help, I fear,' said Will. 'He is Harcourt's brother Richard. And Sir Robert is Steward of the University. Their word is law in Oxford.'

'Then we have no choice,' said Kate impetuously. 'Master

Doll, do you know of a back way into Sir Robert's house in New College Lane?'

The old stationer considered for a minute or two. 'I don't know if I should encourage you in such a perilous venture. But there is a snicket to its kitchen yard from the Turf Tavern. Sir Robert gets his barrels of ale brought in along it.'

Kate turned to James. 'Suppose you and Will go to the door of the house and ask for Sir Robert. Make up some story about having a letter for him. They won't let you in, but while their attention is distracted Tamsin and I can creep in at the back and find Peter and Sukey.'

James and Will looked dubious and Tamsin didn't blame them. She had never heard such a hare-brained scheme. It was a measure of Kate's desperation that she had suggested it at all. She thought for a moment. It was vital that they evened up the odds against them. Which meant getting as many men out of the house as possible. Then she had an idea.

'James, suppose you knock boldly at the door, and tell them that you were riding into Oxford from the west and that you came across Sir Robert at Hinksey. Say that his horse's hoof went through the planking on the bridge over the Seacourt stream and threw him. And that he's broken his leg and wants them to come with a litter to bring him back to Oxford.'

James looked at Tamsin with respect. 'That might just work. But it would be good to have more strength on our side.'

'If strength is what you need, then you couldn't do better than Cabal,' said Doll.

'Cabal! I almost forgot,' exclaimed Tamsin. 'Could I have a slate and some chalk, Master Doll? He needs it to answer my question.'

'What question?' The dry grating voice made them all start

in surprise. A tall figure in the habit of a Dominican friar emerged from the darkness of the back of the shop.

'Ah, Brother Pietro,' said Doll. 'There you are. Here are travellers from London. They are acquainted with the Dowager Duchess of Suffolk, but are in pursuit of Sir Robert Harcourt. He has it seems kidnapped this lady's son.'

'I wouldn't put anything past that devil's cur,' said Pietro. 'And is Princess Alyce also in Oxford?'

'Not yet,' said Kate. 'But she is on her way here to confront Sir Robert.'

'She is also searching for her great book,' said Tamsin. 'Full of the stories her grandfather wrote about a pilgrimage to Canterbury. It was stolen from Mistress Moulton's shop in London. She thought perhaps Cabal had it among the other things in his pack.'

Brother Pietro shook his head. 'I'm afraid she is wrong. The contents of Cabal's pack have long been distributed to their allotted carriers, loyal Lancastrians all. There was no such book among them. But I am glad to hear that your mistress is on her way to Oxford. I need to warn her again against her enemies.'

'What enemies?' said Tamsin.

'Chief among them is the queen, ever greedy for land. There is also Lord Tiptoft. He covets her library as much as the queen covets her estates. But he would do nothing dishonest to obtain it. Sir Robert Harcourt's motives are blacker than either. He hopes to convict Princess Alyce of treason, though quite how I am not sure, except it has to do with books. And the young duke is Harcourt's pawn. He is foolish enough to think that his mother's downfall will be his own advancement.'

'How do you know all this?' asked James.

A wintry smile crossed Pietro's bony features. *'Di riffa o di raffa*. Italians, be they bankers or ambassadors, pardoners, musicians or legates from His Holiness, are adroit at absorbing information. And we share it with each other. Centuries from now, the truth will not be sought in such biased chronicles as John Hardyng's but in the letters we send back to safe archives in Rome, Milan, Florence and Venice.'

'What books, Brother Pietro?' said Tamsin. 'When I left her, she was about to examine bundles that she found in Job the Smith's attic in Wallingford. Mistress Pailton told her that Denis Pailton's books were there and said she could have them.'

'She has already taken Pailton's books to Ewelme? Then it may be too late. They will be her undoing. They are forbidden texts, packed with salacious pictures of unnatural ways of intercourse. Pailton was engaged in a profitable business with Joan Moulton, a business on which the Church must officially frown. As soon as he realised that he was being watched, he sent his exemplars and copies to the Wallingford smith, a friend of his mother's. But Harcourt knows about them. Pailton confessed before he died. Harcourt got hold of Pailton's mother and told her that the Dowager Duchess of Suffolk was responsible for her son's death. And that she could revenge herself if she could trick her into taking the books hidden in Job's smithy to Ewelme. Then he took her to tell Lord Tiptoft about them. I predict that the constable and his men are already riding for her palace. If they discover them there, they'll arrest her for possessing obscene writings. Tiptoft will probably confiscate her entire library. He is book-mad.'

'How do you know all this?' asked Tamsin.

'Because the Italian secretary Lord Tiptoft brought back

with him from Padua is an old friend of mine. He overheard Tiptoft talking to Alison Pailton.'

'If Lord Tiptoft has reached Ewelme, Lady Alyce may not be allowed to come to Oxford,' said Tamsin.

'Pray God that she understood the warning I hid among her plants,' said Pietro, his long fingers passing rhythmically over the beads of the rosary that hung at his belt.

'So if we're going to find my son, there's no time to be lost,' said Kate. 'If Princess Alyce and her men may never arrive, we must hazard all on Harcourt's men believing you, James. Tamsin and I will take Wat and Cabal with us along the snicket from the Turf Tavern. With luck we will steal Peter and Sukey safely away while they are riding for Hinksey. Can we come back here, Master Doll?'

The old bookseller looked uneasy. 'Sir Robert is a hard man when crossed, my dear. And he knows of my friendship with Lady Alyce. Is there nowhere else you could go?'

'What about the Golden Cross, the Earl of Oxford's new house in Cornmarket?' said James. 'He did say when he left us at Windsor that we would always be welcome there.' He felt in his pocket. 'Look, I still have his token.' The silver star glittered like a promise.

'Perfect,' said Kate.

'First we need to ask Cabal if he will help us,' said Tamsin.

'Leave that to me,' said Brother Pietro and went out into the street.

Ewelme

Lord Tiptoft rode thoughtfully at the head of his retinue as it trotted through the hamlet of Russell's Water, halfway between Henley and Ewelme. If Harcourt was to be relied on, the duchess's fabulous library was his for the taking. He'd counsel mercy towards her – a severe penance, then banishment to a nunnery. He was not really easy in his mind as to what he was planning, but comforted himself by reflecting that she was, after all, of an age when Boethius' *The Consolation of Philosophy* would be more suitable reading than the subversive writings of Christine de Pisan she talked so much about. As the road began to descend into the beech woods of Ewelme, he saw two carthorses labouring to haul a wagon up the slope. He shouted to his men to pull to one side of the track and the wagoner nodded a thank you as the cart passed them. As it did, a thought struck the constable. He held up a hand and the wagon slowed to a halt.

'What are you carrying, my man?'

The weathered driver gave him a broad grin. 'I'd have thought you could smell it, my lord, for all we covered it over. Manure from the cows down in Long Mead, going to the barns at Stonor Park.'

Tiptoft remembered seeing the smoking chimneys of a great house a few miles back. He lifted a corner of the cover with the point of his sword and wrinkled his nose in distaste as a stench rose from the cart's still steaming contents. He waved the wagoner on, then clapped spurs to his horse and trotted on towards Swyncombe. From what his watcher at the smithy had reported, Princess Alyce had fallen for the lure of Pailton's bundles. They must be at Ewelme by now. His conscience pricked him again. Confiscating Alyce's entire library on the grounds that she was in possession of lewd books was one thing and would benefit his own collection immensely. But Harcourt's determination to incriminate her as well as the Earl of Oxford in treason could put her life in danger. Sir Robert had insisted that Edward would never go so far as to execute Alyce, but Tiptoft was not so sure. He remembered the malice in Queen Elizabeth's eyes when she talked of her. And Edward was often too lazy to oppose his wife when her mind was set on something. But then he remembered what Simon Brailles had revealed when the rack gave his limbs a second tug. He had no idea as yet of the significance of Newton Montagu, but that it held a guilty secret was sure. In all likelihood a secret that threatened the House of York. He felt easy in his mind once again. This was no time for niceties. Loyalty was paramount. And Chaucers had been bred-in-the-bone Lancastrians for three generations.

His troop rode another mile along the top of the steep chalk escarpment, then turned off to the left. Below them, like a jewel held in a great green hand, was the Palace of Ewelme. No wonder Harcourt coveted it. Labourers working their strips in the huge field sloping down from the track looked up as they passed. A man said something to a lad and he scuttled diagonally across the field and towards the palace like a small hare. Tiptoft imagined the scramble in the household when they heard that a noble company was approaching. And where, he wondered, would Princess Alyce have hidden the books? She must have examined them by now and have realised the danger of harbouring them. But she wouldn't have known how imminently Nemesis was descending on her.

To his surprise the outer court of the palace was utterly tranquil when he rode in. Suspiciously so, he thought to himself. Could its mistress have been warned of his coming? A portly priest and a wimpled woman in a rich fustian gown hung with a chamberlain's chain of office were waiting to greet him. The priest stepped forward and spoke as he dismounted.

'Welcome to Ewelme, my lord. I am William Marton, Master of the God's House, and this is Mistress Purbeck, Ewelme's chamberlain, whom you may remember from last September. Princess Alyce rode for Oxford an hour ago. She will be sorry to miss you. We had no word of your coming.'

Tiptoft nodded. 'I sent none. We are here to search the palace. Do you know the whereabouts of the books that the Duchess lately brought here from Wallingford?'

The priest looked mystified. 'Wallingford? I thought they were from London. They are in her great chamber, waiting cataloguing by Master Brailles when he returns.'

'Show them to me.'

He followed Father Marton into the palace and strode across the gleaming heraldic tiles on the floor of the great hall, enjoying treading heavily on the lions' heads of Suffolk but instinctively avoiding the Catherine wheels of Chaucer. He regarded the works of Alyce's grandfather as the greatest poems in the English language, particularly his translations from the Italian.

When Marton opened the door at the top of the stairs, he had to stifle a gasp. He had forgotten its glories. The tapestries on all but the windowed walls glowed red, blue and gold, their colours intensified by the western sunshine. Benches padded with embossed leather ran under the windows. A high desk with a shelf below it stood beside the largest window and several books lay on the central table. Tiptoft opened them in turn. A few account books. A prettily illuminated psalter and several other books of sacred writings. All exquisite in appearance, but irreproachable in content.

He turned to Father Marton. 'Is this all there were?'

'As far as I know, my lord. I was in the God's House when

her grace returned, and did not get a chance to speak to her before she left for Oxford.'

'And does Princess Alyce keep books anywhere else?'

'Her library is in her tower closet,' said the priest. The main stairs go up from the hall, but there is another door to it behind the arras.' He waved a hand towards a lively representation of Salome offering John the Baptist's head to Herod on a platter. Tiptoft walked over, pulled back the tapestry and tried the handle of the small door behind it.

'Locked. Who has the key?'

'Princess Alyce keeps it on her. But Mistress Purbeck has a spare one.'

Tiptoft looked at the delicately carved door and felt an urge to barge it open with his shoulder. But violence felt wrong in this calm, elegant chamber. 'Go and get her. I will wait for you here.'

After Marton left, he walked over to the desk by the window. There was a single small book bound in blue velvet on the shelf below it. He took it out and opened it. Slanting italic writing covered most of its pages. French verses. With a lovely lilt to them.

He heard Marton returning and pushed the book back on the shelf.

'Here it is, my lord,' said the priest. He held back the arras and turned the key in the lock. When he opened the door, Tiptoft saw narrow spiral steps winding upwards.

'Wait for me here,' he said and went up the staircase. The octagonal turret at the top of the tower had narrow windows to the north, south, east and west. Below them was oak wainscot, above a vaulted ceiling painted in deep blue and studded with gilded stars. In two of the windowsills, brick-lined holes provided safe places for charcoal heaters. Sconces for candles stood in the other two. The only furniture was a high-backed chair and a prie-dieu. The floor was covered with a plaited rush mat, made to fit it exactly and between each of the windows were curtains stitched in the bargello style he remembered from Paduan palazzos, a rippling of subtle hues. He drew one aside and saw behind it several sloping shelves, on each of which were books. Methodically, he looked through them, replacing each carefully in its place. When he had finished, he sat down in the chair and drew a deep breath. There was no bawdry here, only a treasure house of literature.

As he sat, covetous and frustrated, Marton's voice called up the stairs. 'Are you all right, my lord?'

'Yes,' he called curtly.

There was still hope, he reflected. Had he been the duchess, he wouldn't have dreamt of allowing the filth found at Wallingford invade such a sanctuary of learning. She must have hidden Pailton's books somewhere else. Taking one last envious look around, he went down to the solar.

'I'm afraid my men are going to have to search the palace, the church, the school and the God's House, Father Marton. But I will tell them to respect both property and persons.'

He bowed and went down to the courtyard, where his retainers were lounging at ease. A barrel of ale had been rolled outside and two servitors were filling tankards from it and handing them to the men. It was all a little too good to be true. He began to have an uneasy feeling that the search would not elicit a single sheet of the bold bawdry that Alison Pailton had guaranteed.

Oxford

Tamsin followed Kate along the narrow snicket to the picket gate that led into the kitchen court of Stanton Place. Cabal, Will and Wat were going to wait in the tavern for them, ready either to help them get Peter and Sukey to safety, or come and find them if they didn't come out within a half hour. The courtyard was empty, so the two girls quietly opened the gate and closed it behind them.

'What do you hussies want with Stanton Place?' The voice was slurred and drink-sodden, its owner invisible. 'Come over here where I can see you properly.'

They walked towards the porch of the kitchen. Sitting on a bench inside it was a coarse-faced man in the homespun tabard of a porter, a full ale mug at his side.

'We're looking for work, your honour,' said Tamsin, bobbing a curtsey. The man belched.

'And what sort of work would that be? This is no house for honest women, I warn you.'

'Washing or looking after children,' said Tamsin. 'Do you have any here?'

'The only one we have has a maid already. Skinny little waif, but the lad clings on to her like a limpet.'

Just then they heard a loud knocking at the front of the house. The porter sighed and rose.

'No peace for the wicked. Wait there and when I've answered the door I'll find out if there's any laundry work to be had.' He disappeared inside. Kate looked eagerly at Tamsin.

'That's James and Will. This is our chance. Let's see if we can find Peter and Sukey.'

Heart in mouth, Tamsin followed her as she slipped into

the empty kitchen and looked around. On one side of the huge hearth there was a winding stair leading to the floor above.

'They might be up there,' Kate whispered. 'Follow me.'

As they climbed the stairs, they heard feet tramping across the hall and men's voices talking loudly.

'I think it's working,' hissed Tamsin. 'They're all leaving to rescue Sir Robert.'

They reached a small landing and saw a door. Kate put her ear to it, and then turned to Tamsin with an ecstatic smile.

'I can hear Peter's voice!' Before Tamsin could stop her, she had wrenched open the door and entered the room behind it. The people inside, two men, one with a weeping girl in a grubby green gown on his knee, and a small boy hand in hand with a gawky girl, froze like a tableau from a Whitsun pageant. Then the boy hurtled towards Kate.

'Mamma, mamma, I've missed you so much!' He clutched her round the waist and looked up at her with joy.

The bigger of the two men shoved Amice off his knee and stood up, smiling lazily.

'Lady Arderne, I assume. Just in time to bless your son's union with little Betsy Harcourt. She and her father will be arriving soon.' He turned to the younger man. 'Go and see who they've brought with them, Abel.' He walked over to Tamsin and took her chin in his hand.

'You look familiar. What's your name?'

Tamsin set her lips stubbornly. Without warning, Savernake smacked her face so hard that she reeled backwards onto the floor. Kate rushed to her side.

'Tamsin, are you all right?'

Tamsin looked up at Savernake with fury. 'Know, sir, that I am in the service of the Dowager Duchess of Suffolk and that Lady Arderne has powerful friends. You will have cause to regret harming either of us.'

Savernake stared at her, then gave a snort of amusement. 'By the Rood, I remember you now. You're the young wench we almost rode over in Clerkenwell. Well, my dear, the duchess is in no position to help you. Even now I would think she is being taken to Wallingford Castle in the charge of the Constable of England.'

Tamsin glared at him. Then in one swift movement, she leapt up and ran to the open window. Leaning out she shouted as loudly as she could before Savernake seized her and hurled her into a corner of the room. Then he strode over to Peter and picked him up. He turned to Kate.

'Who was she calling to? Are there others with you?'

The door opened and Abel returned. 'There's no one I can see, Rufus. I think they're alone.'

A slow smile spread across Savernake's face. 'Then we can have some fun. One for each of us, eh?'

Desperate to free Peter, Kate picked up a poker from the hearth and rushed at him.

'Stop that, you hellcat,' he snarled, grabbing the poker with his free hand and pulling it out of her hands. He swung it at her head and she collapsed like a limp doll.

Feet thundered up the stairs and Cabal and Wat entered like angry bulls. Behind them came James and Will. Quick as thought, Savernake strode to the window and held the whimpering Peter over the sill with one huge hand. Sukey screamed and the rescuers fell back. Savernake gave the boy a little shake and Peter clutched desperately at air. Laughing, he turned back into the room with Peter held to his chest.

'Long way down,' he said with a sneer. 'Now get out of here

all of you. Unless I see you walking away down the street, the boy falls. You can leave the wenches to us.'

Utterly outmanoeuvred, the rescuers were turning to go when they heard Abel give a warning shout and Savernake a choking gasp. He had dropped Peter on the floor and was desperately reaching behind his back. Wat rushed forward, grabbed Peter and shoved Savernake backwards. He lost his balance and fell on his back, driving the dagger that Amice had just plunged into his back deeper into his body than the girl's own feeble strength could ever have done.

The rescuers looked at Savernake's outstretched body, blood seeping from under him and an expression of furious amazement etched on his face. James bent over Kate, relieved to see her eyes flicker open.

'Are you all right?'

She nodded. 'Where's Peter?' Before James could reply the boy was hugging her tightly. Hugging him back, she looked at Savernake's body.

'What happened?'

James pointed to Amice, who had crumpled into a ball on the floor.

'Amice crept up behind him while he was jeering at us and stabbed him. Then Wat pushed him over.'

'And is he... is he dead?'

'I... I'm not sure. I think so.'

Tears poured down Kate's face and she began to tremble. James took her in his arms, crooning over her bent head and Sukey put a comforting arm around Peter. Will went over to Amice and helped her up. Then he looked round the room.

'But where's Abel?'

'He sidled out of the door as soon as he saw Savernake fall,' said Tamsin.

'No doubt he will give the alarm,' said James. 'We can't stay here. Harcourt may return any minute. The Golden Cross is our best chance of safety. We'd better separate. Exeter, my old college, is close by. Cabal and I will take Kate and Amice and the children there, then double back to Carfax when the coast is clear. Peter, you can ride on Cabal's shoulders and Sukey on mine. Will and Tamsin, go straight for the Golden Cross and warn them that we're on our way. And that we may be being pursued. Here's the Earl of Oxford's token.' He felt in his pocket for the silver star and handed it to her.

'But which way is the Golden Cross?' said Tamsin.

'I know,' said Will. He grinned at her. 'Like old times, us rushing to save the day, Tammie.'

She managed a shaky smile, remembering their September ride to Swyncombe to warn of the coming of Harcourt's men. He took her hand and they slipped down the stairs into the still empty kitchen and went out into the courtyard and into the snicket. Passing the Turf Tavern, they reached the lane that ran along the foot of the city wall and followed it until it reached the North Gate, where the Cornmarket began.

Golden Cross was the largest house in the street. It had a huge gilded cross mounted above the oriel window over its entrance. But its great iron-bound doors were closed. Will raised the brazen knocker on the small door set in one of them and gave two sharp raps. A panel behind a grill slid opened and a man's face peered at her.

'What's your business?'

'We seek refuge. For ourselves and some others,' said Will.

Tamsin held up the silver star. 'Lord Oxford said that we would be welcome here.'

'My orders are to admit no one. You could have stolen his lordship's token.'

'But you must let us in,' Tamsin said pleadingly. 'Lives depend on it. And the safety of a child.'

'What child? I see no child.' The porter began to close the hatch. But before he could do so, a girl's voice, clear and authoritative, sounded.

'What's going on, Ivo? Who has my lord's token?' The face disappeared and the panel in the door slid shut. Tamsin raised the knocker and crashed it down several times. The little door opened and the surly porter appeared.

'Stop that knocking, wench. My lady says you should come in, so come in you shall, but let it be remembered that I was against it.'

Once Tamsin and Will were inside, Ivo closed the door again and locked it. Then he disappeared into his lodging, muttering sulkily to himself. Tamsin found herself looking into a pair of periwinkle-blue eyes, set below exquisitely arched brows in a heart-shaped face. A cloud of starched muslin floated around a horned headdress of cloth of gold which concealed all but a few wisps of fair hair, and a cloth-of-gold houppelande flowed down to two small feet in silver-gilt slippers. Tamsin gasped. This was a princess from a fairy tale. The vision giggled.

'Aren't I grand? This is my wedding gown. It's a gift from my brother George. He saw the style at the court of Burgundy and ordered a dress for me. It should have been here weeks ago, but storms in the Channel delayed it. It only arrived in Wapping three days ago. And I'd left London by then to oversee the unpacking of the cargo being sent on my lord's barge. But dear George brought it to Oxford himself. It'll need a little alteration. I'm so tall that the hem will have to be let down. Now, show me my lord's token. And tell me why you are here. And whose lives are in danger?'

Tamsin suddenly understood. 'You are Meg, then? Sorry, I mean Lady Margaret Neville. His lordship talked of you without cease when we were with him on his barge.' She held out the silver star.

The vision's eyes softened as she took it. 'My dear John. If you are friends of his, you are friends of mine. But don't call me Margaret. It reminds me of being naughty as a child. Lady Meg, if you will and perhaps just Meg when we are better acquainted.'

'I'm only a servant, my lady. Tiring maid to the Duchess of Suffolk.'

'My godmother!' said Meg. 'Is she in Oxford too?'

'We expect her very soon,' said Tamsin. 'But until then we are hoping to find a safe haven with you.'

'A haven from whom?'

'Sir Robert Harcourt.'

All the laughter left Meg Neville's eyes. She looked wary. 'Harcourt? Is he in Oxford, then?'

'He was and he will be again shortly,' said Will. 'It's a long story, my lady.'

'And who are you?'

'William Stonor, of Stonor Park.'

'An honourable family,' said Meg, with an approving nod. 'But before we talk, I need to make myself comfortable.' She looked appraisingly at Tamsin. 'Come with me, tiring maid. You can tell me what your name is and all about your troubles while you're helping me take off my dress.'

Half an hour later, they descended to the courtyard again. Meg had listened to Tamsin's tale with fierce concentration while she took off her wedding gown and put on a practical day dress of blue linen embroidered with daisies.

'The next thing is to tell Arblaster to prepare for more guests,' said Meg. 'His chamber is this way.' They were crossing the court towards the steward's room when the brazen knocker sounded again. Tamsin turned eagerly.

'That will be our friends,' she exclaimed as Ivo came truculently out of the lodge again.

'Or Harcourt,' said Meg. 'Ivo, see who it is.'

Ivo slid the hatch aside again and peered through.

'Party of four. And a boy. And Cabal and Brother Pietro are with them.'

'Then open up and let them in. But admit no one after that. Save it be my godmother. Say to anyone else that there is no one here.'

Tamsin introduced James and Kate to Meg, who greeted them courteously. She nodded cheerfully to Amice and Sukey and winked at Peter, who had pinned his father's brass wyvern badge to his doublet and was clutching his mother as if he would never let her go. She gave Cabal a wide smile and turned to Brother Pietro, a query in her eyes. He gave a barely imperceptible nod and relief flooded her face. Finally, she beckoned to a tall man in the dark gown of a steward, who had come out of the house and hovered uncertainly, waiting for orders.

'Arblaster, take these ladies and little Peter into the house and make sure they have everything they need. They are our guests for the nonce. Tamsin, Master Danvers, Cabal, Brother Pietro, perhaps you will come with me.'

Tamsin followed as Meg led the three men into the steward's

346

chamber and waved them to be seated around a long table strewn with papers.

'We need to make a plan,' said Meg, no longer a fairy-tale princess but an incisive commander. Tamsin remembered that she was after all sister to the Earl of Warwick, the man men nicknamed 'Kingmaker'. 'There are hardly any men here now as the crew of the barge have gone back to Windsor. If Harcourt comes in force, it may be difficult to deny him entrance. He lived here once and he knows the house well. But forewarned is forearmed. We will barricade the gate.'

Tamsin's brain was racing. So Lady Meg knew Cabal and Brother Pietro. And, perhaps, Agnes Quincey and Sir Thomas Malory. She remembered the canvas-covered mountain of luggage the barge had taken on at Syon. What better way of moving a printing press to safety? If the printing press from Clerkenwell was now concealed in the Golden Cross, no wonder Lady Meg was horrified to hear that Harcourt was in Oxford.

But there was no time to make a plan. Thunderous knocking sounded from the courtyard. They stood stock-still, listening to Ivo trying to deny Sir Robert entrance.

'Open up. Or my men will break the door down. Murder has been done and justice must be served.'

The Eastgate warden bowed low as the Dowager Duchess of Suffolk's dainty roan palfrey trotted over the drawbridge. He reflected sourly that its trappings alone would keep him and his family alive for a year. She acknowledged him with a nod and rode on, her face set. He sniffed as a dozen armed retainers clattered past behind her, calculating the pennies lost.

Of course, lords and ladies and their trainbands were exempt from ordinary mortals' tolls, but a penny wouldn't have been too much to ask for a poor man wounded in the French wars who did his job dutifully day and night. But as the last man in the retinue came level with him, a coin fell at his feet. Not a penny, either, but a silver shilling. Gratefully, he stooped to pick it up. When he straightened, he saw young Ben Bilton, his own wife's nephew, smiling down at him.

'How goes it, Connor? Those twin whelps of yours behaving themselves? It won't be long before your family is guarding all the city gates.'

Connor smiled ruefully. 'Not unless I have the favour of the new steward. And they say he's a hard man.'

'Have you seen him recently?'

'Aye, he passed in around noon. With a motley company. Little lad in tears and a couple of shabby wenches.'

'And men?'

'Only his henchman and a groom.'

'Thank you. Any other arrivals of note?'

'Two young gentlemen in a hurry. And another pair of wenches with a lad running beside them. They all asked after Sir Robert, just as you did. Been up to mischief, has he? Nothing new in that.'

'What you don't know won't hurt you,' said Ben, tossing a bonus penny to a delighted Connor and clapping his heels to his horse's sides. The old warden watched as he drew level with the duchess and bent his head to speak to her. Then he beckoned to his deputy, who was dozing on a stone seat set in the opposite side of the gate.

'Take over from me, Roger. It's time his excellency knew what's afoot.' He limped off into the city.

'Help me dismount, Ben,' said Alyce as they drew level with John Doll's shop. 'Then wait outside with the men. I'll find out if Doll has seen them.' But she had barely placed her foot on Bilton's cupped hands when the shop door was opened and Doll emerged.

'Princess Alyce! Thank the Lord. I hope you'll be in time. I told them not to attempt such a madcap scheme, but the young lady was past reason.'

'What scheme?' said Alyce, heart sinking.

'The young gentlemen were to lure the men away from Stanton Place and Lady Arderne and your Tamsin were to get in at the back on some pretext and find the boy.'

'Alone?'

'Not entirely. Cabal and the mooncalf who came with the girls were to stay nearby. And Brother Pietro heard all. Though whether he went with them or not I don't know.'

'Brother Pietro? Here in Oxford?'

'Yes, my lady. Said he had business with Lady Margaret Neville at the Golden Cross.'

Alyce was even more amazed. Meg was here, then, not in London preparing for her wedding.

'What were they planning to do if they found Peter? Come back here?'

Doll reddened. 'No, your grace. I told them to go to the Golden Cross. They had a token from Lord Oxford. I thought it safer.'

'Safer for you too, to be sure,' said Alyce. 'But you were right, John. A bookshop is no place to defend against such ruffians. Thank you.'

She straightened in her saddle. 'To me, men,' she called to her troop, rapped her horse's rump with her crop and rode as quickly as she could along the crowded High Street towards Cornmarket. People scattered as the horsemen followed with warning cries. 'Make way! A Chaucer! Make way!'

When they reached the Golden Cross, its great gates were wide open and the courtyard was a mill of men. Meg Neville stood defiantly at the entrance to the house. Scarlet-faced, Sir Robert was bellowing at her.

'I tell you, my lady, that you are harbouring villains and assassins.'

Clattering hoofs stopped him in mid-sentence. So too did the triumphant joy in Meg Neville's face. He turned to see Princess Alyce at the head of a troop of men.

'That I doubt,' she called out imperiously. 'But you, Sir Robert, have abducted a child illegally. Peter Arderne is no longer your ward. His mother has every right to take him back.'

'But not to mount a murderous assault on one of my men. An assassin knifed Rufus Savernake in the back. He must be found.'

'Say rather she.' To Sir Robert's amazement, a trembling figure in bedraggled green dress stepped out from behind Tamsin.

'I stabbed him, the foul beast. And I am glad of it. He deserved to die a thousand times. And if by stabbing him I made amends for betraying my mistress, I will go to the gibbet happy. I have nothing to live for now.'

'Hush, child,' said Alyce, marvelling at Amice's courage. Dismounting, she put her arm around the girl's shaking shoulders. 'I'm sure you had good cause for your action.'

'She did,' Kate called out. 'And she saved us all. Savernake was threatening to drop Peter out of the window.'

Alyce turned to Harcourt. 'You have repeatedly broken the law, Sir Robert. And now you trespass without cause. Amice has confessed and it is not for you to punish her.'

'As I can attest.' Their heads whirled around. A portly figure in the black and purple robes of an archbishop stood at the entrance to the courtyard, with another dozen men.

'George!' exclaimed Meg in delight. 'I thought you had left Balliol for Windsor already.'

'I might have, had it not been for a timely word from the warden of the East Gate. Sir Robert, having overheard both what the duchess and you have had to say, I suggest that you leave. Tempers on all sides need to cool, so that we can establish the sequence of events for the coroner if there has been a death. Remember that you are Steward of the University and you need to preserve your good name. I'm sure you won't want to become so tangled in legal proceedings that you miss the celebrations at Windsor. I look forward to seeing you there.'

Harcourt looked furiously around, speechless with rage. At last he found his voice.

'Meet at Windsor, we shall,' he snarled, glaring past Archbishop Neville to Alyce. 'I may have lost the Arderne lad, but the greatest prize will still be mine.' He turned and strode out of the courtyard, followed by his men, and a babble of joyful voices broke out.

Alyce watched him go uneasily. What new mischief was he brewing?

Windsor

Sprawled over its hill above the Thames, the golden stone of Windsor Castle loomed above the blossom of the orchards on its western flanks like a gigantic lion asleep in a field of pink-tinged snow. From the highest turret of its central keep, a royal standard flapped lazily. King Edward and Queen Elizabeth and their court had arrived some days earlier, but wagons from local manors heaped with provisions for the feast to come were still queuing to enter the main gate. Barges were moored three-deep along the river and servitors were unloading the countless necessities and luxuries that accompanied royal progresses.

Early in the morning, Alyce, Tamsin at her side, rode towards the castle with Meg, her brother Archbishop Neville and a mixed band of Neville and Suffolk retainers. They had spent the first night of their journey at Stonor Park with Thomas and Jeanne Stonor. James had allowed Will to go home for the summer vacation, and he had impressed George Neville so much by rattling through a welcoming oration in fluent Latin that the archbishop had suggested that he enter his service after his legal training was completed.

Late that night, when the rest of the company had gone to bed, Alyce had sat beside the fire with Thomas Stonor.

'Did you do as I asked?' she said.

He smiled, raising a quizzical eyebrow. 'Books are not easy to destroy, Lady Alyce. And a request to do so from a bibliophile of your renown puzzled me greatly. I'm afraid I couldn't resist opening a few. Which made all clear. Not Lollard texts, as you said in your letter. They were presumably your husband's. Certainly not for the eyes of ladies.'

Alyce nodded noncommittally, guiltily recalling that unexpected thrill. 'But they have gone now, Thomas? Gone for good?'

'Sunk with stones in the sacks to the bottom of the mill pond. Water will destroy them more easily than fire and more discreetly.'

She sighed in relief. 'Thank you, Thomas. But for you, Lord Tiptoft would have found them at Ewelme.'

Thomas grinned. 'Your carter said that he passed him on the road. Luckily that canny old chamberlain of yours had suggested he spread manure over them. His lordship held a pomander to his nose and passed on.

'I am in your debt.'

'I have always been in yours, your grace. To your kindness I owe my wife, the love of my life.'

While they talked, Tamsin and Will were on the roof of the highest tower of Stonor Park, gazing out at the brilliant display of stars in the night sky. 'Do you know their names,' he asked. 'The only one I know is Orion, the hunter. Chasing his quarry across the heavens. Just as I chase after you.'

She smiled. 'I know some of them. Princess Alyce once had a skilled astrologer in her service. He used to point them out to me from the turrets of the palace. Until... until he was disgraced.'

She shivered and he put his arm round her. She felt the warmth of his chest, his beating heart.

'Tamsin – I have two things to tell you.'

She looked up at him, revelling in his closeness. 'What?'

'Firstly, that each time I see you I long to see more of you. Things you say stay in my memory; you haunt my thoughts. There's a Greek philosopher called Plato who believes that everyone has another half somewhere in the world, but few are lucky enough to find it. I feel that we have, that we are two parts of one whole. If only I wasn't who I am, or you weren't who you are, I would ask you to be my wife. But that's impossible.'

Her heart, which had soared at his first words, sank. 'And the second thing?'

'It is my parents' wish that I be married. To Elinor Golafre of Fyfield. It is not at all what I want. But they say it is my duty to... to take to wife a well-born wealthy woman who will give Stonor a suitable heir.'

She cringed inwardly, all her daydreams dashed.

'I wish you most happy,' she managed, then yawned. 'I'm for bed.' Pulling away from him, she went down the spiral stairs of the tower and into the bedchamber allotted to Alyce, who was already fast asleep. Soon she was in her own truckle bed, weeping into her pillow.

They had spent the second night of the journey at St Mary's Priory, near Runnymede, less than an hour from Windsor. When they entered the castle gates, grooms rushed to help the ladies and the archbishop dismount. Hambledon, the castle chamberlain, stood respectfully at attention, flanked by a trio of pages. Alyce was pleased to see that he had kept his position despite having served Henry VI man and boy for forty years. Keen as the queen was to install her own placemen in every royal palace in the land, she had not risked removing this redoubtable authority on both the niceties of royal etiquette and the complex domestic arrangements of the castle. He bowed low and consulted his accommodation list.

'Princess Alyce and Lady Margaret, you are to be lodged with your maids in the queen's apartments. Archbishop, you and your servitors are in the east tower. Your brother of Warwick has already arrived.'

As Alyce and Meg set off towards the west wing of the castle, Hambledon walked quickly after them.

'By your leave, your grace,' he called.

She turned and gave him a lopsided smile, half pleasure at seeing him, half sadness at the memory of all that had changed.

'I wondered if you knew that your son was here already. He rode in late last night.'

Alyce paled. Jack here? But why? He had not said that he was coming to the wedding. He was a friend neither of Vere, nor of Meg. She remembered Cis's words uneasily. And Wenlock's. But of course – the king and queen were celebrating the anniversary of their own marriage and would expect both Bess and Jack to be present.

They reached the wide stairs up to the queen's apartments. A flock of the queen's ladies-in-waiting thronged around Meg.

'You are to use the queen's own bathing tub, Lady Margaret.'

'And where is your dress? I can't wait to see it.'

'Your aunt the Duchess of York is waiting for you in your chamber. She's been so worried. It appears that she called for you at Warwick Inn and was told that you had left a week ago. Where have you been?'

Alyce saw Meg's face fall. She didn't wonder. Cis Neville's wrath was legendary. She squeezed Meg's arm.

'Don't worry, my dear. I'm sure she'll curb her tongue. She won't want a red-eyed bride disgracing the family. Tell her that you decided to visit me and all will be well.'

Alyce was proved right. When they reached Meg's allotted room, Cis rose and embraced her niece with no more of an admonition than an arched eyebrow and compressed lips. And when she was told that Meg had been at Ewelme, she nodded understandingly.

'Very seemly. Though a message would not have gone amiss. Anyway, here we all are and God is shining on your union with fine weather. There are so many Garter Knights present that the handfast before witnesses tomorrow will be in the porch of St George's Chapel. Your brother Richard will escort you and your brother George will officiate at the nuptial Mass in the chapel itself. And tonight, you and Vere are to receive your gifts in an audience in the Rose Chamber with the king and queen. Princess Alyce and I will also be there and a few others. After the gifts have been admired, you will follow the king and queen to the great hall and their anniversary feast will begin. Now, you must dress.'

She delivered Meg over to the queen's ladies and beckoned to Alyce to follow her. Tamsin and two of Cis's own maids followed them at a respectful distance. As they passed through the string of presence chambers, Cis bent towards Alyce with a whispered question.

'Have you discovered what Harcourt's threatened evidence against you and Vere is? He was at dinner here last night, looking much too pleased with himself for my liking.'

Alyce opened her mouth to say yes, but then shut it again. Damaging as the bawdy books would have been to her reputation, they did not concern Vere.

All her sense of triumph evaporated. 'I… I thought so. But it has just struck me that the plot I foiled had no relation to the Earl of Oxford whatsoever. Unless…'

'Unless what?' said Cis anxiously. 'Did it concern a traitor Neville?'

Alyce thought back to Meg's guilty face at being discovered in the Golden Cross and of her evident familiarity with Brother Pietro and Cabal. And of the *Silver Star*, laden with the tightly wrapped bundles taken aboard at Syon Abbey. And of Tamsin's notion, whispered to her as they were riding back to Ewelme, that they had been the dismantled parts of the printing press that had vanished from Clerkenwell Priory. She'd scoffed at her maid at the time, but perhaps she had been right. For if Vere was indeed loyal to Lancaster, then surely Meg would be. The long Neville roll and the hesitant line she had drawn under Meg's name came vividly into her mind's eye. Of course. Meg was the traitor Neville Cis dreaded. And since Hardyng had pointedly omitted entering Vere as her husband, he must have expected his imminent arrest. But on what grounds? And how could they possibly involve her too? She decided that denial was the safest policy.

'No,' she said. 'My best guess is that Pailton believed the Earl of Warwick's dislike of the queen was inclining him away from loyalty to Edward.'

'That old rumour,' Cis said with a sigh. 'My nephew Richard knows better than to betray the man he himself made king. But here is his squire.'

Alyce turned to see a fresh-faced young man in the red and gold livery of the Earl of Warwick. In his arms was a large irregularly shaped object swathed in velvet. He bowed to Cis.

'Your grace, Sir Richard would know if his sister is arrived yet. And where this, his gift for her and Lord Vere, should be taken.'

'Tell him Lady Margaret is dressing for this evening's feast. And that tomorrow he is to be in the presence chamber to lead her to the chapel when the bell tolls eleven. As to his gift, surely he knew enough to hand it over yesterday to Hambledon, the castle chamberlain? Take it to him directly.'

'How should I know him, your grace? I have never attended his lordship at Windsor before.'

Heaving a sigh, Cis signed to one of the ladies who trailed in her wake. 'Take this ignorant boy to Hambledon, Imogen. And then hurry back to my chamber. I must attire myself. And so must you, Alyce.'

Happy in the prospect of her own magnificence, Cis swept away, followed by her remaining ladies.

Alyce looked ruefully at Tamsin. 'I fear your idea about Meg's and Vere's involvement in the printing press may have been right. Worse, I still don't know what mischief Harcourt is planning. We must just hope and pray, child. It's too late to do anything else now.'

At the sight of Imogen and the bundle that Warwick's henchman carried, Hambledon groaned.

'Don't tell me. Another last-minute gift. Which means I have to unlock the doors yet again. What is it? A salt? They already have two. Though by the size of it, this outdoes both in splendour. Follow me.'

He led them to the ornately carved doors that led into the Rose Chamber, most splendid of the new painted rooms added to the castle by Edward III. Tables covered in red damask had been arranged around its walls and gifts of all shapes and sizes were displayed on them.

Hambledon considered for a moment.

'From the bride's renowned brother. He will want it in the place of honour, before even the gifts from the king and queen, I don't doubt. He has the pride of a Turk. But I cannot risk offending their highnesses. I wonder. Let's have a look at it.'

The henchman took off the velvet wrapping. Hambledon's eyes widened. It was a huge ceremonial salt holder made of gold in the shape of a ship in full sail, with every detail of its rigging complete and waves full of leaping fish rippling around its hull. Flags with the devices of Neville and Vere flew from its masts and the figurehead was in the form of a mermaid in the arms of a muscular Neptune.

'It outdoes everything in magnificence,' breathed Imogen.

'Dangerously so,' muttered Hambledon. He gazed at the central table, the natural home of this tour de force of the goldsmith's art.

'I have it. The queen herself told me that special place was to be made for the gift from the bride's grandmother, the Duchess of Suffolk, for all it is merely a book. So I've placed it between the gold chalices from the king and queen. I'll put the Earl of Warwick's salt behind it, but on a plinth so that it towers above everything. That should satisfy everyone.'

While Hambledon fussed about, adjusting his arrangements, Imogen gazed at the intricate carving of the chalices and their lids, one the boar of Vere, the other the Neville bear and ragged staff. Then her eyes fell on the great folio book that held the place of honour. Its binding was a riot of gold leaf flourishes and enamelled flowers. Curious, she put forward a hand to open it. Hambledon smacked it back sharply.

'No meddling, child. And now we must go. There are a thousand and one things still to be done.'

When Alyce reached the Rose Chamber, several of the Garter Knights were already standing at the back of the room. Place was quickly made for her among the Garter Ladies, who were seated separately, and she found herself between Cis and Margaret Harcourt.

Margaret greeted her warmly. 'What a splendid occasion, Alyce. Robert has been immensely excited about it. It seems to have brought him out of the rage he fell into after the failure of the Arderne match.'

'What went wrong, Margaret?' Alyce asked her old friend, curious to know how much Harcourt had told his wife about his machinations.

'Oh, it turned out the boy was half-witted. He made a murderous attack on one of our henchmen. Nor did he have half the fortune rumoured. It was a lucky escape for our daughter.'

Just then more spectators came in. Among them was Sir Richard Roos, whom she had not seen since the gay days at Greenwich when he made up cryptic riddles to delight the ladies of Queen Margaret's court. She had thought him a prisoner, but it seemed that Edward had decided to free him. She waved to catch his eye. His face lit up when he saw her and he nodded meaningfully, as if reassuring her. That was odd. Then she froze as Sir John Tiptoft, Earl of Worcester, entered the chamber. Sir Robert Harcourt followed close behind him. And behind them was Wenlock, supporting a limping Jack on his arm.

There was a blare of trumpets, and knights and ladies alike

rose as the king and queen entered, followed by John de Vere in a splendid cloak powdered with silver stars, a great gold chain of interlinked boars' heads around his neck. Beside him was Meg in the gold chevrons on scarlet of Neville. Boars and stars.

The conversation she had overheard at Temple Place came vividly back to Alyce. 'Here's to the success of our pursuit of the boar and to falling stars.' It had been between Harcourt and Jack. A premonition of disaster came over her.

Once they were all settled in richly gilded chairs of state, King Edward looked benignly at the young couple. Beside him, Queen Elizabeth had a glint in her eye. After Meg and Vere had taken up position, Vere on the queen's right, Meg on the king's left, the queen rose. She raised a hand for silence, then she turned to the bridal couple, gesturing towards the red damask-covered tables and the gifts.

'Around us are tokens of the honour and respect in which you are both held. Most of them speak for themselves, but I would like to draw my lord king's attention to one in especial, for it concerns him nearly. It is the gift of the bride's godmother, the Dowager Duchess of Suffolk.'

Alyce gasped. She had already given Meg her wedding present when she had stayed at Ewelme on the night before their journey. It was the magnificent necklace that Thomas Montagu had given to her on their wedding day. And Meg was even now wearing it. She saw Meg's puzzled frown as her hand rose to the necklace.

She watched as Hambledon stepped forward importantly and walked over to the centre of the display of gifts. What was he picking up? A great folio book. Extravagantly decorated with panels of enamelled flowers and gilded edges. Just as Joan

Moulton had promised for her rebound *Tales of Canterbury*. Hambledon handed it to the queen, whose perfect face assumed a melancholy expression as she turned to Edward.

'However, I was told this afternoon by Sir Robert Harcourt that there is matter in this book which is much heavier than its gay cover promises,' she said. 'Fortunately word has come of it before Lady Margaret's marriage. It proves her intended husband to be beyond doubt a traitor to York.'

Alyce saw Vere flush scarlet and Meg pale to snow.

Enjoying the effect of her words, Elizabeth continued. 'And that his partner in treason is – Alyce de la Pole.'

Edward looked wearily at his wife.

'What proof can a book hold, my dear?'

'See for yourself,' said Elizabeth triumphantly. 'Read the dedication.'

Alyce felt dizzy. She swayed, but a strong arm gripped her and she managed to remain upright. She looked round to see that her mainstay was Wenlock, grim but determined.

'Courage, my lady,' he murmured. 'All is not lost.'

And beside him Jack gazed at her, his expression an utterly unexpected combination of contrition and reassurance.

The king opened the book's cover and read out the lines inscribed on its first page.

Flee from the crowd and dwell with truthfulness,
Let your thing suffice, though it be small;
Hoarding brings hatred, climbing fickleness,
Praise brings envy and wealth blinds overall;
Savour no more than 'tis good that you recall;
Rule well yourself, who others advise here;
And truth shall deliver you, have no fear.

Trouble you not the crooked to redress,
Trusting in her who wobbles like a ball.
Well-being rests on scorning busyness;
Beware therefore of kicking at an awl;
Strive not like the crockery with the wall.
Control yourself, who would control your peer;
And truth shall deliver you, have no fear.

He turned to the title page and then opened the book in several places. Then he looked up at his wife, puzzled.

'I don't understand, dear heart. What treason is there in this? It is a splendidly illustrated herbal and these words are only a timely exhortation to newlyweds to avoid social climbing and hold to the truth. Lines written, if I recall rightly, by Princess Alyce's revered grandfather Geoffrey Chaucer. Most apposite.'

Elizabeth snatched the book back and scanned the dedication herself and turned to its title page. Then she looked across the room at Sir Robert Harcourt.

'What means this, Sir Robert? You assured me that there was treasonous matter in this gift.'

The burly knight lumbered forward, took the book into his own hands and scanned the dedication. He too leafed through a few pages. Then, purple with rage, he thrust it at Hambledon, who carefully restored it to its position of honour on the table. Muttering a request to leave, he bowed low to the king and queen and stalked out of the room.

Alyce turned to look at Jack. He met her gaze squarely with an anxious but hopeful smile, looking so like his father had at the beginning of their courtship that her heart turned over. Never had she seen him look at her with so much respect and affection. Perhaps, just perhaps, a new era was dawning.

Ewelme

'Explain it all to me again,' said Alyce, seated in her favourite chair by the long oriel window of her great chamber, her slim fingers caressing her *Tales of Canterbury*. 'Who stole it from the strongbox? And who wrote this dangerous dedication?'

Joan Moulton put down the copy of Christine de Pisan's *Treasure of the City of Ladies* that she had been admiring and leant back in her chair.

'Margaret Grafton. With the connivance of my apprentice Ned. Harcourt paid her to. He sent your *Tales* to Sir Richard Roos, who was kicking his heels in prison in Windsor. With it was a forged letter from you asking Roos to inscribe it with a poetic call for the Earl of Oxford to rise against York. Which he did. If the *Tales* had appeared on the gift table as your present to the newlyweds, it would have seemed that you were inciting treason – and that Vere was open to the idea.'

'But how did it come about that the herbal that appeared on the table in its place was in an identical cover?'

Joan gave a slightly smug smile. 'That was down to my insistence on perfection. The first binding we made for your *Tales* had a flaw – the enamelling of the frame of the central motif was uneven. So I had another made and put the first aside. But the scheme to put the first cover on a herbal and substitute it for your *Tales* was dreamt up by Farhang.'

She looked across at the aged Persian, contentedly ensconced on a fireside settle. He took up the story.

364

'I'd bought a splendid herbal from Brother Pietro and Joan was going to have a copy made for me, which I planned to give you to make up in small part for the loss of your *Tales*. It was about the same size as your book and Joan suggested she use the first, slightly imperfect, binding she had made. I liked the idea, as if your *Tales* were found they would make a fine pair. When we discovered what Harcourt had done, I had the idea of substituting Pietro's herbal for your stolen *Tales*. We had to remove the surgical treatise bound in with it, as it wouldn't suit a wedding present. As a finishing touch, Guy copied out your grandfather's most improving words on Truth on its first page.'

Wenlock gave a cough. 'You must tell the whole story, Amiri. You've left out how we found out Harcourt's plot.'

Farhang frowned and shook his head slightly. But Wenlock continued.

'It was thanks to your son Jack. Farhang talked to him after his boar-hunting accident and discovered that Harcourt had filled his head with lies about you. As George Neville had also warned him that your downfall would ruin him, Jack told Farhang about Harcourt's scheme. He came with us to Windsor on Tuesday and managed to persuade the royal chamberlain to substitute the herbal for your *Tales* on the table displaying the wedding gifts. Don't be too hard on him, my lady. He is all contrition now. He gave me the *Tales* to bring to you at Ewelme and returned to London. He's determined to win glory in the Smithfield tournament against Burgundy next month carrying your own favour as well as his wife's.'

Alyce sighed. 'Matters won't mend properly between me and Jack until the truth about his father's murder is established. I realise now how remiss I have been in not investigating it thoroughly. But I needed to be cautious. Keeping royal favour took all my energies.'

She turned back to Joan. 'But I still don't understand the connection between the Sign of the Mole and the illegal printing press.'

Joan looked at Wenlock, who shrugged. 'Best tell her, Joan.'

The normally ebullient bookseller looked shamefaced. 'If I'd known things would come to this…'

'Never mind apologies,' said Alyce. 'Just tell me the truth – as scarce a commodity these days as it was in my grandfather's, it seems.'

'The press was based in Clerkenwell Priory and run by Sir Thomas Malory and Agnes Quincy. I thought it was just printing bawdry for me, which customers like John here bought up eagerly. But it was also printing anti-Yorkist propaganda, which Cabal and Brother Pietro and my network of chapmen spread around the country. Wenlock found a broadsheet still wet with ink, and when he heard from Tiptoft that Pailton had confessed on the rack that there was a press in London he put two and two together and guessed it was in Clerkenwell. But Francis Thynne told Agnes that the hunt was up, and with Vere's help they took the press to Syon Abbey by barge before the king's men invaded the priory.'

'And from there in Vere's barge to Oxford,' said Alyce with a wry smile. 'Under our very feet.'

Joan gave a wink. 'Only some of it. But it's already gone from there. It's on its way back across the narrow sea to Bruges. So are the parts that were left at Syon. The time is not yet ripe for printing in England. But I'll soon be importing new treasures for discriminating customers. Who keep a still tongue in their heads.'

She glared at Wenlock, who groaned. 'Worry not, Joan. You've got me over a barrel. Since your companion in mischief Madame de Chinon has suborned the affections of my secretary, none of my secrets is safe. If Queen Elizabeth discovered that I'd got such an... interesting library, I'd be expelled from court. I've no option but discretion.'

Joan looked at him searchingly. 'It isn't just self-preservation that's been guiding your actions, though, is it? The truth is you're slipping off the fence you've favoured for far too long. You're inclining to the cause of Lancaster.'

He pressed his lips together in an infuriatingly inscrutable expression.

There was a knock on the door of the solar and Tamsin entered. 'My lady, Sir Gervais Arderne has just arrived. With him are Lady Kate and Peter and James Danvers. And Brother Pietro and Cabal.'

'Show them up, Tamsin,' said Alyce. 'I hope they have resolved everything satisfactorily.'

A few minutes later, footsteps sounded on the stairs, some quick and light, some slow and heavy. Peter led the way, tricked out like a tiny squire in velvet doublet and breeches and with a real little sword sheathed at his side. Behind him came Sukey in a new nursemaid's gown and Micky, transformed into a smartly dressed page. Then came Kate, her face radiant. Then Sir Gervais, with James. Then Pietro and Cabal and, last of all, Amice, eyes downcast.

Joan held out her arms and Kate rushed into them.

'Godmother, I can never thank you enough,' she said. 'Without you I would have lost everything.'

'I too am in your debt, Mistress Moulton,' said Sir Gervais. 'I now realise that the Arderne family has a fine young heir.

And Lady Katherine is going to come to Langley with me and meet my wife, Peter's grandmother.'

Tamsin was wondering what would become of Amice, but before she had a chance to ask, Kate went to her errant maid and put her arm round her.

'And Amice was exonerated by the coroner. It appears that Savernake had committed all manner of mayhem in London and was himself being pursued for not one but two murders. I told her that I forgave her for betraying me, but she has decided that she wants to enter a nunnery.'

Alyce looked up. 'I recommend the sisters at Godstow. Alice Henley, the abbess, will value Amice's talents as a needle-woman. If you wish, I will give her a letter to take to her.'

'That would be kind, your grace,' said Kate. 'She is deeply bruised in body and soul.'

Alyce signed to Tamsin to fetch writing materials as James stepped forward.

'Sir Gervais has asked me to travel with them to Langley, to be a protective escort. And he's going to tell his wife that Peter has a worthy mother in Kate.'

He looked at her lovingly, then added daringly, 'Who will one day I hope become my wife.'

Joan wagged a finger at him. 'Too soon for that, young man. Marriages based on gratitude have a way of not lasting. And you'll have to change your ways. No more carousing with the likes of John Paston.'

Blushing, James glanced at Kate. To his relief she was smiling.

Farhang looked across the room to Pietro and put his hands together in a gesture of apology. 'I'm sorry about the sacrifice of your herbal.'

Pietro inclined his head. 'I am happy that it has served a great purpose. I care not for the things of this world. Nor do I have long to enjoy them. A crab is eating at my lungs. But I shall spend my last breath in the furthering of the cause of the rightful king of England, the saintly Harry of Lancaster.'

Alyce looked across the room to Wenlock, who was now lounging on a window seat with characteristic elegance. He raised his eyebrows, then shrugged. As a papal emissary, Pietro was untouchable by English law. Moreover, Joan's surmise was a shrewd one. Sir John was inclining to Lancaster once again. Since his marriage to Elizabeth Wydeville, King Edward had shown too little respect for the lords who had won him his throne. There were even rumours that the Earl of Warwick, the man whom all Europe credited with making Edward king, was growing disaffected. And Wenlock regarded Warwick as the greatest living Englishman. And Denzil Caerleon was in the Earl's service. Who knew whom Fortune's wheel would next raise on high?

He stood up. 'Your grace, Mistress Joan, I am expected at Rycote to overnight with the Quartermains. Then Francis and I will return to London. I am travelling to Calais with the Earl of Warwick in a few days' time, on an embassy to Burgundy. But I hope that our paths will cross again in the near future.' He bowed at Alyce, winked at Joan and left, followed by Thynne.

Joan sighed. 'What an infuriating man he is. Always coming and going of a sudden, never still. I don't know why I put up with him. Still, one can't steer one's heart; it follows a course all its own, for good or for ill.' She gave Tamsin a knowing wink and looked round for Monique.

'Monique, I think it's time we too went on our way. If the

369

Sign of the Mole is going to continue to flourish, there is much to be done. I'd like to stay here tonight, if we may, Lady Alyce. And if Brother Pietro and Cabal could put off their departure a while, we would welcome their company on the road back to London.'

Alyce did not reply. She was lost in thought as she folded up the letter she had written to the Abbess of Godstow. So Wenlock would be in Calais with Warwick. Dare she ask him to take a message to Caerleon? She imagined Wenlock's knowing smile, his eyes alert with surmise if she made such a request and dismissed the idea. If her and Denzil's paths were to cross again, it would have to be by chance.

'Lady Alyce?' It was Joan. 'Did you hear what I said?'

Alyce blinked, realising that everyone was staring at her. She smiled brightly and nodded at Joan, totally unaware of what she had agreed to. Then she unfolded the letter and turned to Amice.

'Here, Amice. You can read it for yourself. There is nothing to fear. I have just told the prioress that you are sorely in need of physical rest and spiritual comfort. And that I stand surety for you.'

Tears welled up in Amice's eyes. She shook her head word- lessly and rushed out of the room.

Tamsin rose to follow her, but Kate put out an arm and stopped her. 'I think she needs to be alone. As to reading your letter, Lady Alyce, she isn't able to. All that mattered to her was appearance. Hopefully this second chance will be the making of her.'

'I will visit her from time to time,' said Alyce. 'Joan has taught me, among much else, that kindness works miracles.

By the way, where is Simon? Did he come with you from London, Joan?'

'He did,' said Joan. 'Having played a most useful part in finding out what had happened to little Peter. Perhaps he is in your book closet. He was muttering all the way from London about having neglected his duties as your secretary. He'll be glad to be back at your side.'

So why hadn't he told her he was back? Alyce wondered. She called Tamsin over to her.

'Tamsin, could you go and find Simon and bring him to me?'

Tamsin nodded obediently and headed out of the chamber. She looked in the buttery and the pantry, then headed for the menservants' lodgings, calling his name as she went.

Simon looked down at her from the topmost turret of the gatehouse. How confident and complete in herself she had become. While he felt more unsure of himself than ever. Lord Tiptoft now had an unbreakable hold over him. He was doomed to betray Lady Alyce. Perhaps he had done so already. Wearily, he descended and walked out into the courtyard. Tamsin saw him and went over to him.

'Simon, Lady Alyce wants you. Where have you been?' Then she saw the deep lines of misery in his face.

'Simon, what on earth is the matter? What has happened?' He shook his head and walked wordlessly towards the solar to attend, Janus-faced, his beloved mistress.

Afterword

The plot of this instalment of my series about Alyce Chaucer was inspired by the puzzling dedication in the front of the richly illustrated Ellesmere manuscript, the most famous surviving version of *The Canterbury Tales*, now held in the Huntingdon Library in San Marino, California. Given in full in this book's Prologue, the dedication is generally believed to be a coded exhortation to the Earl of Oxford to fight in the cause of King Henry VI. Nor was the restoration of the 'once and future king' a hopeless cause: on 3 October 1470, Henry VI was restored to the throne by Richard, Earl of Warwick – albeit for a mere six months.

Printing presses soon spread from Gutenberg's in Heidelberg in the 1450s to Cologne, Bruges and Italy. Most history books say they first came to England in 1476, when William Caxton moved his press from Bruges to Westminster in 1476, but an interesting article in the Oxford University Press blog by Ian Gadd examines the possibility of Oxford being where they made their English first appearance (blog.oup.com/2013/11/caxton-england-first-printing-city-oxford-history).

The idea that Sir Thomas Malory was involved in spreading Lancastrian propaganda was inspired by the fact that he was among only eleven people exempted from Edward IV's general pardons of July 1468. Exempted too were a scrivener called

William Vernon, the author of a prose romance called *Hugh Mill* and a chapman called Thomas Philip. My biography of Sir Thomas Malory (*Malory: The Life and Times of King Arthur's Chronicler*, HarperCollins, 2006) tells more of their story.

Malory is central to the last book in the trilogy, *Murder Will Out*, set in 1469. In it, Alyce, Joan and Tamsin journey to Cornwall because vital clues have been discovered concerning the mystery of the murder of William, Duke of Suffolk, in 1450 – a cold case if ever there was one. Simon Brailles finds himself running into danger in the legendary castle of Tintagel, and Sir John Trevelyan, now fully restored to health, reappears to help and hinder. Both Denzil Caerleon and Will Stonor play their part. Not all the loose ends are tied up, but such is life, as well as art. If you would like notice of its publication, planned for November 2024, please contact me via my website: www.christinahardyment.co.uk.

If you are interested in finding out more about Alyce and Ewelme, I recommend John Goodall's *God's House at Ewelme*, Routledge, 2001; H.A. Napier's *Historical Notices on the Parishes of Swyncombe and Ewelme in the County of Oxford*, James Wright, 1858; Karen K. Jambeck's article 'The Library of Alice Chaucer' (*The Profane Arts of the Middle Ages 7*, 1998), and Rowena Archer's article about her in *The Dictionary of National Biography*. My own initial inspirations were Cynthia Harnett's *The Writing on the Hearth* (Methuen, 1971) and Margaret Frazer's series of novels about Sister Frevisse, supposedly a cousin of Alyce.

Acknowledgements

With thanks to Claire Bodanis, Nicolas Soames, Fiona Maddocks, Martin Meredith, Richard Mayon-White, and my daughters Daisy Griffith, Susie Billings, Tilly Connor and Ellie Danby for their encouragement and helpful criticism; to Joe and Lenny Billings for website work; Profesor Peter Field, the greatest living authority on Sir Thomas Malory, and Dr Joanna Laynesmith, biographer of Cecily, Duchess of York, read the book in proof and made useful contributions, though not altogether agreeing with the liberties I have taken. It was also read by Dr Linda Clark, editor of the fifteenth-century volumes of the *History of Parliament*, Gillian Crampton Smith and Philip Tabor. Professor Nicolas Orme gave advice on the medieval church, and Katherine Swift of Morville on medieval gardens. Once again, Ros and Phil Danby lent me Aunty Lucy's bungalow in Arnside to escape into, and Lucy and Andrew Penny allowed me to roost unsociably to write in the sunroom of Clwyd-Waen-Hir and enjoy their cooking and company of an evening.

And thanks again most of all to Lucy Morton and Robin Gable of illuminati book design & editing, for making the second *Alyce* look as lovely as the first, giving much invaluable advice and correcting innumerable errors.